DAUGHTER OF ASH

THE AWAKENED BOOK 4

MATTHEW S. COX

DIVISION ZERO PRESS

Daughter of Ash

The Awakened Book 4
© 2014 – Matthew S. Cox
All Rights Reserved

DIVERGENT FATES
—A—
—NOVEL—

Cover illustration by Jackson Tjota

ISBN (Ebook): 978-1-949174-30-4

ISBN (Print): 978-1-949174-31-1

The Awakened Series

CONTENTS

UNTOUCHABLE

Destruction and neglect marred every surface in this part of the city. Peeling sheets of plasfilm fluttered in the wind, clinging to decaying structures, posts, and vendomats broken longer than Kate had been alive. Some advertised local bands; others pushed merchandise that had gone out of production before the takeover of flying advert bots. The majority bore the eager, smiling faces of missing people. Most looked like high-school ID images, though a handful were adults who had the simple misfortune of working too close to the creeping rot spreading outward from a disavowed sector. They'd lingered too long after civilization had enough and left. Kate had stopped paying attention to them. The youngest of those teens would be twice her age now or more, assuming any remained alive. People could vanish for many reasons in East City, and none of those reasons smelled any better than the alley in which she'd slept the day away.

A baleful droning *whirr* passed overhead. A forlorn advert bot as big as a large, legless dog cruised amid the downpour in search of a mark it calculated would buy whatever items ComTec Corporation programmed it to sell. Sparks sprayed every few seconds from a flattened dent/scrape on one side, suggesting a recent duel with a careless hovercar. She shook her head when it performed a loop and raced off in an erratic spiral.

No wonder the damn thing's out here in the grey, its nav's gotta be fried. She tilted her head back until it touched the wall. *You'll fit right in here, little guy. This is where broken things live.*

Kate stood in the shadow of a fallen thermacrete slab, which jutted six feet out from the second story of an abandoned residence tower, blocking the rain. She tucked up to an alcove beneath it to get out of the weather, hiding in a lingering cloud of steam. Across the street, scraps of plastic fluttered from exposed rebar teeth, stealing moments with their mesmerizing dance. Ruined, derelict skyscrapers gaped like skeletal jaws at the overcast sky, rendering it a jagged grey glow. The howl of distant wind mixed with the occasional gunshot or scream. Metal creaked to her right, the twisted remnants of decades-dead cars bristling at the touch of nature.

A paper cup skittered along the sidewalk, its faint scrape ending when it met the side of her foot—and burst into flames.

"Fuck you, too," she whispered, kicking it into a burst of ash.

Splattering streams of rain ran through cracks in the slab, forming an intangible cage around her. She looked down, no longer wondering how long ago the building had been abandoned. Her maroon skirt hung still at mid-thigh, in flagrant disregard of the gusting that tossed her hair about. Water seemed afraid of her black boots; a shifting zone of dry wavered around her on the concrete walkway, the wet never less than an inch away. The foulness of low tide, a decaying mixture of vegetation, fish, and rot, clung to the air.

Five locals, barely men, rounded the corner and headed her way: black coats, guns on their belts, and the look of the hunt in their eyes. All wore the insignia of the Wharf Rats. The lead ganger's hair shifted in an endless cycle of rainbow colors; violet overtook red, and by the time it reached the ends by his shoulder, blue crept out of the roots.

They made no subtle show of checking her out, staring at her legs and the exposed skin between her skirt and the hand-wide strip of dark fabric over her breasts. One reached toward her jacket to pull it aside for a better view.

Her head snapped up in a wave of auburn; the group jumped back in unison as though the sight of her face hit them with the force of a physical shove. Leering became fear. A man's fingers paused an inch from contact with black leather. He flashed a disingenuous smile as the hairs on the back of his hand withered.

"Hey, Parrot. You guys look desperate."

Parrot lowered his arm and took a step away. "Kate. Didn't know ya for look."

"I rarely wear the same thing twice." She shifted her weight to thrust her chest forward, stance accentuating her hips. "I'm right here if you're in the mood."

Nervous laughter rippled among the Wharf Rats.

"Uhh." Parrot grimaced. "'Preciate the offer, but uhh... Catch ya 'round." He winked and 'shot' her with a finger gun before moving past at a brisk walk.

The rest hurried off.

"It's not my breath, is it?" Kate cracked up laughing and flipped her left arm over to glance at a small screen embedded in a thick, off-white band around her wrist. A few droplets on the glass caught the light and glimmered. "Damn rain."

She left the shelter of the hanging debris and got up to a brisk walk, chased by the incessant sizzle of water dripped onto a hot skillet. Darkened monoliths passed on both sides; she trudged through the downpour, a trail of low-lying steam in her wake. Given the hour, people in this part of town stayed out of sight unless they hunted for food, chems, or something to fuck... or didn't know to keep their head down. Whispers made her look up. Two dirt-smeared urchins crouched in the shadows of a third-floor window, watching her and whispering in Spanish. She smiled at the boys, who disappeared into a tangled mass of girders and junk.

"Hey, let's have the earrings," said a feminine voice, as nervous as it tried to be threatening.

Kate glanced over her shoulder at a stairway leading to a half-basement below the abandoned apartment tower. A teen girl in tattered clothing, plain shirt and pants, emerged from the shadows with a small handgun trained on her.

"If you think I'm going to feel sorry for you, you're about to make a mistake."

The teen put her other hand on the pistol. "E-earrings, now."

Kate set her hands on her hips and sighed. "Okay, perhaps I do feel sorry for you since you're still breathing. Fuck off."

"That's a fancy watch too."

Kate narrowed her eyes. "Sorry bitch, the earrings don't come off and there's no way you're taking my 'mini."

The girl fired; the shot caught Kate in the cheek like a punch, knocking her back into a stagger. She whirled with the force of the hit and landed on all fours. The teen started out of the recessed stairwell to search her kill, but stopped when Kate grumbled and shook off the dizziness; molten lead dripped from her cheek.

"If that left a bruise, I'm going to kill you slow."

The girl screamed, backing up. "W-what the fuck? Y-you some kinda vampire?"

Kate wiped at her cheek and flicked her hand to shake off the liquefied metal. Red light glimmered in her eyes. She stared at the gun, focusing heat into the magazine. A second later, the pistol detonated with a flash of blue fire. The girl hit the ground in a ball, cradling her mauled fingers and shrieking.

Kate got to her feet and stalked over. Blue serpents of fire peeled away from both hands, coiling around her arms. The girl scooted away amid concrete debris and trash.

"P-please don't kill me... I d-didn't believe them. I'm sorry." She sobbed. "I'm s-sorry!"

Kate glared. The girl looked younger with such wide eyes, barely sixteen. Killing her would make her feel better, but leaving her alive could mean one more person telling people to leave her alone. She left her arms burning while she pondered what to do. The flames rippled audibly in the wind, surrounding her with heat blur. A couple of guys ran over, hands up. Both turned pale; a dark-haired man a month or two past twenty seemed unable to speak.

The other one looked about the same age as the girl. "Kate... hey, give her a break, huh? She's new. Only been here a couple days."

"Y-yeah," added the dark haired one. "Kid just got kicked out. You been here a long time too, you know how it is."

A pile of trash on the ground less than a foot from her leg smoldered. She moved away from it, glaring. The fire shrank and died as she willed it out. A gasp came from the wounded girl as one of the boys helped her sit up.

Kate let her arms fall slack. "She shot me in the damn face."

The younger boy scratched his head, offering a cheesy smile. "Manners... Tiffany kinda lacks 'em."

The other laughed at his friend's observation, but looked too unnerved at seeing a gunshot reduced to causing a bruise. His eyes glazed over at witnessing rumor proven true. Kate squinted at the whimpering teen, focusing until a telepathic link formed to the girl's thoughts. She hadn't believed all the stories, the ones that built Kate up as some mythological figure not to be trifled with. This girl had thought it made up. Fear got the better of her under Kate's utter lack of worry while staring her down. The gun went off unexpectedly, a result of nerves and an electronic trigger with a half-millimeter travel. Terror at what was about to happen to her dominated the rest of her attention, as well as the stinging pain of having a gun explode in her grip.

A dark smile spread over Kate's lips as she extended a hand. "Truce then; might as well shake on it, especially since you're bleeding. I should cauterize that before you pass out."

Tiffany scooted away. "Please, no."

"S'ok Tiff, Kate just likes it when people are scared of her." The oldest winked at Kate. "Ain't that right?"

"Yeah," said Brown-hair. "We'll get her to a med center. She's still under eighteen, so it's free."

"You're damn lucky I'm feeling lazy tonight." Kate took a few steps back, touching at her cheek. "If you ever get tired of living out here, point a gun at me again and I'll make sure all your problems go away."

They kept quiet, save for whimpers of pain from the girl, as Kate trudged off down the street. Her heartbeat throbbed in her cheek where the bullet had struck. She clenched and released fists, annoyed at holding on to her pent-up anger. Her reaction to pain had always been to annihilate the source, even if it was her fault for walking into a solid object. A clump of trash paid the price for the girl's insolence; flaming rats scurried into the rain, vanishing to faint smoke trails in the dark.

She checked the time once again on her wristband, adding urgency to her stride. The 'black zone,' an area of the city so lost to gang warfare and decay that even the military shied away from it, ended within the next few blocks. No clear demarcation point existed where it became a 'grey zone.' The evolution from complete decay to a few traces of civilization followed an irregular path, an organic shift based on how much bad happened to who. Some people had more balls than sense, while others cleared out as soon as the first thug walked by their front door. Where 'black' became 'grey,' buildings appeared less damaged—some even still had power—and the number of people on the street increased. Almost no one but Wharf Rats showed themselves within the heart of the areas blacked-out on the NavMap system.

Cybered-up gangers dwelled there for the most part, free from the scrutiny of authorities who would deem them mentally incompetent and take their 'ware away. Bodies more metal than flesh propped against walls or sat around burn barrels. Most had crude street-tech cyberware: bulky, utilitarian, and anything but aesthetically pleasing. Luminous eyespots in the dark widened or narrowed as she passed. The telltale grin on one man gave away his use of high-resolution thermal. At the sight of his obvious excitement, the man next to him slapped his arm and shook his head.

"Not that one, man. No way," he whispered.

"Burner?" asked the lecherous one, rubbing his crotch while squirming.

The first man laughed. "Yeah… you could say that."

These people did not know her as well; she seldom left the safety of the place she had gone from frightened teen to hardened woman. The Norms, even cops, were terrified of setting foot in a black zone for a few minutes, but she had called one home for almost ten years.

Kate grasped the open flaps of her jacket, moving her arms as if to pull it closed over her bare stomach. The material reacted a second slower than her gesture, covering her, though the icy needles of falling rain continued striking her and exploding into puffs of steam. She tossed her hair back, glaring defiance at the gangers. Trash couldn't scream. Unspent anger waited to be unleashed, any one of them would do.

A CyberBurger lit up a street corner four blocks deep in the grey zone. Kate headed right for it, waving both arms at the pair of automatic, sliding doors as if she were some manner of old wizard. Patrons, of which she counted about six, smirked at her and shifted so they didn't look right at her.

Three Class 1 dolls, obvious artificial humans made in the image of teenagers, waited behind the counter. All wore the same unchanging smile permanently molded onto their plastic faces. At the far left end, a thin strung-out woman attempted to argue with a somewhat pudgy middle-aged Hispanic man who wore the uniform of a manager.

"…patties keep getting thinner and thinner."

"We have not changed the assembler patterns in forty years, ma'am. The food you got today is the same food we made before you were born."

The manager glanced over at the new arrival. Kate smiled at him and winked. All color fled from his cheeks as he wet himself, shaking where he stood.

"You look good, Alfonso. I hope business is doing well." She waved her wrist-mini at him. "Don't worry, sweetie; I'm going to pay."

He covered his mouth with both hands, withering to the ground and curling into a weeping ball. The thin woman looked back and forth between them, speechless as Kate approached one of the teen dolls.

"I'll have four double-orbitals and a large fry."

The doser looked her up and down. "Bitch, where you gonna put all that?"

Kate waved her bracelet over the reader, causing it to beep. "I have a bit of a metabolism issue."

"No shit." The woman shook her head, moving closer with a sideways gate unsure if she were predator or prey. Whatever chem she'd taken caused her left eye to twitch. "Don't blame ya. This shit'll fuck you up. These bastards been skimmin' beef off these things for years."

"You know this isn't real meat, right?" Kate shifted her weight onto her right leg. The smell wafting from the doser made her glad she couldn't taste food.

"That's just what they want you to think. The rich are saving the OmniSoy for themselves, leavin' us poor people to eat real cows from the Badlands 'cause they all full of radiation and disease and shit."

Kate blinked. "Yeah, good point." *Shit nuts. Not worth the argument. I'd kill someone for real beef.* Her mouth watered at the memory of fresh venison. Real meat didn't ash over so fast; that, she had gotten to taste. *Has it been that long?*

The doll put a plastic tray on the counter, bearing four enormous hamburgers and a carton of French fries. Of course, all of it came from OmniSoy tweaked at a molecular level to approximate meat, bread, cheese, lettuce, and tomato. She had no idea what the dark green chips were supposed to be. A half hour from now, her magnificent feast would devolve back into the same beige slime. Cyberburger used cheap machines. As Alfonso had said, probably the same machines they installed forty years ago.

"Can I get a metal tray?" Kate didn't bother smiling at the robot. "Please? I promise I won't steal it."

It stared at her with the only facial expression it could make: a vapid smile.

"Do it," yelled Alfonso from a back hallway.

The doll obeyed, transferring the food to a metal tray and holding it up. "Thank you for dining at CyberBurger."

With her food in hand, Kate walked to the middle of the dining area and frowned at the plastic molded seats. She ducked out via a side door that led to a fenced-in area full of graffiti and broken playground equipment. A frigid steel bench elicited a squeal of discomfort upon contact with her ass. Smoke peeled from the bun as she took hold of the first burger, racing to eat it before it crisped to charcoal in her hands. The strange woman crept out the door, edging closer as burger number three died a rapid death. Kate took a few breaths, preparing to suck down number four, and glanced up at the woman as she moved closer to the bench.

"I wouldn't…"

The other woman's rear end made contact with the steel for all of two seconds before she leapt up, screaming and dancing.

"The metal's thin," said Kate, before attacking the last burger.

"What the fuck?" shrieked the still-flailing chem-head as she waved a hand over her backside. "You could cook on that sumbitch! How the hell are you sittin' on it?"

Kate swatted blackened crumbs off her hands. "Like I said, I have a high metabolism."

The woman held a hand a few inches from the bench. "Shee-it." She reached closer to Kate's leg. "Praise the Lord, what the hell? You is burnin' up! What you get them clothes made of that they not on fire?"

"Magic." Kate winked. "They're made of magic and wishes."

THE BUILDING'S SHADOW CONCEALED KATE FROM A BLUE AND WHITE Division 1 patrol craft parked three blocks farther into the city. She had gotten close to the end of the grey zone, where civilization proper once again took hold. Dread came, fear of that which she could not see. Were *they* still looking for her? Would *they* find her if she moved into range of the little cameras all over everything? People said the police ran the citycams, but the people who'd made her could do what they wanted and didn't care about trivial things like the law, or cops. The brown haired man she saw on the back of her eyelids appeared in her mind again, staring down at her. No matter how old she got, he always towered over her as if she remained seven.

A gust of wind brought a shiver. She leaned against the wall, coarse and scratchy on her arm and shoulder. Her gaze fell once more on her jacket, skirt, and boots, searching for the reassurance that came with the appearance of clothes. Fat droplets patted to the ground from the corner of a green and white awning. She reached out and caught one; the droplet hissed and bounced over her palm, fizzling away to steam in seconds. As a little girl, she'd wondered why the water didn't like her. Now it just made her angrier. She shoved off the building with a grunt, stomping around the next corner into a familiar alley.

"Hey, Silva. Got somethin' weird comin' this way on thermal."

The upper half of a broad-shouldered man emerged, leaning around from the far side of a trash compactor. He tilted his head, right eye open wider than the left. Patches of metal poked out of the collar of his suit, where skin gave way to augmented arms. Cold plastisteel hands opened and closed at the ends of his sleeves.

"No weapons, but, uhh…" He shot a sideways glance at someone out of sight. "She's ridiculously hot."

An unseen man laughed.

The big guy frowned. "No, you fucking tool. Heat hot. Like almost seven hundred degrees."

Kate stopped a few steps from a side door, smiling up at him. The top of her head almost reached his chin. "You're too kind."

A thinner guy, short for a man—about her height—extended his arm and banged on the door with a closed fist twice. "It's okay. She works for the boss."

"Afternoon, Silva."

He winked. "It's night."

The big man shifted. "On thermal, she looks—"

"I am." She grumbled. "Don't fuckin' remind me."

She kicked at trash on the way to the door, leaving the new guy pondering how her boot left a char mark on a piece of wet cardboard in the shape of a bare footprint. A dim, cramped corridor made an abrupt right turn three steps in, leading past the kitchen of a restaurant. Kate tiptoed along at a brisk pace, trying not to touch the floor longer than necessary in any one place.

At another turn, this time left, a stationary sentry gun swiveled to aim, tracking her motion. Her bracelet chirped, the sound echoed a split second later by the sentry. It resumed its slow side-to-side panning as she trotted into another hallway. Here, exposed concrete let her slow to a casual walk as she passed doors leading to large cooler rooms on either side. Two augmented men guarded a plain door at the end. Kate offered a professional nod, but her eyes hardened at the grin one of them flashed. An image of her drawn in white upon his surface thoughts revealed every contour amid a wavering inferno of reds and oranges.

"High resolution thermal, huh?" She asked, staring at the floor.

His grin fell flat. "Uhh, sorry. I forgot—"

"I can see your thoughts?"

"Show a little respect." The other man swatted his associate on the shoulder. "She helps the boss out with problems."

"Yeah, yeah," he mumbled, holding his hands up. "Standard procedure to scan… We don't usually have such beautiful ladies come through here."

She winced.

"What? I'm tryin' to be nice." He flashed a cheesy smile. "Sides, it's true. You're gorgeous, like those European runaways the boss brings in."

"You mean *buys*? Oh, sorry… *covers the travel expenses for.*" She studied the floor for a moment. "Oh, well… if you think I'm pretty." Kate's gaze shot upward, with a manic-eyed grin. "We can duck into a room if you want? Have a nice quickie? Maybe you could take me home, show me off to your buddies."

"Uhh…" He leaned into the wall.

She reached up and put her hand on the Epoxil paneling trying to pass itself off as wood. Smoke peeled from her touch. Hissing, melting plastic sizzled, filling the air with an eye-watering chemical stench. The augmented bodyguard stood on tiptoe, cringing away from her proximity.

"Just once, I'd like to reach the end of a day without some idiot reminding me of what I can't have."

He stared at the wisps peeling away from the black handprint, speechless as she went through the door.

On the other side, as plush an office as the surroundings allowed took up the entirety of a repurposed storeroom. Slats covered the windows, breaking the glow of an outside streetlamp into shimmering bands of floating dust. At the center, a thin, older man in a black suit sat behind an ornate metal desk: two kneeling succubus nudes sculpted in chrome holding a slab of obsidian over their heads. He nudged a white hat up in a gesture of greeting and extended a dark caramel-hued hand as if to indicate her seat.

A few quick steps spared the linoleum and brought her to a field of thick, white tiles upon which waited a metal chair marred with the blued discoloration of repeated exposure to high heat. Kate sat and crossed her legs. She picked at her wristband, the off-white material identical to the substance underfoot. Her chair creaked. Even covered by holographic clothing, she still felt naked. Despite knowing him for years, she always felt exposed sitting in front of him. A Syndicate underboss could make anyone cease to exist over business, even if he liked them.

Some manner of game involving rectangular scraps of paper and colored chips between two men paused as they glanced in her direction. Off to the right of the desk, they sat in downdraft of a slow-spinning ceiling fan and seemed as likely to run as they did to pull guns on her.

"You look sad, my dear. The usual"—he waved his hand about, searching for the right words—"fire in your eyes is dim."

Kate kept her head down, unsettled by the eerie glow her clothing gave off in the dim light. "Shitty morning."

He drew a sharp breath. "What happened to your face? Who has forfeited their life?"

The sound of his voice, deep and dry, brought back a sense of confidence. "Thank you for your concern, El Tío. It's nothing to worry about."

"Look at me."

"I do not want you to think I pry into your thoughts." She closed her eyes and lifted her chin, posing so he could see the bruise.

"You have such magnificent cheekbones. I will find this dog that struck you."

"It's not worth your attention. No one struck me."

El Tío's eyebrow went up.

"Some little bitch punk shot me. It was a misunderstanding." In an effort to avoid eye contact with the underboss, she watched the two men.

They shifted, hands moving away from their guns.

El Tío laughed, patting the desk. After his hand came down twice, he went stone-faced. "I should envy your ability to forgive mistakes, but I don't. Mistakes cost lives."

Kate let her gaze fall into her lap again. "It's done."

A terminal on the desk came to life, tinting El Tío's face and making his hat glow bright blue. He swatted his hand at the terminal, paging over a series of screens; the hat flickered orange. Kate waved at her bracelet, causing a holo-panel to spread open a few inches above it, and poked at the intangible controls. The miniskirt shimmered and changed into jeans while her top grew into a baggy T-shirt. Despite showing no skin beyond face and hands, she still felt exposed.

Her bracelet beeped. A text message indicated a deposit of fifty thousand credits to her account. 'Emily Ramirez' was doing well for herself. She ran her fingers over the solid part of the device, careful not to touch the screen. *How silly that something so small could be so important.*

"Well done. The entire building too… That was rather thorough."

"Sorry, El Tío. Anger management issues."

He chuckled, this time letting the emotion run its natural course. "I'd like for you to consider staying somewhere nicer. I would sleep better knowing you weren't out there in the blight."

"And do what? Curl up on heat tiles in my own little corner of an expensive apartment I couldn't enjoy? I'd feel like a dog in a kennel."

"I promise not to lock the door." He winked.

"Thanks, but it would be a waste. You'd spend a lot of money on a fancy place where I couldn't touch anything in a part of the city where I'd be near people who'd try to shake hands or grab my ass and run away screaming. It's better for everyone if I just stay where I am."

El Tío steepled his fingers, lifting his upper lip in thought. "Very well. There is another matter I need you to attend to. An unintelligent man is making and selling Nightcandy in my part of the city."

He made a gesture as if grasping something from his holo-terminal and throwing it at her wristband. The small device beeped. She held her arm up, swiping past a series of ghostly faces.

Kate ignored the wisp of smoke from the chair as she stood and let her arm fall at her side. "How many need to die this time?"

He sat back with a casual smile. "Only about a dozen."

2

METHODICAL

The rain had stopped by the time Kate got several blocks deep into the grey. A mobile NavMap client on her wrist confirmed the address. The cartoon thumbtack wobbled back and forth with a faint chirp, indicating she neared her destination. Red warning text scrolled across a boundary along the top of the map, where void obscured city detail. It made her smile; there she felt safe.

Kate closed the navigation software and fiddled with the interface for her apparel app. A few pokes of a finger later, her jeans and shirt turned black. Light faded as she dropped her arm; the holo-panel shrank away to nothing. About a block and a half ahead, four armed gang members stood near the door to what once had been an electronics shop. Civilization had cleared out of there years ago; bullet holes and missing windows a testament to the turf war that caused evacuation.

They didn't look like Wharf Rats, too new and too disorganized to have colors yet. Guns, however, they did have, as well as the nervous jitteriness of men who expected to piss someone like El Tío off.

A dull ache spread over her cheek as she eyed their weapons. The runaway's little pistol had hit her like a stiff punch. The artillery these people had would likely knock her senseless. A head-on confrontation in the open would hurt. She crossed the street and jogged to an alley. The majority of structures in this area consisted of one or two stories of commercial space with residential apartments above them. Sizzling squeaks squelched with each step on the rain-soaked plastisteel surface, followed by the reek of incinerating foulness. More than once, she winced at the texture of slime boiling out from underfoot.

I'll never get used to that.

When the NavMap showed she'd reached a point behind the building across the street from the drug operation, she stopped. A chain link fence surrounded a space recessed into the first floor, large enough to accept a small delivery truck. She climbed it with practiced ease, leaving a few glowing orange spots. At the top, she perched like a cat to evaluate the ground on the other side. Years of living in the forgotten parts of the city taught her to look before she stepped. Picking broken glass out of her feet was not an experience she wanted to repeat.

I'd kill a busload of people to be able to wear shoes.

Unable to find an appealing place to jump, she swung herself over and climbed down, tiptoeing through debris. Once clear of the crud stacked against the fence, she trotted to a loading dock with a single rolling door that had not opened in decades. To the left, a person-sized door fluttered in the wind. The soft, ghostly moan of a breeze emanated from a building with no windows. She grabbed the top of the loading dock, at chest level, and lifted herself up. The poured concrete structure was in no danger of catching fire, and afforded her the chance for a few easy breaths. Lacking dirt, stone made the best bed—at least until she met Greg.

She thought about him with a smile, one of the few people in the entire mess that was East City who had always been nice to her without ulterior motives. Kate leaned both hands on the wall, letting her head hang as she pictured his smiling face. Just once, she'd like someone to hold her and tell her everything would be okay. Whenever she fantasized, anyone who dared to be nice melted into a screaming puddle.

With a snarl, she leaned back and kicked in the door. In the garage, racks of mildewing clothing still shrouded in packing material mocked her. She glared at the once-clear plastic, yellow with age and grime. Most of the inventory looked like kids' clothes. None of it would fit her even if she could touch it without destroying it.

Guess this place was another casualty of delivery bots.

Navigating a field of such flammable items proved tiring. Plastic melted and shrank away from her, and quite a few times, the old garments combusted. The fire Kate did not need to see; she *felt* it. Each time it winked into existence, she willed it away. Her observation post couldn't be allowed to burn; at least not yet. She crouched at the doorway between the front and the storeroom, clutching a thick fireproof door.

The desperate had looted the place long ago; a few freestanding racks remained, some tilted over. Scraps of fabric, a sock here, a boy's necktie there; damaged and useless things lingered amid a milieu of security tags and windblown debris from outside. For a moment, she locked eyes with a little girl mannequin holding a sign about a summer swimsuit sale. The racks on either side of it were empty. Someone had even taken the swimsuits. *A bikini beats nothing.* She scowled and crawled forward, savoring the overwhelming stink of mold, the stagnant air a comfortable blanket. Her passage left a series of blackened toe marks, knee smears, and handprints on what had once been thin carpeting; the concentration necessary to prevent lighting the room aflame left her unprepared for a sudden meeting between her head and the radiator along the front window.

Kate recoiled backward, twisting to sit with a hand on her face. Carpet smoldered and charred under her ass for a second or two while she bit back the urge to blow the entire building apart for the insolence of a radiator daring to hit her in the face. Once her anger ebbed, she scooted closer to the window and leaned her back against the metal, cradling her forehead in both hands. The rug beneath her caught fire until she gathered her wits enough to quench it. The people across the street didn't appear to notice the smoke, too engrossed in the video games on their NetMinis to pay attention.

Eventually, the dull pain in her forehead faded and she shifted around to all fours again, peering over the top of the ancient heating element. Glass bits sparkled before her eyes; the demise of the store's giant window had covered it with silica snow.

She listened in on their surface thoughts, mostly images of shooting aliens off the outer hull of a damaged space battleship. Every so often, one of the punks would pause his game to look up and around at the street. In those seconds, she caught one man's worry that their boss—her primary target—would be there within the hour. The brief flash offered no clue as to why the man would be angry, only that something inside the lab hadn't gone right.

This area was too far inland to attract the notice of Wharf Rats, probably why they thought they could handle a high-value product like Nightcandy.

Even the Rats, as established as they were, avoided the stuff. That chem hadn't made it as high up on the police's hate scale as Lace; the cops didn't perform summary executions on those caught selling Nightcandy. Unlike most 'soft' chems, the cops *would* arrest people for selling it. Still, the Syndicate controlled the heavy chems in the east. Sometimes, they had to remind little upstart gangs like this about that fact.

For an hour, she sat curled against the radiator; head sideways atop her arm stretched over the metal. She snorted at the fumes of paint burning from the steel wherever her skin made contact. With her eyes closed, she could fall asleep if she let go. The rug below her had burned off to bare concrete, no longer requiring constant focus to keep fire away. Such places had been her home for most of her life.

A *thunk* from a car door jarred her out of her catnap. Her head popped up as a PubTran cab scurried off down the street, departing the grey zone fast enough for its wake to tear the hat off the man it had dropped off. She recognized the face from El Tío's file. The mark. Kate hadn't even bothered to look at his name.

Marks didn't need names.

She shifted her weight onto the balls of her feet, faced the window, and clutched the edge of the radiator. Of the four idiots outside, one had a large submachine gun slung over his chest. Her gaze tried to bore a hole in the ammunition reserve; she concentrated on the spot, feeling for the sensitive propellant wrapped around the caseless ammunition.

The mark went inside after a terse greeting with the outside men. Manufacturers had gone to great lengths to make ballistic propellant stable. The focus needed to set it off with heat rather than an electrical spark required a lot of concentration. A wisp of blue flames burped from a gap in the weapon's housing an instant before the entire magazine erupted in a crackling deflagration. Pings and zips echoed from slugs and fragments spraying everywhere, sending the other three diving for cover as the owner of the gun crashed to the ground holding his gut.

Kate stood, holding her hands out to either side. Flames enveloped her arms from elbow to fingertip in a sheath of burning that shifted from orange to blue as it gained intensity. A casual swipe launched a head-sized comet from her left hand across the street into the back of the nearest ganger. His clothes ignited on contact. She flung her other hand forward, sending another fireball into the next man's face. They screamed and spun, trying to swat away the burning spots.

Her mind called to the flames, building the lingering low burn into roaring columns of dark blue that engulfed both men. Howling figures staggered about for only seconds before they collapsed. The fourth man ran for the building, squeezing off haphazard shots from a pistol over his shoulder. Kate dove to the ground and curled tight to the radiator. When bullets stopped bouncing around above her, she crawled to the side and peered past the metal frame of a door that once held glass. The large man who had the submachine gun had gone from moaning in pain to vomiting at the sight and smell of his former compatriots' corpses.

She raised one hand and pulled at the air, tugging at the sense of combustion within the smoldering bodies. Gouts of yellow-orange fire burst from the charred husks and lapped over the survivor. He collapsed with a shriek, trying to guard his face. Kate slouched, hair touching the ground as she caught her breath.

This is easier when I'm pissed off.

A sharp snap of her head threw her hair back. She crawled through the bottom half of the old door and stood outside, brushing off the debris that did not burn away from her knees. The big man moaned and tried to drag himself away. Shouting from inside the improvised lab preceded another man running out with an assault rifle. He aimed it left and right, surveying the street as he walked past the dead. When he saw Kate, he pointed it at her, but tilted his head with confusion.

Hands up, she offered a demure smile while concentrating on the air behind him.

"Ain't choo a fine piece."

One of the corpses squeaked as trapped gasses seeped out of holes in his flesh. The man shifted away from the body, grimacing. He tried to look tough, and grinned at her. Even a non-telepath could read his thoughts from the way he ogled.

She covered her mouth with both hands and widened her eyes, staring past him. He whirled around to see what had 'scared' her. When he no longer aimed the rifle at her, she exerted herself. A cyclone of azure fire materialized around him, causing an immediate scream and reflexive automatic gunfire into the building. Kate poured energy into the flames until his motion brought him around, at which point she leapt for the cover of a nearby car. She tucked into the wheel, arms wrapped around her legs as the shooting and screaming continued for several more seconds.

Paint smoked away, leaving two bare-metal handprints where she grasped the side of the long-dead vehicle. The rifleman had collapsed on his back, still burning. Inside the building, the mark shouted at the top of his lungs, demanding answers for what was going on outside. Kate rounded the front end of the broken car and jogged across the street.

The ground floor room held a mass of folding tables covered in chemistry equipment. The mark, and two of his guards, stood near a handful of people in sealed white plastic protective wear with dark grey facemasks. All of them looked at her. She locked eyes with the mark, honing in on his surface thoughts.

Shit, it's that Syndicate freak. I got somethin' for you, puta. His arm flew up, pistol in hand. *Indirium bullets, bitch. Melt this!*

Kate let gravity take her down, falling hard on her knees while twisting sideways to take cover behind the wall by the door. Gunfire rang out, painting the lab in flashes of azure. Dust and sparks burst up from the floor, spraying her with grit. When the barrage stopped, she peeked around the doorjamb and induced a blast of flame in midair, inches from his face. The mark flinched, raising his left arm to guard his eyes. Breathing masks muted the screams of the chemists at the sight of combustion; in their panic, they plowed into the armed men as they scrambled for the door.

She gestured, pouring power into a standing wall of orange flames, backing them into each other at the doorway. Muted shouts of "other door" drowned in a subsequent rush as vapors ignited; a backdraft sucked her flame wall and air deep into the broken shell of the former electronics store. Kate wobbled to her feet as she forced a surge of psionic energy into the burning, amplifying it.

Boom.

The explosion knocked her flat. Instinct stopped her from breathing; while the blast of fire going overhead felt comfortable, it carried toxic fumes. Debris, however, was less pleasant. When the concussive wave ended, she lay in silence, basking in the sting of dozens of cuts, serenaded by car alarms from several blocks away.

Who the hell has a working car here?

She sat up, pulling bits of metal and glass out of her body and dropping them one by one. Years ago, she learned her curse, as she called it, only heated the outside of her skin. The lesson had come painfully; soon after entering the city, fifteen-year-old Kate had stepped barefoot on broken glass, never having encountered it before. Once something pierced her skin, like shards of glass, she could not melt them out. Whatever subconscious process kept her 'on' all the time also prevented self-injury. Of course, glass didn't melt at her touch anyway. She could force it to, but her constant temperature wouldn't dull painful splinters underfoot.

Crackling flames consumed the lab, burning in swirls of greens, blues, purple, reds, and yellows from the different chemicals. Each separate pocket of combustion glimmered in her mind, a sense beyond sight or hearing. Her consciousness mingled with the intensity of the burn; she felt the heat as a sentient mind, almost as if the flames breathed and desired to consume more, but starved. Kate slouched and exhaled. The effort to detonate the entire ground floor left her seriously considering sleeping where she'd fallen.

Someone moaned inside.

Dammit.

She forced herself upright and staggered over to the abandoned assault rifle. Unlike the handguns, the magazine went in the top part of the stock away from the pistol grip, so she didn't worry about touching it.

The comfortable, rubberized pads on the grip melted between her fingers as she picked it up. She walked fast, putting a bullet or two into all the bodies strewn about, moving or not. Draped half out of the building, one man reached up, his molten face fused to his chem mask. Bloody slime oozed from the filter unit dangling at his chin.

"You poor bastard."

She shot him in the forehead and stepped over him. The heat and flame in the lab didn't faze her, though she remained close to the door, squinting from the fumes. She pumped four shots into the mark, just to be sure, and one each to the remaining chemists.

"Oi, Kate. There you are, luv. 'Ave a minnit?"

She jumped at the sudden voice from behind, slipping and sliding in blood-laced chemicals that boiled on contact with her feet. A dark-skinned man, a mixture of African and something Latin, emerged from a hiding place among trash boxes. His gun remained in his belt, and he had both hands up. Heat from the chemical fire caused her bracelet to falter and her clothing to flicker in and out of existence for a second. She rushed out into the cool air, aiming the rifle at him and waving the armband to cool it.

"Have you ever 'eld one of those before, luv? You're 'olding it like a bloody action holo star what barely knows which end to point at the enemy. Stock to the shoulder, look over the sights. You'll not hit a damn thing like that."

"I'm shooting dead men. They don't dodge much." Kate blinked.

"What's with the funny accent?"

"Funny?" He gasped, adopting the hands-on-hip stance of an annoyed debutante. "It's not funny. It's British!"

"Oh." She lifted the rifle. "No offense… It's just a job."

"Wait. I'm not one of these tossers; I'm a woman inside."

Kate pursed her lips. "We all got our issues. I don't have anything to say to that. If you're trying to make me feel bad for having to kill you—"

"Bugger all, you're not listening! I need to talk. I'm only borrowing this idiot."

His surface thoughts rattled on in a woman's voice; somewhere beneath it, a man gurgled, making mental noises as if constipated. Kate took a step back, holding the rifle in a way to minimize how much she destroyed by touching it.

The man shivered and twisted, staggering forward in a zombie gait. His shirt rippled and tore open; the skin on his chest stretched out into the hollow upper body of a topless woman with no hair. Arms to the sides, the flesh apparition smiled.

"There we go." The creature's voice sounded feminine and seemed to emanate from nowhere in particular. "Does this make it easi—?"

Kate learned where the full auto selector was.

The recoil knocked her on her ass, but she held the trigger down until the magazine ran dry. More than half the bullets went off into the sky, sparking and clanking into a skyscraper a block away. A nude woman with paper-white skin, generous hips, and shin-length blonde hair appeared in the midst of a cloud of glowing vapor behind where the perforated corpse hit the ground. Kate screamed like a schoolgirl, and released an expanding torus of blue flames.

"Oh, hell," said the woman.

When Kate opened her eyes, she found herself alone with the scent of burned meat. Patches of fire clung to anything flammable, fluttering in the wind. The wail of distant sirens got her upright in a hurry. She looked up at the stars and over at flames inside buildings on the far side of the street.

"Bastards probably saw that on satellite." She backed away from the former drug lab. "Shit."

Flashing blue and purple lights reflected on the glass of a building several blocks distant, high in the air. She darted into the nearest alley and headed for the black zone.

She needed to get somewhere safe.

3

OUT OF THE INFERNO

K ate stumbled down an empty street where the line between grey zone and civilization blurred. The few people she encountered seemed absorbed in their own worlds. One man sprawled on the ground talking to a hallucination of his dead grandmother. A woman with bright pink hair reclined on a public bench, her face lit blue by ViewPane glasses, lost to a virtual simulation. From the muttered sound of her conversation with another player, she played some manner of vampire game. Another man sat on the ground like a wide-eyed five-year-old boy with marbles, only he picked at the bottoms of discarded synthbeer cans to get at the coolant chemicals. A small cry of victory preceded him raising one to his nose and snorting up a puff of white vapor.

The odor of boiled blood followed her, tickling here and there as it steamed away from her skin. She had crossed the dangerous zone, Sector 2629, though the decay had spread at least a mile into the surrounding areas. Sector 2577, adjacent to the south, had the unusual trait of being rather mild in terms of grey zones. Whispers claimed local businesses threw large sums of credits at the police, resulting in a quicker response time and even the occasional patrol. Cops almost never showed up in the grey; that she had seen one or two here in the past few months had proved the rumor to her.

With that arrangement, Sector 2577 had the distinct oddity of going from an area blacked off the NavMap to a close-to-civilized hybrid of gang-controlled territory and operational small businesses that did surprisingly well given their surroundings. Delivery bots experienced strange malfunctions here, except for large orders to local merchants. The sniper rifles had quieted as of late, as ComTec Corporation removed the sector from their delivery availability.

She staggered into a lean on a lamppost and hung there in an effort not to faint. Her mind derailed from finding her way home to pondering the corruption of the world. The cops only cared about this place because they got paid to. Merchants only survived because the national delivery bot system stopped coming here. Gangs thrived because dolls and machines took most of the low-educated jobs away and guns were cheap and legal. Perhaps everything worked as intended after all; those in power encouraged the unwanted to kill each other. A self-cleaning infection.

Kate wound up laughing. The corruption kept her working. She was part of it. Born from it, escaped from it, and suckered right back into it.

"You okay?" asked a man who had snuck up on her.

She shoved off the pole and stumbled on. "Yeah, fine."

He followed. "Looks like you can barely walk. You sure you don't—"

"Don't touch me!" she yelled, yanking her arm away. She walked backward for a few steps, hands raised. "Seriously, just... don't."

Scraggly black hair shifted over a dark, skin-tight shirt as he cocked an eyebrow. He raised his hands. "Suit yourself."

Kaos, I think. One of Fiona's heavy hitters. Kate stopped, letting her head hang. "Kaos? Sorry, bad night."

Kaos chuckled. "You gonna be okay?"

For a moment, she looked him up and down, all seven feet and change of him. Not many people out here could muster anything close to genuine concern in their eyes, and the way he looked at her made her want to curl into a dark place and forget the world. No matter how much she *wanted* to let him carry her home and hold her, she could never touch him. Never mind the minor detail of Kaos having a boyfriend... err, husband.

"Yeah," she muttered.

Her tone made him back off with an apologetic face, as though he did something wrong. She trudged down an alley, heading for the oscillating shimmer of peachy-pink-toned light. The street-side of the building looked unremarkable, with an appearance that all but matched every other abandoned residence tower in this part of town. However, on the alley facing, a striped green awning over a deep porch held up pink letters that spelled out *Tanked*. Around and through the logo, a holographic couple floated and spun as they made love in defiance of gravity.

Kate went up the steps onto the porch, careful to walk on the narrow strip of metal between the stairs and the door. Greg put that there after the fourth time she burned footprints into the false wood. The stink of molten Epoxil could linger for weeks.

At this hour, the bar room stood empty, save for Greg, the bouncers Harley and Joan, and one of the waitresses everyone called 'Nice.' Harley leaned against the wall on the far side of the bar, arms folded. Between eyebrows and beard, she couldn't tell if his eyes were even open. Joan busied herself—at least, everyone assumed Joan was female—at the GravPokit machine. None of the regulars had the nerve to ask, and Kate didn't give a shit. Greg had gotten a cheap game unit, it didn't use real balls, but the device simulated a click whenever the holographic ones collided. Joan had gotten good at banking shots off the lower plane into the top corners. The mere sight of twenty-four three-inch spheres floating in three dimensions made Kate woozy.

"Shit, girl, what the hell happened?" Greg started to run out from the bar, but stopped at a raised hand.

Kate didn't look at him or slow down. "Need two stims, a shot, and a nap."

A door at the back end of the bar led into a narrow corridor that looked like something from an old prewar hotel with dark brown fake wood walls and brass fixtures. To the left, a wiry older man sat behind a counter in an alcove. He looked up with an open mouth ready to speak, but when he saw Kate, he went back to what he was doing.

"Hey, Phil."

"Kate," he muttered.

She forced herself to trot in an attempt to minimize damage to the carpet and gasped each time her weight came down. Every cut, bruise, and embedded glass splinter pulsed with each step. The narrow corridor ended when it joined a wider hallway running left and right. Greg had gone to great expense to dress it up in the image of a high-end twentieth century hotel. Kate ignored the décor she had seen a hundred times before and wobbled as fast as she could to the last door on the right. A chirp emanated from the wall panel as she waved her bracelet near it, and the door slid to the side with a hiss.

A large, clear cylinder dominated a room with a non-flammable tile floor, four feet high and filled with peach-hued slime. The thick metal disc at its base whirred and blinked with filtration systems and status readouts. A matching metal disc mounted to the ceiling above the tank would receive the two-inch-thick cylinder when it closed. Metal stairs wrapped around one side, leading up to the edge of the tank. Kate collapsed on a bench by two cabinets intended to hold the clothing of whatever amorous couple rented the room. To normal people, the tank offered a zero-g sex adventure.

To her, it was home.

Her face reddened at a knock.

"Kate, it's me, Greg. You okay?"

"Yeah, come in."

The electronics responded to her verbal approval and opened the door. Greg entered carrying a tray, thigh-length dreadlocks swaying behind him like a cape. He set the stuff on the small table near the cabinets and spun to face her with a four-inch red Stimpak clutched in each hand. Kate laughed at the shower-slasher way he held them and looked down.

"Don't tell me you're embarrassed? You look dressed."

"Yeah, but I know you know I'm not." She gathered her hair off her shoulders and bent forward. "Remember—"

"Yeah, yeah, I know. Do it quick like, jabbin' ya. So'z they don't melt." He approached, standing close behind her. "Hey, girl. Relax. I seen enough tittie workin' here to last me till I'm dead fifty years. Kinda funny."

"What's funny?" She switched the bracelet off.

Naked.

"For someone 'oo neva wear nothin', yer awful shy." Greg's energy diminished, he let off a sympathetic sigh. "Dis place drainin'. De city no' be kind tae da' forest nymph."

Maybe I should go back out there. Kate slumped forward, rubbing her face. "Yeah, well, maybe it bothers me because I don't have a fucking choice."

"Oi, lady!" He gestured at dozens of bleeding cuts all over her, revealed when her clothes vanished. "What the 'ell 'appened to yas?"

She made a pinching gesture. "Tiny explosion."

He stabbed her in the shoulder with one of the Stimpaks. "T'aut you was untouched by fire."

"Ow, dammit, not so hard." She reached back and rubbed the spot. "Fire I can stop from hurting me; flying sharp shit, not so much."

Greg picked at a few larger pieces of shrapnel in her back, tugging them out and waving his hand to cool it. When her wounds ceased shrinking, he jabbed her with the other autoinjector. The pneumatic hiss drowned in another shout of pain as a whiff of chemical fumes drifted by. He looked at the tip, a metal nub the size of a pinky finger with a small hole in the middle.

"Na melted dis time. I gettin' better at dis."

She shivered as the last of her external wounds stitched closed. *I wonder if those little nanobots know they're millimeters away from destruction.* He moved the tray to the bench next to her, a plate of raw chicken breast and a shot glass with a dark whiskey in it. She ate, cooking the chicken by touch, consuming it far too fast to care what it tasted like. Greg shook his head, chuckling.

"For a little ting, you eat like 'Arley."

"Greg… are you really from Jamaica or do you fake that accent?"

"You know damn well where I'm from." He chuckled. "Works, doesn't it?"

She leaned back, looking up at him. "Yeah." She opened her mouth, but hesitated. After a sigh, she let off a wistful laugh. "That's the problem."

Greg poured the shot of whiskey into her mouth; she clamped her jaw shut, swallowing the puff of flame. She got up and wandered to the cabinets, setting the bracelet inside as he went for the door.

"Greg?"

Before it could close behind him, he leaned a foot back to catch it. "Ya?"

"Thanks again for letting me crash here."

"No problem." He winked, and walked off, letting the door close.

Kate made her way to the tank while examining herself for injury. Blood had become black streaks smeared here and there, flaking off as ash while she moved up the stairs. She sat on the edge of the metal deck and dangled her feet into the syrupy gel. It bubbled and popped, like some kind of volcanic muck. After letting all the air out of her lungs, she shoved off, suppressing the urge to squeal at the brief presence of cold all over.

She went fetal and sank. After a few seconds to prepare herself, she inhaled warm goop. Many people were uncomfortable with breathable gel. Even those who had military training for jump travel took years to become acclimated to aspirating liquid. A few weeks ago, the idea of being inside a tank again had frightened her more than breathing the slime. She weathered the memory of screaming and uncurled once she adjusted to inhaling and exhaling syrup. The huge entertainment tank had at least a ten-foot diameter, plenty of room for a foursome. She swam to the bottom, where it projected a holographic control panel through the clear wall. One button closed the cylinder against the ceiling; another filled it to the top.

She skipped the sexy music.

Weightless in the dense gel, she let her limbs go wherever chance took them. Everyone else that came to Greg's establishment sought a few stiff drinks and the novelty of fucking in a tank, some manner of kink started by military people who'd spent far too much time in deep space. For Kate, this placed offered a sealed tank, a locked door, two bouncers, and a friend between her and the world. As much as floating in a cylinder made her feel like a caged science project all over again, she couldn't argue it was more comfortable than trying to curl up on a slab of concrete.

Here, she could sleep.

The constant heat stopped whenever she lost consciousness. Living on the street, she would wake up every hour or so when she got too cold. With consciousness, came warm comfort. Ever since she had found Greg, she could make it through a whole night again. She daydreamed about him touching her, sliding her hand up and down her arm while pretending it belonged to him. Her imagination whispered his fake Jamaican accent over her shoulder. *Et gon' be all right, girl.*

She wrapped her arms around herself, closed her eyes, and tried to feel safe.

MECHANICAL THRUMMING PERVADED THE GEL. THE FACES OF TWO MEN IN white lab coats, one dark and one light, morphed and stretched in the curved glass as they leaned close. They stared at her while peeking at datapads and rubbing their chins. Three other men in coats stood farther back. Kate swam to the wall of the tank, palms pressed to the surface, flashing a wide-eyed smile at them. Her reflection had no shape: no chest, no hips, and a wide-eyed 'please like me' face she hadn't made in years. Stringbean limbs swished back and forth amid a floating cloud of auburn hair. Sometimes the boredom got so bad she made friends with her reflection, pretending she had a sister trapped in a backward world she could talk to.

The oldest of the men, wrinkled face and silvery hair, walked up between the nearer two. They argued, but she couldn't make out more than warbling tones due to the thick material. The urgency in his expression seemed strange. She listened to their thoughts.

The older man shook his head. *Absolutely not. We've put far too much effort into this project.*

Doctor Solomon, are you forgetting the purpose? asked the man on his right. *The genetics team can't explain or correct her persistent skin temperature. We can't use her for anything. The project is a failure.*

The old man gestured at her. *Look at her. She's only seven. Psionic or not, she's still a little girl. I won't be a party to killing a child. Scrap the project; I'd like to work with her on my own time. Who knows what a few years could do? You're so worried about hitting milestones, you've lost sight of the long-term picture.*

Horseshit. The younger scientist scowled. *You're a sentimental old fool.*

Kate's smile collapsed into a grimace of terror. She shivered and tried to slap the glass, but the viscous fluid did not allow her hands enough speed to make noise on impact.

We've been unable to find a way to mitigate her constant pyrokinetic emanation, said the younger one. *Her external temperature is enough to damage or destroy most anything she touches. Equipment, disguises, vehicles... she is completely unusable.*

She doesn't melt through metal, said Solomon. *Her external temperature ranges from 600 to 800 degrees. There are materials that can withstand that. There's got to be a way.*

Oh, fine then. We'll make her a metal dress. That won't stand out. The man on the left rolled his eyes. *You're too close, old man. This isn't your granddaughter; this is a weapons project. Have you forgotten that?*

Her pathetic, begging expression went from man to man as she read their minds: the two younger ones were terrified and wanted to kill her, the middle one didn't care at all, and the dark one hated *it.* Only the old one thought of her as a real person.

Kate stared at Doctor Solomon, sending her voice into his mind. *Please help me!*

Solomon whirled on the dark-skinned man, red-faced and screaming. *She's a human being. She's just a little girl. How can you even suggest what you're suggesting?*

The man on the right poked a finger at his datapad. *She is too dangerous. We can barely contain her now. What's she going to be like at puberty? What kind of abilities is she going to have as an adult?*

The younger pale scientist held up a hand. *We have no idea if she will experience the usual peak in the younger teen years we so often see with telekinetics. Her powers may weaken, grow, or stay the same. We're in uncharted territory, Ramesh.*

Ramesh frowned at her. Kate paddled away from the tank wall, not liking the look in his eyes. *I cannot risk what may or may not happen. If she does surge, we'll have no way to predict how to deal with her. We have clearly done something beyond any previously recorded pyrokinetic.*

Pale shook his head. *Agreed, her test data is off the charts... However, all that is meaningless if she cannot interact with the world without standing out.*

Solomon fumed. *We could try treating her like a damned person. If she thinks of us as family, we won't need to control her. Her side effect might even go away as she matures. W-we could develop some kind of heat-mitigating bodysuit. Indirium threads ought to do the trick.*

Ramesh waved him off. *Even if we went to that expense, the suit would be as hot as she is. She still couldn't touch a damn thing... and forget thermal sensors. The assassin everyone sees coming from orbit.*

The old man sighed, head down. *Please, Ramesh, I can't in good conscience be part of destroying a child. Let me work with her on the side, out of my own budget.*

The Director isn't willing to wait another seven years based on a maybe. Ramesh had no trouble looking right at her, even when thinking about killing her. *We're going to scrap this attempt and try again.*

Her best pleading stare had done nothing. Ramesh wanted to end her life; he reached past the curved shell toward a button out of sight. In his thoughts, a killing liquid seeped into the gel she breathed. They weren't even going to let her out of the tank. Her safe place, her bed, changed in that instant to a death trap. She wailed in silence, breathable gel unable to produce sound as it passed over vocal cords. Solomon pounced on Ramesh, wrestling him away from the kill button. Pale jumped into the fray.

Kate clawed and kicked at the glass, desperate to get out.

Armed guards rushed in and subdued the old man before dragging him away into the hall. Dr. Solomon screamed loud enough for Kate to hear him call them monsters. The other two stood, fixed their coats and shirts, and Pale wiped a trickle of blood from his nose. Both of them glared at her as if it was somehow her fault.

Terror became anger.

Kate floated in the center of her tank, glaring at Ramesh, hating every inch of him. Tiny hands balled into fists. She wanted him far away from her. She wanted him not to hurt her, wanted him to go away. His dark skin turned red, blisters appeared all over. Some swelled to the size of oranges and burst, releasing bloody steam as all the fluid inside his body boiled. His wailing gurgled to a halt as he collapsed, twitching and dead, leaving a bloody hand smear down the outside of the tank. Vapor peeled from his lifeless mouth.

In a moment of lapsed anger, Kate attempted to scream at the sight of what she had done, and burst into tears. She calmed in a moment as the need to escape overpowered her repulsion at the gore. The silence of her fluid-filled capsule left her heartbeat thunderous. She looked at Pale, projecting a telepathic shout.

Let me out!

Pale leapt away in horror.

I promise I won't hurt anyone if you let me out.

He shook his head so fast his glasses flew off.

Kate pointed at what remained of Ramesh. *He wanted to kill me. Do you still want to kill me?*

He stared, backing away. *Oh, God, kill it. Kill it!* "N-no."

Kate closed her eyes and curled up, head to knee, hands clasped under her chin. Panic took her; they were going to leave her locked in here until they could kill her. She looked up and down at the metal discs at either end of her clear prison, blurry from the peach-hued slime. Most of her life had been spent stuck in the tank, which used to feel safe. The outside world had always been scary, and whenever the men let her out to play 'games' with funny machines, she longed to go back where she felt protected.

Now, she wanted out more than anything.

She stared past her toes at the wavering dark lines of vents in the floor. The gel escaped that way, perhaps she could too. She swam to the bottom, laced her fingers among the metal slits, and pulled. Her feet slid over the slick plastisteel, and her effort did nothing but terrify her more. Pale edged closer to the tank, reaching for the bad button. Kate snapped her head up to stare at him; he leapt back, screaming. Finding the floor useless, she kicked off and floated up to eye level with him.

She pressed her hands on the cylinder wall, pushing and banging. The man continued backing away. Kate sobbed in silence, trapped in liquid, looking all around her for anything she could do to run away before the men came back to hurt her. A flash in her memory brought back the image of a small metal can. They asked her to hold it, but seconds after she grasped it, it burst and sprayed her with something they called 'soda.'

Kate braced her hands against the wall and closed her eyes. She focused on her desire to generate heat. Power flowed into the slime around her; before long, the thick syrupy gel flowing into her lungs became too painful to inhale. Kate held her breath and kept pushing. The gloopy sputtering of boiling gel grew deafening in the narrow cylindrical prison. Sparks arced and snapped in the liquid as the millions of nanobots that fed and tended her met their demise.

Her eyes opened to slits. Red light flashed outside as an alarm went off in the room. A digitized woman's voice said something about temperature limits. The trembling scientist crept closer to the tank, another try for the kill switch. Kate thrust her legs down; a mute scream of terror displaced the gel from inside her. All of her fear spiked into a psionic outburst.

Splintering cracks raced down the cylinder wall with ear-piercing squeals; a split-second later, it exploded. A torrent of thousand-degree viscous perfluorocarbon fluid boiled the skin from Pale's face in an instant; arm-length shards of tank glass impaled him before he could scream.

Kate flowed with the tidal wave of deadly slime, by some minor miracle avoiding more serious damage than a few small cuts. The flow carried her against the wall, under the lockers where they kept the silver hot suits the men always wore to 'handle' her. She lay on her side, staring at the skinless, poached corpse studded with razor spears of glass. Blood swirled in the steaming gel around him.

She tried to scream, but sputtered gel and choked.

Whenever they took her out of the tank, one would hold her upside down by the ankles so she could drain her lungs. She liked the men in white coats before they wanted to kill her. Even if they had to dress head-to-toe in bulky silver suits to do it, most were willing to play with her. Up until that moment, they had been nice. Kate scowled at the smoking wreckage of the tank. Maybe it wasn't nice that they left her in there so much.

With no one to help her clear her lungs, she gasped and coughed, spitting out gel until she cried from how much it hurt. Elbows and forehead on the floor, she wailed as fluid leaked from her mouth. For minutes, she remained in that pose, trying to listen to the rush of air in her throat over the blaring alarm. Her first attempt to stand ended with her foot flying out from under her and her body landing flat on her chest with a squish. On the second try, she fell hard on her butt. She dragged herself on all fours through the slippery fluid, searching for a dry spot to stand. Realizing the entire room had flooded with two inches of goop, Kate sat back on her heels and tried not to look at the dead men as she scooted on her knees toward the exit. When the door opened, she offered a neutral face tinted with pleading at a man and a woman in green camouflage. They gawked at the carnage.

Kate flashed an innocent face and waved. "Hi. I'm sorry for breaking the machine." She pointed at Ramesh. "He wanted to hurt me."

Her hope shattered when they reacted with fear and aimed rifles at her. She shrieked, raising her arms, wanting them to go away. A tornado of azure flames burst forth from the space between her hands. Both soldiers howled and fell in place, their uniforms burning.

Snarling and gasping for breath, she crawled over the bodies to the open door. Charred handprints seared into flesh as she pulled herself out from the muck.

Why does everyone want to hurt me? What did I do? Am I bad?

Slime steamed away from her skin as she crept to the edge of the peach colored puddle and found footing on bare metal floor. Kate held her arms up, watching the liquid sizzle away to flaky, white powder that she brushed off. Her hair lofted in a noticeable breeze in the hall, though she still felt warm.

A man in a lab coat rounded the corner, his casual stroll a clue he was unaware of what had happened. Again, she tried an innocent smile and wave, but he screamed. The sight of her out in the open, uncontained, terrified him. Everyone in white so far had wanted her dead.

She wouldn't let them kill her.

Kate leaned at him; the stomp of her foot sent a wet slap echoing as she screamed, "Go away!"

Fire erupted out of the air and coiled around him like a snake. He shrieked and flailed, falling over seconds later with ghastly burns. Kate bit her lower lip as she crept up to the moaning body. She stood near his head with her feet together, swaying side to side as if playing with a dress she couldn't wear. The sight of what she could do to people horrified her. Small test robots and target plates didn't smell this bad when she made them burn. Kate stared at the floor; part of her felt guilty, but nothing in the 'play room' had ever tried to kill her. A glance around at featureless, sterile corridors offered no clue which one would take her to the place they always took her to play. Maybe if she went there and did what they wanted, all of this would stop.

The man wheezed. Blood welled out of his mouth, pooling on the floor. She crept backward as it seeped closer and closer to her toes.

"I just wanted you to go away," she whispered.

Tears fizzled from her cheeks. *Is this why they all hate me?*

He gurgled, trying to crawl.

You want to hurt me, said Kate, with telepathy. *That's bad.*

The scientist shook his head, still trying to slide away from her. *No, no, no.*

Kate peeked at his surface thoughts, but found such agony she recoiled with a shriek and hid her face in her hands. Red hair swirled as she shook her head. The man convulsed, gasped, and went still.

She tried to talk to him with her mind voice, but sensed emptiness. The puddle of blood continued expanding, forcing her back in tiny steps until her shoulders met the frigid wall. Kate tried to press herself into the metal, more afraid of him dead than alive. The odor of burning paint made her turn; black lettering smudged wherever she had touched it. Curious, she dragged her fingers over the wall, erasing the writing like wet ink, but leaving the shiny silver wall unscathed. For a moment, she played with the funny letters, oblivious to the dead man behind her.

A loud klaxon went off in the compound, snapping her out of her finger 'un-painting.' She looked at her hands, swatting them together to clear off ash. Eyes closed, she took a few steps, refusing to look until she was sure she wouldn't see the body. Sirens blared; the normal bright lights cut out. The hallways became a nightmare of blackness, punctuated by flashing crimson.

Kate remembered this game, and did not like it. She couldn't see in the dark, but the men with the black masks could find her. The last time they made her play this game, she tried to run into the maze and hide, feeling her way with hands on the walls. The men chased her, shooting her with painful darts that made her woozy and sick. To win the game, she had to stay away from them, not be caught, but she couldn't see. The fourth time they dragged her to that awful game, they left the lights on—and the dart guns stopped hurting her. Whenever she saw them shoot, the chem darts melted on contact.

After what she'd done to the bad men, she feared they'd use something worse than darts on her now. Trembling, she sniveled and ran forward. This whole place was evil; everyone here wanted to hurt her. They never let her spend much time out of the tank, leaving her with no idea which way to go. Being out of the tank without six men directing her every move felt almost as scary as the button Ramesh wanted to push.

Kate whirled around, whining at the sameness of every corridor. Having no better ideas, she ran in the direction she happened to be facing already. Sterile metal corridor zoomed by, a door here and there she didn't spare a second look. She slowed to a creep at the sound of boots squeaking on the tiles around the corner of a four-way intersection.

Whispering came from the right hallway. Kate looked down at the floor; the faint hiss of tears boiling off the tops of her feet louder than the men approaching.

They want to hurt me too.

She raised her head, glaring at the open space in the junction.

Why does everyone want to hurt me? Little hands made fists. *I hate it here!*

The air between her and the corner ignited in a flash, and she pushed the whirling cloud of fire around the bend. She flinched at the sound of screaming and several errant gunshots, but kept her mind locked on the presence of the flaming cyclone. Each shriek scared her more and made the fire hotter. When all sounds of men stopped, she relaxed and the burn went out. She put a hand over her nose, a pitiful shield against the stink of scorched meat and plastic. Tiny fingers curled around the wall. She trembled, afraid to look at what she had done.

For a minute, she stood there bawling, ashamed of what these people made her do.

The blaring alarm urged her forward. She held her stomach at the sight of bodies collapsed over each other. At least five soldiers lay in a smoking heap. Tiptoeing over the nasty muck, she raised her arms and tried to get past them without touching anything. With nowhere else to go, she had to step on one man's chest; a small charred footprint seared into muscle. She whimpered at the feeling of flesh boiling underfoot and almost slipped as his skin peeled away. The body moved, startling a yelp out of her. A glove flew to her leg, grabbing her about the ankle and lifting. Melting skin clung to her sole and tangled in her toes, stretching into thin strands.

Smoke poured from the armored glove. The soldier's attempt to crush her ankle stalled when the material melted. He screamed as his fingers made contact with skin, and threw her leg upward. Kate fell backward, landing on top of another corpse, which ignited at her touch. She shrieked, flailing about in an uncoordinated attempt to stop touching the dead man.

The dead man she'd created.

Terror feasted upon her guilt, growing into a specter of doom. She *had* to get away from the dead bodies—she couldn't *stand* touching them—before they came back to punish her.

She drew in a breath to scream.

A chirp froze her in place. The man sat up, a bright red patch of muscle in the approximate shape of a small foot in the center of his chest. He pointed a massive pistol in her general direction with his uninjured hand, sweeping it back and forth as though he couldn't see her with the warped visor fused to his head.

Total panic washed over her. She shut her eyes and screamed as loud as she could, wanting the bad people gone. A thunderous *boom* resounded in the metal-walled corridor, and a rush of air from the side pushed her over. She sprawled on the floor, landing on dry crumbles instead of squishy dead.

Her eyes snapped open. Blackened bones and ash scattered around her, all that remained of the soldiers. The metal walls had blued from heat damage, and patches of steel glowed. She pulled her knees under her chin and stared at a smoking skull. Everyone she met in here would try to hurt her. She sat and rocked, teetering between sorrow and anger. What did she do so wrong that they wanted to hurt her?

After a deep breath, she got to her feet and glared at nothing in particular. *I'm not gonna cry. There's nothing wrong with me. They're the ones who are bad.* A woman in a white coat carrying an armload of datapads skidded to a halt as she spotted her. Kate stared a challenge right back. It took only seconds for the scientist to drop the pads and beg for her life. Kate stomped forward, moving without fear in the wake of the fleeing woman. That scientist didn't want to hurt her, only wanted to get away. Kate's lip quivered, but she didn't hurt the woman.

Inferno consumed room after room as her rage lashed out at everything as well as anyone she saw who didn't run away or beg. Anyone who wanted her dead, she surrounded in flames. She wandered lost, for a time forgetting her hunt for a way out and searched only for things to destroy. Offices burned, computer terminals went up in smoke, and blue fireballs incinerated anything that looked combustible. Hunger growled in her gut, and the scent of chicken soup on the air made her change course and move up to a jog down the corridor from whence it came.

Amid the silence of the facility, the patter of tiny bare feet on a metal corridor seemed the loudest sound in the world.

She jogged amid the pulsing red light from emergency flashers, heedless of the scent of smoke in the air. The fragrance of food led her to a pair of double doors, which she shoved aside on her way into a large cafeteria hall with long, metal tables. Three steps into the room, she caught sight of a man. She looked up at a soldier a second before a shot rang out. The impact hit her in the chest like a punch, swatting her to the ground. Molten lead dribbled over her ribs to the floor. Paralyzed from the strike, she stared at the ceiling tiles, unable to breathe or move. Tears sizzled off her cheeks. She wheezed, curling onto her side, and burst into tears, wailing like a child who'd skinned her knee. Boots tromped up behind her. A man in green camouflage hovered, a shaking pistol levelled at her face.

"Oh, man... What the fuck are they doing here? It's just a kid."

His boot touched her shoulder, nudging her flat on her back. He gasped at the sight of a giant bruise rather than a gunshot wound. Her crying ebbed to a snivel. She grunted, making him jump. A childish response to the source of her pain manifested as a scream and torrent of blue fire from an outstretched arm. Uniform and flesh blew off char-blackened bones, floating away as flakes of ash. From the thigh down, the man's legs remained untouched. Everything above had reduced to scorched bone.

Kate rubbed her chest, whimpering, testing the bruise with her fingertips.

She looked at what she had done to him and didn't know how to feel.

"They're going to be mad at me for breaking soldiers," she whispered. After a moment of consideration, she knocked one of the legs over and frowned. *They tried to kill me, so I don't care.*

Unsure if she wanted to throw up, cry, or hide, Kate stood and limped among the tables with one arm tucked to her chest over the sore spot. Everything in here looked metal; aside from a few stacks of napkins, her power couldn't ignite anything. A door at the far end led to an industrial-sized kitchen, and she soon found a storage compartment filled with slabs of ground beef sealed in plastic. The slabs were longer than her height, three inches thick, and wide enough for her to use as a mattress. She dragged one out onto the floor, and squatted over it, savaging the opportunistic meal. Her fingers pierced plastic and seared the meat on contact.

She glommed down handful after handful until she didn't want to move. A gasp from behind startled her away from watching grease burn off her skin. She whirled, staring up at an older woman in a blue uniform coat bearing a white nametag. Flame surrounded Kate's hand, incinerating a few squiggles of vat-grown beef.

"Hey, child. Easy. Where are your clothes?" The woman slipped her coat off. "I'm not going to hurt you. I work in the kitchen."

Kate lowered her arms, staring without words as the woman wrapped the garment over her.

"There. You shouldn't be running around na—"

Smoke peeled from the fabric a half second before it ignited in several places. The woman gasped and stepped back. Kate remained motionless, making a face that asked the woman why she was dumb. Burning cloth slipped to the floor around her and became ash.

"They didn't make me right," mumbled Kate. "I'm not useful."

"Aww." The woman reached to pat her on the head, but thought better of it.

"Back away from the girl. Do it now!" shouted a man.

The woman jumped. Kate edged about in a slow turn to face the door.

A soldier pointed a rifle at them, taking cover in the entrance of the mess hall. The woman moved to get between them, but stopped before she took full step when Kate shrieked.

"Leave me alone! Stop making me hurt people!"

Her rage exploded as a cloud of fire in midair by the door, blasting the soldier off his feet. Blue muzzle flare spat from the weapon; bullets raked over the ceiling, far from hitting anyone. He slid out of sight, screaming. Kate looked up at the kitchen worker. The kindness in her eyes had faded into the realm of terror.

Kate folded her hands in front of herself. "You're nice. I'm not gonna hurt you."

The woman forced a smile. "It's not right. What they do here is not right."

Kate left her there and padded back across the mess hall to the door with one hand on her full belly.

The dream blurred through a dozen more dead soldiers and screaming scientists. Kate stared at her little fingers clutching a door handle. She pulled and shoved, and the grey slab swung away. Wind lofted her hair and made her squint as she stepped onto a metal porch amid the glare of sunlight.

She raised an arm to shield her eyes from the majesty of nature she had never seen before. Pine trees waved back and forth in the wind, highlighted with bits of white settled on the needles. Fresh air smelled funny, but it carried away the stink of burned flesh. The touch of a breeze on her skin mesmerized her. Moving air had always come straight down from above, never a sideways gust. This wind still made her shiver, but she marveled the way it made her feel free.

Rows of parked trucks sat in a snow-covered dirt lot at a wall of trees. Far off in the distance, the silhouette of an enormous city segmented the sky into blocky patches of blue. She looked at her feet, stepping with care on her way down the four steps until her toes met loose soil. A giggle escaped as she explored the feeling of standing on a surface other than shiny metal.

Flickering drew her attention to a dozen little red dots swarming on her chest. Soldiers, hidden among the vehicles, aimed rifles at her. A young man with light hair and a long, sand brown coat emerged from a dark car closer to the building. A leather-gloved hand waved at the soldiers to hold their fire.

Kate bit her lip and ground her toes into the dirt as he walked over. She looked up when the red dots vanished and his shadow fell on her.

"Hello, Katie. I'm Agent Perrin."

"Why don't you have head voices?"

He chuckled. "For my job, I have to know secret things. I have a machine in my head that helps me keep secrets. Please don't try to peek. It will hurt you if look too hard. I don't want you to get hurt."

"I don't want people to hurt me!" she shouted, stomping.

All of the soldiers shifted.

"Shh." Agent Perrin raised one hand. "No one is going to hurt you, Katie. We can't let you wander off alone. The world is a dangerous place for a child your age to be alone. If you promise me you'll behave yourself, I'll make sure no one hurts you."

Kate glared at him.

"Would you like a nice dress?"

She folded her arms. "No, I'll destroy it."

"What about a pony?"

"I'll kill it if I touch it."

"You don't want to be alone, do you?"

Her face twisted up to cry, but she held it in. "I don't wanna die. I think you are lying. Those green people want to hurt me."

"Katie, you are a special little girl with special abilities. Bad people in the world will try to use you as a weapon."

She tapped her foot. "Isn't that what you want me for? They said I wasn't useful."

"Well… Certain issues have presented themselves, which makes training you as a field operative a tad awkward. We will change plans and learn from you instead. No one is angry with you for what you've done. We're… curious now. You'll be safe here. No one will hurt you."

"You wanna put me back in a tank and lock me up forever. No. I'm going away. I don't wanna be here!"

Kate ducked around him and started to run, but halted when all the red dots found her chest again.

"We can't let you leave, Katie. You may be a little child, but you are too dangerous. Power like yours is not meant for a mind so young. I'm sorry."

"No…" She looked down, trembling at all the red fireflies on her bare chest. "*I'm* sorry."

A low rumble began from inside the building and fire was everywhere.

4

COLD

K ate jolted awake, still floating in gel. Momentary panic resulted in silent screams and clumsy flailing. At the realization she was no longer a child and not *locked* inside the tank, she went limp. A rare sense of coldness surrounded her each morning, created by the several second delay between waking and her subconscious furnace firing up. The morning chill seemed stronger today, pronounced enough to make her shiver and curl into a ball. It intensified over her shoulders, spreading across her back. Her mouth opened in a silent scream, but the unnatural cold faded.

She lost all feeling in her left arm.

Seconds later, it moved of its own accord, stroking her hair.

I'm so sorry, Kate, said a voice in her mind. Female. British.

She blinked, unable to sense or move the limb, which continued its reassuring caress.

What the hell is happening to me now?

Her left hand moved to her shoulder, hugging herself. *Trying to make you feel better, luv.*

Why is my arm numb? She grabbed the renegade limb by the wrist and held it out.

The voice in her mind sighed. *It's what you want, isn't it? No one can touch you. I was just trying to be nice and make it feel like someone was comforting you.*

She shivered. *Are you a ghost?*

I suppose that's close enough for the moment. Sensation returned to her arm; a warm glove sliding up from her fingertips to her shoulder. *I hopped inside you. Please don't panic.*

Her hands explored her body, looking for anything out of the ordinary.

Will you relax? I'm a friend. I want to talk, that's all.

Kate swam to the bottom of the tank and waved at a sensor, which created a holo-panel inside the gel. One button initiated the release sequence. She flipped upright and kicked off the bottom, gliding to the wall by the stairwell.

What about? asked Kate, keeping her head below the surface of the draining fluid.

You're not as alone as you think you are, said the voice.

Once the fluid level stabilized at the halfway mark, the tank wall lowered into the floor. Kate climbed up onto the metal porch, turned around, and bent over the pool. As soon as her skin met air, the layer of viscous fluid whitened to an ashen film.

Oh, no thank you, luv. I'd rather not share that feeling.

Her attempt at gracefully exhaling the fluid back into the tank turned into a shuddering coughing fit as ice-cold vapor exuded from her back. Kate held on to the edge to avoid falling head first into the goop again, cringing at the sensation of her lungs draining. After a few coughing breaths of air, she sat up bleary-eyed.

"Fuck that hurt. You *had* to make me choke?"

"Sorry."

Kate startled at the woman's voice so close behind her. A tall figure, white as new-fallen snow, moved past the end of the curved stairs with the grace of a ballerina. Hair the color of lemons hung down to the backs of her calves. Her curvaceous hips and full bosom brought a full on blush; the sight of all-black eyes caused a momentary stunned silence.

"You're naked," whispered Kate.

"Well, you're one to talk." The woman looked around. "Or hadn't you noticed your lack of apparel as well?" Her tone went playful. "Then again, I expect these rooms were intended for two, weren't they?"

"I don't have a choice." Kate covered herself with her arms as best she could.

"From the looks of that dream, it didn't always bother you."

"I'm not a damn kid anymore. What's your excuse?" Kate looked down. She hadn't felt shame until she'd come to the city, until people saw a naked girl and tried to do stupid things.

The woman spun hard enough to cause her hair to furl outward. Her body disintegrated into a cloud of fog, which slid through the tank and materialized on the other side. Kate clamped a hand over her mouth to suppress a gasp.

"I can't take things with me when I go play with ghosts." The woman winked. "I'm Aurora by the way."

"Put something on." Kate looked away.

She gestured at the empty cabinets. "Sure, I suppose I'll just nick something from your expansive wardrobe."

Kate shot her a glare.

"Sorry, sarcasm is my first language. You don't need to feel awkward; I'm not ashamed of my body." Aurora winked. "Normally, I rather enjoy making people uncomfortable, but I'm trying to be sensitive to your feelings."

"Are you hitting on me?"

"Not by intention. Would you like me to?"

Kate brushed particles of incinerated gel off her arms and legs, swatting at her rear end as she moved down the steps and over to the small closet where her bracelet waited. She made it a point not to look at Aurora.

"I wouldn't care," muttered Kate. "Man or woman... I just..." An unremarkable outfit, plum sweatshirt, jeans, and basic shoes appeared around her as she clipped the bracelet on. "Hate being alone."

"If you wouldn't melt my skin off, I'd go for a toss with you, but..."

"Are you saying that purely to piss me off?" Kate whirled on her, making fists.

"No, I'm being sincere." Aurora glanced at the door. "Bother. You're about to have guests."

The strange woman imploded into a cloud of silvery mist and sank into the floor. A second later, the door buzzed.

"Kate? Are you decent? It's Paul."

"Yeah, come in."

A beep signaled the door reacting to her words, admitting a tall man in a dark suit. He was almost as dark-skinned as Greg and looked like he could pick up a PubTran car. At first, he hesitated, but once he noticed her 'clothing,' he looked at her.

"Sorry to bug you at, uhh, home... but El Tío needs you."

She sat hard on the metal bench, wiping the last bits of sleep out of her eyes. "Who needs to die?"

"Oh, you'll love this one." Paul chuckled, removing his hat and holding it to his chest. "A geneticist is in the middle of a, uhh, corporate relocation procedure." He leaned away from her withering stare. "Far as we know, no connection to your, uhh, past. His former employers would like him terminated before he gives away proprietary information."

"What's the catch?" She examined her fingernails. "There's always a complication with corporate jobs. What is it this time? A dozen guards? A cyborg? Kids in the way?"

Another man edged in the door. *Leo?* He also removed his hat. Like most of the population, his skin had a light brown tone. Unlike the majority, he was every bit as big as Paul. She looked down; the oddity of seeing clothes but feeling floor under bare feet took her mind away from watching two huge men walking on eggshells in her presence, as though they'd faint if she yelled.

"Uhh," said Paul. "He's got a lot of protection. El Tío doesn't want a bloodbath. Needs it done surgical this time. We know those scientist types are a sore point, but we can get you inside."

"Dress up like a whore again?" She picked at her nails.

"Sorta," said Leo. "They got a lot of gear. You'll never get close to them since they got thermal shit everywhere. Real pros. Mercs."

"We got an idea." Paul seemed to lose his fear as he got into explaining the plan he probably thought up. "Boss said you don't burn when you're sleepin'. We give you somethin' to knock you out, carry you in there like you've had too much Sandman or something."

"Fuck that," said Kate. "I'm not going into a place like that helpless. Who knows what they'll do to me when I'm out."

"We got it covered," said Leo. "We'll have a guy with you all the way to the room. Yeah, he'll be unarmed, but he'll have an ampule of wake up juice just in case. You gotta be out to get past their thermal. They got so much security on that place it's ridiculous."

"Oh, come on. Mai or Ricky could do it. Either one of them could get in there."

"Both of them are freelance, expensive, and neither has El Tío's complete trust. This guy's got bank. He could turn 'em. Besides, they're going to be moving the mark in a few hours and they've already ordered a call girl for him."

"Freelance? Yeah, sure." Kate let all the air out of her lungs in a slow breath. "Who's going to turn down a request from El Tío? Especially one paying eighty grand."

Paul gave her a meaningful look.

"Yeah... right. Okay. What did you do with the hooker?"

"In the van," said Leo, pointing over his shoulder.

"Dead?" Kate blinked.

"Nah. Catch and release." Paul laughed. "Provided she can keep her mouth shut."

She stood, chasing them away from the door with her advance. "Fine. Mind if we stop so I can eat first? I'm starving."

KATE SAT ON A THREE-FOOT SQUARE TILE IN THE BACK OF A BARE METAL cargo van. She picked at the edge, hating the way it made her feel like a *weapon in transit.* El Tío was the sort of individual that had scary connections. The ease with which he'd gotten his hands on heat insulation from interplanetary shuttles scared her. She kept one hand clasped over her face, muffling cheeseburger-flavored belches knocked loose by a bumpy ride. Up front, Paul coughed at the lingering smoke from charred bread.

A terrified girl a few years her junior, probably not even twenty yet, clung to a frame of empty shelves bolted to the passenger-side wall, wearing handcuffs and underwear. Leo sat on a rear-facing bench seat against the partition between the cargo area and the front, sorting through the other woman's clothes. In the passenger seat, a young Indian man fiddled with a number of holo-displays and strange electronics that bathed the area in green and blue light. A wire connected from behind his left ear to one of the boxy contraptions on the dashboard, but he had not surrendered his awareness to cyberspace.

Kate's fingernails clicked at the edge of the thermal material. "How'd it go with her?"

Paul didn't look up from what he fiddled with. "We intercepted the entertainment."

"No shit. What about the driver?" Kate's eyebrow climbed. "Let me guess, he was stupid."

"Nope. Pimp was cheap. Made her take a PubTran." Paul laughed. "Hitesh locked 'er down and drove her right to us."

The man in the passenger seat waved.

Kate scoffed. "A PubTran? Seriously?" She sighed at the woman. "You need a new pimp, girl."

Their captive kept her head down, evidently too afraid to make eye contact—or a sound. Everyone jostled about as the van took a stiff turn. The prostitute sniffled and raised her head, staring into Kate's eyes, pleading. She held on to the shelves because El Tío's men had chained her arms through them, probably also to avoid being thrown around the van. A mixture of contempt and envy in Kate's expression made her look away. Of all the things to be jealous of, she envied the girl's complexion: skin the color of mocha coffee and long, black hair. Whoever she was, she could blend into society and escape notice. She was one of the ninety percent.

Gingers stood out like a sore thumb.

Kate felt every bit as unnatural as she was. Only people who wanted to stand out went to the gene clinics and got their bodies changed. Porcelain-skinned redheads were the 'in' thing about six years ago; lately, the fashion world swayed in favor of ebony princesses. Anyone with two hundred grand could look like whatever they wanted. Everyone except someone terrified to enter civilization.

The more Kate stared at the unlucky prostitute, the more she envied her.

Leo's threat to kill her if she made a sound was more effective than any physical gag. The girl cringed away from Kate's stare, shivering.

Calm down, bitch. We're not going to hurt you if you can keep your mouth shut. Sorry about your clothes though. They're not gonna survive.

The woman stared at her, gobsmacked. "What? Oh, God, you're psionic."

She struggled against the cuffs as if they'd chained her to a post as a sacrifice to a lion. Leo looked up. Kate waved him off.

"Leo won't hurt you either. Stay quiet and do as you're told, and you walk away without a scratch. No, I'm not going to melt your brain. That's a load of bullshit."

The woman gave up fighting and sagged. "Okay."

"She could melt your brain, but she'd have to go through your skull to do it."

Kate squinted at Leo. "You are not as funny as you think you are."

"She's seen our faces," said Paul from the front.

"Your fault for not blindfolding her," Leo muttered.

"Will you two knock it off? Don't torture the bitch." Kate glared at them before lowering her voice. "They're assholes. You do appreciate how unhealthy it is to interfere with El Tío's business, don't you?"

"Yes. I know of El Tío. I know what he does to his enemies. P-please, I swear I won't make trouble. W-what are you going to do with me?"

"We need to keep you out of sight for a little while." Paul pulled himself to his feet. "Ready?"

Kate sat with her elbows on her knees, watching particles of sand and grit slide forward in the grooved floor as the van decelerated. The prostitute tucked herself into the back corner, head down, shivering with dread.

"Paul?" asked Kate.

"Yeah?" He fumbled with a green autoinjector.

"When I go out, you two better be on your best behavior." She looked up at him. *If I'm not awake the first time I have sex, I am going to kill you slowly.*

He seemed hurt by her lack of trust. "Shit's sake, Kate. The thought never crossed my mind."

"Sorry. Okay… hit me."

Paul stooped down and poked her in the shoulder. The autoinjector felt like a stimpak shot, except it didn't create a spreading patch of cold.

The van blurred to darkness.

FOR A FEW FLEETING MINUTES, KATE SAW HERSELF ALONE IN THE FOREST, not quite ten years old. She'd gone elbow deep in a smoking deer carcass, shoveling handfuls of meat into her face, the first time she had killed one and didn't feel sorry for it. Its head lifted and turned to face her.

"Oh, man. This girl is wasted."

The shock of a talking *dead* deer sent her back to reality. A decorative raised ceiling swirled in a mess of chestnut brown and artificial light. Pain radiated from a small point in the middle of her right forearm. She managed to get her eyes open, finding herself lying on a Comforgel bed, dressed in the prostitute's clothes: a tight foamy-plastic wraparound that felt like hands grabbing her boobs, miniskirt, neon blue luminous fishnets—everything but the unmentionables.

Kate focused on a blurry smear of metallic green on her forearm, which sharpened into the shape of a metal wasp about three inches long, perched with its stinger embedded in her skin. It waved a thin foreleg at her as the needle retracted; a drop of yellowish liquid lingered on its rear end.

Antidote.

Whisper-silent wings lifted the tiny bot airborne, headed for the open patio door. She gathered her arms tight to her chest, savoring the feeling of solid clothing against her skin. A contented moan escaped her.

"Oh, you're awake," said a man.

She moaned again, the need to get out of the bed before she set fire to everything failed to motivate limbs that didn't want to move. *Ugh, I'm not burning. So dizzy. Clothes feel... amazing. I need to do drugs more often.*

"Hey, uhh. Are you really a working girl? If those idiots just kidnapped some random woman off the street and drugged you, I don't wanna..."

Trying to reach for the edge became falling; Kate hit the rug on her face.

"Oh, shit, are you all right?"

The man grabbed her arm, pulling her around into a seated position. Without thinking, she squeezed him, clinging to human contact, not caring who he was or why she was in here. The embrace lasted all of four seconds before he yelled and threw her off.

"What the fuck?" He danced around, flapping his hand. "The hell did you burn me for? I had nothing to do with it!"

Kate pouted at her lap as the pink skirt blackened to ash and the clothes went up in smoke. A few sparks came from the power source of the light-up fishnets. Her top melted to liquid that ran down her stomach, sizzling and bubbling off into a foul plastic stink. She turned on the bracelet and stood. Burning bits of fabric slipped away from undamaged dark pants and a loose grey shirt.

"Sorry," she muttered, swatting the remains of physical clothing away. "That was an accident."

He stopped waving his burned hand, staring at her with confusion. Somewhere in his middle-to-late thirties, grey devoured the brown of tight, dark curls. The few extra pounds he carried had distributed well enough to overlook. His being nice was less easy to overlook.

"What's going on?"

Kate changed her running shoes from red to black. "Optimus Health is pretty upset with you for running off."

"You're here to kill me?" He sized her up, seeming confident at her lack of firearms.

"I'm sorry. You seem to be a nice guy. It would've been easier if I woke up to being pawed." Kate glanced at the wall. "Though, that probably wouldn't have been very good for the building."

"Tyrel Zahn."

She blew air through her lips. "Yeah, I know who you are. Look, you're probably a sweet guy, but El Tío is getting paid. It's not my choice."

Tyrel's right pupil turned yellow and lit up. "You don't have any cyberware. You're pretty. Redhead, huh? That couldn't have been cheap. Look, just go home. There's no need to posture; I won't touch you if you're not willing."

"Oh, I'm willing." Kate took a step toward him. "You got thermal in that eye?"

The yellow dot faded to a dull violet. Tyrel's jaw dropped. "There's no way that number's right."

She gestured at the footprints she had charred into the hardwood. "It's right, and I never really cared for scientists. Especially ones that dick around with genetics."

Kate summoned a sphere of blue fire in her right hand and held it up. Ripples pulsed over the orb, drawing back along the length of her arm. Tyrel tried to scream, but only managed a squeak.

"P-please, don't." He backed away. "Fentel-Mars is offering me a huge enticement. I'll split it with you."

She advanced another step. Carpet burst into flames around her intangible boot.

"Okay, you can have it all… Four million!"

The fireball leapt to her other hand. "Four million credits is tempting, but there's a problem."

"What?" he yelled.

"Well, first of all, I can't buy anything nice." She winged the fireball into the face of an armed man rushing in. "Secondly, do you have any idea what El Tío does when people abuse his trust?"

Tyrel trembled, eyes locked on the dead man standing in the doorway. Blackened skull stared at him from what had once been a face. Without muscle to hold them, two metal eyes fell out of their sockets. One thudded to the ground while the other dangled on a bit of frayed wire. The body went over backward, smoke peeling from the head.

"Okay!" Tyrel backed into a tiny bathroom, landing seated on the toilet. "I'll go back to Optimus!"

The sound of footsteps grew louder.

"As if they'd trust you not to leave again." She closed her eyes, focusing on the air in the hallway outside the room. A deep rumble in the distance built into a rush of azure flames by the door. Strong wind whipped her hair to the side as the hallway backdrafted, cutting short numerous screams. "Will you get off the toilet? So undignified."

"L-look, I'll go off to some colony. No one will ever find me. You can say you killed me."

"El Tío took care of me when no one else would. Even if I was convinced he would never find out, I couldn't betray his kindness."

Tyrel screamed.

"And... I never did care much for scientists."

She hesitated for a moment, a tiny thread of guilt snapped under the weight of her memory of Ramesh. A fireball formed in her hand. Kate offered an apologetic look and drew her arm back to throw it. Desperation flared in his eyes a split second before he lunged. Kate got her arms up in time to shield her face from a punch, but he grabbed her by the wrists. Tyrel's cry of rage became pain as he clenched down. Reflex shoved her away.

Arms flailing, she landed on her back. Tyrel whimpered at the molten flesh stringing from his raised palms. Kate rolled onto all fours and leapt upright, turning in time to catch a chair across the head. The blow staggered her sideways; smoke rose in wisps from where her hands had touched floor. He loomed over her, raising his improvised weapon high.

She pushed up, pouncing at him and wrapping her arms around his thigh. His pants ignited. The chair fell out of his grip; he waved his arms to keep his balance. A desperate punch left knuckle skin stuck to her temple, but knocked her flat to the ground, dizzy. Tyrel collapsed as well, howling from savage burns all over his leg.

Kate clasped one hand to the side of her face, the other searching for flat ground to push herself upright. Scraps of his skin and fabric slid over her chest, crinkling to white ash. Tyrel hissed and moaned, rapid breaths launched saliva from between his teeth.

For a half-second, they locked eyes.

He screamed as blue fire formed around her arms and shot down his open throat. His sides burst outward; flame belched from charred openings between each rib followed by foul-smelling smoke. The former scientist collapsed in a lifeless heap, trails of grey rising from his mouth and nose.

"Ouch." She slumped on the ground, rubbing where he'd punched her. "I shouldn't have talked to him."

When she held up the bracelet to take an image capture, the voice of El Tío emanated from behind her, tinny and small.

"No need, my dear. I've been watching."

The electro-wasp hovered a few feet away. She scowled down as the floor caught fire around her feet. Eyes closed, she basked in anger. This world of normal people was not for her. Woozy from multiple hits to the head, she grabbed the chair to steady herself as she stood. It too caught fire.

Whirring drew her attention to the door, where a dog-sized robot rolled in on tracks. A tiny tank swiveled toward her, aiming a gun the size of a rifle. Her first instinct, a fireball, had little effect on the shining silver machine. It twitched, perhaps a result of startling the operator. Kate dove into a somersault behind the Comforgel bed as a hail of automatic fire rippled through the room behind her.

"The area is heavily reinforced." Hitesh spoke from the wasp as it landed on her shoulder. "There's two dozen coming up the elevator now and Division 6 is on the way."

Kate huddled low to the ground. "Can you do something about that bot?"

The wasp shook its head. "No. It's controlled via a local PCM transmitter. No GlobeNet link."

"Fucking archaic shit." Kate grumbled.

"Actually, it's brand new stuff. Hacker proof." Hitesh sounded offended.

Whirring tracks drew close. Kate eyed a small silver door on the exterior wall, plain except for bright red letters spelling *Fire*. She almost laughed at the irony. The bot's shadow stretched past the corner of the bed. She thrust one arm forward between her knees, wreathed in a glove of flames to the elbow. When the bot's front end emerged, she poured psionic energy into a stream of burning. A projection of deep blue faded to white and narrowed into a rushing roar. The machine chittered and sparked, small electronics fried under its warping hull. It swiveled sideways in an effort to protect sensitive components. Patches of plastisteel glowed red. She'd damaged it, but the bot would take more than that to put down.

Not worth the damn effort. Hate bots. Hate cyborgs.

Kate let the flame disperse, panting and sweating from the effort. Shouting from the hallway left her no time to think. She sprang to her feet, leapt the bot, and ran for the emergency door, a trail of bullet gouges chewing up the Epoxil floorboards behind her.

5

FIRE ESCAPE

The temperature of Kate's skin got in the way of a great many things in her life. The inability to wear clothes, have human contact, enjoy comfortable surroundings, and an amped up food intake were the usual annoyances. With a great amount of concentration, she sometimes managed to turn it off for a few seconds or dim it. Most often, she did that to enable drinking water even if it made her tired fast. Swallowing steam would cook her insides. While hurtling down a tube intended as a fire escape, she found the requisite amount of concentration difficult to maintain.

A vertical shaft embedded in the hotel's wall led straight from the roof to the ground level, filled with a snug plastic sleeve designed to retard the falling speed of fleeing guests. Alas, the flexible tunnel did not slow down a body much when it melted on contact. She fell in fits and jerks whenever her focus lapsed. During each period of free fall, she clawed at the wispy translucent shroud racing by.

Paul, or maybe Leo, had carried her into the building while she had been unconscious. She had no idea what floor the target stayed on or how long the fall would be. Molten plastic smeared over her arms, between her fingers and toes, and got all tangled in her hair. Claustrophobia mounted, as if she drowned in gooey tatters, unable to see more than a hand's width in any direction. On the way down, she negated her genetic defect for a few seconds at a time—enough to slam into a pit full of foam chunks at a sub-fatal speed.

Shock from impact ended all mental focus, and her safe landing turned into a trap. She grabbed and struggled to stand, but the hunks of padding melted to liquid so fast she couldn't grasp anything but liquid. A goopy mass of semi-molten cushioning and caustic fumes threatened to drown her. Adrenaline kicked in, giving her the strength to wade through the thigh-deep miasma and climb a metal ladder out of the pit. Liquefied foam ran down her legs in sizzling trails as she sprinted toward flashing red lights by the exit door.

"Oh, shit."

Opening the fire exit had set off alarms, which would attract the cops as well as emergency services. She ran her hands over her chest and arms, slinging the bubbling ooze off as much as she could. It hit the wall, solidifying on contact into organic filaments resembling dried noseblow. Squawking sirens outside blared louder when she stiff-armed the door open.

"Vagrant 5," she muttered to the bracelet.

Her holographic clothing shifted to the rags of a street dweller. Several dozen homeless people sifted among trash or sat around in the alley behind the hotel. Against every instinct telling her to get out of there, she staggered to the other side and collapsed against a building. Grime seared away from the wall where her back touched it, and bits of trash burned out from under her. In seconds, the scratchy traction-coated metal under her bare butt warmed to comfortable.

A squad of armored mercenaries swarmed the corner, heading for the fire exit. Kate kept her head down. She peered past strands of her hair, black courtesy of the holo-projector, watching and waiting.

One of the men waved his rifle around. Approaching sirens lent urgency to his voice. "Any of you shitheads see a woman run outta that building?"

Several of the homeless people pointed down the alley, one man pointed the other way. Kate faked a congested cough and waved in the same direction as the majority. Whatever dried liquid she'd sat on burned off to such a horrible smell, the mercs kept their distance. She clung to the hope that her heat would kill germs, trying to avoid throwing up at the idea of sitting in a puddle of someone else's bodily fluids. The police jogged off to her right, the officer leading them muttered to someone over a comm link about an aerial unit.

Blue and white Division 0 patrol craft swarmed in, soon joined by an enormous flying fire-suppression machine. Kate remained in place, cradling her bruised face and happy for a chance to breathe. The attempt to burn the sentry bot by pushing fire to white hot had left her ready to pass out from exertion. She touched her temple, trying to understand how her brain could melt a bullet on contact as a reflex while she had to work so damn hard to consciously destroy the little machine. El Tío had once likened it to attacking a tank with a flamethrower.

A small bit of lead isn't armor plating.

Police boots tromped past her. Acting the part, she pulled her feet in close and muttered incoherently at them, as if annoyed by their presence.

"Well that's irony for ya," said a scratchy-voiced female officer. "Some asshole sets the fire escape on fire."

Kate found it difficult to suppress the urge to laugh.

The wasp zipped unnoticed around the legion of police and came in to land on Kate's knee. It looked up for a moment before hopping to her shoulder and hiding in her hair.

"You should leave soon," said Hitesh. "They've called in Division 0. Hotel security saw you burn that hallway. You're slipping; only one of them died."

"I wasn't trying to kill them all, just keep them away. El Tío asked for surgical, didn't he?"

One of the Division 1 officers stepped in front of her as she got up. "I need to ask you to stay in the area until we are finished taking statements."

"It was the Martians." Kate held her hand at stomach level. "Little grey fuckers, this tall. About a dozen of em."

He shifted his weight to his left leg. "Have you been drinking, ma'am?"

"Drinking? No. I wish. Got any?" She flashed a broad grin and peeked at his thoughts.

This is useless, damn vagrants. I don't have time for this crap; the Zeros can read their fucking minds.

She gasped, covering it up with a cough, and focused on a spot of air at the front of the hotel, by a cluster of police vehicles. A loud detonation of orange flames set off dozens of car alarms. When the officers looked, she took off running, screaming that the Martian invaders were attacking.

The alley led to a sidewalk packed dense with bodies. Kate had no choice but to wait for an opening. Touching anyone would attract unwanted attention. She altered the hologram to project unassuming street wear and conceal her hair under false blonde. Opportunity presented itself in the form of a man carrying a large metal box. She lunged at him, shoving the parcel and knocking him on his ass. The brief confusion afforded her a gap to the street, and she darted across traffic to the other side and the safety of an alley.

A half hour and several blocks later, she'd made it far enough into the grey to consider the cops a non-issue. She shut off the holographic alteration of her hair, letting it go back to normal—a necessary badge of identity in her black zone—and ducked through an unlocked fence into a lot behind a disused building. The rear door still bore the fading logo of a long-dead franchise fast-food place, one of the companies who refused to replace a live workforce with unpaid dolls. That dated the area to at least forty years abandoned. Kate huffed, leaning forward to catch her breath.

"What the hell are you grinning at?" She frowned at the smiling rendition of an older man in a white suit holding a drumstick.

Her fingers snagged an inch into her hair on gooey plastic. She picked and peeled at herself in an effort to get rid of it all. The more she plucked away, the more she found.

"Screw it."

After a look around to make sure no one watched her, she removed the bracelet and walked a few feet away from where she set it down. A column of flame erupted around her, creating a deafening roar and thick, black smoke. She let off on the burn only after she no longer smelled scorched plastic.

"Most impressive," said a female voice.

Kate gasped, covering herself as she whirled. A short woman with white hair in a pixie cut lurked beyond the gate. Both of Kate's hands filled with fire and her face turned as red as her hair.

"You must be Kate. I—"

The woman let out a yelp as she jumped away from flames striking the fence. Kate walked sideways to her bracelet, another flame orb poised.

"Bloody hell! Do that again and I'll break your little toy."

Kate stooped to grab it, never taking her gaze off the shadow in the fence. Once the comforting presence of holographic clothing shrouded her, she lowered her guard a little. "Who the hell are you?"

"Well, I can certainly understand why you have so few friends. You're such a charmer."

"Fuck you." Kate backed away, looking for an escape route. She had a choice of boarded up window or climbing the fence. She edged for the window.

"I'd rather not. Are you dressed yet?"

"Stay back." Kate whipped the second sphere into one of the boards, focusing on the lingering fire to amplify it.

The woman stepped into view around the fence. "All I want is a moment to talk. I'm Anna."

Kate leaned against the wall; the burning board went out with a *whoof.*

Hello, thought Anna. *Looking at my head are we?*

You're looking at mine. Kate's eyes narrowed as she sensed Anna pondering a blast of lightning to knock her senseless. *You can make lightning?*

Anna smiled. *Don't act so surprised; you make fire. Please don't let me see any more.*

"You know that freaky bitch?" Kate grasped the edge of the windowsill behind her. "The white one?"

"Yes. Aurora's unique. So… I won't zap you and you don't burn me. Deal?"

Kate narrowed her eyes. "What do you want?"

"Deal?"

"I'll think about it."

"Come on, we need to get you out of sight." Anna moved away from the gate, boot heels clicking on the alley.

"Who are you?"

When she got no answer, Kate pushed off the wall and ran to the fence. Anna waited a short distance away, too far to talk. The look on her face turned pitying by the time Kate had crept close enough for conversation.

"Don't look at me like that."

Anna gestured at a passage into a parking garage. "It's not too often I run into someone who makes me think I didn't have it so bad coming up. I'm sorry."

Kate raised her hands, expecting an attack. Anna shook her head.

"I'm sorry for what you went through. I'm not going to harm you."

Anna jogged down the street to a ramp entrance, stopping a few steps into a sunken space full of cars with an expectant glance. After a moment of feeling exposed in the alley, Kate followed. Puddles flashed to steam as she stepped in them, running to catch up. Bare footprints rendered in dry where combat boots had trod.

"We should have a little privacy here." Anna started to smile, but let off an exasperated sigh. "Oh, will you please relax. You're like a beaten dog waiting for the next fist."

Kate blushed at the ground, glaring up a moment later. "I don't need your pity."

"Some friends and I have been trying to find you for a long time. You're not as alone as you think."

"Freaky bitch said that too. So what *is* your deal?"

"You know you're psionic? Please tell me you don't think you're using magic or chi or some such nonsense."

"Duh." Kate rolled her eyes. "Who'd believe that?"

Anna smiled through her fingers. "You'd be surprised. Well, you and I… we're not like normal psionics. We are a higher order. Those men who made you were trying to create a perfect weapon."

Kate faced away, biting a knuckle.

"I'd have killed them too. People like us need to stick together. We can help each other."

"Help each other do what?"

Anna leaned against a car. "There is a very smart man who is trying to make a better way for us. He wants to create a world where those with gifts are not hunted, exploited, or killed. A world where The Awakened make the rules."

"Awakened?" Kate looked back at her. "People like us?"

"You're a pyrokinetic. Most people with your talent make ordinary garden-variety fire, but yours is blue. You are many times more potent than anyone the authorities have seen before. Electrokinetics can't throw lightning through thin air; they have to use a conductor." Anna reached out and sent a twenty-foot arc into a nearby light fixture, which exploded in a shower of glass and sparks. "I can do that."

"I've got El Tío to look after me."

"Aurora's told us all about him. Like everyone else in this world, Kate, he's just using you as the weapon they made you to be. Maybe he does feel some sense of pity or affection for you, but at the end of the day…"

"Yeah." Kate kicked at the ground.

Squeaking boots echoed over the parking deck. A cat-sized hover bot slipped into view from behind an elevator bank, pivoting to face them.

"Bollocks," grumbled Anna.

Five figures in grey armor followed it, the same brand of corporate mercenaries who had been protecting Tyrel. Kate muttered a few choice words as she clawed her hands in the air away from them. A handful of shots rang out in the seconds before a standing wall of blue flames rose in their path and wrapped around. Bullets came close, spraying her with fragments of glass from wrecked cars, though she didn't flinch.

"Damn," said Kate. "They don't know when to call it a day."

Patches of inferno turned yellowish white as she intensified the burn. A *crack* louder than a gunshot disrupted her concentration, snuffing the flame wall to a curtain of smoke. The fleeing bot careened into the ceiling, chased by a blue-white lightning thread from Anna's hand.

"Where were we?" Kate brushed glass from her hair.

One of the mercenaries moaned. Kate glared, and patches of flame around the bodies burst into a roaring bonfire. She snarled at them until the twitching stopped.

"You just killed five people." Anna blinked. "With no more reaction than…"

"They would've killed me. It's just a job. I do it. I get paid. People die. Who cares?" Kate squinted. "What do you mean Aurora might've been right?"

Anna forced a polite smile. "In polite society, telepaths don't eavesdrop."

"I'm not part of polite society."

"Great, another feral." Anna sighed at the ceiling. "Cripes. At least the last one was sweet, if not a bit petulant."

"I don't bay at the moon or piss on trees, you know." Kate nibbled on the tip of her finger. "At least, not anymore."

"You're taking the Mick, I hope." Anna frowned. "We don't have time for that. You certainly don't sound like you grew up wild."

"Whatever that means. El Tío made sure I got somewhat of an education." Kate moved close enough for her visitor to lean away from the heat. "You've got my attention. Tell me more about this smart guy of yours."

The area rumbled with the weight of six-wheeled armored vehicles, tires visible through the gap between wall and ceiling at the street.

"Crap," said Anna. "Police assault units."

"Damn interruptions." Kate held her hands up, ready for a fight.

"Are you nutters? That's Division 6. They don't talk." Anna leaned back, eyes half-open. Her arms shot out to the sides, and a barely-visible pulse of energy rushed away from her.

Kate's bracelet faltered and shut off, making her gasp. Dead lights above them flickered with eerie violet-blue light before they exploded. The cascading effect raced outward in a circle, following the pulse and leaving them in the dark.

Kate covered herself with her arms, glaring at Anna. "What the hell did you do that for?"

Anna squinted at the electronic device. "To buy us time to get out of here. I tried to leave your thing out of it… Oh, bother."

Kate tapped it twice and it came back online. She slumped with a sigh of relief as a ghostly mesh of blue gridlines wrapped around her and turned into opaque clothing a second later.

"Run, Kate. Get out of here." Anna jogged backward. "We'll catch up."

Outside, men and women yelled, most of them cursing faulty equipment that all failed at the same time. A thick-voiced woman yelled about an EMP weapon, which seemed to worry them. Kate sprinted across the garage to the far side and leapt up, grabbing the lip of the wall. Her toes slipped on the smooth concrete, so she pulled her weight up with only her arms. For a moment, she squatted atop the wall in a gap too short to stand in, looking back at the shadows of assault police moving among destroyed cars. Before any got close enough to see her, she ducked out onto the sidewalk and blended with the crowd.

6

LOST AND FOUND

Seated at the edge of a long plastisteel pier, Kate dangled her feet over the edge and swung them back and forth. The reek of fish, algae, and saltwater kept her breathing shallow. A hundred yards off to the right, the flickering effect of an acetylene torch lit the windows of an old warehouse. The tainted wind played with her hair, making her shiver each time it danced over her back. She shivered not from being cold, but from feeling exposed.

Behind her, East City loomed, a great monolith of technology shadowing the docks. Light flickered and moved along the numerous elevators and stairways connecting the city surface, some seventy meters off the ground, to the natural earth. She lost a few moments watching workers in exo-armor drag a cargo container the size of a PubTran bus onto the most massive elevator slab she'd ever seen and begin the long trek to the surface.

A distant voice bellowed from the deck of an ancient oil tanker berthed two piers to the left. Off-gridders had converted it into 'luxury' housing, replacing the cavernous holds with walls, floors, and hundreds of society's unwanted. Their lookouts paced the deck, small rifles tucked close to their chests. None of them noticed her there, a redhead in black.

The wind gusted with a howl. She curled up, hugging herself, the touch of her fingers on bare skin made loneliness heavier. Gunshots rang out in the distant dark. She looked in the direction for a few seconds and let her head sag forward. Such sounds made up the routine background din of the black zone; anyone who reacted to a far-off firefight stood out as a newcomer. Out on the water, the hollow, semi-skeletal figure of an ancient statue caught the glow of faltering lights. They'd shut down the holographic replacement for some reason or another… maintenance probably. Some years ago, a senator had campaigned for money to rebuild the statue. He'd pocketed most of it and bought a giant holo-emitter instead.

Kate huffed.

"Yeah, right. Tired and poor are all we have left."

She ran a hand over her leg, staring at the light blue rings around where her fingers pierced the hologram. For years, she had done without the bracelet, hiding in the shadows of the places sane people were afraid to go. At first, she didn't know any better. She had no idea what could happen to a solitary woman out here, much less a teen girl. Aurora had mocked her embarrassment. True, she hadn't cared about being naked all the time until after she'd arrived in the city and everyone she met made a big deal about it. Though she never bayed at the moon, she had watered a tree or two.

Kate smiled.

The punks didn't know what she was. Memories of gangs running in terror made her laugh while thoughts of kindly people burning themselves trying to take her hand made her angry. She pulled her feet up and lay sideways, using an arm for a pillow. Fingernails scratched the wet, tarnished metal, creating thin lines of dry as well as steam. The bracelet rested inches from her eyes. Cyan numbers on the curved, black screen read: 02:41 a.m.

Another burst of wind gathered enough strength to push past her aura of heat for an instant, causing a shiver. She curled tighter, anger building. Tyrel was one of *them*. A scientist. One of the horrible people who cursed her with an existence at arm's length from the world. She picked at the heat-resistant band around her left wrist. His nice act hadn't fooled her. No, she refused to feel guilt for murdering a man seeking only a better life. He wasn't a man—he was a scientist.

The kind of man who could push a button to kill a little girl in a tank, because she failed. No, she hadn't failed. *They* failed in making her right. It wasn't her fault she couldn't turn it off. But still, they blamed her.

Anger lapsed to exhaustion, and she shut her eyes.

KATE LAY ON HER SIDE, CURLED UP LIKE A NEWBORN BABE IN A CONCRETE vault. At once, she recognized a dream. Her bracelet was gone, her body younger. She remembered the smell in the space she had made home, a sour-sweet mixture of garbage and rotting food from squatters on the upper floors. Her teenaged self had taken over a space under the ground floor of the emptiest building she could find, close to the western edge of East City. She laughed inside her head. Her mind had taken her back to about a year after she had grown lonely in the forest. One day, she decided to keep going east until she found people, and the city.

Her hands squeezed into her stomach after she sat up, trying to weaken the hunger that haunted her each morning. Rats had not been as filling as wild deer. She crawled to the square hole leading out of her chamber, stood, and stretched. Inches of ash lined the ground floor, the lunar grey disrupted here and there by the remains of furniture that had not burned all the way. All the trash packed into the place had gone up in smoke the first time she walked in.

Kate stepped with care around metal and glass and went to a hole in the wall where a door had once hung. She remembered her teeth chattering that day out on the street. Pain wracked her muscles; lack of food had caused her to cool. The idea seemed solid to the mind of a sixteen-year-old. If she ate less, her body would run out of excess energy and stop burning. Unfortunately, her metabolism did not like the idea. Rather than cool off, she starved.

Long, wild hair brushed against her legs as she ran. Voices behind her teased and whistled, but only from a safe distance. Kate never let them know how much she wanted to be touched. When she first entered the city, a few tried to force the issue and learned agonizing lessons. After a year, rumors had spread and the gangs left her alone. A few felt bad for her, some even brought her food.

The whole sector knew her, and stayed away.

That night, she hunted for food. No deer existed in the city, but she had found a substitute. When she got close to the edge of the grey zone, she stuck to the shadows. Her lack of clothing always caused problems. She didn't want to hurt the people who tried to offer help, but she still ran away. If she accepted help, *they* would find her. The man in the black coat and everyone he worked for wanted to put her back in a tank—a tank with a kill switch.

She crouched behind a row of garbage pods, under a cloak of hair, watching the street at the end of the alley. The back door to a CyberBurger, one she had raided several times, waited. Acrid smoke stung her eyes from whatever substance sizzled out from under her toes. At the instant pedestrian traffic left the alley unobserved, she bolted from cover and ran to the wall. The metal touched her back, cold for only an instant, slimy for a second more as the grime seared away.

Against the building, she had shelter from the street, and enough hair hanging over her to look like a dress from a distance. For several minutes, she pressed herself into the plastisteel wall, cringing at every loud hiss whenever she made contact with more grease. A noise at the wrong time would ruin her hunt.

At long last, the entrance opened. Kate vanished in shadow behind the door as it swung toward her. A dark-haired man in his middle thirties with a coffee complexion carried two massive bags of trash to a dumpster. She darted around the door and slipped inside, shifting sideways with raised arms to duck through a narrow hallway without touching anything. Hanging smocks, shelves of spare parts, and a stock of cleaning chemicals, any of which would ignite if she made contact.

Once in the production area, she went straight for the industrial food assembler. She kept one eye locked on the reflective surface of a refrigerator-sized OmniSoy reservoir, watching the door. CyberBurger manufactured each meal as ordered; the huge machine sat idle at an hour too late for breakfast, but too early for lunch.

A few quick taps at the holographic console got the machine producing. She lost herself in the ecstasy of food, grabbing burger after burger as they slid along a conveyor. Kate managed to inhale three before a man shouted at her.

"Hey! What the hell are you doing in here?"

She whirled on him, desperate eyes staring over the sandwich while her attempt to speak turned into a series of pleading whimpers.

"Oh for shit's sake," he grumbled. "Why are you naked? You kidnapped or something?"

Kate shook her head, grabbing another burger.

"Hey, stop that… Someone's gotta pay for those. Policy won't let me comp you. Hell, I can't even pay for it myself. Corporate thinks it'll attract more vagrants. You want me to call the police?"

She shook her head again, harder, packing the burger into her mouth with both hands.

The manager froze as she took another, noticing the smoke that peeled from her touch. "What the hell are you?"

"Hungry," she muttered.

He yanked a long, metal bar out from between two machines, a flange at the end gleamed as he brandished it. She reached for another burger, but he shouted and advanced. She shied away. He backed her into a corner, pointing the bar at her while yelling for someone named Jennifer Three. Kate licked bits of food out of her teeth, eyeing the door. A rickety teenage doll appeared in an archway leading deeper into the building.

"Yes, sir?"

"Call the police, now. Report a burglary."

"Yes, sir." The doll took on a vacant stare.

"Go away," said Kate.

She took a step for the door but he slid to his right, blocking her.

"Don't move, kid. I don't know what the hell is going on here—"

He screamed when her right hand ignited, cradling a blue fireball. Kate cocked her arm back as if to throw it, and advanced. Rather than run as she hoped, he roared and charged. She flung the incendiary missile into his chest and jumped aside as his rush became a fall. The manager hit the ground, howling in agony. She tiptoed to the side, edging along the wall of machinery. He rolled onto his back; his chest, neck, and some of his face had become a glistening red mass devoid of skin.

Jennifer Three walked around the counter and stopped nearby, tilting her head with an overdone girlish giggle. "Mister Alfonso, should I request an ambulance as well?"

He wheezed.

"Yes," said Kate, reaching for more food.

"I am sorry, miss. I am not authorized to accept commands from customers."

Kate shrugged, knocked another four burgers apart to grab only the 'meat' patty, and carried them out the back door while concentrating on not burning them. She skidded to a halt on her heels, staring at a big man in a black suit and violet hat.

In the real world, sleeping Kate smiled at the memory of her first meeting with Paul.

"Hey, Kid," said Paul, raising a hand.

She stuffed the burgers in her mouth, expecting him to take them.

"Whoa, slow down. I ain't here to steal your food."

Alfonso wailed in the distance. Paul leaned past her to peek, holding a hand a few inches away from her shoulder. Kate sidestepped. She remembered reading his mind, finding no intent to hurt her.

"The boss wants to talk to you. We could use someone wit' your talents…" Paul rubbed his chin. "Course, we gotta do somethin' bout that naked thing. Lucky for you, El Tío knows people."

COLD DRAGGED HER OUT OF THE DREAM. KATE GAGGED AT THE TASTE OF low tide in the air. The feeling of freezing, experiencing the world as it should be, lasted only seconds. She sat up, clutching herself, wishing it longer. Once her metabolism caught up, the continuous bubble of warmth she lived in resumed.

She rubbed her face, cursing, and stood. The squeak of a shoe on the metal ground made her spin, hand aflame.

"Hey," said a skinny boy of about thirteen, dressed in a Wharf Rat coat and baggy blue pants with side pockets on the thighs. Dirty-blond hair hung in a wild tangle around light brown skin and almond-shaped eyes that seemed too young for this place.

Kate let her arm drop; the fire went out. "What the hell do you want?"

7

DRESSED YOUNG

The boy's smile vanished, replaced with a determined grunt that lasted all of a second. He stumbled to the side, caught his fall, and resumed smiling. Kate went to grab him, but thought better of it at the last moment. A spike of anger lit fire to a dumpster a few feet away.

"Damn, this little bastard's got a lot of willpower." He smiled for a few seconds before rolling his eyes. "Oh, same to you, kid."

Kate squinted. "Aurora?"

"Indeed. I was hoping you wouldn't kill a small one. The boy is kind of cute, even if he's got a foul mouth."

Kate laughed at the diatribe of swear words going by in the combined surface thoughts of a woman and a kid. A few made her cringe. After a moment of it, Aurora seemed to have had enough and growled. The sense of the boy receded.

"What was that?" asked Kate.

"I can't carry on a conversation with you while I've got him gnawing on my ear. He's fine, just tucked away for now. Anyway, Archon wanted me to reach out and see how things were going."

"What the hell is an archon?" Kate brushed sand and grit away from her legs. "Come on, I can't sleep out here."

"Who can?" The boy laughed, and fell in step at her side. "Archon's the one who's trying to help us."

"It's cold. When I'm unconscious, the heat stops. I wake up freezing, get warm, go back to sleep, wake up again. It's a pain in the damn ass."

"That explains the sex tank." He scratched his head. "I was wondering about that. Given your background, I'd imagine you'd rather hate them."

"Archon, huh? I'm guessing his parents didn't name him that." She hung a right turn, swearing under her breath.

"What're you cheesed off at now?"

Kate scowled. "I hate walking everywhere."

"Don't fancy an autocab? Uhh, sorry, you call them PubTran here. I still can't get used to that."

Kate stopped, pinching the bridge of her nose. "If I could ride in one without burning it to fuck, I would."

The boy backed away from increasing heat. "Right, sorry. Sore point. I get it. So you walked all the way from the facility to the city?"

"Obviously." Kate stomped ahead. "I didn't go right away, spent a few years living like a wild thing in the woods."

"Sounds almost like a storybook." He looked up at her.

"Oh, yeah. Maybe a horror. Melting down deer, tearing them apart with my bare hands. Sneaking into Scattered Lands towns and stealing food when I could. I had to run away from anyone who saw me. The nice ones invariably wanted to hug me and wrap me in blankets, which would've burned them to shit. The bad ones... well, those I didn't always run from."

"Yes... Anna mentioned you're easy with killing."

Kate shrugged. "So, what did she mean by saying you were right?"

"Oh, no offense, but I told Archon recruiting you wouldn't work in his favor."

"What makes you say that?" Kate glanced over as they reached a corner crossing.

The boy blew all the air from his lungs, flapping his arms in a noncommittal gesture of indecision. "Just a hunch. The future's not always clear and obvious. At best, your tendency to give in to anger over reason could create problems. At worst, you might turn on him."

"Is he planning to grab my ass?"

He laughed. "You're hardly his type."

"What is his type? You? That other... umm, electric one?"

"He fancies a big..." The kid started to hold his hands over his chest, but touched a finger to the side of his head. "Brain. As well as a woman who can look down on those not of her station, but always regard him as her superior." He sighed.

Kate came close to grinning at his expression. "So, the other one?"

He shrugged, looking down and kicking a spent autoinjector off to the side. It hit the building with a *click* and fell out of sight into a drift of trash. "Anna's quite smitten with him. Oh, bother. Why did I do that?"

Kate turned left, strolling down the centerline of a road packed with dead cars. No functional vehicle had come this way in decades; traffic signals were all dark, many long since used for target practice. She weaved among the wrecks for a few minutes in silence, trailed by the possessed boy. Several faces watched them from shaded alleys and broken windows. At the sound of a blade sliding out of a sheath, Kate flung her arm out in that direction.

The interior of a derelict car exploded in a flash of bright orange and ash. A horrendous howl escaped the lips of a charred figure that managed to drag himself halfway out of the window before succumbing. A knife that verged on a small sword slipped from his fingers and hit the road with a metallic clatter. Some of the watching faces sank into darkness.

"Guilt kills," said Kate. "I'd be dead if I hesitated. I'm still alive because they know what happens if they try anything. So, I'm guessing this Archon guy wants me for the same reason everyone else does?"

"To a point, yes." The boy kicked another empty synthbeer can, sending it rolling and bouncing. "To fulfill his vision may require a spot or two of violence. Though, I would like to think that is a preparatory concern more than a plan."

"Doesn't he want to take over the city or something? Kill everyone who gets in his way?"

"Oh, heavens no." He stopped, staring down at himself.

"What?" Kate paused, a step ahead, looking back.

"I don't understand this sudden urge to kick trash. I've never worn a little boy before, must be a thing."

"Has anyone ever told you that you're fucked up?"

He beamed. "Thank you. It's nice to be appreciated. Though, it does feel awkward having a todger."

"A what?" Kate held up a hand. "Wait. Never mind. You just used the kid to stop me from killing you on sight... Why not drop him?"

"I don't have a fancy bracelet. Clothes don't follow me through the astral world. Nothing that isn't part of me goes. A nuisance, really."

Kate looked at him, covering her mouth.

"My lot's by choice," said the boy. "Course, as a matter of practicality, perhaps not so much."

Kate resumed walking. "So now that I won't kill you, why not leave him behind?"

"And traipse about starkers in a black zone? Are you completely touched?" He cringed. "Sorry, that means crazy... I know you're a mess over that whole touchy-feely thing."

"I've gotten used to it." Kate tried to stick her hands in pockets that didn't exist, and snarled. "So, why make contact with me anyway if you think it's such a bad idea?"

"Well, sometimes I think things are bad ideas, but Archon never listens to me. Even after that other mess. You know... if you want me to let the kid go, I could always wear you."

"Uhh, no thanks. So if you think it's such a bad idea to have me along, why not ignore him?"

He grinned with a weasel's delight in his eyes. "Because I want to watch the show. What's the fun in setting up a maze of dominoes if you don't tip them over?"

"You a precog?"

"I've been called worse." He kicked another can. "Dammit."

"Will it kill me if I join you?"

He looked her up and down, and rubbed his right shoulder. "Probably a close call, but I doubt you'll die."

"Darn." Kate looked up at a trio of passing advert-bots. "So when can I meet him?"

8

DISTANT PROMISES

A pleasant chime rang out as the glass doors slid aside. Kate waved at Alfonso, sending him scurrying for the back room. She moved to the end of the shortest line, leaving a comfortable gap between her and a short woman about her age. Envy made her glance away from tight faux-leather pants and a jacket, jealousy that deepened when the woman looked back. Kate couldn't understand what people fancied about pale redheads. The brown-skinned woman gave her the same jealous smirk.

Someone who looked like everyone else wanted Kate's complexion, but couldn't afford the procedure. Kate wanted to be unremarkable, but couldn't set foot in a Reinventions clinic. Medical people would know something was different with her, and *they* would find her. Her train of thought derailed as a guy in a shimmering dark suit slipped into the gap between her and the woman, cutting into the middle of the line.

The four people behind Kate yelled at him. He ignored them, focused on a conversation over an implanted link. She leaned closer, blackening the material of his suit. Casual, hands on her hips as if in her pockets, she hovered until his clothes burst into flame. The fire called to her; she felt its presence as though it were a living being to which she could talk. At her behest, the flames crept over his shoulders and along his arms, dribbling down the front of his jacket.

At last, he noticed, and ran for the street screaming. Kate looked in the direction of the manager's office. The door was empty, and the sound of a man weeping echoed out of the hallway.

Probably under his desk. She shook her head.

KATE RECLINED ON A THICK, CONCRETE SPAR THAT HUNG AT AN ANGLE FROM the ceiling. She laced her fingers behind her head, staring up at the crisscross of exposed wires and rebar from where one end had fallen years ago. She slid her foot back and forth, teasing at a loose bolt in the grit with her toes. The holo-bracelet chirped at the arrival of a text message from an unknown sender.

"Five minutes."

Idle fingers picked at the holo-panel floating over her wrist. Her frumpy sweatshirt shrank and changed color into a military jumpsuit, then a skin-tight cat suit, then a white dress. A twist of a virtual knob cycled it among various colors. She changed it again to jeans and a t-shirt. Each shift made her angrier.

Her stomach rumbled.

One hand patted her belly. "Sorry I only had four... A girl's gotta watch her waistline."

Sunlight glinted over metal at the far end of the floor. She rolled her head to the left without lifting it. A small hovercar nosed in via the broken windows of an abandoned office tower. Dust spewed in its wake as it glided to within ten feet. Fender doors rotated open to reveal ground wheels, onto which it settled. Aurora waved from the driver's side, visible through the inch-thick resin windscreen. Anna got out first, the *clicks* of her high-heeled boots echoed in the entire level. Despite being bundled in a long, white coat, she shivered. Aurora had dressed like a corporate executive in a jet-black skirt suit sporting a row of silver buttons. She pulled dark glasses down and waved with her fingers.

Kate looked away. "You're late."

"Sorry, luv," said Anna. "I had another meeting that ran a bit long. I never miss an opportunity for good sushi. Have you ever tried it?"

"I can't eat sushi." Kate swung her arms down, using the momentum to pull herself sitting.

Anna fished out a NetMini and smiled. "It's really not that bad."

"No... I mean I really *can't* eat it. By the time I chew twice, it's no longer sushi; it's cooked."

Aurora burst out laughing, scaring a flock of pigeons away from the north ledge. Anna gave her an exasperated look and set her NetMini flat atop a large chunk of displaced concrete. The head of a man in his middle forties with shoulder-length chestnut hair and a meticulously trimmed goatee appeared above it. The last inch of neck shimmered with the rainbow light of a hologram; above that, he looked solid.

"Kate, this is Archon," said Anna. "The man who would save us all."

"Melodramatic," mumbled Aurora.

"So, this is Kate...?"

"Just Kate," she said. "No last name. No family. No friends."

He frowned, for a moment looking annoyed.

Kate leaned forward, elbows on her knees. "How do we get started? I might have to do the occasional favor for El Tío now and then, but I'm a free agent."

The head rotated to face Anna. "Who or what is El Tío?"

"Local Syndicate underboss," said Aurora. "She's been cleaning up messes for him for quite some time. The man's got connections in more places than mold."

"Really?" Delight gleamed in his eyes. "Do you understand what you are?"

"Some kind of biological weapon, I guess."

"Allow me a moment."

The holographic head stared at her. She slid her arms back until she grasped her knees, feeling uneasy at the sudden change in the air. The sense of a fourth sentient mind became apparent, centered on the hologram of Archon. Several seconds later, a telepathic connection started.

Relax yourself. I am only peering in to see what we have to work with. I promise I will not do anything but look.

She tensed, putting one arm over her chest and the other in her lap.

I cannot see under your hologram, but you feel exposed anyway.

Scenes from her past leapt to the forefront of her mind. The exploding tank, burning bodies in the facility, running through the woods free, sleeping on mounds of burnt pine needles and dirt, hunting deer, her journey into the city at fifteen, El Tío, and everything up to the now.

"I believe Aurora is correct. You are one of The Awakened. It would be an honor to count you among us."

Kate gazed into her lap until the individual threads of her false jeans stood out. "Are you sure you want me? I can't do anything fancy like them. All I'm good for is killing. I can't even touch people."

Anna's eyes reddened. She pivoted away.

"You are Awakened, Kate. You are part of the greatest evolutionary peak humankind has yet reached."

"She may have a point, James." Aurora made a cute little cat-scratch gesture. "I did warn you about Althea, and look what happened."

He scowled. "That one was a handful. She refused to accept her greatness. Kate here is ready."

"Who's Althea?" Kate mumbled, still studying her lap.

"Another feral child," said Archon. "Perhaps when she is older, she will come to understand. Alas, we may not have the luxury of time." He froze, one eyebrow raised. The dawn of an idea spread over his face. "Perhaps... Yes, perhaps indeed."

Aurora opened her mouth, but closed it without saying a word. She glanced at him, hesitated, and wandered a few paces to the side, rubbing her hands. Anna shook her head at Archon.

"I may be able to offer you that which you most desire, Kate."

"She doesn't strike me as the money, fame, and power type," said Anna.

Archon flashed a Cheshire grin. "I was thinking something less grand. Perhaps a pair of trousers and a nice angora sweater?"

Anna moved between Kate and the hologram. "James, please leave that girl alone. Did you forget what she told you? The next time she sees you, you're going to die."

Archon rolled his eyes. "Oh, Anna. That girl is incapable of killing anyone."

"Actually..." Aurora leaned her head left to right, making her hair dance. "I said she will watch him die. Not necessarily the next time they meet, and I ever said anything about her killing him. It could be forty years from now."

"It could also be next week," mumbled Anna. "I'd rather not risk it."

Kate jumped up and advanced on the NetMini, staring into holographic eyes. "Are you telling me there's a way to make this... heat shit stop?"

"He's getting ahead of—" Anna tried to grab her shoulder to hold her back, but pulled away at the last second. "Feck!"

"This poor woman has never known the touch of a mother's love, or a warm bed." Archon's face adjusted itself into an imperious stare. "I cannot say beyond a doubt; however, I was able to elevate myself from an ordinary psionic to the—"

"Most powerful telepath in the world," said Aurora, twirling her finger.

"Thank you, Lauren." His withering stare returned to a smile at Kate. "There are several possibilities. In most cases, someone who is born as an Awakened has an oddity. Thus far, in all cases I have seen, the effect tends to be visual changes or mild annoyances. I dare say C-Branch did a rather cack-handed job of it."

Anna shivered, looking around. "Don't say that too loud. They've got bots everywhere."

"I thought I was the paranoid one." Archon chuckled.

"C-Branch?" Kate blinked. "Is that—?"

"Yes. The man you remember as you left the building." The eyes in Archon's hologram head turned to white static. "Agent Perrin. Interesting."

Kate held her head, almost too dizzy to stand. A dozen voices screaming filled her mind. For a moment, she became her seven-year-old self again, at the center of a roaring inferno that used to be parked trucks and a platoon of soldiers. Fire died down and cyclonic winds whipped her hair. She stood at the center of a picturesque forest snow globe, only the flurries falling around her were ash instead of ice. A charred man in a black coat dragged himself out of sight into a ditch. Little Kate walked among the falling embers into the woods, free.

The past melted into the present, trees turned into bare concrete and wires.

"Do not feel remorse for them," said Archon. The voice existed in her mind and in the room at once. "For what they did to you, for what they almost did to you"—the fear of toxin seeping into the gel in a tank she could not escape returned—"they deserved to burn."

"I…" Kate, woozy, staggered to one side, arms waving to recover her balance when she stepped on a jagged rock. "Dammit!" She rubbed her foot. "I'd kill them all over again for a pair of goddamn boots."

"They were trying to make a weapon with a pretty disguise. Doll you up and send you in. No cybernetics to hide from scanners, no guns to conceal, you would have been the perfect assassin." Archon scoffed. "Fools."

"C-Branch is military intelligence," said Anna. "They got their hands on DNA from Ekaterina Myshkin and tried to reproduce her gift. Their effort to amplify it didn't work."

"I know a couple people who'd disagree with that," mumbled Kate.

"Anna," said Archon, "this woman spent her formative years consuming wildlife and running about the woods starkers. She would not know the Myshkin woman from a clod of dirt."

"Wait, so you can"—Kate rubbed a hand up and down her stomach—"make it so I'm not always like this? I-I wouldn't destroy everything I touch?" She looked at Aurora who made a flicking gesture, as if starting dominoes. The long-dormant urge to cry welled up. She held it in, though her hands shook as she covered her mouth. "What do I have to do? Just tell me."

"First, I will need you to come to West City. Once I get a better look at you, I can answer the rest of your questions."

"Let's go." Kate jogged over to the car, bouncing.

"You'll burn us out," said Anna.

Aurora raced to the driver's side door. "We need to go."

Kate almost grabbed Anna by the shoulders. "I don't burn things when I'm asleep. Knock me out and throw me in the back."

"No time," said Aurora as she got in. "We need to get out of here right this instant. Kate, stairs, blue door. Use the air intake to go into the basement and wait in the shaft."

"Sorry, luv." Anna ran to the NetMini, hanging up on Archon's protest. "I've learned not to second-guess a precog."

"But... But..." Kate grabbed at the rear door. Her fingers melted through the plastic handle, unable to pull hard enough to open it. "You can't just leave me here after that."

Anna slipped into the passenger seat. "Sorry, no time. We'll find you again."

Aurora started to pull away, but spun to look at her with worry in her gloss black eyes. *It's not his fault. Remember that. He was only a boy then.*

Kate squeezed her hand into a fist, forcing the goopy plastic to exude between her fingers as the hovercar shot out a giant hole in the wall on the opposite side of the gutted floor. She flung the smoldering glop to the floor with a contemptuous growl as she shied away from the rush of wind and debris. At the sound of other approaching vehicles, she sprinted for the stairwell.

Panic stole the care from her stride as she raced down, leaving a trail of burning trash. She stepped on several harsh reminders of her boots being illusions, each time screaming in anger. Half of her wanted to run back upstairs and melt down whoever had showed up and chased Archon's emissaries away. Something about Aurora's reaction of fear checked her murderous urge, reducing it to a momentary pause. Kate glanced over her shoulder at the flames behind her and willed them quiet.

Four floors down, she found a large grated intake duct as Aurora said. She stuck her fingers into the gap, pulled it open, and crawled inside. The echoing clamor of metal striking the wall flooded the stairwell from overhead. She reached over the grate and hurled a stream of flames farther down the stairs to create a false trail. After tugging the cover closed, she crept backward.

In a vent shaft, her holographic clothing surrounded her in an eerie glow. To hide, she shut it off. It didn't matter if she wore light or darkness. Two meters in, the shaft opened into a vertical drop. Kate leaned forward, shifting her weight onto her hands and slid her legs down. Her toes found no purchase but slick metal; she hung on fingertips as ten men in black armor tromped by. A few seconds' worth of flashlight flicked around the ductwork. Fear gripped her as she questioned if she would be able to pull herself back up.

Aurora's directions to find this vent replayed in her mind. Her fingers went numb, her body shook, and she pressed her face into her arm to muffle the urge to make noise. She looked up at the featureless dark metal; shadows shifted from movement outside.

The men were doubling back.

Did she mean for me to hide in here or drop?

She shifted, trying to look down. Her feet continued their involuntary search for something to stand on. Below, darkness awaited. Even if she had wanted to, her arms refused to pull her up. Her grip faltered. Somehow, she managed not to scream as her fingers slipped free and she fell. The drop ended seconds later on a curved metal elbow. Her skin squeaked, butt sliding on the steel duct; she skidded to a halt a few feet from the bend.

Owwwww... Fuck.

A moment passed before she could move, mouth frozen in a silent scream. She bent forward over her legs, forehead to the ground, struggling to contain her usual response to pain—anger. Weak light glimmered in the shaft, not enough to see much more than where she had come from. Her hands explored the walls. Cold metal covered in a layer of grit enclosed her in a square shaft too small to sit up in.

"Well," she whispered. "Guess I only got one way to go."

9

TRAPPED

Minutes of crawling in duct tunnels past a series of turns, dead ends, and unclimbable vertical shafts brought her to a grating in the floor. Unable to see, she groped about, testing the floor. The stink of burned fuel wafted up from below. A few sharp shoves failed to move the grate, so she crawled on. No sooner had she put her second knee down than the floor gave out.

She screamed for a two-second fall, her cry of surprise cut silent as she crashed onto more metal, which broke from the force of her impact. Soot filled the air, making her choke and gag as she brought her arms up to shield her face. A head over heels somersault ended with an impact on more duct wall. It, too, collapsed from the force of her hit. Horizontal became a diagonal as one end of a longer shaft fell, leaving her sliding on her chest down an incline over gritty metal until it leveled off.

Kate curled up, clutching her breasts and whimpering a series of choice words. Her head hurt from several strikes against metal, her entire front felt chafed raw, and somewhere along the line, she had whacked her ankle, leaving her left foot numb. Metal creaked.

"Shit!"

She scrambled up to crawl, but the duct gave out. For seconds that felt like minutes, she hung weightless. Her body crashed on an unforgiving surface, a bed of horizontal bars amid the clatter of broken ductwork. The hit knocked her breathless; every gasp filled her mouth with the taste of soot, oil, and rust. Coughing, she fumbled around in the dark, gripping a series of parallel pipes, each about as big around as her wrist. Sitting on top of them made her feel like a slab of meat on a grill. Her knuckles clipped something metal and sent it flying. A clatter like small bits of plastic falling deeper into a metal enclosure followed. Kate muttered curses into the crook of her elbow, covering her mouth and nose in a futile attempt to stop tasting oily ashes.

For some time, she lay flat on her stomach, gagging, in a chamber large enough to let her stretch out to her full height. Panels of sheet metal strewn over her made banging noises as they warped from the heat. Once the sediment settled enough for her to attempt to breathe without covering her mouth, she shifted to check on her bracelet. It ignored her hand wave, filling her with dread at the prospect of having to make her way back to Tanked with nothing on.

Ten years ago, El Tío had given it to her. Her holographic projector stopped her from attracting attention, stopped gangers from killing themselves trying to attack her, or well-meaning people from causing a scene when they tried to 'help.' To a point, it let her feel normal.

Even if it was a lie.

She cried as though a beloved pet died and grasped the pipes to push herself up, cautiously trying to bring her feet under her. The grill offered nowhere to sit without a pipe going somewhere uncomfortable. Kate squatted on the frame, balancing on the balls of her feet as she reached around to explore her environment. Above, smaller pipes crisscrossed, studded with holes. A small orange flame appeared at her behest, hovering over her outstretched right hand.

Soot smeared her skin in more places than it remained pale. Six feet away, a rectangular hatch offered a way out of what appeared to be an ancient boiler or furnace. In front of the door, a grid of rebar sat over the bones of dozens of rats and burn-gel cans. From the look of it, someone had been cooking here. Her stomach growled. Live rat meat tasted better than OmniSoy hamburgers.

She ducked, glancing up at rows of narrow tubes beneath a smashed water tank and a complicated tangle of broken ductwork. *No way I'm climbing back out of here.* She edged forward, careful to test her footing before putting any weight down. When she reached the hatch, she leaned up to peer out a small four-inch strip of grimy glass.

The basement of a former commercial property appeared dark and empty. A pair of toothed metal bars extended from a geared hub at the center of the hatch, keeping it secure. She grabbed on, ignoring the oily, flaking dirt squeezing between her fingers. Tugging at it failed to move it. Both hands pulling on one side did not fare better, nor did bracing a foot against the wall accomplish more than burning off a spider web.

Kate pounded on the hatch, drawing a breath to scream, but stopped. The men trying to kill her might still be out there somewhere. The rat grill provided a less painful seat than the old boiler pipes, though it remained far from comfortable. A few half-hearted kicks at the hatch made her feel more confined. She huddled in the dark, grateful at least for not feeling cold.

"This was her damn idea; the freaky bitch better get her ass over here to let me out."

Her head sagged forward, hair draped over her shins, and she traced her fingers over the tops of her feet. The stink of the boiler no longer registered, only anger at captivity and the vulnerability that came with it.

Kate sat in silence, shifting every few minutes to keep the grill marks from becoming permanent on her rear end. Eventually, Aurora would show up or perhaps whoever used this place as a cooking fire... assuming they still lived.

She sighed, running her fingers through her hair in rhythmic strokes. The urge to destroy something grew close to uncontainable, manifesting as a blanket of fire around her body. Kate glared at the immobile bar mechanism holding the hatch closed, hating it and whoever built it. Wavering blue firelight illuminated a tangle of crud-encrusted gears, none of which looked as though she'd be able to move them with her bare hands. She despised the scientists who cursed her with life, as well as the city and everyone in it. Rat bones beneath her smoldered and smoked. She hated the lack of anything in easy reach she could make scream in agony.

A shift of weight startled her out of her building anger; the grid upon which she sat softened enough to sag. Eyes closed, she clenched her fists and attempted to calm down. Wrathful woman traded places on and off with fearful child as she drifted from being livid at getting trapped and terrified she'd never get out.

With no sense of time to guide her, her rusting prison became intolerable after what felt like hours. She abandoned worry of mercenaries, and yelled, "Hello?"

The sound of her voice echoed over and over itself into quiet infinity.

She sighed, head bowed. Angry, she slammed her palm into the door, and winced.

A *clank* of metal, like a pipe or rod falling over outside, made her lean up to the door and peer out the tiny window. A wavering flashlight beam emanated from the right, held by someone out of view, sending long shadows stretching over rusting metal walls smeared with streaks of dark liquid. Her breaths came shallow; anticipation and fear knotted in her stomach. It had seemed like an eternity she'd sat there in the old boiler. She doubted the mercs would still be out there looking for her after so long.

She contemplated fixing her embarrassment by killing whoever opened the door. Guilt added to her nerves, causing an anxious shiver. *Maybe he'll try something and give me an excuse.* She brushed the dead bracelet, mourning the loss of her only possession.

It chirped.

The sound made her jump enough to scrape and bang inside the enclosure. Hasty swipes cleared the screen, revealing a dense layer of oily soot covering it—enough to block the sensor that reacted to her gestures. Something moved in the window, followed by two metal-on-metal taps.

"Somethin' in there?" asked a male voice.

Crap!

"Casual One," she whispered to her wrist.

Holographic clothing shimmered into existence around her: dark sweatshirt, loose pants, and black athletic shoes. The eerie glow from the faux garments lit the eyeball of a pallid man peering through the tiny window. His grey-blue iris thickened as the pupil shrank.

"By the maker…" he gasped, backing away.

"Help!" she yelled. "Open the door. I'm stuck in here."

He remained silent.

"I'm not a ghost, moron. It's a hologram."

She shifted her weight onto her feet, poised by the door, gaze locked on the gear nub.

"Please?" She knocked on the hatch. "Open it." *I promise I won't hurt you.*

The eye returned, widening. "I know you! You're the Firefly."

"No one's called me that since I was a kid. Come on, open the door. I fell in from the vents and can't get out."

An ear-splitting screech rattled the boiler as the gear moved. The rag-clad man dragged the hatch open, allowing a blast of cleaner air in. Kate lunged, sliding out the narrow opening and walking on her hands until she could get her legs free. After a brief crawl, she stood, rubbing the discomfort out of her butt, and limped around in a circle.

The man peered at her from behind the half-inch slab of metal, dirt-stained knuckles whitening. Pale as a corpse, and almost as thin, he flashed a nervous attempt at a smile before he looked away.

"Thanks." She glanced around at the basement. "What's the fastest way outside?"

He pointed at a small concrete stairway leading to a door.

I wonder if she knew he'd show up. Kate argued with herself on the way out, trying to make up her mind if she should be angry or grateful.

Several blocks and quite a few ignited dumpsters later, she still had not gotten the essence of soot out of her mouth. Her illusory garments hid most of the dirt, but knowing a thick layer of boiler grime covered her bothered her as much as looking like it. The smell of rust clung to her fingers, making the idea of touching food unwelcome.

Fires erupted in trash at random as she stomped down the alley, wherever a piece of flammable material caught a whiff of her anger. She did not care enough to put them out, figuring a metal city built on metal plates wouldn't mind a little burning. *Why did I ever come to the city? I should've stayed out in the wilds.* She snarled at a trashcan, which exploded skyward at the head of a trail of flames, with a deep concussive *boom* that echoed into the distance. *I'm no less lonely here. Having no one around was better.* She picked at her fingernails. *Well, at least I don't have to kill deer.*

Kate closed her eyes, thinking back to the feeling of Aurora controlling her arm. The sensation almost fit how she imagined being touched would feel, even if it had been her hand under someone else's control. Archon had offered her the one thing she wanted more than anything, and she had no way to get to him. West City... on the other side of the continent.

Another pile of debris roared into a bonfire.

I can't take a damn shuttle to the west coast; I'll light the seats on fire. She scowled, daydreaming about shipping herself as cargo in a metal box. *No, they'll find me on the scanners.* The alley ended at a cross street with a sparse crowd. Three blocks down, the flashing sign for Tanked lit up the night. *I can't walk across the damn country.* Several people leapt away from her as she stormed into the bar. They cried out from the heat and glared, confused and angry. Any pretense of caring for others had gone out the window; her usual habit of giving idiots space was an extra effort she disregarded.

Greg looked up from the bar as she slipped into the hall leading to the gel tank rooms. Repetitive *thuds* from an occupied suite darkened her mood further with a reminder of an activity she could not know. Curtains smoldered from her barely-contained anger as she rounded the end of the corridor and entered her room.

The bracelet landed on the bench and she plunged into the gel, keeping her head above the surface as she scrubbed herself. Nanobots in the fluid avoided direct contact due to her temperature; however, wisps of black grime disappeared when they got far enough away. Kate dunked her head, holding her breath and closing her eyes. The microscopic robots got to work in seconds, clearing her hair of dirt.

In the muted void of sound and darkness, the voices of arguing scientists echoed. They could not understand why the little girl was too hot to touch, yet her hair remained cool and unburned. The old man, the only one of them she still thought of as human, tried to use it as justification for continuing. He surmised her brain had subconscious control over the heat, and if they could figure out the mechanism behind it, they could 'turn her off.'

Kate lifted her head out of the gel and gasped for air. Images of soldiers dragging Dr. Solomon away while she floated helpless in the tank reddened her eyes. Kate didn't often cry; crying was a plea to the world for comfort, and no one would comfort her. She slid out of the tank and sat on the edge, as clean as someone who couldn't use an autoshower or touch water could get. Whiteness spread across the coating of peach colored slime until it flaked off as dust.

Kate stewed about the scientists, her life, and Archon's improbable offer. Anger built on itself. She glanced across the room at the bracelet, the sight of her 'key to the normal world' muted rage to quiet resignation. Grumbling, she fell into the goop, in dire need of sleep.

DULL GREEN CARPET IGNITED WITH EACH STEP, BURNING DOWN TO A blackened footprint seconds later. Pale yellow lights faltered overhead, as if the building feared her approach. Kate locked on to two men in Wharf

Rat jackets loitering by a door, taking pulls on Flowerbasket inhalers and discussing the pros and cons of Siege Corporation's firearms compared to high-end Deutsche Technik Firma guns. Their debate paused as they sniffed smoke, and both glanced at her.

"I need to see Robbie."

The closer man held up his hand. "No can do right now. He's busy."

Kate let her head sag forward. "I'm seeing Robbie. Do I need to kill you two in order to do it?"

They leaned back, reaching for guns.

"Yo, I thought you was cool with the Rats," said the far man.

"I'm not a very cool person," she muttered. "I need a favor that I'm not prepared to wait for."

"This Syndicate bang?" asked the near man.

"No, it's personal."

"Yo, Rude, this bitch is nuts," whispered the far man.

"I'm also not deaf." She stepped closer. "Get out of my way."

The Rats scooted away from the door.

She glanced from it to them. "Shall I burn it down?"

Rude leaned in, as if putting his hand too near a hungry lion. He poked at the silver control square, and the door slid open with a faint pneumatic *hiss*. As soon as it did, he leapt back.

"Thanks. I just need to ask him for a favor. Don't shoot me in the back." She grasped the doorjamb, blackening a handprint into the painted Epoxil trim. "I'll melt your balls off and leave you alive to enjoy it."

Neither man's surface thoughts contained an inkling of intention to attack her. She winked at them and went inside. After climbing six flights of stairs, she headed down a hallway to Robbie's apartment and let herself in. Smoke rose around her legs from the thick pile carpeting as she strode through the living room into the back hallway of an apartment once considered nice, before the sector turned grey. The sound of a holo-bar led her to a bedroom where a thick-bodied, naked man reclined on the bed, engrossed in the drama playing out on a ninety-inch slab of light. He might've had a few extra pounds, but his bronzed tan and sculpted body hair got her mind diverting to places the rest of her couldn't go.

He glanced at her as she walked in, raising one hand in greeting. "'Sup, Kate."

"Hey, Walt. Where's Robbie?"

"You okay, girl? You look fit to be tied. Not that a rope could hold you." Walt slapped his leg, laughing. "Really, what's up? He's in the tube."

"I'm having a bad day. I need to do something I should've done a long time ago."

"Righteous." He leaned back, returning his attention to the movie.

She stared down at her 'sneakers,' focusing psionic energy on suppressing the carpet's desire to burst into flames. A few minutes later, a short Hispanic man, chest covered in tattoos, emerged from the bathroom with a coral-colored towel around his waist. As soon as he saw Kate, he stumbled backward.

"Hey, Robbie." She didn't look up.

"What the fuck are you doing in my house?"

"It's not a house, Robbie. This is an apartment. It's not even an apartment really since you're squatting."

"You semantic bitch." Robbie laughed. "I'd hug ya, but…"

She snarled.

"Whoa…" He raised his hands. "Sorry, forgot. Shit, I can't believe you're still sober after all that. If I was you I'd have overdosed years ago."

Kate wandered to the dresser, the edge of her light-clothes shimmered bright blue where they touched the floating display panel. The dresser top held an assortment of derm patches, which she looked over before picking a lone coffee-colored hexagon up. She set it on the underside of her wrist, turning so Robbie could watch it melt, catch fire, and burn away to ash. Whatever chem saturated the pad tinted the fire deep emerald.

"If I *could* use drugs, I'd be high all the time."

Robbie advanced on her, waving and growling. "You just scorched five hundred creds worth of Stardust. You planning to pay for it?"

Walt covered his mouth to hide the grin.

"Sorry," she said, in a flat tone.

"Sorry? You barge into my place and singe the fuck out of my carpeting. Then, you waste a dose and all you can' fuckin' come up with is 'sorry'? If you was anyone else, I'd be callin' Edmond to get your corpse outta here about now."

"I need a favor, Robbie. You still play in the net?"

"Whoa, whoa, whoa." He waved both hands at her. "We're not past the five hundred credits you owe me yet."

She looked at the collection of drugs on the bureau.

"Wait!" he yelled. "Don't."

"I want to know where the CEO of Laughlin-Reed Innovation lives."

"Can't you get that from the VidPhone directory?" Robbie paced back and forth, one hand holding his towel in place.

"I don't know their name. If it was public information, do you think I'd be here right now?"

Robbie looked at Walt. "You have such fucking awesome timing. We were about to—"

Fire pooled at her feet, shimmering along the carpeting like orange liquid rolling down from her legs. She glared at Robbie.

"Okay... Okay... Fuck's sake, it's not my fault you can't—"

Walt threw a pillow at him. "Rob, stop. You ain't making her any happier."

Kate shuddered with rage, but stilled the burn. "Please, Robbie. All I'm asking is for you to find the son of a bitch and I'll leave."

10

EXECUTIVE DECISION

Darius Reed leaned back in his chair, savoring the aroma of twin lobster tails. He rubbed his face and stretched out the fatigue of a fourteen-hour long day of meetings. A grin spread over his face as he studied the plate, turning it a little to get a look at the whole presentation. To his left, his eleven-year-old daughter stared at her dinner, pushing her lower lip out in an expression of indecision. On his right, his younger son attacked the unrecognized morsel with wild abandon.

"Ashley, you know I've talked to you about your choice of clothing before." The girl tugged at a pink shirt, hanging too low off her shoulder for Daddy's comfort. "I expect you to put on something presentable before we leave."

She poked at the food; a series of quick pouty glances failed to change his mind.

"There are people in this world that would be willing to kill you to eat that."

"If you get to have your hair like that with a suit, I should be able to wear what I want." She stabbed a fork into the lobster tail. "It's a giant bug, Dad. How is it a delicacy?"

His wife Margaret laughed. Darius looked across the table at her, unable to resist the urge to smile. "Your mother put a lot of effort into cooking for us tonight, Ash. She's rather good at it. At least try it."

"Wait, this was alive?" The girl scrunched up her nose at her mother. "You killed some poor animal? Why do people go to culinary school anymore anyway? Machines do the cooking."

"Oh, now we feel guilty about it? I thought it was just a bug." Darius chuckled, gesturing at the boy. "And it's her hobby, like Charlie's art."

"Isn't it illegal to kill real animals for food?" She looked back and forth between them.

"Some animals, yes," said Margaret. "Lobsters aren't one of them. There's no shortage."

The girl gawped at her plate. "If this came out of the ocean, it's toxic."

"Farm raised," said Darius, digging in. "And cooked perfectly."

Margaret winked at him. He grinned and wagged his eyebrows at her. An hour or so from now, the kids would be on their way to his parents', leaving him and Margaret nice and alone… for a whole weekend.

Charlie held up his thumb, unable to speak due to a full mouth.

A *thud* at the door drew their attention.

"Oh, ignore it. Let Marcus deal with whoever it is." Darius worked his knife, separating the second tail from the shell with a surgeon's touch. "The only problem with this dinner is that I want more."

"You can have this one," said Ashley. Her mother's sad face made her pull the plate back. "Sorry."

The girl sectioned off a tiny piece and tasted it.

A man's scream in an outside hallway preceded a gunshot. The family jumped in unison. Margaret leapt out of her chair, racing to the VidPhone on the wall. Both children ran to their father. The apartment door, on the far end of a lavish room and enormous black leather sectional, slid open to reveal a hallway filled with grey fog.

Marcus, the head of the Reed family's security team, staggered in. He raised an arm to Darius, wheezing smoke from his lungs, and collapsed. Darius froze in place as a stunning auburn-haired woman in a dark jacket and tight leather pants stepped over his long-time friend. A cartoon punk rabbit on the front of her hot-pink t-shirt raised two middle fingers. She had no weapons, but her gaze drilled through him.

KATE GLANCED AROUND A ROOM TWICE THE SIZE OF ROBBIE'S ENTIRE apartment, at a two-hundred-inch holo panel showing a paused cartoon. Plants, both fake and real, sat everywhere possible to put them between shelves of useless decorative objects and furniture. A tall black woman in a pink dress had one hand out toward a VidPhone, inches from hitting the emergency button. On the other side of an obsidian table, the man she had come here looking for clung to a pair of kids. Dreadlocks hung to the shoulders of a twenty-thousand-credit suit, but he looked only in his mid-thirties.

He had everything she could never possess: wealth, an opulent home, but most biting of all—a family.

"Who the hell are you?" Darius reached out with one leg, trying to drag a briefcase closer.

"You don't recognize me?" Kate circled left; a hard stare chased the woman away from the VidPhone. She frowned, opening her hand to reveal a fist-sized fireball a second before flinging it into the briefcase.

Darius lurched back, sliding in his chair. "N-no! I don't."

"Daddy!" shouted the daughter; she hid behind his chair, cringing from the glare Kate sent her way.

She forced her way into his mind, wading through his fear in search of any recognition or knowledge of the secret project. "I don't know why I'm surprised. Since when do executives have the first clue what the rank and file are up to?"

"What the hell are you talking about? What do you want?"

"I've come here to kill you, Darius. For what your company did to me."

"No!" screamed the little girl, jumping in front of him. "You can't hurt my daddy!"

He grabbed her shoulders, nudging her toward his wife. "Margaret, take the kids. Get out of here."

The woman didn't move.

"No!" screamed the daughter.

The boy sobbed, hiding his face against his father's chest.

Darius fixed Kate with a calm stare. "I don't know what was done to you, but… Whatever you do to me, please don't hurt my family. They had nothing to do with it. Ashley, Charlie, go with your mother."

Kate gathered a fireball as big as her head in one hand. The roaring flames drew a shriek from Charlie. Ashley trembled, but continued to fight her father's attempt to push her away.

"Margaret, get the kids!" yelled Darius, not taking his eyes off Kate.

As still as the woman stood, it seemed she no longer breathed. Darius pushed his children to the side harder, but Ashley growled and held on.

He gave up trying to push the girl away. "What did they do to you?"

"Something terrible." Kate gazed over ripples of light blue fire sliding across the top of the sphere. "They made me." She remained silent for a moment. "How old is your boy?"

Darius clasped the child's head in his hand, pulling him close. "He'll be eight in three months."

"Your company wanted to kill me when I was younger than him."

"Go to your mother," whispered Darius. Both children refused to budge. "That's got to be more than ten years ago. My father ran the board then. I was still pursuing my doctorate."

She held the seething orb closer to her face, mesmerized by the patterns. "Twenty-five years ago, your company conducted a genetic experiment with DNA taken from some Russian woman, trying to make a weapon. They got me instead. Eighteen years ago, they called me a fuck up and tried to kill me."

Darius broke out in a sweat. "Look, miss. Twenty-five years ago, I was in seventh grade. I had no more to do with what happened than the people next door. I accept that my corporation wronged you, and if there's anything I can do to help—"

"Help?" She shouted, flinging the fireball over Darius's head into the wall. Curtains went up in a flash. "Your company wanted to *kill* me when I was a child. Do you honestly think I'm going to trust them? Even if they had the ability to fix me—which they don't—as soon as they had me helpless, they'd bury their mistake like I never existed."

Darius leaned his chair back on two legs. "Kids. Go to your mother."

"Don't kill my daddy!" Ashley shouted. "It's not his fault."

"Why should I care about *your* father? His company took mine."

"Please…" Darius set his jaw, hiding his fear in clenched muscles. He pushed at the kids. "Run."

"She's bad!" shouted Charlie. "We didn't take your dad! You never had one; they made you in a jar!"

Kate's anger manifested as a cyclone of orange flames, coiling around her body and rushing to fill the room behind her. The sudden conflagration caused a severe wind that dragged the nearest plate to the floor and whipped her hair back.

"You dropped my mom's dinner," said Charlie, pointing.

Kate stared into the reflected blaze in his wide, brown eyes.

Darius gave her an apologetic look before twisting away to shield his kids.

"Don't look," he whispered. "Don't watch."

Ashley cried.

Kate played with a flame between her fingers. "I don't want to harm your kids, Darius. Please ask them to move."

"You're going to make them watch?" His voice cracked. "They don't deserve that any more than you deserved what happened."

"I'm not going!" yelled Ashley. "If I let go, she'll kill you."

Charlie sniveled, unable to speak.

It's not his fault. Aurora's odd telepathic statement replayed in her memory. Both children sobbed. Kate turned away from Ashley's accusing stare.

"Margaret, come take the kids and go to your mother's. I won't use my family as a shield."

Kate let the fire on her hand go out. "You don't have to."

He lifted his head with a hesitant look.

"You're right." Kate stared at her fingers. "It wasn't your fault. I, uhh…"

Darius closed his eyes, squeezing the kids. "Margaret…"

Kate whirled around at a sudden crash in the outer hallway. A flickering red light danced in the corner of her eye. Margaret Reed's finger had pierced the holographic panel by the VidPhone, impaling the emergency call button. She withdrew her arm, covering her mouth, trembling.

"Sorry I interrupted your dinner." Kate let her arm fall limp at her side.

She collected all the fire: the curtains, patches on the floor, and the inferno hanging in midair over the sectional. The flames collapsed into a scintillating orb, which she directed to a halt a few feet inside the door.

Four Division 1 police officers burst through the smoke, pistols rising. Kate pushed with her mind, detonating the energy sphere into a wave of concussive force that knocked her back two steps, and bounced the police off the wall to the floor. She ran over them and looked back at Darius holding his family; tears of jealousy steamed away from the corners of her eyes. He bowed his head, relieved.

"Wrong house. I was looking for a government weasel."

A gloved hand closed around her ankle, but released with a howl of pain an instant later.

Kate jumped into the hall, sprinting for the stairwell.

11

OFF THE GRID

Thick, foul-smelling muck sizzled out from under Kate's feet as she descended the ladder. Squealing and fizzling preceded puffs of smoke that stripped the air from her lungs and brought a tear to her eye. The cops had been on her heels for several blocks, no doubt tracking the intense heat source they could not explain. Out of breath and in pain from lack of food, she had sought refuge in the one place she hoped the police would not follow—The Beneath.

East City rested atop a layer of massive metal plates, each a hundred meters square and twenty-five meters thick. The fifty-meter gap between the bottom of the city tiles and the natural Earth was known as The Beneath. Depending on how angry they got, the law *might* chase her into a black zone, but they would never go down here. Kate wasn't even sure she wanted to.

At the bottom of the ladder, she stepped shin-deep in more black slime. The awfulness bubbled and popped around her with a sound as though someone had dropped an air hose into a vat of syrup. The stink of burning sour raspberries mixed with industrial chemicals brought momentary relief from the feeling of hunger.

She expected difficulty getting out of the muck and pulled her leg up too hard, causing her to flail and grab the ladder not to fall. The intense heat of her skin boiled the substance away before it touched her, leaving a thin layer of steam between her and the ooze. Hindered only by the stench, she covered her face and rushed to the edge of the puddle. Narrow corridors lined with pipes and gridded floors led off in several directions.

Luck had been with her; a wet patch of sidewalk had caused her to wipe out while taking a corner and sent her sliding into a storm drain. The last time she had gone below the city, into the guts of the tiles, was over a year ago. That time, El Tío's contact provided them with a hacked code to open a police hatch. Circumstance, in the form of a broken sewer pipe, let her in today.

She went straight, choosing the largest corridor, and let off a yowl as soon as she stepped on harsh grating meant for thick boots. Arms raised to the sides, she crept forward, gasping and wincing each time she eased her weight down. Rectangular LED lamps reacted to her motion and flickered to life, illuminating a flaking yellow placard warning about the requirement to wear safety gear at all times, including a helmet, goggles, and metal-toed boots. She held out a middle finger to the sign.

"Fuck you."

Having had enough of walking on upraised dinner forks, she jumped up and grabbed on to a dark pipe small enough to get her hands around. The next thing she knew, she lay flat on her back, on the grating, convulsing. A glop of molten plastic slid away from a hand-sized patch of bare wire and landed on her chest. Smoke peeled out from under the dancing blob as it zipped left and fell to the floor.

"That... wasn't... a pipe."

A thousand tiny steel daggers stabbed her back, butt, and legs, but she dared not move. Once the paralytic effect of the shock wore off, she eased herself upright. Kate glared at the patch of naked wire. Fortunately, the heat-resistant bracelet didn't conduct, and her NetMini survived.

"Aren't they supposed to label those damned things 'high voltage' or something? I should complain to the city."

Kate gritted her teeth and hobbled to the end of the passageway, where it connected at a T to another hall with a mercifully smooth floor. A cursory pat down found no blood, despite her having been certain falling on that Hell-spawned grating had torn up her skin. She sat on the floor, rubbing her sore feet and waiting for the pain of the near-electrocution to fade. After several minutes of sitting idle, the need in her gut outweighed her inertia.

At least the cops aren't going to come after me down here. I shouldn't need to stay underground too long. I don't think any of them saw my face.

Aimless, she roamed along a series of corridors. Technically, she hadn't yet entered 'The Beneath.' She considered staying within the plate interior, which could be safer, and avoided ladders in either direction, searching for a place where her NetMini could pick up a signal. After an hour, 'signal interference' had become a swear word with which the bracelet mocked her.

She froze at the distant echo of voices and listened. When their volume didn't change, she figured the locals weren't walking around and decided to creep in the direction of the sound. The scent of cooking meat reawakened the monster in her belly, urging her up to a full run. She brushed aside dangling cables and cobwebs and approached a reinforced hatch-like door. It stood ten inches off the floor and sealed by means of a mechanical wheel, like something out of an ancient submarine. She ducked to squeeze past, while stepping over the lip at the bottom. A four-foot corridor connected to a matching door, suggesting a join point where two city plates met.

Jumping through the second hatch proved to be a mistake as the large chamber on the other side had an inch of water on the ground, which boiled off on contact. Her feet shot out from under her with a sizzling *hiss* and she slid out of control, landing flat. The cloud of steam at her back robbed her of all traction and sent her sliding like a stone on ice. A dozen and change people, unshaven, unwashed, perked up like meerkats as she careened ass-first into a huge pile of wet boxes and junk.

Kate rolled onto her front and folded her arms under her forehead, furious to the point she could not form the requisite thought to stand. Her curse had forced this life upon her. It had made her wipe out in a puddle twice in one day, walk barefoot over a medieval torture device, and nearly electrocuted her. It also came close to making her traumatize two children. *Shit, I probably did that already. Screw 'em. Compared to me, they have a perfect life. So what if they have nightmares about fire for a few years.* She kept her head down in an effort not to summarily destroy the first thing she saw capable of screaming in agony.

"Yawrite?" whispered a female voice. "Nassa fall ya took."

Kate spoke into the hollow between her arms and the ground. "Bad day." Her stomach growled. "Got any food left?"

"Jash came back from a huntin' bit ago. He got some big ones. What ya got ta trade?"

"Need anyone killed?" She pushed up and sat back on her heels. The girl standing nearby looked in her later teens. A filthy, threadbare tartan-pattern coat, blue and white, covered less-intact rags, and she wore one boot and a sneaker that had to be forty years old. "I don't have much else."

"Nice joo-ree." The girl indicated the bracelet.

"I can't trade that."

The girl spun about and trotted off. Kate stood, following her over a field of debris, broken pipes, and support struts. People had made a campsite of this chamber, hanging clotheslines and building impromptu walls to section it off into living spaces.

"I'm Cady. Evar-wun jes call me Cee. Talk ta Gene." She waved in the general direction of a few men sitting around a crate of synthbeer cans on her way to a makeshift table consisting of a slab of metal on boxes. "He's inna middle."

Cee moved around behind the table and retrieved a large dead rat from a box, which she proceeded to skin and clean. Kate glanced up at the metal roof, wondering if the police were still out hunting. With one hand on her stomach, she meandered over to the three men and sat on a section of shelf repurposed to a bench. Having neither the interest nor the ability to trade what they would most likely ask for, she remained quiet.

"What are you hiding from?"

Kate glanced at the man nearest her, not sure what to make of the grungy clothes or the drawn, wrinkled face. His eyes, like beads of glass set in the side of a leather satchel, glinted beneath a spray of thick brows. She leaned forward and squeezed both arms into her stomach in a futile effort to weaken hunger.

"Not much of a talker, eh?" He leaned back into a long swig from his can. "Most people aren't much for talkin' at first."

"You Gene?"

The man laughed. "Well, that's not really my name." He lowered his voice. "I'm Ajit, but these people think I'm a genius."

"Are you?"

"Perhaps by comparison." Ajit took another swig and winked. "Well, maybe a little."

"Police might be after me. You know any way to get to Sector 2629 from here without going topside? I have no damn idea where I am."

"Yeah. Not a great place to be, that. Specially not for a woman... or anyone that ain't half metal. You sure?"

"I got friends there."

She sat up as the bench buckled from the heat. Seven men glanced over with varying degrees of curiosity and interest. One hand patted the bracelet, ever so grateful for it. At the same time, she felt resentment at being so far from normal. Archon's offer replayed itself in her mind. *Stupid. What the fuck was I thinking going after Darius? Now I'll never get to West City. I'm going to spend the rest of my life underground with the off-gridders. Shit!*

A loud bang silenced everyone as a portable cooking surface exploded, followed by Cee's screams as globs of burning fluorescent-blue thermo-gel showered her. Each point of flame resonated in Kate's mind as the feeling of a single heat mass fragmented into dozens of small flecks. They winked out as she willed them dormant.

"I just tapped it!" The girl kept screaming as she flailed and fell in a smoking heap, unaware the fire had already gone out.

Kate shrank into herself as the off-gridders clustered around Cee. Shrieking became sobbing while they tended to a few minor burns.

One of the younger men waved a large wrench at the whimpering teen. "I told you was a bad idea lettin' this idiot near the cooker. Now she's broke it."

"I'm sorry!" wailed Cee. "Ah jus' tappa lid t'open it, and it went off."

"Easy, Zeb," said Ajit. "You're the one that made her cook for everyone. You can't blame her if the parts you scavenge are crap."

"The explosion was my fault." Kate stood. "Leave her alone."

"Oh, that one's funny." Zeb wagged the wrench at Kate. "Alla way over there." He grabbed Cee by one ankle and dragged her close. "This stupid clumsy bi—"

Ajit grabbed Zeb's arm at the exact moment a blue fireball sailed past his face. Everyone froze; heads swiveled at the *whoosh* of the fire.

Kate bounced an orb of fire over her hand like a baseball. "Go ahead, Zeb. Hit her."

They all stared. Cee kicked her leg free and crawled backward, taking cover in a chamber cordoned off by hanging sheets.

Ajit let go of Zeb and approached. "Psionic, right?"

"Yeah. Things tend to get warm when I get pissed off." She squinted. The splattered blotches of thermo-gel ignited. "Sorry about the cooker."

Zeb retreated to his bunk, grumbling.

"Charming fellow, usually," said Ajit. "Likes to bend your ear about how anything that goes wrong can be traced back to a woman."

"If you want him out of your way, I'll kill him for some rat meat."

Everyone got quiet again.

"No, no, no." Ajit held up his hands. "Please, no violence. It's dangerous enough for us down here without going after each other."

She let the fireball go out. "I need to get to West City. I can't stay here."

Ajit tapped his lips. "We can probably sneak you into a terminal."

"I can't use a shuttle." Kate edged around him to the makeshift table and picked up a hunk of raw rat, which sizzled on her palm. "I've got a slight issue with touching things."

The smell of cooked meat drew Cee out of hiding, awestruck.

"Mind if I eat this?" Kate hot-potatoed it from hand to hand to keep it from charring black.

"Uhh..." Ajit waved, speechless.

"Thanks." Kate sat on the bench, devouring the rat to the bone. "I haven't had rat in years."

When she looked up, Cee hovered inches away.

"How did you do that?"

While munching, Kate gave them the short version of her curse.

"We could get something to knock you out and hide you on the shuttle," said Ajit.

"Only if you let me kill Zeb first. I don't feel like being unconscious around him." Kate licked grease from her fingers. "Would you mind if I swiped another? I'm starving."

Cee blinked. "Ya jes' ate whole rat. I k'eet half a one, barely."

"Fast metabolism." Kate glanced at Ajit. "I'll cook the lot for everyone in trade."

"She's gonna touch it?" asked a man somewhere in the back.

Kate blinked. "You're down in the plates, covered in dirt, eating rats, and you're worried about what's on *my* hand?"

Ajit chuckled, holding his fingers over her arm. "I don't think germs would survive on her. Well, there is another option." He followed her to the table. "Roadway Corporation runs transport caravans out to Scattered Lands city states. You could sign on with them, ride on the top of an armored truck. That could get you to the river at least, but you'd have to walk across the Badlands."

Cee skinned and cleaned another rat.

Kate tossed the meat from hand to hand, cooking it. "They take on passengers?"

"No, they don't. You'd have to sign up as a mercenary looking for guard duty." Ajit handed the cooked meat to the first off-gridder in the line that formed.

A sienna-skinned woman in her mid-forties emerged from the cloth room where Cee hid, carrying a metal disc.

She approached, waving it. *"Cocinar en esta, es más higiénico."*

Cee looked up from her work on the next rat. "My mama say you cook on that."

Kate hefted the plate. "This is too heavy for me to hold up." She glanced around and took a seat on a nearby piece of junk, resting the disc on her lap while holding the sides.

Ajit hovered nearby as Cee cooked, astounded by the sight of a surface hot enough that bits of meat charred to ash where they stuck.

Kate stared, mesmerized by the sizzling rat. *Way to go, Kate. You're a goddamn stove now. I gotta get out of here.* She snagged another piece, earning no objection from anyone. "So, Ajit... Tell me more about this Roadway thing."

A THIN LINE

The code Ajit gave her worked. Kate dropped the metal rod she had used to poke the buttons, cringing from a spray of rubber-scented air as the hatch plate opened. She climbed, pulling herself out into a modest breeze gusting down the alley.

"Ow, shit," rasped Ajit from below. "The ladder is hot."

She squatted near the hole. "Sorry. Thanks for everything."

"I hope you find what you are looking for."

Between the morning sun and the dark depth, she couldn't see him, but waved anyway. The hatch beeped and closed on actuated struts. She looked down, reading the diagnostic message on the hatch plate's screen for a moment before closing her eyes and crossing her arms.

"Yeah, me too."

She changed her outfit to green-on-brown military pants, a grey tank top, and a loose camouflage shirt. With her gaze on the ground, she trudged out of the alley and went left. This early in the morning, the sparse pedestrian traffic left her ample room to avoid passing too close to anyone and arousing suspicion. Fear, uncertainty, and doubt warred for prominence in her heart. Ajit had been willing to take credits to play tour guide, ten thousand and he'd spent the past several days leading her through The Beneath to the western edge of the city.

A CyberBurger proved too strong a distraction. She ordered four double-orbitals, requesting a metal tray. This one had no play area, so she wound up standing by the window while she ate. Two drunken idiots bet each other a hundred credits over whether or not the 'skinny chick' could finish everything she ordered.

Kate ignored the resultant fistfight as she dropped the empty tray on top of the de-assembler by the door on her way out. Having no police show up caused as much fear as it did hope, urging her to move at a jog to the end of the block. The cross street was a main east-west artery that traversed the middle portion of the city, six lanes in either direction. From there, the open green of the Scattered Lands stretched between a handful of tall buildings near the edge of the elevated construction. Her destination waited at the bottom of a ramp connecting the city to the ground seventy-five meters down, past a massive open lot filled with cargo transports.

She trudged along, the only pedestrian on a walkway so narrow it had to be an afterthought. A lump formed in her throat as a car shot past, triggering a daydream about what it would be like to ride in a vehicle or feel the touch of real clothing. *I don't care what I have to do to make that happen.* Halfway down the ramp, she stopped. *This is silly. I should let them drug me and put me in the trunk of a hovercar.* Another vehicle rumbled by, this time a box van. Electric motors in the hubs whined as the driver leaned on the brakes. Sparks flickered within the wheels, visible in the gap between the moving rubber and stationary center.

Hovercars don't fly over the Badlands. They can't go as high as shuttles. Walking again, she gazed at the clouds, pondering rumors she'd heard about shuttles always going above the clouds. *Why do they have to fly so high?*

Flashing blue lights from behind made her freeze. She started to glance over her shoulder, but leapt against the chain link fence, cringing away from a hail of wind and dust as a huge blue van rumbled by. She raised a hand, squinting at police insignia emblazoned with a large, white 1 on the rear doors. Her weight shifted off the fence onto her feet as the transport reached the bottom and pulled into the gate at the Roadway Compound.

Great. Those must be my future co-workers.

For the remainder of her journey down the ramp, no other cars went by. Kate walked with the solitude of the whistling breeze in her face until the ground leveled off. A lone guardhouse stood to the right of a person-sized gate. An obvious doll made to look like a generic security guard in blue looked at her.

"Please state your business, Ma'am."

"Miss." Kate grumbled to herself about not being old. "I'm only twenty-five, dammit. Guess they skimped on your personality module, huh?"

"Please state your business, Miss."

Don't get angry... "I'm interested in signing up as a guard for a Roadway run heading for the St. Louis Protectorate."

Its irises glowed amethyst for a few seconds and dimmed. "Records located. Good morning, Emily Ramirez. No security flags raised. Please pass along our respects to your uncle."

She pursed her lips, a knowing smile, as the gate opened. "Thanks. I'll let him know."

"Follow the white line." The doll gestured at the wall, as if pointing at the ground outside.

The long ribbon of worn paint led her to the face of a huge warehouse-style building. She followed it around the side past twelve loading docks, ten enclosed in high-security fencing and razor wire. Whistles and howls came from six men on top of one of the long trailers. Bodies massed at the front into a tangle of orange jumpsuits and dingy white armor vests as they tried to get a better look at her. One man held up a boxy assault rifle, tethered to the truck by a metal cable, and howled.

Kate paid more attention to the texture of the concrete underfoot than she did the sex-starved convicts. After being in the city for so many years and walking on metal, she came close to enjoying it. The stripe led her to a pair of automatic doors and a small lobby decorated in military chic. A Vendomat stocked various brands of synthbeer while another sold ammunition. The reception area extended from the far right corner, with a hallway going around it to the left, deeper into the building.

Behind a shimmering field of faint blue energy, a young woman stared with vacant eyes at a holo-terminal screen. The sight of another person with rich light-brown skin and long, black hair caused Kate to swallow an upwelling of jealousy. A reminder of how different from everyone else she was. *At least my nose isn't that big.*

Her patience gave her all of six seconds before she knocked on the energy field. Cyan ripples spread out from where her knuckles touched. "Hey... are you alive?"

"Just a sec," said the girl, shifting and squinting.

Kate leaned to the side. "Are you playing a goddamned game?"

The teen didn't look at her. "Hang on, I'm the healer. I gotta focus or people die."

"You're raiding at work?" Kate rubbed the bridge of her nose.

"Well... *yeah*," she said. "What kind of idiot *volunteers* for this? I don't work with the cons. You're the first person I've seen in six months." Emotion appeared at last as she smashed a holographic button several times. "Crap, stop distracting me. I almost lost someone."

You're about to lose a whole lot more. Think your priest spells will cure burns? Kate covered her face in both hands, turning away and muttering. *Gotta do this. Archon can fix me. Stay calm.* Kate repeated the chant in her mind for several minutes until the sound of triumphant music behind her caused her to look.

"Okay." The girl looked up. "Sorry about that, what are you selling? Oh wait, you don't look like a sales weasel. Are you one of those people giving out religious crap? Selling cookies?"

The plastic plant on the shelf in front of the energy field melted into a puddle. The clerk blinked at it. Kate reined in her temper before visible flames appeared.

"No. I want to sign on as a guard for a run to St. Louis."

"You?" The girl cocked an eyebrow. "Uhh, no offense, but you don't really look like the type."

"Is there someone I can talk to about getting on a truck headed west?"

"If you're just looking to score with some hot convict, you should know the drivers have cameras. They see something going on an' they'll stun the crap outta both of you."

Kate slammed her eyes closed as the rage whirled around her mind. She focused on hologram-Archon promising her a cure. *Calm. Calm. Calm.* When she opened her eyes, she found the clerk under a table behind her desk, screaming. The outer lobby looked fine, save for a black smear on the tiles around her feet.

"I'm not looking for convict sex. Before you say something even more idiotic that pushes me beyond the limit of my ability to swallow my temper, please point me to someone who can do something more than play video games."

"W-what was that fire?" The young woman crawled out, sheepishly taking her seat. "Was that a hologram?"

"Did you feel heat?"

The girl's eyes widened. She sat still for a moment, jumping to hit a button on the desk as if startled. Kate tilted her head, slow tapping her right foot while waiting for a reply. An Asian man in a grey Roadway Corporation polo shirt and black BDU pants appeared through a doorway at the end of the hall and wandered over.

"I'm Brian. Can I help you?"

Kate covered her breasts with one arm, grabbing her right shoulder, and put her other hand over her crotch, an unconscious reaction to his stare. "I am looking to ride as a guard out to St. Louis."

Brian looked her up and down, rubbing his chin. "Well, no offense, but you look more like a runway model than a mercenary. However, Roadway Corp isn't a company that discriminates against anyone based on appearance. I do have to ask about qualifications though. Come on."

She followed him a short distance into the corridor, hesitating at the door to his office.

"It's okay. You can come in."

"Look, Brian. Before this goes any further, I need to know if you can keep certain information confidential."

"Your record is clean, right?" He shot her a nervous glance.

"Yeah." *As far as I know.* "There's a complication. Your employer has an arrangement with my employer and it would be better for everyone involved if the usual channels were bypassed. My uncle's a nervous guy."

"So?" He cocked an eyebrow.

"My *uncle.*" She stared at him.

Brian opened and closed his mouth, humming. "Mmm, yes. I see your point. Very well then, what is it you need to tell me?"

"I need to go west. I can't touch most things without destroying them." She pinched a leaf off the plastic plant by his door. "I wasn't sure if the non-convict guards have to wear those vests, but it would be a horrible idea for me to touch one."

"Only the prisoners wear the fragmentation devices, though we can provide DuraFib armor vests without the explosives if you like."

The idea of wearing something real lifted her eyebrow. "What's the heat tolerance of that stuff?"

"It's designed to melt on purpose to trap projectiles in a gooey tangle of indirium threads."

"Oh." She frowned. "Never mind then. All I really want is a ride west. I'll do the guard thing, but I can't use a rifle either."

"The housing is metal; you should be able to carry it around for appearances. Besides, they're mounted to the truck. You can leave it in the holder."

"You people have a lot of faith in the convicts to give them artillery like that."

Brian flipped through a few screens on his terminal. "The driver has a master arm, and the guns don't work if they're oriented toward the transport." He looked up. "You acknowledge that Roadway Corporation is in no way responsible for injury or death resulting from your contract employment as a caravan security agent. Furthermore, you indemnify Roadway Corporation against liability for damaged, lost, or stolen property that may or may not occur during the course of your employment."

"Yeah, sure."

"Additionally, you hold that Roadway Corporation is not responsible for the conduct of rehabilitative security agents, up to and including assault of a physical or sexual nature." Brian looked up. "Of course, if someone tries anything, feel free to kill them."

"I'm not worried about that."

"Furthermore, if you plan to bring personal weapons in addition to the RCR-52C rifle provided by Roadway Corporation for your convenience, discharge of said personal firearms is strictly forbidden during the course of your employment without authorization from the driver."

"Does your personal weapons policy include fireballs? Or just firearms?"

"Fireballs?" Brian blinked. "Please don't tell me you're nuts and think you're in an MMO."

Kate made a fist-sized sphere of blue fire. "I guess if you're seeing this, you're crazy too."

"Holy shit!" He jumped out of his chair.

"Oh, relax." She closed her hand, crushing the orb into a wisp of smoke. "I promise to behave."

KATE MADE HER WAY DOWN A NARROW CORRIDOR WITH A BARE CONCRETE floor and armored walls. The upper half of the left wall had a transparent barrier thick enough to seem bullet resistant. She crept forward, watching Division 1 police officers corral men in orange jumpsuits into different holding cells. The convicts looked at her; she couldn't hear them through the barrier, but they all gawked after someone pointed her out. Some winked, some seemed blasé, and a few made rude gestures.

She felt sick for a moment as she thought back to her break in at Darius Reed's apartment. If the eighteen police officers on the other side of the wall knew who she was, she'd be over there with the rest of the caged animals. Her freedom felt as ephemeral as her clothing.

The hallway ended in a cavernous space three stories high. Automated cargo loaders whirred about, carrying boxes like mice running a maze with invisible walls. Brian had made a change to the schedule, moving up a run to St. Louis to happen today rather than in two. He figured the cons wouldn't know better or care, since it meant more time out of jail. His attempt at reassuring her they were all considered low-risk offenders on good behavior was pointless. She hoped someone tried something. After that idiot at the front desk, she wanted to make someone scream.

Kate found Dock 8 right where Brian said it would be, between seven and nine. She rolled her eyes at his lame joke. A passing lift truck came within three inches of flattening her toes. Once the initial shock wore off, she jumped back with a howl and pressed herself into a support column.

"How the hell did something so big sneak up on me?"

She glared at the lift as it drove into the open trailer, dropped a palette of boxes, and reversed back out. Watching it handle the cargo as if it was all Styrofoam scared the breath from her chest.

"Hey!" shouted a big man who looked like a correctional officer. He came trotting over. "What the hell are you doing?"

Kate looked up at him. "I'm signed on for this run."

"They forget to tell you about the lines?" He pointed at the floor. "Don't walk in any of the red areas."

She looked down. The tips of her 'boots' stopped an inch away from a patch of ground outlined and filled with red painted diagonal lines. Red areas took up the majority of the floor. "Uhh, lines?"

"The red areas cover where automatic lifts operate. Yellow zones are safe walkways."

"Yeah… They forgot. Sorry." Another lift shot by fast enough to pull her hair to the side in the breeze. "Do I get an assigned spot?"

"Well, guess you're either an adrenaline junkie, nut case, or an idiot." He leaned down close, whispering, "Normal people don't sign up for this sorta thing."

She looked at a two-person armored perch atop the back end of the trailer. "I'm not normal."

"Didn't think so." He chuckled. "Go on and take any of the stations. You got the coffin at the ass end, two pods on each side, and the eagle nest at the front on top of the cab."

"Coffin?" She eyed the armored box "Because it looks like one?"

"Nope. It's at the back end of the trailer. When pirates attack, they usually have a crew come up from behind and another group pull out ahead. The rear perch is the easiest target, and it's where they tend to fire first. Side pods are harder to hit. Seventy percent of our fatalities occur in the coffin."

"Oh. I thought it would give the best angle to shoot back from."

"It does. Depends on the driver you get. Sometimes they wait too long to arm the guns."

She smiled. "Can I hop up there now?"

"You're gonna be stuck on top of that thing for two days at least, no point rushing it."

"I'm set. I hit the cafeteria already."

The yellow paths got her close to the door, but she couldn't see a way to get to the ladder on the back without going across the red. She waited for an opening in the train of lifts and rushed across a safe-looking gap to a metal ladder on the right side of the trailer. The top had to be at least fifteen feet off the ground. An armored hatch let her crawl into a metal-walled enclosure designed as a shooting platform. Two large rifles sat tucked in holders at the center. Thick metal cables secured them on five feet of tether, making the space look like an ancient carnival attraction.

All of it was bare metal, no cushions or comfort. She smirked at the footprints she left in the dust, smudging them to avoid awkward questions. With time to kill, she folded her arms atop the rear-facing wall and squatted to watch the cargo loaders scurry about. The barrier would come up to her neck if she tried to assume a kneeling shooter's position, but the awkwardness didn't bother her.

Sleep had almost taken her when a loud buzz sounded in the warehouse. Four Division 1 officers in shiny blue armor escorted a single-file line of men in orange jumpsuits. All had been fitted with the Roadway Corporation security vest, armor that could kill its wearer as easily as protect them.

The prisoners stopped in the red area behind the trailer, still in single file. Kate made eye contact with the man at the head of the line. Broad-shouldered, coffee-colored skin, shoulder length black hair, and a wiseass grin. Anger, her usual reaction to fate teasing her with a treat she could not touch, faded as she read his surface thoughts.

What's a pretty girl like that doing here?

One of the officers moved between them and the truck.

"We got anyone new?" He leaned taller, looking them over before checking a datapad. "Doesn't look like it. I'm gonna skip the long, bullshit speech since you've all done this before, but I'm legally required to cover the usuals. You know the drill. Driver arms the rifles, don't shoot each other. Your life is in your hands, and so on. We've been told this is a schedule change, so you'll be going out to St. Louis. An extra two days of open sky."

A few of them cheered, clicking handcuffs as a form of clapping.

Motion drew Kate's attention to a pasty-faced man in a grey Roadway Corporation polo and black pants. He had a datapad tucked under his arm and scurried along with a nervous twitch as if afraid to look at anything but the ground. He stopped by the police, casting a cursory look at the prisoners before he caught sight of her in the coffin.

"Why's that one out of her restraints?"

Kate stood, leaning both hands on the railing. The look she gave him made him shrink behind the police.

"That one's an outside merc, Bernie."

"Oh." The driver found a shred of courage in that and gave her a mixed look. "Don't try anything unprofessional"—he waved the datapad at her—"I can see everything."

"No, Bernie, I didn't pick the coffin because there's enough room in here to fuck. I expected to get stuck with a chickenshit driver that'll wet his pants if we get attacked and wait too long to arm the rifles. Looks like I might have good intuition."

Chuckling spread among the convicts, even the cops. Bernie grumbled, scurrying past the gap between the trailer and the wall in a speed-waddle for the driver's compartment seventy feet away. He looked even shorter by the ten-foot front wheel as he climbed the handholds in the hub. The driver's door closed with a *thunk*, followed by a metallic *clank* as it locked. At the center of each prisoner's vest, a cluster of red lights flashed yellow. A moment later, they went green with a series of chirps that swept down the line from front to back.

The police removed the men's restraints and led them one by one to the platforms around the truck. Kate sat and leaned against the back corner, as far from the hatch as the space would allow. Clanking and grumbling seemed to come from everywhere. The face of the man who had smiled at her appeared in the opening. He grinned and climbed up, taking a seat and pulling the hatch closed.

"Hey." He extended a hand. "I'm Esteban."

"Kate." She looked at his hand. "Sorry, I don't do the touching thing."

"Fair enough. Is this your first time?"

She realized her posture must have portrayed a sense of cowering in the corner, and tried to relax. "Yeah. First time."

13

CONVOY RUN

K ate sat with her back to the side wall, feet apart, arms draped over her knees. Esteban faced the rear, tall enough to see over the armored plate even while sitting. He pulled the closer of the two rifles out of its holder and examined it. On either side of the housing above the pistol grip, a panel glowed bright red. Raised metal along the barrel guard formed the logo of Siege Arms Corporation.

He grunted as he pivoted it over to examine the oversized magazine that made it look more like a squad-level support weapon than an assault rifle. The number 243 floated in green hologram along the top of the weapon, in clear sight while firing.

"Hope it's enough ammo." He tapped the magazine. "Can't reload."

"That's stupid."

Esteban laughed. "They're afraid someone will jury rig a bomb if they can get the bullets out. You're right. It's stupid. Anyone volunteering for this caravan shit is on a short stint anyway. They wouldn't be interested in making a run for it."

"What's up with Bernie?"

"Some of the drivers get big heads. I guess having eight men's lives at the tip of his fingers makes him feel like a god. He's not the only one. Most of the drivers are like that."

Kate gathered her hair to keep it out of her face from the wind. "You know he can probably hear us."

"Yep. He's not going to set off my vest just for insinuating he's an asshole. Without an immediate threat to his own life, the company would consider it murder. Plus, you'd get caught in the shrapnel blast."

"Charming." She jostled back and forth as the truck hit a series of holes. "Seems like not a whole lot of incentive to volunteer for this."

He slid the rifle into the holder and stretched. "It's a couple of days of fresh air. Even if they make us sleep on the truck, it beats a metal cube and artificial light. We don't get paid, but they knock a few weeks or months off the sentence each time we do it."

"That's not fair." She gazed at the clouds. "Bet the driver gets a hotel room for the stopover."

"Yep. He thinks we're less than people since we had a scuffle with the law. Animals on exploding leashes. More than twenty meters away from the truck, it goes boom. Had a guy get bounced out of his pod last run." Esteban stared into the distance. "He rolled a couple of times, screaming, then popped like roadkill." A faint smile twisted half his lip. "He took one of the bandits with him though. Splatter on the windscreen; made him crash."

"Sorry."

"Eh, he was reckless. They told us not to stand up. Of course, the transport was going too fast. They're not supposed to go over forty."

Their conversation stalled for a little over an hour. Some of the other men shouted back and forth, discussing the sexual prowess of Bernie's imaginary sister. The utter wrongness of some of their remarks got Kate laughing. She stayed seated, not caring to watch the scenery pass by and suffer the agonizing slowness of thirty-five mph.

"So, what's your story?" Esteban glanced at her, at last ending the long silence between them.

Self-consciousness at her legs-apart posture made her shift to face the rear, giving him her side rather than a full frontal. "I need to go west, and I can't take a shuttle."

"Afraid of flying?"

"Something like that."

"I won't say anything if you want to keep your head down."

"That's awful knightly of you, but I can handle a fight."

He grinned. "I get the feeling there's more to you than you let on. Takes a special kind of crazy to refuse the armored vest." When she said nothing, he chuckled. "Mind if I ask you an awkward question?"

"Ask away, but don't expect an answer if it's too awkward."

"Your shadow…" He pointed at the silhouette of an obvious breast. "Doesn't seem right."

She tucked her legs to her chest as his shadow finger teased her shadow nipple. "Trick of the light."

"Right."

Over another quiet half hour, the increasingly raunchy banter behind them brought her to blushing. A voice much deeper than the rest had started involving goats in the orgy with Bernie's now-nymphomaniac fictional sister. Esteban craned his head around and yelled at them to give it a rest. Kate thought about her immediate circumstance and how things might go down if they got attacked.

She looked at him. *Esteban?*

He jumped, raising an eyebrow. "Did you just say something?"

"No." *I'm psionic. Don't flip on me.*

Esteban lost control and laughed himself to tears.

She glared. *What's so funny?*

Moments later, he regained the ability to breathe. "When I was little, far too young to even think about girls, my grandma made me promise never to get involved with a psionic. She pulled me aside one day, I think I was seven, and she's all like 'Now Esteban, I need you to promise me when you grow up you won't marry a psionic girl.' Now I'm sitting here wondering what I can say so I don't sound like an idiot to you."

She hid her face in her knees, waiting for the rage to subside.

He raised his hands in a gesture of surrender. "I didn't mean to offend you. My grandmother was opinionated, and not in good way."

Kate took a long, slow breath and let it out. "You didn't."

"Good." He mimed wiping sweat from his brow. "I'm not like the rest of my family. I got nothin' against people who're… umm… yeah."

"You first," she said. "What'd you go in for?"

"Oh, nothing impressive. My brother and I used to own a garage. We tweaked performance on hovercars and land cars."

She furrowed her eyebrows. "That's a crime?"

"Well, some of the parts we used belonged to the police and aren't legal for civilians to own. Had a cousin inside their motor pool stealing parts. They didn't appreciate that. We got three years, course Jimmy got fifteen as well as fired from the force. Like I said, the guys they let do this caravan thing are low-risk."

"What about smiley back there with the mohawk? He doesn't seem all there."

"Oh, Wilma? He likes killing people. Apparently, they believe doing this satisfies his urges and keeps him passive while he's in custody. He's a model prisoner, maybe the only lifer they let out of his box."

"I guess it's a good thing the rifles don't fire on the truck."

"Oh, he's too careful for that. He'll only kill the people they let him kill. Otherwise, they'll put him in a small, dark place and take away his recreation."

"This is his recreation?"

Esteban sputtered. "Yep. Okay, your turn."

She stared into his eyes, hating how his face reminded her of her curse. To prevent eavesdropping, she projected her voice into his mind. *I'm an overclocked pyrokinetic.* She held her hand out. *Don't touch me. Just reach close.* As expected, he yanked his hand away when he got within an inch.

"What the?"

I'm like six hundred degrees or something stupid like that all the time. I can't turn it off. He gave her a meaningful look. *Yes, that means I'm not wearing anything but holograms right now.*

He looked away, whistling.

"I wanted to tell you in case it gets rough. Don't try to grab me if I go flying."

"There's no way I'm going to let you fall on the road... especially with nothing between you and the pavement."

You have no choice. If you grab me, your skin will melt off and I'll fall anyway. Don't worry. I'll stay down.

The day wound into evening, and she found herself opening up about her isolation. While she avoided any mention of being a government experiment, she confessed her bitter loneliness at not being able to touch another human being. He offered a sympathetic ear, exaggerating his complaints about his ex-girlfriend to comic levels.

"When she said she wanted to go to an off-Earth colony and have two dozen kids, I figured she was going to be high maintenance."

Kate laughed, then got quiet when she couldn't remember the last time she had a genuine laugh. "You're making it difficult. You seem like a decent guy."

"You can call me Steve if it helps cool you down." He winked. "I use Esteban with the pretty ones."

"Hah." She chuckled.

The truck slowed and came to a halt on the side of the road.

"Attention. We are stopping here for the night. Pods one and three have first watch. Two and four, second watch. Coffin and Nest, one man on third watch and one on fourth. That includes you, miss special. If you need to relieve yourselves, there's paper with the rations. Remember you have twenty meters. If you hear a chirp, you're getting too far away."

A voice near the front moaned. "Aww, we can't use your executive bathroom with the gold toilet seat?"

"Bernie-man would wet himself if the doors opened," grumbled a closer voice.

Wilma's cardinal red hair appeared over the wall. Kate glanced up at the hulking figure; her muscles tensed at the eerie calm on the face of a man who killed as a hobby. His size made her feel as if she were a small child.

He saluted them with a brown plastic ration. "Hello, sir and madame. Your magnificent feast is at hand. Chef Jacques has assured me that he has perfected his technique." He opened his hands.

Two food pouches clanked into the metal between them. Wilma cast his gaze upward as if pondering the nature of humanity. After a few seconds, he walked away. Kate watched the rim of the coffin until the sound of boots on the trailer roof ceased.

"He's a strange duck." Esteban helped himself to one of the pouches.

She melted the other pouch open with a finger as if using a laser scalpel, causing a number of smaller silver packets to spill out.

"Dammit."

Esteban squeezed one into his mouth and glanced sideways at her while he chewed. "What? You get the omelet or something?"

"It's all in plastic pouches. I can't touch them. I've eaten some awful things, but goopy molten plastic... ugh." She glared under her eyebrows at him. "What is that smell?"

"Tuna salad"—he glanced at his food—"I think."

Kate crossed her arms, careful not to touch the screen of her NetMini, and tried to drill holes in the armor with her glare. He set his food aside, took the largest pouch from the second ration, and peeled it open.

"Here, lean back and open your mouth."

Her face reddened.

"Come on. You don't have to cheep at the sky like a starving bird, but I'd smile if you did."

The blush intensified, but she laughed. "It's..."

He sniffed the packet. "I think this is tikka masala chicken, but it might be a hamburger."

She looked at him. "Those two aren't even close."

"It's a military ration pack. It's all OmniSoy anyway. I don't know what they do to it to prevent it from degenerating back into slime, but taste isn't high on their priorities."

"Prevent it? It *is* slime."

"Good point. Come on, I can't make you watch me eat."

After a long sigh, she tilted her head back. He squeezed a bit of food onto her tongue, cocking his eyebrow when it sizzled. She couldn't look at him for the first few mouthfuls. After eye contact, she couldn't stop laughing. Food dribbled off her chin as he tried to feed her despite the giggles; she caught some of it and cracked up again at the face he made.

For a quiet moment, their gazes met.

She looked away first, frowning at her lap.

"You got a little on your, uhh." He pointed at a wisp of smoke rising from her shirt.

"Oh." Kate flicked a nugget of charcoal from her breast, still moping. "Thanks."

Esteban scooted back to his side and resumed his meal. "So, which was it?"

"What?"

"Chicken or hamburger?"

Her hand slid up and down her shin. "I couldn't tell. I don't taste much."

He finished his tuna and tucked the empty packet back into the main pouch. "Did I do something wrong?"

Yeah, you're nice. "No."

"I get it." Esteban shifted his weight, looking for a comfortable position to sleep in. "I can't imagine what it's like not to be able to touch anyone. I'm sorry if I reminded you of that. I understand it's no small task for a girl to keep their hands off me." He winked.

"I could put my hands on you if you want," she purred, crawling toward him.

He flattened into the wall and slid down. She hovered over him, swiping her tongue across her lip.

"Knock it off, you two. No fraternization on company time." Bernie's voice crackled from a tiny speaker in the center of the rear wall.

She sat back on her heels, tucking her hair over her ear. "Relax. Just repaying a tease with a tease. We're not going to do anything." A sigh slipped from her nostrils. *We can't.*

Esteban sat up and closed his eyes, breathing slow and deliberate.

"Why are you thinking about an old woman in her underwear?" asked Kate. "Oh, wait... never mind. I think I understand."

He laughed.

"I might not always be like this," she whispered, stretching out on her side with an arm between her head and the metal floor. "There's a doctor in the west who thinks he can turn it off."

Esteban settled against the wall, shifting and squirming. "I hate these damn vests."

With the sun down, her camouflage outfit took on a ghostly luminescence. She picked at the heat-resistant band, dreading the sound of Bernie's voice demanding she get rid of whatever is making the light. *If I stay down, nothing should see me.*

"I don't think many people would enjoy wearing a bomb."

"Thanks for reminding me of that. Damn thing is rigid, and locked on. Not comfortable. Try to get some sleep if you can."

"Yeah..." Kate sighed. "I'll try."

🐿 🌾 🏯 ☄ 💬

SHE AWOKE TO THE SOUND OF HER TEETH CHATTERING SOME TIME LATER. IT took a few minutes for her curse to kick in and chase away the cold of nighttime. Esteban snored. Whispering voices above and behind debated which of the two men on watch stood a better chance of getting her in bed. Fortunately, they sounded intent on trying to talk her into it rather than force the issue. Kate shot a dirty look at the wall and tried to go back to sleep.

🐿 🌾 🏯 ☄ 💬

A HAND SQUEEZING KATE'S SHOULDER WOKE HER. ESTEBAN LEANED OVER her, a look of confusion on his face. Before she could think, she leapt up and rushed a clumsy kiss. He jumped back, rubbing the side of his neck where her arm had made contact.

"Ouch." He looked at his hand, finding no blood. "That wasn't as bad as you made it sound."

Crimson-faced, she averted her gaze to the distant sunrise. "It takes a minute to get going after I've been asleep. I'm sorry; I don't know why I did that."

"I'm used to it." He turned to catch another pair of ration packs thrown at the coffin. "Ladies can't resist the *Esteban*." He laid a thick Spanish accent over the name. "Steve, not so much. Not bad for a first kiss."

She attempted to become part of the wall.

Wilma goose-stepped to the end of the trailer, rendered a Nazi salute with a ration pack, and dropped them. He spun on his heel and ran off giggling like a twelve-year-old girl.

"Palak paneer or tuna mushroom casserole?" He held the pouches up. "Which one do you want?"

"Uhm. What the hell is that?"

"Indian. If you can't taste what you eat, you might as well take the tuna."

Kate moved closer. "Okay. Actually I meant *that*." She pointed over her shoulder at the wall. "What's his damage?"

Esteban laughed. "The head-doc at the prison can't even tell. He's probably just doing it on purpose. It's too far over the top. You're the psychic, why don't you take a look?"

"Uhm. No thanks. Some doors are better left closed."

After eating, Bernie gave them ten minutes to use nearby bushes to relieve themselves. Much to Kate's surprise, the men were respectful and turned their backs to her. Once everyone had returned to their cubbies, the truck got underway, giving her a great view of a dust cloud in their wake.

"I wasn't expecting them to be so polite."

Esteban laughed. "Everything that happens here is on camera. Except for Wilma, every one of us is hoping for early release. Those corrections shitbags would dock us three months for sneaking a peek."

"Oh, damn. I almost thought they were decent human beings."

"Some things are worth three months." He winked. "Perhaps they are."

Several hours passed in relative silence. A few burned-out buggies on the side of the road contained blackened skeletons draped over hollow tube frames. Off to the south, a walled-in settlement stood sentinel amid a sea of grass. The road leading to it passed by soon after, decorated with more destroyed vehicles.

"Don't feel sorry for them," said Esteban. "They're pirates and raiders.

They'll kill you without hesitation to steal whatever we're carrying. Even if it's a truckload of toilets."

She laughed. "Why?"

"The only law out here is inside those settlements." He gestured at it. Indistinct figures moved along the wall, rifles obvious. "Scattered Lands isn't much different from the Badlands to be honest, 'cept there's no runaway cyborgs or strange mutated things. Settlements are a lot bigger too, but they're all independent."

Kate looked at her hands. *Maybe I should stay out there. I think I qualify as a 'strange mutated thing.'*

"What are you thinking? You did sign on as a guard… You can get in legal trouble if you don't help repel an attack."

"Nothing… That's not a problem. I've killed before."

"Really? You don't look like a killer. Couldn't have been too long ago if you're still making that face at the idea of it."

She looked up in a slow, deliberate gesture, staring into his eyes. "I was seven years old the first time I killed a man. I don't regret it. They were going to kill me."

"Umm." He scratched his head. "I have nothing to say in response that won't sound stupid or patronizing."

"It's okay. Like I said, killing doesn't bother me." She leaned on the railing, squinting into the wind at the road ahead. "I'm no Wilma, though. I don't get off on it… it's just something I have to do sometimes."

"Yeah."

"You have a girl?" *Why am I bothering?*

"Already told you, Gina ran off to some colony to make babies. No joke. Some corporation was paying big for wanna-be mothers. She wanted a big family like in the old days, and she wasn't gonna get that on Earth. Free ride, too. Helps she's got a degree in finance."

"Oh."

"Now what's wrong?"

She stretched up on tiptoe for a moment and leaned against the inner wall with one foot braced against the opposite rim. "I'm angry. I never thought I'd meet someone who didn't freak out about what I am. Talking to you reminds me how much I hate my life. I hope what you're thinking about me isn't all based on pity."

He coughed.

"Yeah, I am reading your mind." She glanced at a herd of deer bounding through the grass to flee the rumbling behemoth. "I suppose that's rude of me, but I'm not going deep. Only what's on the tip of your brain."

"You're definitely not a pity case, at least by looks. No, I'm not trying to flatter my way into your pants."

"Don't even say it. You're trying to set up for a 'you're not wearing any' joke."

He held his hands up. "Sorry, just trying to lighten the mood. If you spend your whole life angry at the world and the man upstairs, you'll never be happy."

"Man upstairs?"

"God," said Esteban. "He made you that way for a reason."

Kate lowered her foot from the railing, unconsciously covering up again. "I don't know much about religion, but it wasn't anything divine. I was made by a bunch of morons in white coats."

"Mmm. Oh, well... I had to try. My grandmother always said that whenever I got upset. Thinks there's some divine intelligence guiding humankind, and whenever something bad happens, she said it was part of his plan."

"Think she's right? Or, do you think she's ignoring reality?"

"I don't think about it at all." He went to pat her on the shoulder, but reconsidered. "If it makes her feel better, I'm not gonna pop that bubble."

Kate glanced up at puffy, white clouds. "I'm not gonna bother. I got too much blood on my hands."

"I think you're about to get a little more on them." He hauled one of the rifles out of the holder, shouting over his shoulder. "Incoming!"

A cluster of small buggies burst from the billowing mass of dust, flanking an old pickup truck with slabs of armor welded to the body. Two compact cars took the lead, both with the roof cut away and replaced with machine guns on posts.

"Bernie, arm the fucking rifles!" shouted Esteban.

"The unidentified vehicles haven't closed to within policy threat range," said the tinny voice.

"Look at them," shouted Kate. "They're not coming to ask for directions."

Esteban's rifle chirped and buzzed as he tried to shoot.

The buggies accelerated and spread out, filling all six lanes of highway. A goggled, bald head peered up over the roll bar in the pickup, a manic grin spread over his face. He looked at the convoy truck, down at something in his hand, and back up. Behind him, a camouflage-painted metal box, far more modern than the vehicle carrying it, extended upward and pivoted.

"They have some kind of missile launcher," shouted Esteban.

"Come on, you idiot!" roared one of the other cons.

"Wilma hears the call," said Wilma. "I am coming, Father." He looked skyward.

"Unidentified vehicles have not crossed into threat range," said Bernie, triggering a cascade of profanity from everyone but Wilma, who smiled. "We cannot assume everyone out here is hostile."

"Yeah, maybe they're on the way to the mall," said an unidentified con.

She looked back and forth between the speaker and the road. "Those buggies have old engines. I can feel the fire."

"If he doesn't arm these rifles, we're in deep shit," said Esteban.

The truck picked up speed, edging up to forty miles per hour. The pursuers kept pace. Goggles reached up and slapped the roof twice, causing the driver to veer left and step on the accelerator.

Kate focused on a buggy right in front of the pickup. Her concentration snuffed the engine, and the little cart decelerated as hard as if he'd stomped the brakes. The pickup rear-ended it, knocking the small aluminum frame sideways. Wheels caught the road and sent it rolling like a log. Screaming, the driver spilled out of his seat as the metal cage jammed under the pickup's bumper in a shower of sparks.

A long red smear emerged along the road.

Esteban's rifle continued to buzz error tones. Azure flames coalesced into a sphere above her right hand, which she hurled at the closest buggy. The driver swerved out of the way, gaping at her wide-eyed.

"What are you doing?" barked Bernie. "They're still beyond minimum engagement dist—"

"Fuck your engagement distance," yelled Kate, throwing another fireball. "You ever hear of Darwin? You're about to prove him right."

Her attack scored, immolating the exposed driver. Molten skin separated from his face, flapping in the breeze on either side of his skull. He shrieked loud enough to be heard over the roar of engines and veered off the road. Ancient concrete debris clanked and scattered as the buggy tumbled into a ditch and exploded. Her psionic reach pulled at the expanding cloud of ethanol fire in an effort to focus it at another car, but the convoy passed before she could get the conflagration to the highway.

Bernie lost his mind, screaming at her about protocol and liability, most of which degenerated into unintelligible sounds.

The pickup skidded to a halt, backed up, and drove around the wreckage. Goggles, covered in black soot, lifted his eye protection, exposing a negative-raccoon effect. He thrust his hand down, out of sight, and two circular holes opened on the front of the pod.

"Bernie, they have missiles," said Esteban, sounding far too calm for the situation.

"There's no law out here!" shrieked Bernie. "We can't kill them for having weapons."

Kate threw two fireballs at the pickup, doing little other than darkening the paint. "You are an idiot, Bernie. You're going to get us all killed!"

"I have to follow policy!"

"I can't burn metal," she rasped at Esteban.

From the farthest lane, what would have been oncoming traffic centuries ago, the pickup maintained distance as the missile pod rotated toward them.

Esteban kicked the speaker. "They're going to fire it at us, Bernie! Guns. Now! They're staying out of range on purpose. They're exploiting your fucked policy."

"I can't see the damn missile," said Kate.

"What's that got to—"

A line of smoke appeared in an instant, connecting the launcher to the ten-foot tall left drive wheel on the cab. The sense of combustion appeared and ended in less than a second, too fast for Kate to interfere with. With a great *boom*, the massive vehicle jerked to the right as if kicked by a giant. Sparks and debris flew out from the electro-motor core, through a hole she could've climbed into. Two-foot-thick rubber treading snagged on the road as the motor failed and stopped on that side, dragging the truck into a severe and unexpected swerve to the left.

Bernie screamed over the speakers and overcorrected. The swaying truck flung her to the ground inside the coffin as the sound of automatic weapons fire erupted from everywhere. From the floor, she looked up at Esteban, struggling to keep from getting thrown out of their kill box. The arming light went green and he held the trigger down. Tiny flakes of metal foil snowed out from the bottom of the rifle. A fusillade of metal clanks preceded a softer *bang* and the crunch of great metal hunks tumbling over grass. Clicks and clanks hit the metal wall behind Kate's head, bullets failing to penetrate the truck.

"Pickup's down." Esteban ducked a spray of bullets; one caught him on the shoulder, stalling in the vest with enough force to knock him backward. "Son of a bitch that's going to bruise." He blinked. "I guess this really *is* armor."

Kate scrambled to get up. He used the rifle to push her down.

"Don't. They're firing wild."

Wilma let out a long, "Yaaaa-hooo," and opened fire.

The driver's effort to fight the dead wheel dragging them to the left caused the truck to thrash side to side like an angry serpent for a few seconds before the wheels on that side lost contact with the ground. Bernie's whimpering became a scream as the eighty-ton transport rolled to the right. Esteban floated up into Kate, and howled as her skin burned holes in his prison jumpsuit for the few seconds they remained in contact.

Screams from the two men in the gunnery pods cut out as the truck slammed down on its side. Their metal enclosures crushed like empty synthbeer canisters.

The coffin filled with a deafening *whump* and the grinding scrape of metal on paving; gravity shifted and she fell on top of him again. He shrieked, but she pushed away from him, bracing hand and foot against the metal, standing with her back to a wall that used to be the floor. Sparks streamed away from the new floor as the truck continued sliding. Esteban flew out, clinging to the tethered rifle. He kept his legs raised, trying to balance like a turtle on its back so the vest took all the abuse from the road. His orange jumpsuit darkened to red in a spray of gore coming from under the trailer that used to be two men.

A prisoner who had been in the eagle's nest bounced by on the road, snagging Esteban's leg with a wild, desperate grab. He held on for a second before slipping loose, vanishing under one of the compact cars racing closer. A man leaned from the passenger window with a submachine gun, spraying at Esteban.

Bullets clicked off the ground, clattering into the coffin. She screamed and ducked, terrified of catching a bullet she didn't see coming. Esteban swiveled, kicking at the road in short bursts to avoid shredding his legs as he aimed and fired. Smoke billowed from the little car's tires as it braked, but their evasion came too slow. A scattering of holes decorated the little car's hood as the truck shuddered to a gradual halt. Esteban kept firing at the compact, until the driver slumped over dead.

His moment of relief lasted only seconds before he scurried in a backward crabwalk. The now-driverless car continued to roll. Kate cringed back, flattening against the side as he dove in next to her. They both shouted "Shit!" as the car crashed into the truck, trapping them. The mangled metal bumper halted inches from her leg.

"They *had* to call this a coffin, didn't they," she whispered, gagging on smoke laced with the stink of burning oil.

"Well." He gasped, covered in sweat and bleeding from road rash and burns. "I survived a truck roll and now I'm trapped in a confined space with a beautiful naked woman while being shot at. I don't think life will ever top this moment."

Kate's gaze fell, checking to make sure her holo-projector hadn't broken. "Shit, you scared me."

Buggies buzzed like wasps, circling the stricken semi, trading gunfire with the three remaining convict-guards.

"You're worried about your fake clothing right now? Figured you'd be used to it."

She winged a fireball through a gap in the wreckage, setting off a fuel explosion in a passing buggy. "You know how they always say you want what you can't have?"

A wave of burning ethanol lurched forward over the driver. The shrieking raider jumped out of the vehicle without slowing down, rolling into the scrub at the side of the road, motionless and burning.

"Yeah." He stuck the rifle around the left wall, shooting. "Is this car going to explode?"

"No. I won't let it." She missed the next buggy. "Being naked never bothered me until I went to the city and people started *looking* at me like that. Alone in the wilds, I didn't know any better. I never felt cold. Now I can't stop feeling embarrassed. It's more about what people think than being seen."

Esteban held down the trigger, swinging his aim to the right, reducing the second compact car to a bullet-riddled husk. Kate lobbed a fireball into the window, igniting the interior as it careened off the road. Ballistic propellant saturated the coffin with an acrid chemical vapor.

"Something wrong with the other rifle?" He fired a hasty burst, ducking as a spray of bullets hit the metal by where his head just was.

She dropped to all fours. "Trigger's plastic."

"Oh, right. Hah." He popped up, firing a series of rapid single shots until something exploded. "I feel like an action hero or something. Stay down, I'll protect you."

"I'm not some helpless princess." She climbed onto the hood, burning the paint to bare metal wherever hand or foot touched. "We're gonna die if we stay in this damn box."

Kate squeezed through a narrow gap between the coffin and the car, crawled over the roof, and jumped to the road, crouching by the driver side door. Blood and automotive fluids leaked from dozens of holes, sizzling away from her toes. Three buggies circled clockwise, trading shots with the convicts still alive on top of the trailer. Her position behind the car kept her out of sight as another roaring engine came around the rear. Behind the driver sat an enormous clear plastic tank. Kate grinned as she focused.

Greasy black smoke oozed from a ten-meter fireball that engulfed the rickety vehicle. The driver's screams lasted only seconds. The charred buggy wobbled on melting wheels into the ditch. A howl of terror came over the speaker from Bernie, accompanied by a repetitive bashing noise. Kate whirled to her left, staring down the length of the truck carcass at the goggle-wearing raider from the missile truck. He attacked the windshield with an enormous medieval style sword.

"They're everywhere," the driver cried. "Escape! They're escaping!"

"Bernie, no!" Kate yelled.

Goggles looked at her, grinning at what he mistook for an unarmed, helpless woman. He gave up on the windshield and stalked in her direction. With a wild howl, Wilma jumped down from the top of the trailer, landing behind him with one arm across his throat and the other around the wrist of his sword arm. The men struggled for a few brief seconds, though the mohawked convict seemed far stronger than the raider, and controlled him with ease.

Humming, Wilma proceeded to waltz the raider around in a circle for a moment before crushing the man's wrist, causing the blade to clang to the ground. They danced for another few seconds in front of the cab, Wilma vocalizing his best attempt at classical music.

The one convict still atop the trailer roared as he took a bullet in the leg; he fell seated but continued machine-gunning a buggy passing what had been the top of the truck, out of Kate's view. Rippling clanks became wet splats and then a roaring burst of flames, sending a billowing cloud of smoke over the trailer.

Wilma planted a kiss on the grimy sweat-covered side of the man's head and flung him face-first into the windshield.

"I want you ta apologize ta Bernie, mate. Wasn't nice o' ya ta stick the truck wif' a missile." He held the bandit against the glass, ripped a knife from the man's belt, and drove it into his back. Goggles struggled for another few seconds. His cries sprayed blood on the glass before he went limp. "Aat's a right proper 'pology, I fink."

Bernie's scream rang louder than Goggles', even over tiny speakers. Kate blinked at Wilma, stunned wordless, not moving until she whirled at electronic beeps from the coffin.

"Shit!" Shouted Esteban. "That fucking jackass triggered the vests!"

"Come out here now!" Kate jogged along the trailer toward Wilma, waving at the last man. "Hey! Come down, get close to me."

One man from the Eagle's nest abandoned the rifle and jumped to the road nearby.

Two smears of red painted the road, twisty trails that lined up with the crushed remains of gunnery pods on the side in contact with the pavement. She slipped, cursing under her breath while skidding across one as the liquefied man steamed out from under her foot. Wilma looked to the clouds, holding his arms out to the side, bloody knife still in hand. A cluster of red lights flashed at the center of his vest, blinking in time with beeping.

Esteban grunted and heaved the compact car out of his way. He rushed out of the coffin, catching up as she held up a hand to keep Wilma two steps away. Shots rang out from above, followed by clanks and squealing tires. The last buggy broke the circle, speeding off down the road in the direction they came from.

Kate set her feet in a wide stance, held her arms out, and concentrated on the area around her. Psionic energy shimmered in the air, creating a sphere similar to heat blur around her. *No burning.* The convict on top of the truck panicked as the pace of the beeping reached the point where it sounded like a single tone. He shouted at Bernie and clicked the trigger at the cab, but the gun didn't go off.

"I am coming," said Wilma, at the clouds.

Esteban waved at him. "Mack, get do—"

The tone ended with a muted *thump* from above and a shower of gore. Most of what had been Mack rained on them. Bloody tatters of orange, two legs severed at the thigh, flopped onto the road. Esteban looked down at his vest, sagging with a sigh of relief at the dark lights.

"Fucking hell," said the man from the eagle's nest, wiping blood and chunks from his face. "Bernie, you cocksucker…"

"Don't," said Kate, in a zombie's tone. "If you get too far away from me, it'll go off."

Wilma peeled his gaze from the clouds, raised an eyebrow, and laughed. "It seems he will wait for me still." He eyed Kate up and down. "Perhaps you and he will meet."

Her eyes shifted toward him. "Don't distract me if you want to stay alive."

"I see it in your heart, little one." Wilma leaned close enough to make a face at the heat. "He'd like you."

"Back off," said Esteban.

"I am merely having a conversation about theology." Wilma held his hands up, smiled, and took a step away.

"We can't fucking stand here forever."

Esteban flapped his arms at the man from the eagle's nest. "Yeah, Kurt. Right on point with the obvious again."

"Right here." Kurt grabbed his crotch.

"I wanna twist that little weasel's head off," said Esteban. "Let's move as a group to the front. Kate, can you walk while doing that?"

"If I step in Mack and fall, you all die."

Wilma laughed. The others gagged.

Kurt's face froze in a warp of confused anger. "Wait a minute, how are we still alive?"

Esteban pointed. "She's psionic. A pyro."

"A pyro?" Kurt turned pale. "I didn't think they could *stop* fire… much less bombs."

"Gift horse," said Wilma. He grabbed the man's vest and spun him around.

"Hey man, I ain't into that. Get the hell away from my ass!" Kurt struggled, but Wilma held on.

"Shh," whispered Wilma. He clamped one hand on the vest between Kurt's shoulders, and the other around one of the struts. "This won't hurt. It'll be over before you know it."

"Oh, shit!" Kurt screamed through clenched teeth.

Wilma turned red, veins rose in his forehead and arms. A weak cracking sound came an instant before a spark flew out of the joint. The shoulder strap popped open with enough force to throw it airborne, over the trailer. After catching his breath, Wilma broke the other side. Kurt slipped the vest off over his head and threw it at the cab.

As soon as it flew about fifteen meters away from Kate, it detonated, launching a blast of fragments. Spiderweb cracks raced across the reinforced windscreen.

Kurt recovered his balance and ran to the break, kicking at it. "Bernie, you little shit. Turn off the fucking detonator."

Indistinct murmurs sounded inside the cab, like someone shrieking underwater.

Kurt glared at the clouds for a moment. "He thinks I'm escaping."

"So kill him," muttered Kate. "Never really liked that asshole."

He shrugged, and got to work kicking the glass. Wilma broke Esteban out of his vest and carried it a little farther away from the truck while waving at Kurt to clear away from the cab.

"Give us a little room, what? Got a nice little somethin' for the Bernster." Wilma winked.

Once Kurt cleared out, Wilma hurled the vest so hard he took two involuntary steps forward. The vest detonated on impact with the windshield, which flashed opaque white in an instant from millions of cracks. Kurt ran back over and put his boot through the armored glass, peeling it out like a wall of stacked snow. He reached in, hauled the bloodied Bernie out, and threw him on the road. After a parting kick to the side, Kurt crawled into the cab.

A few minutes later, he yelled. "I think it's off."

Esteban jogged over. "We need more than *think*."

Kate crept toward the cab. "What's the release code, Bernie?"

Bernie dragged himself over crumbles of glass and blood. "I don't have it. There isn't a business need for drivers to know the ERV codes." He shrieked when Esteban grabbed him by the boot. "They shouldn't have tried to escape!"

"I can't disarm a damn thing," said Kurt as he emerged from the cab. "It's an immediate trigger. Truck computer isn't showing any active links to explosive restraint vests. It thinks we're all dead."

Kate grumbled.

Esteban waved Wilma over. "Might as well try to break it."

With Kurt pulling on the vest from the front, Esteban holding on to the back plate, and Wilma shoving at it, it split in two neat halves, sparks flying. Kate cringed at the sense of nascent combustion, squashing it back into nothingness. They threw the pieces into the field one after the next.

Each one exploded with a sharp *crack* and a shower of dirt and grass. Exhausted, Kate slumped to the road where she stood, panting and drenched in sweat.

"Well, now what?" asked Kurt.

Esteban squinted, trying to peer past the smoke into the east. "We search for what we can scavenge and get the hell out of here."

Wilma grunted in agreement.

14

SOLITUDE

Kate sprawled on the road, trying to catch her breath, inhaling in the scent of burned plastic, smoldering rubber, and charred flesh. The coarse texture of paving below came in handy to scratch an inch or two on her back. A steady serenade of creaking metal, squeaking springs, and cursing rang out as the three surviving cons rummaged among the wreckage. She relaxed for a while, skirting the precipice of sleep. Scuffing footsteps startled her awake as Esteban and Kurt returned with two battered submachine guns and a pistol. Wilma trailed behind them, carrying an enormous metal sword. He grinned from ear to ear while peeling bits of its former owner from the edge.

She stood and stretched before swatting bits of glass off her legs.

"He beckons, and I heed. This was a sign. I will be heading west. My time among the false civilization is at an end." Wilma set the tip of the weapon in the road and bowed to Kate. "He calls for you as well, sister of rage."

She checked her beloved bracelet, relieved to see it undamaged. "You are entirely too happy with that thing."

Wilma laughed and hefted the sword, letting it rest over one shoulder. "The true measure of power is strength. I foresee much joy in my future, and this will not run out of bullets."

"Speakin' of joy." Kurt edged up to Kate. "How 'bout a little head?"

Esteban shoved him. "Hey, she just saved all of our asses. You're not gonna touch her."

Kurt backed up. "Just asking. I weren't gonna do nothin' she didn't want."

"We all want what we can't have," said Esteban.

"Then your wants are too complex." Wilma pivoted on his heel and meandered to the west, whistling like a farmer on his way to the field, the great sword balanced over his shoulder.

Kate sighed at the crashed truck. *I'm out here this far, might as well keep going.* She gave Esteban a meaningful look and followed Wilma. Esteban shrugged and fell in step beside her. Evidently not wanting to be alone, Kurt hurried after them.

Kate went off the road to avoid walking over the glittering field of smashed windshield, muttering at the smoking grass. "Something like that."

Esteban shot her a confused look until her voice echoed in his mind.
No boots. Glass.

Without thinking about it, Esteban reached out to help her back onto the road a safe distance away from the wreck. Kate disregarded him, clearing a ditch with a jump. She frowned at his hand and turned away before she had to look at his face.

Wilma moved up to a jog, overtaking the limping driver who had made it about a quarter mile from the crash site. He hauled Bernie upright by a fistful of polo shirt collar. "Bernster..." The driver yowled. "Be at ease, driver. It is by your grace that my destiny has become manifest. You provided me the chance to play with the natives. Even if you did push the bad button, it wouldn't be proper to leave you to rot."

"Fuck Bernie," said Kurt.

"If you want." Wilma held the driver out to Kurt with one arm. "Don't take too long."

Bernie wept.

"You're a walking psych thesis, Wilma." Kurt shook his head and walked off. "Who names their son Wilma anyway?"

"Dammit, Wilma." Kurt shivered. "I meant fuck in the metaphorical sense."

Wilma marched west, dragging Bernie. Like an overgrown boy, he took great pains to keep stepping on the faded yellow paint in the center of the ancient road.

The hapless driver stumbled along, glancing back at Kate every few steps. He seemed unable to determine if the huge man was abducting or assisting him. Kurt and Esteban flanked him, keeping watch to either side. Bernie whimpered when Esteban fired a test shot from the sub gun.

She slowed to let everyone get in front of her. Arms crossed, eyes locked on her non-boots, she moved only fast enough not to get left behind. Worry of being with two convicts she didn't trust, especially when it got dark enough for holograms to glow, guaranteed she wouldn't sleep. They walked without conversation for some hours. Soon, the earthy fragrance of meadow grass replaced the stink of war. Kurt yelled at the occasional insect that drifted too close for comfort, loudest when something the size of a hen's egg took a keen interest in his hair.

"I changed it," said Wilma, out of nowhere.

"Changed what?" asked Kurt.

Wilma balanced on one leg before leaping a pothole he could have walked around. "My name."

"Why would you do that?" blurted Bernie when no one else had the nerve.

The big man smiled at the sky. "Good for startin' fights."

"Oh." Bernie forced a smile. "I see."

Another hour or so passed in relative silence.

Kate snarled at her bracelet showing a no-signal message below the time. *When did I become so dependent on this thing?* "How far are we from St. Louis?"

"I'unno," mumbled Wilma. "Let me check the navigation system." He glanced at Bernie, waited three seconds, and gave him a hard shake when he didn't say anything.

"Uhh." The driver looked around. "If we were still on the truck, we'd have been there by now."

"If you weren't a chickenshit moron, we'd still be on the truck," muttered Esteban.

Bernie whimpered. "Where the hell did bandits get missiles?"

"You'd be surprised what people can do when they have to improvise." Kate absentmindedly covered her chest.

Esteban winked as Kate drifted closer. "They probably looted a small military shipment or something."

Wilma rolled the great sword over his hand and caught it, making it *whoosh*. "It is futile to worry about where they procured it. Their arrow has already charted the course of our destiny."

"Damn thing hit the truck before I felt it burn," said Kate. "Sorry."

Esteban glanced at her; Kate looked away.

"What's that smell?" asked Kurt.

Kate perked up. "Water. We're near a river."

"Let's pick it up then." Esteban walked faster. "Get inside the wall before it gets dark."

THE COMFORTING SCENT OF WOOD SMOKE WAFTED BY, SPECTRAL THREADS hovered in a beam of light from a tiny window. Kate reclined in an ancient porcelain bathtub, daydreaming about what it might feel like to soak in water. She peered over the side at two thick blocks of wood with black footprints—Esteban's idea to spare the floor. Embers of anger glowed in her heart, the boards a visible reminder of a barrier between her and the world.

At her low angle, the tiny window offered a view of stars. She frowned at the light switch, out of reach. It wasn't worth the effort of standing and balancing on a plank. The plastic lever would melt on contact with her finger and she would still be in the dark. Technology existed in a strange commingling in the Scattered Lands. Holo-terminals sometimes sat next to physical light switches, and modern micro-fusion power cells fed filament-based bulbs.

Kate stretched and yawned. The old tub offered little in the way of comfort or room to move, but at least the porcelain tolerated her temperature.

She closed her eyes, thinking of Esteban, and let one arm slide between her legs. Pleasure by her own hand was nothing new, but having a specific man in her thoughts was. Her mind ran away with impossible dreams as she writhed alone in a dirty hotel bathtub.

A slam from the living room made her sit bolt upright in a frantic search to put her hands somewhere innocent and natural looking. Esteban appeared in the doorway holding a metal box. He had a small backpack over his left shoulder, and his weapon was gone. At the sight of her face, he broke up laughing. Seconds later, the smell of fried chicken followed him.

Kate blushed, her embarrassment too strong to check his surface thoughts to see if he caught her in the act or only assumed.

"Turned off the thing? Uhh, you okay with me seeing you like that?"

"Mayyyybe," she purred.

He sat on the toilet and put the box on the sink.

"Since I have walls around me, I'm saving the battery for tomorrow." She pushed herself up into a sitting position. "I don't like the way it glows in the dark, makes me feel like a ghost."

"You sure it won't run out on you?" He handed her a drumstick. "They might have a charger in town here. It's not completely primitive."

The food sizzled and popped at her touch, but she devoured the chicken before it charred too much. "I made it to like sixteen or something without it. I'll get used to it again. Sleeping on dirt is more comfortable than this tub."

He handed her a second piece and got started on one. "Sounds like you're not planning to come back."

Desperate eyes locked on to him as she savaged a chicken breast, unwilling to stop or slow down until she held smoldering bones. "I want to come back. I just don't know how long it'll take me to find what I'm looking for. Wow, this is good."

"It's real food," he said. "Stephanie raises live chickens. Winds up cheaper out here than anything imported from the real world."

"This is the *real* world." She tossed a smoking bone into the box. "Sometimes I think it's better out here, away from all the corporate bullshit. Too many people stacked up on top of each other."

"I don't think it's a good idea for you to try and walk to West City." He held out a biscuit for her to bite. "I've heard all sorts of horrible stories about the Badlands."

Kate brushed burning crumbs off her thigh. "I'm not helpless."

"No, but... A woman alone, especially if your thing is turned off... You'll draw bandits like moths to a flame."

"You know what happens to the moth when it gets too close to the candle, right?" She smiled into her lap. "Is that concern I hear? You almost sound chivalrous."

Esteban held up a finger in a 'wait a moment' gesture and rummaged around in the backpack.

"I don't have to be as careful out here," she said. "No need to hide bodies."

Stooped to the side, he cocked his eyebrow at her. "Why do I get the feeling you're not kidding."

Kate eyed the box of chicken like a hungry dog. "I'm not."

He handed over another piece. When she ducked to feast, he patted her atop the head. She looked up, startled, and he waved at her with an oven mitt. She laughed at the absurdity of it, but soon found herself fighting the urge to cry when he stroked her hair.

Chicken bones ignited in her hands, burning to ash.

She clung to the side of the tub, eyes closed. The lump in her throat grew too large for any words to squeeze past it.

"I've been with some pretty hot girls before, but I never needed this much protection."

Crying won't change a damn thing. She sniffled. "I'm… I hate this."

"Sorry." He leaned back.

"No, don't stop." Kate looked up. "I mean"—her head sagged forward—"I hate being like this. I'd give it all up to be normal. I'm so tired of being alone, of being cut off from the world. That's why I have to do this. Some people found me… other psionics who think they can help."

"They can dial you down from nuclear reactor to electric stove?" He winked.

She looked into his eyes. "That's my hope. It's what I want more than anything."

His hand slid over her head to rest on her shoulder, thick padding smoldering. Kate's eyelids drooped half-closed. She leaned toward him. Esteban was more than she ever imagined: handsome, confident, brave, and didn't have a problem with her being psionic. She didn't care about his being a convict. Being with him mattered more than anything else at that moment, and compared to the usual sort of people she associated with, installing stolen car parts made him a saint. He hovered so close she could smell his breath. Without thinking, she closed her eyes and leaned toward him.

Esteban howled and pulled back, one hand clamped over his lips.

"I'm sorry!" She grabbed the edge of the tub and started to get up, but he waved her down.

"Myf falf. Not yourf." He fanned his lip where a large blister had already appeared. "Ow. Well, that was stupid."

She collapsed into the tub with her back to the room, head bowed. Tears struck porcelain in a series of faint pats, which drowned in the noise of running water from the sink. It cut off with a squeak, which made her cringe and curl into a ball. The oven mitt patted her on the shoulder. Esteban had a wet cloth to his face, but seemed to be smiling.

Kate shied away from the sight.

"Hey... Don't blame yourself. Maybe that psio cure thing will work. How long do you think it will take?"

She shrugged. "I dunno." *If it even works at all.*

"Wilma kept going. Said something about being called into the Badlands. Crazy bastard didn't even want to spend a night in a real bed first."

Stop crying. You're the idiot for getting attached. You've known him for a day.

"Bernie's at the hospital. Bit rougher out here; no tanks, so he'll be recovering for a few weeks. He'll live though. Course, he's gotta wait for another convoy to show up to go home. I sold the gun for the room and some food, and I talked my way into a job fixing stuff."

"Are you going to stay here then?" She managed not to sound like she wanted to cry, though her voice came off cold.

"Not sure." He rubbed her hair, making her shiver. "No telling what Bernie will claim happened. He's not wound too tight. If he spouts off about us trying to mutiny, I'll be screwed. If he doesn't, and I go back on my own, it'll only help. Might even knock a few months off."

Kate's voice trembled. "How much left?"

"Little over a year." He stood and tossed the smoking oven mitt into a wastebasket by the sink. "Well, the glove's had it. I figured you crazy for wanting to walk across the Badlands, but after what I saw out there"—he chuckled—"I'm not so sure."

"I'm sorry," she whispered, shifting onto her back.

Esteban didn't bother being subtle about appraising her figure. "You're like some kind of deadly beautiful."

"The scientists did that on purpose. I was supposed to be an assassin, so they tried to make me pretty." She waved a hand around her face. "High cheekbones... Anna said something about my DNA being from this Russian girl."

"They did a damn good job of it." He dabbed at his lip.

"Not so much." She folded her arms behind her head as a pillow. "I was no good to them like this. Can't wear the fancy gowns to get into the fancy parties and the wrong people's bedrooms. I can't sneak past thermal sensors." Her voice fell to a mutter. "I can't even hold someone I like."

"So they cut you loose?"

"No, they tried to kill me so they could start over. I got away." She stared at the ceiling, mesmerized by the projected shadows cast by a cloud of moths outside the window. "If there is something up there watching us, I hope it knows I'd give up anything to be normal."

Esteban shrugged. "I'd call my grandmother to say a prayer for you, but they don't have VidPhones out here. Try to get some rest."

"Yeah, sure."

He drifted into the bedroom, pulling the door to behind him. When the old-fashioned bed creaked, she covered her face with her hands and cried in earnest.

15

INTO THE WEST

Kate moaned in contentment as she woke, embraced by cloth. Her eyes fluttered open, and she found a dense blanket packed around her in the bathtub. For a few seconds, she couldn't comprehend the meaning of the strange sensation on her skin. Once realization dawned, she flailed, shoving and kicking at it in an effort not to ruin it. The blanket fell to the floor, with only a few blackened spots.

She'd slept the whole night.

Sunlight glaring in from the dirt-smeared window forced her to squint. She sat up in the bathtub, moaning at sore muscles. It took a few minutes to stretch away the pain from a night of horrible posture. She frowned at the lump of cloth, a painful reminder of Esteban's concern. After a second stretch, she slipped one leg over the edge of the tub onto the thick wooden slab. It smoked on contact, though she suppressed open flame. It extended her reach enough to grab the leftover chicken.

"Esteban?"

The outer room stood quiet and empty, the bed haphazardly 'made' by a casual toss of the bedspread. Echoes of activity outside came through the window, snippets of voices and the occasional rumble of a passing vehicle or barking dog. A small boy shouted at something, a hooved animal from the sound of it, scampering by the door.

She used the corner of the sink to push the power button on the bracelet's embedded NetMini. While waiting for it to boot, she set her feet on the wood slabs and shuffled like a cross-country skier to the front door. Esteban had left a note tacked to it.

Kate, I needed to get out early. The boss wanted to meet me at dawn and get some things settled before his shift started. Hope you're still there when I get back. I'll understand if you've got your mind set on chasing that cure. Good luck, and take care of yourself. –Steve.

A yelp escaped as she noticed her feet covered in flames. Her lapse of concentration let her 'shoes' ignite. The fire dissipated with a soft *whuff* as she willed it out. As soon as the bracelet chimed its orchestral welcome tone, she held it up to her mouth. She paused at the sight of the battery meter full. He had taken it out and charged it while she slept.

"Casual one."

A matrix of blue lines formed around her body for several seconds before they changed into low top boots, a black long-sleeved pullover, and loose-fitting navy pants. She adjusted the baggy pullover with a few tugs, still marveling at how the hologram could react to her attempt to touch it. Relief came with knowing if she only used the bracelet for clothing, it had about a week and a half of power. She took a breath and went outside, stepping off the blocks onto a concrete porch.

Hotel doors went in both directions, forty rooms around the walls of an enclosed parking lot with only two vehicles in it. A little boy chased a baby goat around one of the cars. The diminutive animal wanted nothing to do with being caught and carried. Sunlight glinted from windows, distant metal walls, and a bulbous water tower. She followed the sidewalk around the square, hanging a left down a ramp past a buzzing neon sign to the street.

Buildings looked as though they had a contagious disease that caused a slow metamorphosis from wood and brick to metal. Time and technology had converted old St. Louis—or what remained of it—into a hamlet balanced on the precipice between ancient and not quite modern. She wandered in the general direction of West. Citizens regarded her with curiosity. A man and three boys led a group of goats on chain leashes. The animals shifted, eager to distance themselves from the sense of a predator.

Her attire stood out. Too clean, too modern. Everyone she passed—including the local 'police' force—kept their eyes on her. She found the usual reactions in surface thoughts: men trying to undress her with their eyes, women being jealous or indifferent, she's not local, what's she up to, she's unarmed... what's wrong with her? A complete lack of street gangs or obvious corner chem dealers struck her as odd. Much like the big city, the catcalls continued, though none did more than make rude comments.

What strange place is this where people obey the law?

Two armed men in green military camouflage went by, both eyeing her with suspicion. The St. Louis 'police' force seemed more like a militia than a law enforcement group.

Guess they shoot people here rather than arrest them.

A familiar mechanical whine rose above the din, leading her down an alley to a huge open square by the city's primary gate, which motored open at an agonizing pace. It halted with a heavy *clunk* that shook the ground, and several farmer families dragged wagons made from pickup truck beds in, laden with produce.

She passed two gun stores, an armor repair shop, and two bars before stopping to fire a mournful glare at a clothing merchant. According to rumor, the private sectors—privatized regions embedded within East City—had expensive boutiques where the rich still shopped in person. Ages ago, people considered the convenience of delivery bots trendy. Now, the effort of shopping in person had taken on an air of wealth and superiority.

A moment of staring at flannel shirts renewed her determination to rid herself of her curse.

Ignoring the stores, she crossed to the far side of the courtyard and headed down another street toward the western gate. The militia, men and women, lingered among stacked sandbags arranged around a pair of enormous doors, holding modern rifles out of place with their uniforms. Being this close to the Badlands, the leaders of the town likely wanted every advantage.

She stared out past the gate at a blue badge-shaped sign that bore the number 55 as well as a few bullet holes. Beyond that, a massive bridge packed with dead cars, barricades, and machine gun nests stretched out over the water. Skeletons of tall buildings dominated the skyline beyond; the better part of what had once been a city. Esteban's voice replayed in her memory from their walk in the previous day. Historically, St. Louis spread over both sides of the river, but all semblance of civilization had shifted east after the war. None of the crazy shit that lived in the Badlands crossed the water. No one seemed to know why, though he had made it sound like a campfire ghost story.

All the carnage on the bridge made it seem more real.

A woman yelled from her left. "Hey, where you going?"

Kate snapped out of a daydream of Esteban's sparkling eyes and glanced at a dark-skinned woman in green camo. "West."

"It ain't safe out there," said an older man with greying hair. "'Specially for a lady."

"He's right." The woman waved her rifle at the bridge. "We're close to Fourth Reich territory. Unless you fancy winding up as some genetic throwback's sex toy, you should stick around here where it's safe. Only an idiot walks into the Badlands without weapons, armor, and provisions."

"Never heard of them," said Kate, not slowing down. "And I'm not unarmed."

"Bunch of jackasses," added a dark-skinned man. Nicohaler vapor slid between his teeth, as if a visible manifestation of the contempt in his words. "They're an inbred pack of idiots. Anyone who ain't white, they kill. Girl like you they'd do nasty things with." He gestured at the female soldier. "Her, they'd just shoot."

The woman snarled. "They wouldn't live long enough."

"Over skin color?" Kate stopped. "That's the most ridiculous thing I've ever heard."

"They're still living in a prewar mindset," said the female soldier. "I hear people were like that four centuries ago."

The grey-haired man walked up; her gaze lingered on the name *Alvarez* stitched in black block letters on his left breast. "They're a small, isolated group that keeps to themselves. Corporal Anders is right about the inbreeding. Most are dumber than a bonedog. They don't come too close to the bridge since Rawlins and Morris use them for sniper practice."

"I'll keep an eye out for them." Kate went to move around him.

"It's not safe," said Alvarez, reaching for her.

He grabbed her bicep, jerking his arm back with a yowl an instant later. The woman aimed her weapon at Kate; Anders raised an eyebrow. Alvarez gawked at his palm, smoking and blistered. Kate ignored him, narrowing her eyes at the woman.

"On a list of the ten most stupid things you can do, Vickers, shooting me is around fourth."

"W-what the hell?" wheezed the sergeant.

Private Vickers adjusted her grip. "Don't move."

"Sweet monkey Christ." Alvarez waved his hand. "Stand down, Vickers. I grabbed her."

Vickers lowered the rifle, edging backward. Her eyes seemed ready to pop from her skull. Anders took a long pull from his Nicohaler.

Kate looked down as she brushed ash from her arm. "I can't turn that off."

Alvarez took a small, red cylinder from a belt pouch and stuck himself in the arm. For a moment, his hand resembled boiling creamed coffee as millions of nanobots repaired his flesh. "Care to explain how you did that?" He flexed his fingers and reached near her again, hand hovering a few inches away. "'Cause I ain't got an explanation."

Vickers got close enough to feel the radiant heat, and mumbled something about God.

"I should start charging admission to the psionic freak show." Kate glanced from her feet to the bridge. "Like I said, I'm not unarmed. I'm going west and I don't much care if I make it either." She looked over her shoulder at the town. *Esteban... I can't go on like this.* "Tell Esteban I'll be back as soon as I can."

"Even if you are a psionic..." Alvarez moved out of her way. "I don't want a preventable death on my conscience. You should reconsider."

Kate climbed over a row of sandbags, leaving burned handprints. "Don't lose sleep over me. If I die, it wasn't preventable."

The St. Louis Guard remained quiet as she walked out onto the bridge, following the centerline as much as the barricades and crashed cars would allow, unable to see over either side. Kate kept her gaze down, stepping around broken glass, holes full of jagged rebar, and sharp fragments. Every unnoticed painful object she stepped on added fuel to the fire in her heart.

Slumped over a burned truck, a huge skeleton with a canine head, long fangs, and rusting primitive cyberware all throughout made her pause. Three metal blades on each forearm extended from tubes grafted to the arm bones. Based on their size, they would have given the creature twelve inches of usable weapon. The skull shifted, startling her. A jet-black centipede, as thick as a banana and twice as long, crawled out of the fatal bullet wound in its forehead and vanished into the wreck.

"Okay... that's a big ass bug." She stared at the spot while edging past, ready to incinerate the creature should it come after her.

Once she felt far enough away from it, she faced forward and walked as fast as the treacherous ground permitted. By the time she reached the shattered concertina wire barricade at the far end, she found herself pondering if she should've spared Darius.

So what if he was only a kid himself when they made me, he still represents LRI. I'm just one of the monsters they've made.

She held her hands up, clawing them into fists. *They did this to me.* The surge of anger faded; her arms fell to her sides as she shot a baleful glance into the creaking corpse of old St. Louis up ahead. Metal girders groaned, plastic and wood clattered in the wind, and skitters of life came from the shadows.

If Archon can't fix me, I'll burn the entire corporation... down to the last janitor.

16

ABOMINATION

Old St. Louis seemed deserted. Kate wandered west along an elevated road connected to the bridge. The cloudless sky overlooked a day devoid of wind; the world had yet to wake. Long, crawling shadows stretched from behind her, cast by a sun reluctant to leave its bed in the east. Aside from the sporadic sizzle of unidentifiable muck underfoot, she existed in silence. Her gaze wandered over bullet gouges in the pavement, metal fragments, bottles, and more than a few bloody drag marks. She looked out over a rusted guardrail, at a distant structure that gave her pause. Inside a thick wall shaped like a triangle with a rounded bottom, an odd pattern of brown dirt, reminiscent of a Japanese fan, marked one corner of a grassy field. Bodies, most dismembered, littered the green, as did the husks of old cars. The more distant section had targets set up where a number of figures in grey-on-white camouflage milled about. Most of the space within the thick perimeter wall held seats, suggesting it had been an auditorium or theater of some kind before the war.

Why are they keeping that grass so neat?

She lost interest, swinging her stare to the left at massive open lots on the other side of the highway. The spaces gave way to bizarre paths made of metal rails and littered with vehicles that resembled cargo transports without a cab. Many had been repurposed as dwellings. Kate felt the presence of eyes upon her. Amid the dark spaces lurked a mixture of rifle-bearing adults and pistol-toting children, most of whom wore only dirt.

A boy not yet twelve, pale and brown-haired, sat in the doorway of one of the wheeled boxes, swinging his feet. He might have had fur or leather shorts, or merely a cat curled in his lap. Sunlight glinted from a silver handgun he almost aimed at her. He seemed hesitant and looked up at an old man. His lips moved, but he was too far away to hear, though the question and its answer rang aloud in his thoughts.

Can I shoot 'er gan-paw?

Naw, Boy. She's one of us. Save yer ammo for the bad ones.

Kate pushed deeper into the child's mind. The boy wasn't used to seeing white people outside their group, and *really* wanted to get a chance to shoot one of the 'bad ones'—people with darker skin. Grandpa told him all about how they had lost 'the blood war,' and there weren't many of 'us' left. He had no clue East City—and modern society—existed... he thought the Badlands went on forever.

She shook her head in disgust. Both of them would lose their respective shit in a city of millions where ninety-something percent of the population had brown skin.

The boy pointed at her. *We gon' go catch 'er den? She make a good breeder.*

A'ats a thought. The old man lifted his rifle, using the scope to check her out.

Kate created an azure fireball over her right hand and sent her thoughts into the old man's mind. *I see so much as a single inbred shithead following me, I'll burn every last one of you to ash.*

The old man fell backward off his seat and the boy scrambled inside to see what had happened to him. She let the fireball whiff out and walked faster. Feeling such hate inside the mind of a boy made her contempt for the world grow stronger. She clenched her hands into fists, fuming at how people could pervert the innocence of a child into blind animosity, and debated if it would be a kindness to kill him now. The idea of people hating others didn't strike her as new. Being scorned for her psionic talents at least made *some* sense. She had the ability do things others couldn't. Fear and jealousy, she could understand. Hating someone for not having pale skin seemed so beyond stupid she pondered burning them out for the hell of it. Even middle-class citizens could afford something as minor as a color shift at Reinventions. It struck her as ridiculous as if they hated a person because they wore the wrong color shirt.

Many parallel rows of the same odd metal rails filled the area to her left for quite some distance. Her occasional glance caught women, children, and elders hiding inside the wheeled boxes, watching. She figured them for some kind of ancient cargo transport, but couldn't explain how they moved. The simple containers mounted on wheels had no apparent source of power.

Soon, people emerged here and there. Men edged out of doorways, children appeared on the rooftops, struggling to get away from the women trying to keep them inside. Perhaps one in six had clothing beyond a loincloth if that—yet anyone who looked older than about twelve had a firearm. The locals' thoughts gave away the speed with which word traveled among their kind. They all wanted to see the 'demon' for themselves.

Great, religious wingnuts too. Kate grinned to herself, and locked eyes with a woman who seemed in her early fifties.

Hello. Kate forced her thoughts into the woman's head. *Pauline...*

The woman grabbed her head and shrieked, "Out of my head, devil!"

You know why I've come? The woman looked up, shaking her head. *Your god has turned his back on you for the sin of hatred.* Kate created fire in the air behind her; serpents of low-intensity orange flame circled her. *Your prayers have held me back, for now, but he is very disappointed in you. He gives you another chance. Discard your murderous ways and remember his word, or I shall return bearing the fires of wrath.* As an exclamation point, she lobbed a fireball into the dwelling, aiming for a patch of metal that wouldn't ignite. A brief blast of heat and light scared screams out of a handful of idiots.

The woman shouted and wailed at the others, her ramblings indecipherable from the distance.

Kate turned away before her stern expression cracked to mad laughter. *It's too easy to mess with those people.* The elevated road continued past more large buildings and open lots, and nearly an hour later, she passed by a residential area to the south. Gunshots and shouts tinged with anger emanated from within the old buildings. She debated if anything similar to a divine being existed, and if so, would it be upset with her for impersonating a demon? She glanced over her shoulder at empty road. Thus far, no 'hunting party' had shown itself in pursuit of her.

Maybe they aren't all that stupid, or at least they have some sense of self-preservation.

The land on either side of the road turned lush a while later, a battered sign referred to it as the Highlands. Trees whispered in a light breeze, the thick, dark green of the woods broken up a handful of small ponds, which caught the sun. Kate scowled. Her initial sadness at her inability to swim spiraled into dwelling on her curse.

What does it feel like to touch water?

Sorrow became anger. The memory of Esteban's burned lip flashed by.

Everything I touch, I destroy.

The next few hours passed in a blur of aimless rage. Land on either side of the decaying roadway became greener as nature reclaimed what had once been suburbs. A slab of scrap metal on the road shifted under her weight, spilling her onto all fours. She rolled around to sit, cradling a skinned knee. The wind picked up, carrying a tattered doll out from under a crashed car. The blonde, blue-eyed plastic toy came skittering over the roadway toward her.

Kate frowned at it. Its presence mocked the childhood she never had. Whatever little girl had once cared for it had been gone for centuries. The innocent look on its face didn't stop the fireball. She glared at the deforming cherub as the eyes blackened and the round cheeks developed expanding holes before it melted into a beige puddle.

For some minutes, she scowled at the mess, unable to figure out why she felt guilty about destroying a hunk of plastic. Her imagination said the toy had come to her on its own, as if it wanted a new mommy. The wind went still, taking all the ambient sounds of wildlife with it. The silence left her mind meandering to the conclusion something wanted her to see the doll. She had found innocence and destroyed it out of spite.

"What was that for?" she shouted. When no answer came, she stood and got louder. "Why? To remind me I can't touch it?"

Smoke peeled from the solidifying mass. Kate looked up, stepping past it, shouting at nothing as she walked.

"What did that mean? Innocence? It's a piece of plastic!" She held her face in both hands, trying to catch her breath. "I don't feel sorry for plastic."

She received no reply.

Her fingers slid over her mouth as her arms fell slack. "I was innocent too."

The memory of betrayal, those men she thought wanted to take care of her becoming murderous, brought tears. She closed her eyes and watched the gel tank exploding all over again. Kate focused on Archon's holographic face, clinging to the hope that he could cure her.

With that thought in mind, she walked to the west until the sun set.

KATE SHIVERED AWAKE, CURSED, AND SAT UP. IT HAD BEEN DAYS SINCE SHE
had seen another person. At night, she left the bracelet off both to
conserve power and because the glow could attract danger. Holographic
clothing did nothing to keep her warm, so leaving it on would only waste
battery power. She crawled through the brush, calmed by the fragrance of
burned leaves and grass. Leaves and branches caressing her body
reminded her of her years growing up, a child of nature.

A short distance from where she'd slept, she squatted by the remnants
of a deer she killed earlier. Her hands seared its flesh, tearing and cooking
the meat at the same time. She ate with a feral savagery absent since she
had first wandered to the great city. Loneliness, a desire for human
contact, had made her leave the forest. Had she known then that the city
offered only worse isolation, she would not have gone. Being alone out
here didn't carry the same sense of emptiness as being alone in a city of
millions.

It was easier to be alone without people around.

As much as solitude hurt, nature offered a certain degree of peace.
Kate moved back to the dirt mound she had made for a bed and drifted
off to a dream about a time before technology.

She woke again an hour later, teeth chattering. No sooner did her
brain engage true sleep than her continuous heat faded, leaving her as
cold as an ordinary person curled up naked on the ground in the woods.
The dead deer's lifeless eyes gazed at her, black save for a speck of
reflected moonlight. One hand traced circles on her stomach,
remembering how hungry she had been before killing one for the first
time. Seven-year-old Kate cried over the first animal she hunted. Unlike
them, it had not wanted to hurt her.

Kate couldn't recall the exact moment when she stopped feeling
guilt over killing them. Perhaps around the time she learned how to
make the fireball hot enough to kill it instantly, and they no longer
screamed.

"Sorry for killing you. Thank you for giving your life to prolong
mine."

She wasn't sure why she started saying that. Vague memories of a man
drifted out of her childhood, someone who had spent weeks trying to
coax her out of the woods. She had fleeting images of sitting by a
campfire, listening to him talk about spirits and the Earth. It could not

have been long after her escape, months at most. As hard as she thought, she couldn't recall what had happened to him.

I probably killed him by accident.

Kate snuggled into the dirt and closed her eyes.

"Ironic," said an elderly voice.

She shot upright, fumbling at the bracelet.

"There is no need to be embarrassed." A skeleton wrapped in skin, and the black uniform of a priest, emerged from the trees. "You are like a daughter, Kate."

The device ignored her frantic swatting. She scooted back, overcome by an inexplicable fear for her life. Modesty took a back seat to survival; she leapt to her feet and summoned a fireball.

"Who are you? What's ironic?"

"You are happier here among the wilds than among the trappings of 'modern' society. For so many years, you denied your nature." Dark venous lines shifted in his cheeks as fragile skin stretched into a smile, baring kelp-colored teeth.

The more she looked at him, the more frightened she became.

Kate flung the fireball into his chest. Blue flames wrapped around his body, lingered for an instant, and seemed to draw into him with a rush of air. No scent of burned fabric or flesh tainted the fragrance of early morning vegetation.

"Your anger is beautiful."

What little color Kate had in her face drained away. "W-who... W-what are you?"

He folded his hands behind his back. "You asked what was ironic. The man you remembered. Alas, you did not kill him. He died trying to lure bandits away from what he believed to be a helpless child."

"Ironic because I could've saved his life if he led them *to* me." Kate put her hands on her hips.

The old priest tipped his head. "Indeed."

"How do you know that? What do you want from me, and why the hell should I believe anything you say?"

He buttoned his black coat, hiding his unburned white shirt. "I know many things. Such as why the only hair on your body is on your head."

She fumed, too angry to feel embarrassed.

The priest closed his eyes as if savoring a delicate aroma. "It is part vanity, part early experience. When you first saw yourself, reflected in the wall of your tank..."

"I was too little to have body hair."

"Very good, Kate. Your inner mind sees yourself like that still." He touched two fingers to his temple. The liver-spotted skin on the back of his hand folded thick with wrinkles. "Subconsciously, you don't burn away the hair you think you should have."

She blushed. "What the hell do you want?"

"I know what it is that you desire more than anything. For years, I watched you grow, nursing your anger. Every time raiders found you, their elation became despair." The priest gestured, simulating a conflagration of flames with opening fingers. "Whoosh, and men died. I tried to call you home, but you went east."

"Are you the 'he' Wilma was talking about?" She swallowed. "Are you God?"

The priest hissed into a laugh that leaked saliva over his chin. "In a manner of speaking, I suppose."

"Tell me." Kate advanced, her nose hovered inches from his chin. "Is it true? Can Archon get rid of this curse?"

Foul corpse-breath reached into her nostrils and tried to drag her meal back out. She re-swallowed.

He glanced down at her with an impressed frown. One finger tapped at the corner of his mouth. "No. He cannot. All he wants is to use you as a worm."

Kate blinked.

"Oh, forgive me. I expected you to comprehend a fishing metaphor. He seeks to use you as bait." Red light glinted in his eyes.

She didn't back down. "Bait for what? He lied?"

The priest broke eye contact, wandering in a circle while waving his hand about. "Archon is relying on an unlikely sequence of events transpiring that… in a distant way *might* result in the outcome you desire."

"Might?" She crossed her arms and pouted at her feet. "I…"

"Don't wish to continue living?" The priest winked at her.

Kate shied away, unable to figure out why she feared a man who seemed frail to the point of dropping dead at any moment.

"Archon wishes to make use of your situation. He believes your need could convince a child to return to the city and join his cause—a child who is not a child, but a being that already refused him once, and will again. While I would not mind *it* leaving my domain, I would prefer *it* handled another way."

She looked up. "That doesn't make any sense."

"If it meant freedom from your so-called curse, could you kill something that looked like a child?"

"A blue-eyed blonde," whispered Kate.

"It only appears to be a little girl, but it is not," said the old man.

Like a doll.

"It does not belong in this place. It upsets the balance while preying on the pity of fools."

She shifted her weight. "A demon?"

He grinned again. "Six of one…"

"Yeah. Okay, but you said Archon wants this kid too. If I kill her, won't that piss Archon off? Then he won't cure me."

"Forget Archon." The priest moved up to her in a blur of black and white. Threads of cobweb hair wavered in the wind. "You belong here. This is as much your domain as it is ours."

Kate did not have time to jump away from his sudden motion and gasped when he put his hand on her shoulder. She stared, waiting for the smoke and screaming, but none came. His touch, coarse and calloused, slid to the side of her neck.

"You have every right to be angry at them for what they did to you." He pulled her into a paternal embrace. Rough hands caressed her back. "You do not need Archon to be free, Kate. Accept your destiny, destroy the abomination masquerading as a child, and *I* shall bestow your wish."

She wrapped her arms around him, adoring the sense of contact with a warm body, and let her cheek rest on his shoulder. Bones shifted under cloth as she squeezed him, gazing into the distant west.

All of a sudden, she found herself seven years old again, clinging to him.

"There, there, Kate." His hand patted the back of her head. "Your rage is justified."

An involuntary nod came with a sinister smile. Hate for a child she'd never seen before swarmed through her veins.

The whole world deserved to burn, and she would deliver it into the inferno.

17

BURNING DOWN THE HOUSE

I n the delirium of near-sleep, Kate forgot she had crawled into a culvert beneath a road. The two-day old memory of meeting the strange priest felt like only hours had passed. Her attempt to sit up smacked her head into the top of the corrugated metal pipe. She fell, curled in a ball, and moaned for a moment before shaking off the pain and dizziness. A small motor buzzed overhead, conjuring the image of an enormous mosquito. It sounded like one of the raider buggies that attacked the caravan, a vehicle consisting of a rickety combustion engine mounted to a hollow aluminum frame. The fragrance of ethanol washed over her, bringing with it a memory of Esteban.

Someone needed to die screaming.

Kate crawled to the end of the pipe, squinting at the sunbaked mud outside. She turned on her holo-projector, selecting the same camo outfit she used for the convoy run. The intangible holographic pane made her frown; the bracelet had only a few days' of battery power left. If not for the sound of activity nearby, she would have left it off.

Beneath a dried crust, the river of sediment held moisture. Mud sizzled and popped from her feet as she stepped away from the tiny artificial creek bed, leaving a trail of steaming prints.

Days of walking had turned trees and vegetation to rolling plains dotted by clusters of growth and the occasional destroyed structure. The road surface sat on top of several feet of gravel and dirt, enough to hide behind and watch.

Sure enough, the sound came from a four-wheeled metal buggy. It had stopped about forty yards away from the culvert, parked by a red-walled building at the side of the road. Kate shuffled forward, running as fast as possible while ducking. One man in armor made of leather and metal scraps stepped down from a platform at the rear of the cart, between the two large drive wheels. Two axes crossed on his back; brass-capped red cylinders studded his belt, among several empty loops. He slid a long rifle with a thick barrel and wood stock from an animal hide sheath on the back of the cart and hung it over one shoulder.

Kate moved to a position in line with the buggy and crouched behind the berm. Weeds smoldered around her, but a haze of grass along the edge of the paving blocked her face from view. A woman with wild, black hair down to her waist sat in a pod bolted to the left side, perched behind a large belt-fed machine gun. She remained still and silent as the driver grabbed the roll cage above his head and hauled himself out the opposite way.

The driver's animal hide armor creaked as he moved, metal plates rattling about his legs. He had several knives and two pistols, and a crowbar slung across his back like a medieval warrior's sword.

A burst of wind lofted the gunner's hair to the right, exposing an inch-tall steel collar around her neck.

Gravel shifted under Kate's hands as she tensed. A quick glance left and right along the road at miles of nothing reminded her that in the Badlands, the only law was strength.

"Hep, dern it!" The more distant of the two men skidded to a halt. "Ya fergot ta put the gun on safe."

The driver howled in annoyance and stomped back to the buggy. He bent over the side, pulling up on a lever mounted to the floor. A chain rode over a pulley in the roll cage, drawing the woman's shackled hands up over her head—away from the machine gun. The prisoner remained passive until both men vanished inside the windowless building. Once they could no longer see her, she struggled.

Kate got up and sprinted across the four-lane road to a halt by the huge rear tire. The woman in the side pod squirmed around to look. She appeared about Kate's age, if not a year or two younger. Dead bugs, some the size of exploded grapes, dotted her bare chest. Dark sienna skin glistened with sweat running in trails. Her ill-maintained skirt looked stitched together from scraps of a dozen t-shirts. A length of chain padlocked to either side of an uncomfortable looking metal chair served as a seatbelt, tight enough to leave marks across her stomach. Heavy irons hobbled her legs, rattling over the thin sheet metal pod as she cringed. The woman seemed as angry as she did frightened, fixing Kate with a measuring stare.

What is wrong with these people? Kate examined the rusted Master lock holding the prewar handcuffs to the 'safety.'

The woman froze like a deer in traffic. "*No tiene armas. Volverán pronto. Corre antes de que te atrapen.*"

"Whoa. Too fast," muttered Kate in novice's Spanish. "Do you know any English?"

"Yes." The woman looked away, staring at the building. "They will take you if they see you. Your looks are rare. You have no guns, and they will return soon."

"I hope they come outside right now." Kate frowned at the welded leg irons. "You got a name?"

"I used to, before this." The woman looked down, whispering, "Alejandra."

"Okay." Kate ceased leaning on the pod and patted it. "Wait here, Alejandra."

"Where would I go?" Alejandra wriggled in place. "Hey, stop. Don't be stupid. You should run."

Kate paid little attention to the warnings streaming out of the woman's mouth and approached the door. The scent of food wafted on the air near the opening, mixed with tobacco and age. Smoke seeped between her fingers from the wooden door handle as she pulled it aside to expose a dim interior with a short hallway leading to a right angle turn to a larger room. Three men loitered at the corner. The looks they flashed at the sight of charred footprints made her want to smile, but she wore a threatening glare as she passed.

A little concentration prevented the floor at her feet from bursting into flames as she paused at the entrance to the barroom. Old tables and chairs, in various states of collapse, had been set up around the place. Few matched, as though the owner scavenged them from a dozen different businesses. Kate stared at the tall, silver-haired man behind the bar. His moustache was so thick it resembled a dead rat hanging from his face. Hard blue eyes squinted back; like her, he seemed not to belong to this place.

Everyone in the room, a few women among them, wore the trappings of life in the Badlands. Armor cobbled together from whatever they could find, weapons anywhere they could hang them, and expressions that said they'd kill as easily as talk. At that moment, Kate realized how much like an unarmed, helpless tourist she looked.

Everyone, even the women, looked at her as if trying to weigh how best to take advantage of her.

The men from the buggy sat at the bar, about to attack a plate of food each. No one seemed the least bit concerned at the presence of a pair of raiders.

Remind me to thank those lab rats for making me look like a fashion model. She sighed. *'Just pretty enough' would have been better for infiltration. I stand out. Horny bastards.*

Without saying a word, Kate flipped both arms forward, palms raised. A collective gasp swept over the crowd as a head-sized blue fireball formed above each hand. The desire to kill came easy, riding the wings of an alien rage that swelled in from nowhere. She puffed air, as if blowing out the candles of a birthday cake. The gesture had little to do with her mental control of flames, though it looked as if the burning spheres responded, flying into the backs of the buggy crew.

Leather ashed over on contact; intense heat melted skin and muscle in seconds. Toneless fluttering replaced screaming as their chests ruptured. Kate poured psionic energy into the sense of the burn, adding to the fire and forcing it to invade their lungs until both men belched like dragons, spewing flames from the mouth and nose.

They hit the ground, dead and convulsing, smoke drifting from charred holes that used to be mouths. She drew the remnants of flame into the air, creating a carpet of fire along the ceiling that she pulled around behind herself into a curtain.

"I will say this only once. If one of you knuckle-dragging genetic throwbacks even looks at me sideways, this entire building and everyone in it will be ash."

Kate stared at the people for two seconds before she stopped concentrating; her display of power dissipated with a loud *whoof* of air. She approached the dead men and squatted nearby. Pouches and pockets burned away as she searched their things, careful to avoid putting her fingers anywhere near prewar bullets. She lost a few seconds examining the brass casings out of curiosity. Several minutes passed in tense silence.

Everyone watched her, but no surface thoughts gave away anything more than fear, curiosity, and awe.

At last, she found keys and stood. "These two better be as they are when I return."

No one moved. Kate went outside, back to the buggy. Alejandra had worked up a sweat trying to defeat the mechanism keeping her hands away from the machine gun. When the door swung open, she froze as if caught stealing. Kate smiled at her, approaching with keys dangling from two fingers.

"Alejandra, listen carefully." Kate leaned over her. "I'm going to put the key in the cuffs. Don't touch it right away, it will burn you."

The woman gave her a quizzical look, but nodded.

Kate held it up; the key glowed red-hot.

"My god…" whispered Alejandro. "What are you?"

"Pissed off." Kate stuck the key in.

Alejandra tried to pull away from the searing hand so close to hers. Kate focused on the key, using her command of heat to chill it.

Kate took a step back. "It's safe now."

"What about the—"

"They're both dead." She scratched at her head. "If it makes you feel better, it hurt a lot."

The woman freed her hands and cycled through the keys until she found one that opened the 'seatbelt.' Another key worked on the padlock at her throat and she threw the collar as hard as she could hurl it. Kate went back inside, approached the bar, and helped herself to one of the untouched meals. The breaded slab didn't resemble anything she'd ever seen before. It had enough flavor that she caught a hint of taste despite her inhaling it fast enough to prevent a mouthful of cinders.

"This didn't used to be a person, did it?"

The man behind the counter shook his head.

"Good enough." She didn't care much what animal it came from.

Outdoor light flooded the foyer; making the three men loitering there squint again. For an instant, they seemed eager. After a glance at Kate, they begrudgingly moved to a table. Accompanied by the sound of a dragging chain, Alejandra shuffled into view, rubbing her wrists. She followed the trail of charred footprints to her former captors' bodies.

"No key for those?"

Alejandra frowned at the leg irons. "They are welded on."

"You should take enough to protect yourself," said Kate, fanning her mouth from the heat. "What is this?"

"*Chile relleno*," said the almost seven-foot man behind the bar. His gaze drifted from Kate to Alejandra as she searched the corpses.

"I like it. Meat with actual flavor." She pulled the second plate over and started on it.

"It's not meat," muttered the man. "Got roast Squealer if you want meat."

Alejandra gathered coins from one of the dead men. "How much for a plate?"

"Four," replied the man.

She put four coins on the bar, two copper, two silver. The rest remained in the pouch she tied to her skirt. Kate eyed the prewar money, shaking her head at the inconvenience of currency that couldn't be traded at the wave of a NetMini.

Alejandra grabbed the belt of shells and put it on, and slung the shotgun over her back. She spent a moment pouting at the incinerated armor before taking a seat on one of the stools. Kate finished her second helping, almost feeling satisfied. The battery meter on her bracelet shrank to a worrisome point. *Whatever that old man is, if he can fix me, he should have done it right away. Guess he doesn't trust me to kill that creature without holding it over my head.*

"What?" asked Kate, noting Alejandra's piercing stare. Surface thoughts gave away jealousy. The woman wanted Kate's baggy camouflage shirt. "Oh. Sorry. I can't give you my shirt."

"I suppose I should be grateful that you freed me." Alejandra looked away.

I physically can't, said Kate, telepathically. *Remember how hot the key was? My clothes aren't real. They're a hologram.*

"What is hologram?" asked Alejandra.

"Later," muttered Kate. She glanced up at the bartender. "You trade?"

"Yep." The man nodded.

"Got any shirts?"

"Yep."

Kate stooped to grab four knives from the dead raiders, which she put on the bar. "This enough of a trade for one?"

"Aye." The tall man slid a plate in front of Alejandra.

He gathered the knives, carrying them into a back room. A moment later, he returned with a blue-grey flannel shirt and offered it to Kate. She pointed at Alejandra. The woman took a break from eating to put it on. Kate tapped her foot, staring at the shackles. *I'd hurt her more than the metal. Fuck it; not my problem.* She frowned again at her battery meter, finished the last of her second plate, and walked across the room to the exit. She left a burned handprint as she stiff-armed the door open and stormed back onto the highway.

Kate made it about twenty yards down the road before a voice broke the silence.

"Wait." When she didn't stop, Alejandra yelled again. "Please, wait! Why are you walking?"

I helped you escape; I don't want to adopt you.

"Hey, wait!"

The sound of Alejandra's attempt to run turning into a pratfall made her look back. "Don't hurt yourself."

"Why are you walking away?" Alejandra recovered the shotgun and stood.

"I have to go west." Kate resumed walking. "I don't have time."

"Take the cart."

Rage formed wisps of flame around Kate's hands. "I can't."

"Why not?" Alejandra's yelling drew closer, underlined by the melodic ringing of chain on pavement.

Kate whirled. "Because, I destroy everything I fucking touch…" She fumed, her voice fading to a half-whisper. "And… I don't know how to drive."

Alejandra caught up, out of breath from the ungainly shuffle. "I can show you. I can't get in there with the chain."

"Shotgun it."

The woman shivered. "I'm afraid of hurting myself. Small wounds can kill… long, painful death. Look, I show you how to drive. We go together?"

Kate held her hand over her eyes, squinting to the west. At most, the bracelet would last a few more days before needing a recharge she had no way to obtain out here. The buggy looked like a deathtrap; memories of the convoy run haunted her with a fast, grisly end. Her seven-hundred-degree ass inches away from a plastic bottle full of ethanol seemed like a bad idea. Still, she didn't exactly plan on attacking a cargo hauler, and raiders would probably leave a buggy alone.

A few people from the bar had emerged, checking the vehicle out.

"You know," said Kate. "Most people would use something metal to hold fuel."

"It was what they found. They all this"—Alejandra grabbed her crotch—"and none of this." She tapped her head.

Kate summoned a fist-sized orb of flames. "All right, fine."

She hurled a fireball over the heads of the crowd, clearing the potential thieves away from the raider cart as she jogged up along the right side. Alejandra made her way to the side pod without hesitation. Kate stopped to watch the woman climbing back into a metal enclosure that used to be her prison.

Guess seeing them die made her feel better.

The driver's compartment consisted of a flat slab of metal for a seat and a small steering wheel made out of a bent piece of rebar. The shape of the frame forced the driver's legs down two separate channels, each with a pedal at the bottom. Kate got in, drawing a sharp breath at the brief touch of cold metal on her skin. Rubber pads on the pedals melted and oozed through her toes in seconds. At her size, she barely saw over the shroud enclosing the steering wheel. The buggy sat so low to the ground she felt like her ass would be scraping pavement. All the metal around her should have seemed like armor, but it had the opposite effect, making her feel trapped and vulnerable. She closed her eyes and tried not to think about being stuck inside tumbling, twisted wreckage.

The buggy rocked as Alejandra grabbed the frame and hauled her legs over the side of the gunner pod. She unlocked the rest of the 'seatbelt' and threw the chain and locks overboard. After a dire look at the dangling cuffs, she leaned as close as she dared to Kate.

"Right foot is fast. Left foot is stop. Don't push both at the same time." She pointed at a small stick with a squeeze lever reminiscent of a motorcycle brake. "That is shifter. Squeeze first to open clutch."

A rudimentary explanation of how to drive an ancient, manual transmission followed. Somewhere between 'oh screw it' and confidence later, she squeezed the clutch flange. Everything in the buggy was metal, except for the starter button, the tires, and the plastic bottle full of ethanol. Alejandra leaned over and pushed it; the engine behind them roared to deafening life.

"As far right as it goes, then back into the corner to reverse."

Kate did as instructed, easing off the handle grip until grinding noises rang out and it stalled.

"Need to give it gas." Alejandra went over it again.

"Isn't that ethanol?"

Alejandra pointed at the pedal beneath Kate's right foot. "We call it gas."

Under the glare of several spectators, Kate eventually managed to back the buggy onto the road. With Kate focused on driving, Alejandra kept the mounted gun pointed at the crowd until the cart turned too far for it to reach. Metal protested and scraped as Kate fumbled for first gear, but she managed to get it moving without stalling. The crowd jumped as it backfired; sudden acceleration bounced Kate's head off a plate behind the seat. Grumbling and cursing, she eased off on the pedal and experimented with steering, hoping the unsettling rattle coming from somewhere behind her was nothing more than the empty cuffs hanging over Alejandra's head.

Her hair whipped in the wind as they picked up speed. Each time a strand or four caught in the frame and pulled, she swore. Somewhere in third or fourth gear, she kept the cart on the centerline as much as potholes and debris allowed. A faint *clank* rang out as a giant insect splattered on the bar in front of her, spraying a mess of yellow slime over her forehead. A second later, an intact bug smacked her in the face, exploding like a hurled egg. The impact left her dazed for a moment as several more peppered the buggy. Alejandra's explanation of 'mating clouds' did not do much to make her feel better.

Bug guts boiled away to ash.

"I am sorry for laughing."

Kate grumbled, rubbing the beginning of a bruise. "You don't need to stay with me."

"You want me to leave?" Alejandra's gaze fell.

"I'm just saying I don't want you to think you belong to me now or some screwy tribal bullshit."

"Oh. I don't." She patted the shotgun, seeming happier. "I understood that when you did not stop me from taking this."

An hour passed with neither woman speaking; the constant drone of the unmuffled engine somehow managed to go from annoying to hypnotizing. Alejandra gathered her hair down, keeping one hand on the old machine gun and her eyes on the horizon. Her shout snapped Kate out of a stupor in time to react to an enormous pothole approaching. The buggy went up on two wheels as she swerved, gun pod sparking along the pavement. Kate screamed; if not for the sidecar, the rickety vehicle likely would have rolled. It hit the ground hard, slamming both women to the right before coasting forward. It took a moment to shake off the pain in her arm.

Kate downshifted, gave it a little gas, and got back up to speed. Alejandra didn't even give her a scornful look for almost crashing. She clutched the wheel in a death grip for a few minutes, relaxing once the adrenaline of a near crash faded.

They drove for some time without speaking, the constant vibration of the engine in the harsh seat numbed Kate's butt.

"Strange that they let you operate a gun like that," said Kate, after the quiet became intolerable.

"There are worse things than men who take slaves," Alejandra shouted over the motor. "And the gunner is always first to get shot. They put me here to die. I was always fighting to get away, and I am not pretty enough to be worth the trouble."

Kate swallowed her anger, quite aware that several gallons of ethanol sat in a thin plastic bottle a short distance behind her. "Got a home?"

Alejandra scowled at the horizon, away from Kate. "My husband found a powerful bow that can put an arrow through the shell of a great crawler. The raiders came demanding tribute. When they saw it, they wanted it. He gave me to them instead."

"I..." Anger whitened Kate's knuckles on the wheel.

"Our elders cower like mice before the raiders. They ride into our village several times a year to demand tribute. They take supplies, weapons, and sometimes slaves. All this they say is in exchange for protection, but only from them. They do nothing if other bandits attack. So, no... I do not have a home. I will not go back there."

Shouting over the engine lost its appeal, and the pair remained quiet for the better part of several hours. With the approach of darkness, Kate pulled off the road into an ill-tended meadow between the highway and a decaying strip of old stores. The last vestiges of sunlight gleamed like flames upon shards of broken glass still clinging to window frames. She stalled the engine on purpose and brought the buggy to a halt. Within a few seconds, complete silence gave way to the chirp of innumerable insects.

"Unless this thing has lights, we're stopping."

Alejandra grasped the roll cage over her head and vaulted out of the gunnery pod. While she shuffled away to find a bush to water, Kate got out on the other side and wandered a few steps closer to the old structure. Blue signs mentioned food and fuel; two things she doubted remained in any noticeable quantity. Motion in the tall grass gave away the position of a cautious deer. One fireball seared the skin from its face and charred the skull, leaving the animal dead on its feet and convulsing.

By the time Kate dragged the animal closer to the buggy, the effort to keep the grass from igniting had left her ready to sleep. Alejandra hobbled over, looking worried and wide-eyed.

"My God, you're a ghost!"

"I'm not a ghost." Kate eyed the bracelet. The battery indicator flashed red. "This is why I didn't give you my shirt before."

She shut it off.

Alejandra covered her mouth. "You're naked."

Wow. Thanks for pointing that out. I didn't notice. "Don't remind me." Kate squatted over the deer.

"Let me check you for bugs; the grass is not safe."

Kate muted a laugh as her finger seared the animal's skin open like a blade. "Ticks don't like me."

Alejandra took a knife from a sheath strapped to the side of the buggy and busied herself chipping at the shackle around her right ankle. Kate pulled the deer apart with her hands, tossing the viscera to the side in a smoking pile. Alejandra lost interest in her battle with the welded metal, gawking. Kate heaved a large chunk of cooked venison to her traveling companion before taking enough meat from the kill to satisfy her abnormal appetite.

She ate until she could consume no more, and glanced over at Alejandra who still had not taken one bite. "You should eat."

"I…" The woman shook her head as if coming out of a trance. "Sorry."

"Yeah, so… that's why you shouldn't touch me." Kate threw the uneaten portion of her chunk onto the deer carcass.

"Are you cold?"

"Not right now. As soon as I go to sleep, I'll cool off, then I'll wake up freezing. I'll get hot again, try to go back to sleep and wake up again. It's a shitty cycle."

"I'm sorry." Alejandra nibbled on her food. "Thank you for hunting."

Kate wandered off a ways to relieve herself. When she returned, Alejandra had a crude metal jug in her hands, drinking from it. Evidently, her former owners had brought water along. She gulped down a few hasty mouthfuls and put it down before she boiled it.

With the din of crickets surrounding her, Kate rolled onto her side, curling up. "You don't have to stay out here in this crap. There's a real city in the east, and another in the west."

Alejandra shook her head. "No. To the west is a great wall of flames"—she held her hands up, waving fingers as if to illustrate fire—"that marks the entrance to Hell."

"Damn primitives." She rolled over to face Alejandra. "It's a load of crap. Some tribal probably got too close, got toasted by a laser cannon, and the story mushroomed."

"What is a laser cannon?"

"I almost forgot how comfortable soft dirt can be." Kate reclined, and explained about lasers, technology, and the great cities.

"I am not sure I believe you." Alejandra stretched out, resting her head on her arm. "If this city is as you say, why are you here?"

"I'm searching for a cure," muttered Kate, close to sleeping. "I gotta go West… kill an abomination."

Alejandra's next words blurred into the onrush of dreaming.

18

RUNNING ON EMPTY

Kate sat bolt upright amid the horrendous noise of a prewar machine gun firing. A ratty blanket slid down her chest and gathered in her lap. Out of instinct, she swatted the oily material away before it ignited without recognizing what it was. Awake before her brain could ascribe meaning to the clamor, Kate froze, staring at green-brown bodies swarming out of the tall grass, illuminated by the staccato flashes of muzzle flare. They ambled closer at a slow, staggering gait, some with arms raised, others trudging with their limbs at their sides. Dull green slabs of leathery skin separated by brown-red patches of exposed, dry muscle covered the creatures' bodies. No fluid leaked, though the air filled with the stench of rot.

A dry, crusty hand seized her by the ankle, dragging her into the oncoming throng. The scrape of dirt and rocks across her unprotected front broke the shock of sudden consciousness. Jagged fingernails, yellowed and thick, raked down her back and pressed into her arms and legs. Moaning, shambling figures gathered her into the air; hands everywhere, sandpaper tongues slid over her skin as several mouths bit her.

Kate screamed, for a moment incapable of anything close to coherent thought.

One by one, they ignited as her skin heated up to its usual blistering temperature. A clump of tongue fused to her left bicep, stretching and snapping loose as she wrenched her arm away from one of the moaning bodies. The creature didn't react to having its tongue ripped out so much as it panicked at its hands burning.

"Eww! Shit! Fuck!" Kate flailed at the clump of burning flesh. The army of desiccated humans found themselves unable to hold onto her as their dry skin ignited on contact. Kate swore and screamed as the crowd pinched and squeezed random parts of her body. Seconds felt like minutes as she slipped through their flailing limbs and hit the ground. One dove on her, biting at her throat. She got her hands up, holding him back by his chest. The creature had far more strength than its appearance suggested, and forced its way down with ease. Smoke hissed out from under her palms as it overpowered her. Kate brought her knee up into a blank groin. Its chest burst into flames where her fingers melted skin; its face caught fire when dry lips brushed her throat.

Howling in agony, it dove away and rolled.

"What the hell—?"

Alejandra opened up with the machine gun. The entire buggy shook and rattled with the recoil. Orange tracers streamed overhead. Kate curled into a defensive ball, gripped by a rare moment of terror. Dull, dry slaps came from above and behind her, as did the occasional raking grab for her legs that ended with burning and moaning. Another one fell on her, losing its tongue on her back as it licked. It, too, fell away, on fire. She crawled to the side, heading for the road. Once she got out from under the rain of bullets, she jumped to her feet, shivering in terror at the wall of green bodies.

The gun stopped without warning, triggering an angry, desperate growl from Alejandra.

"Bad round!" yelled the woman, as she scrambled to clear the dud.

Kate stared at the unbelievable horror staggering closer. "H-how do those things even work?"

"The bullets are not old. The bandits make them. They just do bad job."

Panic ebbed as the warmth of her psionic curse chased away the night chill. She gathered a fireball and hurled the seething projectile into the center of the throng. One body immolated in a half-second, becoming a walking torch, a burning man-shaped pile of tinder. She fed the essence of flame, willing the energy to spread to either side.

Alejandra pulled a useless bullet from the chamber, tossed it to the side, and tucked the ammo belt back in place. The discarded round landed too close to Kate for comfort, causing her to scoot away as the woman slapped the mechanism down and racked the bolt.

"Careful!" Kate whirled at a moan behind her.

Dozens more scuffed across the road from the other side, some dragging their legs, others at close to a jogging pace. Kate backed up, startled when she bumped into the gunnery pod. A fireball into the second group ignited a handful, but as fast as they went down and burned, more filled in the space. They swarmed right up to the buggy, trapping Kate on the pod side. One kept walking into it from the right, reaching over the empty driver's spot, as if he could not understand why Alejandra eluded his grip.

The machine gun erupted again; Kate whirled. Bodies in front of the buggy broke apart like stacked dirt. Flaking, chunky bits sprayed wherever the tracer stream went. Every now and then, a bullet ricocheted off a hardened plate of keratin. The sight of biological matter repelling a bullet snapped Kate out of a daze.

"There are more behind us. We gotta run!" yelled Kate, stopping herself from grabbing Alejandra's arm. "Run!"

The woman kept firing. "I can't run. Chain."

"Shit!" Kate threw another blast of flames to the rear, sending four or five to the ground.

A fleeting memory of what she did to the soldiers as a child came back. Her level of fear was sufficient to summon a blast capable of killing them all, but it would take Alejandra too. Kate grumbled, ashamed of the terror these creatures' appearance triggered. *Fucking zombies? Really? This can't be real. I'm sleeping.* She burned ten more, fireball after fireball. Baseball-sized blue spheres occasionally passed clean through their target and ignited one behind it. *Damn scientists; this has to be nanobots or something.*

There's too many. I'm going to pass out.

Alejandra screamed, half out of fear and half out of desperation. The dancing brass serpent in Kate's peripheral vision grew short. Almost out of ammo.

"Fuck." Kate eyed the driver's seat.

She didn't have time to run all the way around the mass of bodies. She could climb over Alejandra and burn the hell out of her, or dive headfirst into the crowd. Kate closed her eyes and ran forward, arms across her face.

Hands grabbed and squeezed anywhere they could get a hold. Fingers scraped down her skin, igniting like matches as they tried to force their nails into her flesh. Inhuman moans of pain bellowed around her; the air stank to the point she gagged. Gaping mouths full of yellow teeth flashed by as she punched one, elbowed a second, and kicked another. A hulking rotter emerged from the crowd, blocking her path. No longer able to hold back the urge to vomit, she leapt into a hug.

This is not fair. This is not what I meant by human contact.

The giant burst into flame and roared. It spun in circles, grabbing at her back and shoulders. Kate threw up again at the sensation of bubbling, burning flesh in contact with her entire body. More hands grabbed at her from behind and ignited. One snagged her hair, pulling her over backward. Her grip on the titan faltered, the melting body slipped out of her grasp with alarming ease, leaving her holding steaming sheets of skin. The hand in her hair dragged her over dirt and scrub. The giant collapsed, body caving in, lost to the consuming fire. Kate reached over her shoulder, seizing the arm by the wrist and squeezed until she seared its hand off at the joint. One grabbed her foot and bit down on her toes, howling with a mouthful of flames. She jerked her leg back and drove her heel into its nose, caving in the skull with a sickening crunch. When she sat up, an arm reached around and clawed at her stomach, retreating with a pained moan before it could break skin.

Dirt gave way to the scratchy presence of paved road as the horde continued to engulf her. She fought her way standing, finding herself fifteen meters from the buggy, surrounded. Coarse hands touched her everywhere, trying to pull her to the ground. Their skin burned away before they could get enough of a grip. Covered in patches of burning flesh, Kate raised her arms. An azure flame appeared between her palms, rolling and expanding into an orb of heat as wide as her shoulders. She cringed as mouths glommed at her sides, legs and shoulders. One tried to bite her neck. She flung the pyroclastic sphere into the ground at her feet, feeding the heart of the flames into a radiant explosion.

At least thirty of the creatures ceased to be, reduced to ash on the breeze. Those farther away didn't evaporate; they fell, howling and convulsing as fire consumed them. She sprinted for the buggy, hurling a small stream of flame into one of the things trying to drag Alejandra out of the pod. With metal surrounding her, the woman fought valiantly to defend herself, swinging a machete through the small opening in the roll cage.

Fire made it lean back, giving Alejandra the opportunity to take its head. It careened over sideways, replaced by another. Kate stuck one leg into the driver's compartment and thrust an arm forward; an arc of flames spread open from her palm and ignited nine more. The sudden flare of heat and light made the crowd retreat several paces. She leapt into the seat and smashed the starter. The plastic button remained solid only long enough to engage the motor before it melted under her thumb. She slammed the gearshift into the reverse position and stomped on the accelerator pedal. Dirt sprayed forward as the buggy backed over four dozen ambling figures, knocking them aside like bowling pins. Kate stared at the destroyed start button, terrified of stalling out as she worked the shifter into forward.

Alejandra stood in her seat, slashing over Kate's head at the armored green and brown bodies reaching at them. A severed hand fell into Kate's lap and ignited. She ignored it, focused entirely on the clutch. Harsh fingers in her hair banged her head into the roll cage as something tried to pull her through solid metal. Alejandra brought the machete down with a *clank,* freeing her. Strips of various colored cloth dangling from the woman's skirt trailed over Kate's chest and smoked.

"I can't see through you!" shouted Kate.

The hips in front of her face lurched several times as metal hit metal and something out of sight moaned. "Just drive. You're straight."

Kate thrust her leg forward, shoving the pedal down. Acceleration pushed Alejandra's side into her forehead, eliciting a wicked scream. The woman collapsed into the side pod, fetal and whimpering. Kate opened her mouth to apologize, but screamed as one of the creatures appeared in front of them with no time to swerve.

It landed on the buggy, clinging to the roll bars with its head an inch from biting Kate on the nose. It seemed unable to comprehend its shoulders exceeded the width of the gap, and kept lunging into the bars like a battering ram, bending them in an effort to bite her. Wild, yellow eyes glowed with hunger and hatred. Much to Kate's horror, it had surface thoughts. Simple thoughts… constant pain and hunger—and Kate looked like food.

They're alive…

She kept her foot on the pedal, ducking her head left and right as each successive attempt to bite grew closer. Watching the creature bending the steel frame by ramming itself into it scared her mind blank for several seconds. When the third bite got teeth on her ear, she howled and grabbed its face, forcing her fingers into its mouth.

Smoke oozed from where she made contact. Dried out skin flaked off, leaving her holding bone. He gurgled and lurched back, instinctively attempting to distance from the sensation of burning. The jaw came off in Kate's hands. Alejandra shouted and brought the machete down. The strike beheaded the creature and sparked against the metal frame. Kate swerved left, tossing the body off the angular front. The buggy rocked as the large rear wheel bounced over the tumbling corpse.

Kate held the jaw out to the side, cringing away from it. She relaxed her grip, but it stuck. A few shakes knocked it loose, but a patch of human leather remained on her palm. Kate held her arm out, waiting for it to burn away.

"Okay. That... was nasty."

Tears streamed sideways in the wind over Alejandra's face. A patch of skin above her right hip had turned cherry red. The woman lowered herself into the pod, ignoring the empty machine gun. Kate cleared her hand and shifted up to the highest gear the buggy had, risking that the moonlight would be enough to spot holes at seventy miles per hour.

Separated from imminent danger, the shaking took over. Her inner voice kept repeating *Goddamn zombies!*

KATE HAD NOT PAID ATTENTION TO TIME, HER MIND LOST AMID THE wandering rumination of what she had just witnessed. Sputtering noises from the engine pulled her out of the trance-like state. She frowned over her shoulder at the empty plastic container. The rising sun spread a bluish-orange tint across the horizon behind them. Feathering the pedal did no good. The tank was empty; the engine choked out a final gasp and died. She squeezed the clutch handle and let the silent vehicle roll forward until it squeaked to a halt. Alejandra had fallen asleep in the pod. Kate decided to join her, leaning back in the seat and closing her eyes.

In what felt like seconds, the sun leapt to the center of the sky, hot and bright. Kate stretched, pulled herself upright with the roll cage, and climbed out. She felt neither reassured nor annoyed by the texture of paving under her feet. She swiped her hands over her body, discarding bits of charcoal that had once been bits of people, as well as several teeth embedded in her skin. Blood bubbled and foamed here and there where the errant tooth or fingernail had managed to leave cat-scratches before burning. The wounds were minor, but everywhere.

She sank into a squat, gathering her knees to her chest. Her stomach wanted to vomit again, but held nothing to project. Their stench haunted her memory. Springs creaked; the buggy rocked. The delicate jingle of chain dragging on pavement announced Alejandra's shuffle around the nose end, past tires thin enough to be from a bicycle.

Kate stared at the road, glancing sideways at the woman's feet when she got close.

"You're naked," said Alejandra.

"Yes. Thank you for noticing," grumbled Kate. "Sorry I didn't get dressed up for the ambush. I kinda got distracted by a throng of goddamn zombies."

Alejandra blinked, seeming unsure if she should laugh.

"I've been stuck like this my whole damn life. Anything I try to wear burns, anything I try to touch... Any*one* I try to touch..." Kate started to cry, but the sadness gave way to anger.

"I'm sorry," whispered Alejandra. "I cannot imagine how awful it is."

Rage weakened. Kate swiped her hand at the bracelet, activating her false clothing. "I know I have some kind of gift... I'd give it up if I could." She laughed. "You know, I'm jealous of your looks."

"*My* looks?" Alejandra blinked, and blushed. "I am so plain. You are..."

"Yeah, I know. I stand out." *I want to disappear.*

Jingling chain moved away to her left, followed by the dull clunking noises of the woman rooting around the buggy.

Kate continued to gaze at the road between her feet. "What the fuck was that?"

"The scout has no fuel. I am taking what I can."

"No." Kate waved an arm to the rear. "Back there."

"We call them rad ghouls." Alejandra shouldered the shotgun on its strap.

"Are they dead?" Kate covered her face with her hands, trying to stop remembering that smell.

"If they were dead, they would not be walking. Rad ghouls have a disease that turns their skin hard, like armor. They are in pain just to move." Alejandra waved a hand around her face. "The pain makes them crazy. My grandfather said they were made by an old army, to be better soldiers."

Thinking of them as living, disease-ridden people was easier to cope with than the idea of returned dead. Alejandra shuffled up alongside. Kate stared at the shackles for a moment, sighed, and stood.

"The shotgun would break the chain."

Alejandra flicked her thumb across the side of the weapon. "I am afraid to do it."

"We're going to have to walk from here. Sit down, put the chain over the barrel, and fire."

"What if it explode in my hand?"

"Explodes." Kate pinched the bridge of her nose. "Sorry. Look… That chain is going to slow us down. I don't have a lot of time left."

"Why are you hurrying?"

"Battery is running low."

Alejandra shrugged. "Imaginary clothes are not important."

Kate cocked an eyebrow. "You don't think so? Take yours off. We'll both go naked."

The woman looked at the ground, red-faced. "I don't want to."

"I thought clothes weren't important." Kate walked on. "Besides, the sooner I do this, the sooner I get cured. Shoot the chain out. I'm not going to slow down for you."

The rattling of guns, jingling of chain, and desperate gasping from behind as the woman tried to keep up brought Kate to a guilty stop not quite ten minutes later.

"Thank you." Alejandra sagged forward, catching her breath. "You are nice."

Kate stared at the white puffy clouds overhead. "I've been called a lot of things, but nice isn't usually one of them."

Once Alejandra recovered her energy, they walked with the sun at their backs. She found the slow pace maddening. With every click of the chain between Alejandra's ankles, Kate's anger grew. As noon approached, Alejandra shuffled off the road to spare her feet from sunbaked paving. Even that few seconds' delay in not traveling west made Kate want to hurt something. She felt like an impatient three-year-old who couldn't wait to get her hands on her new doll—and rip its head off.

What's wrong with me? The irrationality of the rage floated through her consciousness and slapped her. With begrudging guilt, she tried to feel sorry for her traveling companion's plight. That pity twisted into annoyance when a glint of sun flashed from the shotgun's barrel.

"What are you looking for?"

Alejandra's sudden question made Kate jump. "An abomination I have to destroy."

"I do not know what that is."

"Something unnatural that does not belong in this world." *Like me.* Kate paused, painfully aware of how the road felt cold to her. "It has taken the form of a young girl to trick people into thinking it is harmless. I'm looking for a child with bright blue eyes."

"The Prophet?" Alejandra gasped. "You must be confused. The Prophet is not evil."

"You know where this thing is?" Kate pointed at the horizon. "I feel something strange pulling me in that direction. I… uhh… think God wants me to destroy it."

Alejandra made the sign of the cross. "I do not believe that. If He is involved at all, He has sent her to the world to help us. She is a healer. Tribes war with each other to claim her."

Kate stopped, palm upraised to block her companion's advance. "So God sends her here to heal people, but they kill each other over her? Yeah, that worked out. Great plan. Maybe that's why I'm supposed to destroy her. Maybe the world doesn't deserve such a gift."

Alejandra's thoughts contained only rumor and third-hand information. The woman had not met this 'Prophet' in person, but had a great reverence for her. In a land devoid of medicine, she figured such stories could easily take on a mythic quality. Whatever this thing was, its trickery had the natives wrapped up tight.

I'll be doing them a favor.

19

EVIL SPIRITS

The scent of cooking meat tugged Alejandra out of sleep. Kate knelt over the dead animal she had no name to call. It resembled a gopher, though its body looked larger than most dogs she'd seen. She pulled it apart barehanded, as she had done to all her meals since she was small. The lifeless head seemed cuter than deer; Kate couldn't look at it without remembering her first desperate kill.

"What's wrong?" asked Alejandra as she scooted over. "Don't like squealer meat?"

Kate tossed her a hunk of cooked meat. "Nothing."

"You seem sad."

"I must've looked pathetic." Kate sat back with a portion. "The first time I killed a deer for food I was seven. I was so ashamed of myself for hurting an animal, but I was starving. I remember jamming venison in my mouth and sobbing at the same time."

They ate without speaking for a moment.

"It makes no sense. I killed dozens of people to escape, but I only cried about a damn deer."

Alejandra shifted to rub her sore ankles. "The deer did not try to hurt you."

"A man once told me an animal gave its life to sustain mine and I should be grateful. It's silly and superstitious, but for some reason I always do." Kate tolerated eye contact with the dead animal for only a second. "I'm not sure I believe it was willing to do that." She let out a half-hearted chuckle. "Somehow, I don't think 'thanks, little buddy' will make the little gopher ghost feel better."

The woman rolled metal links through her fingers, shame and hatred clear in her eyes. "Wolves do not shed tears over what they eat."

"You know we'll wind up having to run from something."

"Yes." Alejandra let the chain fall. "They do this so we are too afraid to escape. It is… a bad way to die."

"Shoot it. If you nick yourself, I'll burn the wound closed so you don't get sick."

Alejandra shivered. Kate followed her stare at the distant sunrise for several minutes. Eventually, the woman found her nerve and stretched her legs out. She placed the tip of the barrel at the center of the chain and rocked back, legs in the air. Kate scurried around, away from the field of fire.

"Forgive me if I don't put my arm around you."

"I understand." Alejandra steadied herself and slid her finger over the trigger.

Boom.

The sound fell on them from above, crashing to the Earth upon a wave with tangible presence. Alejandra screamed and fumbled the shotgun as the sky burst into a brilliant cloud of orange, yellow, and white flames. A massive sphere of fire and smoke expanded among the clouds, pierced on one side by a spiraling thread of burning. Kate tracked a sparking object hurtling through the sky, generally southwest. After a moment of quiet, a distant *crack* reached them.

"The sky is on fire!" screamed Alejandra.

"Calm down." Kate held out a hand, keeping the woman from standing. "It was some kind of aircraft. From the sound of the crash, it landed far enough away for us not to worry about it. We barely heard it."

"Aircraft?"

"I'll explain later."

Once again, Alejandra assumed the position. She seemed afraid to put her finger on the trigger, staring up as if another great explosion would occur. She pushed forward on the gun, extending the top of the barrel past her feet.

Crack!

The chain split in a spray of dust and metal. Alejandra fell limp, panting.

"See, all that fear and nothing happened."

Alejandra rubbed her ankles. "It hurt."

Kate wandered away. "Yeah, but you can run now."

Alejandra sat up, scowling. "I wish I could make fire like you. Then I could protect myself." She tugged at one of the dangling chains before dropping it with contempt. "I would not be treated like this."

"If I could give it to you, I would."

"That is foolish." Alejandra stood and gathered the blanket, machete, two pistols, and the shotgun. "Would you rather be a slave?"

Kate considered it for a moment. "No, but there's other ways to defend yourself. I could use a gun, or a knife."

Alejandra laughed. "You are so skinny. The raiders, even their women, would overpower you... gun or not. You should be thankful you have such power. It makes you strong out here."

"Yeah well..." Kate frowned at the battery meter. "I don't plan to stay out here much longer."

"The land may not let you leave." Alejandra used the machete to cut the remnants of the strange creature into steaks.

Kate moved to the road and adjusted her clothing to a patternless black bikini top and short skirt to use less power. "What's that supposed to mean?"

Alejandra gathered the food, making a sack out of their one blanket, and jogged over. "My grandfather told us stories about the land, about a great war many generations ago."

The odd pull tugging at her mind led Kate away from the angle of the road onto open scrubland. Alejandra followed without protest beyond the occasional curse when she stepped on one of the loose chains dancing around her feet.

"Yeah, the Corporate War," said Kate, some moments later.

"Many were killed. The land was wounded as well, and it is angry."

Oh, boy. Native superstition. "The land doesn't get angry."

"There are too many stories. Machines stop working for no reason. People wander into the dust and return savage, wanting only to kill."

Kate smirked, unable to think of something to say that wouldn't sound patronizing.

"Do people in that city of yours kill each other like this? Do they make slaves of the weak?"

"Not in the same way. They don't call them collars and chains there... more like jobs and taxes."

Alejandra shot her a confused look. "So it is the same there?"

That got a laugh out of her. "No... I'm making a cynical metaphor."

"A what a for?"

She's ignorant, not stupid... just uneducated. Not her fault. I used to be primitive too. "Forget it. No, it's not the same. But it's not because of some 'angry land spookery,' there are police in the city that keep law."

"There is evil in the dark," said Alejandra, with too much conviction for Kate's peace of mind. "Some can resist it, but most cannot. It wants pain, suffering, and misery. That is why I refused to hate my husband for what he did. It is like a hole in the screen." She wiggled a finger in midair. "It is small, but it lets bugs in. Then, before you know it, you can put your whole hand through." She made a fist, held it for a few seconds, and let her arm fall.

Kate knew something pulled her in a specific direction. The old priest warned her about a demon, told her she was capable of doing God's will and he would reward her with freedom from her curse. Alejandra's tales of evil land seemed so far from plausible, yet the presence pulling her west was undeniable.

It couldn't possibly be the influence of a demon, or of the land.

I've always been this angry.

20

MIDNIGHT SNACK

Kate felt ridiculous wandering the Badlands in a black bikini top and micro skirt, but it resulted in a welcome uptick in estimated battery life. For the past several days, they had walked in the direction of the inexplicable pull. Kate had learned the names of Alejandra's extended family and the peculiar habits of the black chicken with the bum foot. She learned more than she cared to know about prewar weapons, like the shotgun and 9mm handguns they had scavenged. The local woman had grown up with guns; everyone in her home village had to help defend it. Alejandra used the topic of danger as an excuse to slip in more mention of the 'evil land' stories, claiming that anything with electronics in it could fail at any moment—if the land so desired.

An unprompted description of the difference between 'dry' rad ghouls and 'wet' ones that were skinless and coated with a layer of clear slime had given Kate a case of insomnia, even more than usual. Her condition could kill diseases, but would do nothing about radiation poisoning.

Out of sheer boredom, Kate had reluctantly opened up and shared her story. By the time she had gone from lab escapee to Syndicate killer, Alejandra seemed torn between pity and fear.

"Your city is not so different from here. Those who have power and strength attack those who do not."

"Okay, so if this whole evil spirits thing is true, why does this thing still work?" Kate held up her bracelet.

"Is it a weapon or something that can help you travel?"

Kate frowned at her reflection in the rectangle of black amid the heat-resistant band. "No. It just keeps people from seeing me naked and getting stupid ideas." *This skimpy shit is almost worse than not wearing anything at all.*

"Then it is not important enough to break." Alejandra looked up as if she would say more, but remained quiet.

"What?"

"You do not believe, and I do not want to make you angry with me." She hesitated for a moment. "You do not seem like the kind of person who can kill for money."

"I hide my anger well…" *Sometimes.* She sighed. "I guess it wasn't about the money. I felt like I owed El Tío for helping me. I did what he asked because he asked, not because he paid me."

"Oh." Alejandra stared at the distant horizon.

"What were you thinking?"

"The evil grows stronger with hurt. If it would cause you sadness or rage for that machine on your arm to break, it will break when it is most painful."

Kate looked down at her body. "I didn't care about not having clothes until I read lust in people. Being naked doesn't bother me, being looked at *like that* does." *Mostly because I can't…*

"How did raiders not find you?"

"I stayed in the forest, far away from people or anything worth stealing. I didn't even know such a thing as bandits existed. I hid during the day and hunted at night. After that man disappeared, I lived alone for years before I saw another person." Kate's somber expression shifted to a smile. "I used to play in the streams, trying to swim… but all I did was make a lot of steam. Once, when I was little, I thought I could 'put myself out' if I jumped into a deep spot. I hoped the water would cool me off and make me normal. My brain wouldn't stop trying to fight the cold; I got so tired I almost passed out and drowned."

Alejandra reached for Kate's shoulder, but pulled her hand back. "I'm sorry your life has been so cruel."

"Yeah, well. Damn scientists never know when to leave shit alone. Profit margins and deadlines got in the way. They didn't *have* to kill me. They could've studied me… Those bastards only saw a project in a cage to be poked and prodded, not a little kid, not a person. I'm like this because of them. I'd do anything to get rid of it." Kate sank into a squat, close to crying. "I want real clothes. I want to be touched and not have people scream. I want to be able to *enjoy* something I eat, not have to stuff it down my throat before it turns into charcoal."

"You would kill the Prophet for this? But, she is just a little girl."

"I..." Kate ran a finger over a healing tooth-shaped bruise. "I don't know. The priest said it is a creature of evil that only looks like a child. Maybe it made itself look innocent so no one dared destroy it? What if this Prophet is really that evil you're talking about?"

"That is stupid."

"Think about it..." Kate caught sight of buildings in the distance and veered off course. "You say she can heal and wants to help everyone. How many die fighting over her? If you count the number of lives she saves against the number of people who died because of her, which side wins?"

"I... I never thought that before. It isn't her. It is greed that makes them kill." Alejandra stopped walking a few paces ahead, waiting. "The legends say she can cure anything, except death."

Kate looked up. "Anything?" She teased a finger at the dirt by her toes. *Maybe I should talk to her... it first. She thinks the girl is real. What if that priest is trying to trick me?*

※ ⚔ ▥ ◌ ◍

LONG SHADOWS STRETCHED ACROSS THE ROAD FROM WHAT REMAINED OF old buildings littered about open yards of browned scrub and dirt. Some looked like they had been vehicles in a past life. The burned husks of former military trucks clustered together at the end of a long, one-story building painted in white, blue, and bullet holes. Kate stuck her toe under a thin, rectangular piece of dented metal on the road and kicked it over. Enough remained of green paint and white letters for her to read the name of the once-town.

"You can't wear that," said Alejandra. "And it is too weak for weapons. The metal will not hold an edge."

"It's a sign. This place was called Edgewood. We're getting close. It feels like just past the mountains." She looked up at the waning sun. "It will be dark before we can cross. We should shelter here for the night."

"The metal speaks to you?"

Kate spent a moment explaining the concept of written words. Alejandra had never heard of such a thing, but seemed eager to hear about it. Kate's thoughts drifted back to the old doctor teaching her while she floated inside her tank/prison. Holographic projectors had created numbers and letters in the gel with her, so she could do the lessons. Their discussion of the alphabet continued on their walk through the abandoned town. Someone had hung scraps of wood and glass from numerous branches. The chimes shifted in the wind, lending an eerie musical backdrop to the haunted desolation around them. Kate headed onto a narrow road, barely two lanes running north-south. The pull tugged at her; the urge to follow it grew.

A door creaked somewhere out of sight, the sound sharing the breeze with a chattering whisper. Kate stalled, raising a hand to silence Alejandra as she looked around. Daylight had weakened to the point where even simulating black, her outfit took on a spectral glow.

Something is here.

Alejandra jumped back at the voice injected into her thoughts. Chain fragments rang on the paving. She shrugged the shotgun off its strap and held it at the ready.

Great swaths of open ground spread between the ancient buildings, providing little in the way of cover. Moonlit scrub brush cast long shadows over the blue-glowing dirt. Kate squinted at broken windows, long-dead cars, and the occasional drift of shadow she hoped was an animal in the dark.

"You are lit up," said Alejandra. "If we are hunted, they will see you."

"That should make it easier to kill them."

A weak moan emanated from their right. Kate tiptoed in that direction, hands raised in preparation for a fight. She cringed at the clamor of Alejandra's broken shackles when she moved to follow.

"Watch behind us," whispered Kate.

Alejandra whirled about, walking backward.

Beyond a collapsing grey building, a man writhed upon the ground. Whoever lived here had staked out an emaciated, nude man, spread-eagled on the ground with large, blood-caked hooks pierced through both wrists and behind his Achilles tendons. Blood from thousands of small cuts covered his chest, and his mouth was a gory mess of sharpened teeth. A bloody file still sat on his stomach below where someone had started the process of stitching dark brown leather to his skin.

The sight of the mad tailor's work made Kate gag.

A sick, wheezing moan foamed blood over what remained of his teeth as he raised his head toward her. Tight leather also covered the upper part of his skull like a second skin, held to his cheeks by a zigzag of straining black threads. Dilated eyes focused on the light of her phantom clothing. His arms wobbled as he clenched his fingers as close to fists as he could get them. More blood welled out of the point where the hooks pierced; ropes creaked.

"Unggggh…" Thick, bloody goo oozed from his mouth.

Alejandra, mesmerized by the ghastly sight, almost walked into Kate from behind. She gasped, taking her left hand off the shotgun to cover her mouth. Again, she made the sign of the cross.

"He wants me to kill him," said Kate in a near-whisper.

"H-how? That was speaking?"

Kate glanced at her and opened a telepathic link. *I can hear his thoughts. They are an insane scramble of agony. He's barely human.*

Recognition widened Alejandra's eyes. Tears ran down her cheeks. "Thank you for making me shoot the chain. We have to run away, now."

"Why?" Kate advanced on the helpless, writhing figure.

Alejandra stayed at the corner of the building, making noises at her as though she called a cat. "Nibblers. They will eat us. We have to run!"

The man stopped fighting the ropes as Kate neared, laying back on the ground and exposing his neck. Involuntary shivers kept one leg rattling.

"Kate!" hissed Alejandra. "This is their home. They are turning him into one of them! We must leave before they see us."

She locked eyes with the man. One brief instant of sanity returned; enough for him to nod. The first deer had been easy to kill, but hard to accept. The second deer was the hardest kill, harder even than the first time El Tío asked her to help him with a problem. She had almost hesitated killing someone because she'd been told to, but the idiot pulled a gun.

Kate couldn't look away from where the man's cheeks warped at the pull of the zigzag threads. All the times she had killed in the past, why now did it feel almost *wrong?* Even with the man begging for it.

"Kate!" whispered Alejandra, waving. "You cannot help him."

"Yes, I can."

A fireball formed over Kate's outstretched hand, hovering inches from her skin. She concentrated, forcing a buildup of energy, shifting the burn from blue into white. *I don't want him to suffer more.* He stared at it, thrashing his head in a violent nod. Pity made for weak motivation, no stronger than the detached nothing she so often afforded people El Tío wanted dead. They died screaming. She wanted this man's relief to be instant.

Kate thought back to Esteban, the face he made when he burned himself. She held onto the longing and the shame, her anger at being a freak no one wanted near them. An audible whoosh surrounded the orb as it turned pure white. A trace of pain licked at her hand—the fire approached the limits of whatever subconscious mechanism kept her from burning herself. Hurt triggered the normal human reaction to burning and she flung it downward, willing it into a missile more by power of mind than physical gesture.

Skin and leather vaporized on contact, leaving charred bone and empty eye sockets smoldering. Tiny patches of candle flame lingered on the blackened skull. The body jerked twice, and went still. Kate stared at the corpse, lost to wondering if he was better off.

Boom.

She jumped at the sound of a shotgun going off behind her. Alejandra pumped the weapon and fired a second time after a slight correction in aim, earning a wail in the distance. Though the loud and substantial report shook the air, Alejandra barely moved under the recoil. Bodies glided around in the dark, silhouettes flecked with bits of gleaming metal. The shadows had an eerie hybrid gait somewhere between monkey and stalking panther. A scrape of metal on stone pulled Kate's head around to face forward.

A wiry man, covered head to toe in leather except for around his mouth and eyes, flowed around the corner of the building. His outstretched left hand raked the wall with metal claws. Both arms ended in a fistful of five-inch blades, triangular shards of steel grafted onto his fingers—nail extensions from Hell. Their sharpened edges still bore the dried blood of a prior victim.

Teeth, filed to points, oozed liquid two parts saliva and one part blood. Wild eyes regarded her without a trace of lust or attraction. One thought bounced around in his head, a tiny rock rattling around in an empty can: food.

Kate lost a few seconds staring at the claws. Her skin crawled with the memory of the rad ghouls' hands all over her. Fingernails lasted long enough to scratch before they disintegrated; metal claws wouldn't burn. More shadows gathered behind him making chitters of excitement.

Boom. Alejandra fired again.

The jolt destroyed hesitation.

Kate brought her hands together wrist to wrist, fingers splayed, and projected a streamer of flame into the figure's chest. He howled, far higher pitched a noise than she expected to come from anything male, and leapt around the corner out of sight. Kate flung herself into a white door two paces closer to where Alejandra cursed the misfeeding shotgun. A Nibbler leapt off the roof, landing between them with a keening wail, facing Kate.

Alejandra whipped around, bashing it in the back of the head with the butt of the shotgun. The impact knocked it face-first into the wall. She hit it again in the back, and when it turned on her, she cracked it across the face, knocking it to the ground. In the moment of reprieve, Alejandra pulled fresh shells from the bandolier and loaded them.

Kate jumped shoulder-first into the door, succeeding only in blackening ancient paint.

"What are you doing?" yelled Alejandra, shaking the weapon. It went off, liquefying the downed Nibbler's head into a spatter.

"They're everywhere. We need a choke point." Kate bounced off the door again. "Fuck!"

Alejandra, pumped, aimed behind her, and fired. A howl of pain erupted from the distance. She backed up and fired again. Kate fumed, and kicked at the door with all she had. Several black footprints and an intact door mocked her.

"You are a skinny little thing," said Alejandra. "Move."

The next leather-clad figure around the corner bore the brunt of Kate's anger. She never asked to have the body she got; the scientists thought it would help her be a spy. *Idiots.* The nibbler dropped where he stood, cradling his burning chest, face on the ground and ass in the air. *Inconspicuous works better than a red-haired gazelle.* A long, sustained, flamethrower effect forced a pack of whooping crazies racing in from the other side to dive for cover. She snarled, tossing fire left and right in a faltering effort to keep the nibblers away. *Unless they... Of course, I was going to be an assassin. Cozy up to the big boss, get him in bed and...*

Four nibblers to the right went flying as Kate's anger caused a midair detonation.

Alejandra held the shotgun sideways, reared up on one leg, and booted the door by the knob. It cracked, but held. A screeching voice from above preceded a jagged-toothed mouth grinning over the roof. She got the shotgun up as it leapt at her. The tip caught it in the chest as it went off, blasting a hole in the body, which the weapon slid through. His dead weight falling on her knocked her flat on her back.

Kate flicked a fireball into another one sprinting for the pinned woman, killing it in an instant.

Alejandra rolled left, jerking the shotgun back and forth in the corpse to pump it before firing at one charging Kate from behind. She shoved the body away and leapt up, rushing the door with a war cry and a kick that knocked it wide open.

Kate pulled existing fire from a smoldering corpse and backed into the building, gathering it into a sphere, which she hurled at two more nibblers brave enough to run out of the darkness. Dry mustiness hung in the air, though she didn't have time to gawk at the prewar furnishings.

Two nibblers ran for her, claws raking the air as they loped up to a sprint. A few quick fireballs made them jump away; the building shuddered at their impact with the wall on either side of the door. A clatter of metal behind her broke the silence. Alejandra pulled shells from her belt and stuffed them into the shotgun while Kate burned another one trying to follow them inside.

The frantic whooping outside faded to silence. The nibblers seemed hesitant and wary of charging headlong at the door. To the left, the main 'living room' area merged with a kitchen. Three windows and the front door gave them a limited view of the outside. The other end of the room had a narrow hallway leading to a few doors.

"What's that smell?" asked Alejandra, pumping the shotgun and sticking one more round in. Three remained on the belt.

"Smell?" Kate blinked. "Oh…" The fragrance of smoldering linoleum brought a growl to her voice. "Nothing to worry about."

At least the place had a concrete slab instead of wood for a foundation. She grumbled, hating the sensation of standing in sticky goop as the floor bubbled around her toes. A desperate nibbler appeared, running for the door with a trash can lid held up like a shield.

Blam!

It didn't do much against buckshot.

"Are you okay?" Alejandra sounded worried, but in control.

"Just peachy."

The woman lowered her voice to a reassuring tone. "You're trembling."

Kate looked at her shaking hands. "Isn't this a normal reaction to being surrounded by blade-fingered lunatics that want to eat me? The damn curse won't protect me from their claws. I feel naked." *Bullets splatter... will those?* She shivered, not wanting to find out if her subconscious defense against getting shot worked on steel blades too.

Alejandra didn't say it, but her expression did.

"Yeah, yeah... I know," grumbled Kate.

Both women looked up as feet tapped over the ceiling. Kate squeezed her hands into fists, wanting armor... wanting something between her and sharp pointies. She glared out the window over the sink at a nibbler poking out from behind a wrecked car twenty yards from the door, staring. In his surface thoughts lurked a view of the house from outside.

"Kitchen windows," Kate shouted, pointing. "Two coming. I'll cover the back."

Glass shattered deeper in the building before Alejandra could question. Seconds later, nibblers attacked the doors in the rear hallway. Leather-wrapped arms raked their claws, splintering and chewing up the flimsy hollow wood. Dim blue light flickered over the walls as fireballs flew.

Bang, ka-chuck, bang.

Screams and twinkling glass filled the vacuous silence in the wake of the blast. Alejandra covered three windows and the door while Kate kept a burn stream on the ones attempting to enter via the hallway.

Even expecting it, the gunfire inside the house made her jump and her ears ring with each shot. With the back hallway clear, Kate ran to shove the front door closed, but it bounced open.

Alejandra loaded her last three shells.

Another nibbler leapt in at Kate, claws raised. She managed to get a fireball to form in her hand before the shotgun went off from behind, blasting a gouge out of the side of his neck. The limp nibbler's charge became a hurtling dead weight that crashed into her, knocking her down. He smoldered on contact, gasping for air while pawing at his throat. Arterial spurts shot dark streams three feet in the air, covering her in boiling blood.

Kate shoved and screamed; bits of metal worked into his leather shell scraped her skin. She kicked the body to the side and looked up at two more coming in the door. Crawling backward, she hurled flames between her knees.

Alejandra's shotgun went off again. Her last shell cored out the head of the one on the right. She tossed the empty weapon onto the table and drew a pistol from her belt, firing at the kitchen window.

"How many of these fuckin' guys are there?" Kate looked around in a frantic search for options. A gleam of silver gave her an idea. "Get in the fridge!"

Alejandra almost ripped her skirt off trying to get her second gun out. "What?"

"Do it!" Kate screamed.

Nibblers crawled in the windows, chittering and clicking their bladed fingers. Bloody foam oozed through shaved teeth. More emerged from the back rooms as another filled the only door out. Alejandra fired wild at the ones in the kitchen, running for the large metal cabinet in the corner.

Kate waited for the *whump* of the rubber-sealed door and curled into a ball. Not since a platoon of grown men had been ready to shoot a little girl had Kate felt such overwhelming terror. Tempered with age, her fear flashed, a spark in the infinite blackness of her adult mind. Dread became anger: pure, unbridled rage at what the world had done to her. In her mind, a child's scream of terror built into a grown woman's cry of determination to survive. Sounds of stomping, crashing, and breaking glass closed in.

A hand touched her, breaking the calm.

The spark expanded with the sound in a brilliant flash in her imagination. Her body shuddered from an incredible pressure wave and slumped from a tremendous drain of energy. A deafening roar drowned out screaming for several seconds before perfect silence returned. Faint snaps and hisses lingered in the quiet; the all-too-familiar clatter of burning timber raining back to earth brought reassurance and peace.

She uncurled, not bothering to open her eyes as her limp body rolled out on the floor like a meat carpet. The strange sensation of cold floor on her naked skin barely registered. Wind tousled her hair and caressed her front. Fatigue left her paralyzed. Minutes passed in silence until the suctioning sound of the refrigerator door opening brought her out of her delirium. Open, starry sky greeted her gaze.

The entire house had vanished.

Kate rolled her head to look at the refrigerator lying on its back some twenty meters from where it had been before. A steel sink hit the ground with a *clank* farther away. Bits of flaming ash hovered in the air, a snow of embers.

The fridge door flipped up like a casket lid. Alejandra sat up and peered around at the destruction. Every ounce of strength left in Kate's body went toward the act of breathing. When the sensation of cold reached her brain, her teeth chattered, and she laughed.

Alejandra climbed out of the fridge, rubbing a bloody nose. She stepped around small, lingering flames on her way to Kate's side.

"Are you still alive?" she whispered.

"I'm not sure." Kate raised her left arm, breathing a sigh of relief at the sight of the bracelet still functioning. Perhaps her attachment to the thing had subconsciously protected it. "So tired…"

Alejandra mumbled in Spanish, something that sounded like a prayer, as she tiptoed around the burned slab. The only sign nibblers had even been there were a few bones and too many loose metal claws to count.

"W-what did you do?" Alejandra's next question stalled at the sight of the warped steel fridge door; several blade-fingers had stuck in it from the force of the explosion.

"I got scared." Kate propped herself up, sitting. "I have no idea where the shotgun went."

"Everything is gone…" Alejandra moved to the edge of the concrete slab foundation where the door had been. "There is just a big black circle."

Kate rubbed her face. "I'm freezing." She blinked. "I'm fucking freezing!"

Alejandra scurried over, reaching a nervous hand out. Sensing no heat, she touched Kate's shoulder. "You feel hot like fever, but is no burning."

After the woman helped her up, Kate wrapped her arms around her and squeezed. Emotion got the better of her and she bawled like a scared child.

"Why are you crying? We are safe."

"I've never been able to touch someone before…" Kate wiped her face. Sobbing gave way to manic giggling. "I…"

"Need some real clothes," said Alejandra.

"I'm so damn hungry." Kate swooned to the ground. "I… remember this feeling. The time I tried to swim. I need to eat or I'm going to die." She cried again. "It won't last; I'm too weak to make myself hot. The curse will keep trying until it kills me."

Alejandra unwrapped some of the Squealer steaks, which had been fortunate enough to be with her in the fridge. Kate ate three of them too fast to taste, and gnawed on the fourth, despite having no room in her stomach. The gentle hand brushing her hair and rubbing her shoulder kept quiet tears flowing the entire time.

"I'm going to heat up again soon," Kate muttered.

"I'm sorry. It is not fair." Alejandra picked at the blistering patch on her side. "You are frightening in this power you have."

"I've only blown up like that once before." Kate took another bite of steak four. "When I was outside the lab, there were so many soldiers. I was so little, but they were all terrified of me. They would have shot me except for this man in a dark coat. He lied and said they wouldn't kill me, but I didn't trust him." She took another bite. "I'm not sure how I did it, just like this time. I was so scared… and then I got angry."

"You are warming up." Alejandra scooted away.

"Yeah," muttered Kate, staring down. "I shouldn't have hoped."

"Hoped?"

She stood and stretched. "I wanted to believe I might've used up all my power at once."

"Then you would be defenseless. That is not a good thing to be out here."

Kate stumbled to the edge of the concrete slab, curling her toes over. A circular patch of burned ground extended almost thirty meters in all directions; thin trails of white smoke wisped upward from several spots.

"*Madre de Dios,*" muttered Kate.

Alejandra let off a stifled laugh. "*Si.*"

Kate exhaled. *No, I'm pretty sure I'm playing for the other side.* "I get the feeling we should move."

"Yes." Alejandra kept her one remaining pistol at the ready. "Things will have seen that flash."

Yeah, like people on Mars. Kate glanced at the sky.

The strange but welcome chill in the air had ceased; the ever-present shroud of warmth had returned. She stepped among the ashes of nibblers and scrub grass, keeping her eyes aimed down in search of sharp things. Minutes later, Kate reached the paving they had first followed. Her mind ran in circles around memories of the older scientist trying to get her to 'switch it off.' All of his mental exercises had failed. The only effect any of it had was for her to singe her eyebrows off once. It made the old man think she could control it, if only they could understand the subconscious mechanism that protected her hair.

Alejandra followed, making no noise other than jingling.

The thin dirt trail ended at a T intersection by a sign bearing the words 'County Line Road.' Kate glanced left and right. Up ahead past a guardrail, a square concrete culvert offered the promise of shelter for the night beneath a large east-west roadway. Kate squinted at the old highway; the ephemeral tug pulled her from deep within. She would follow the highway; the inexplicable urge called to her. She moved to the edge of the paving, bracing her hands on the guardrail for a moment before climbing it. Alejandra followed her across dry, waving grass on the far side. Smoke peeled around her feet as she crept to the waiting tunnel.

"Why are you moving so slow?" whispered Alejandra.

"I don't want to start a brush fire." Kate stepped onto a patch of dirt by the opening and relaxed. "This road overhead... I want to follow it west. But, I'm about to pass out."

The culvert was tall enough that neither of them had to stoop. Someone, no telling how long ago, had made a home of the place by adding a cot as well as several crates and boxes serving as storage shelves. Kate ignored everything, curling up on the hard concrete. It was far from comfortable, but she couldn't burn it.

Alejandra crouched nearby, holding her hands over Kate as if she were a campfire. They made eye contact; the woman seemed ashamed of herself.

"It's okay." Kate laughed, and turned off the bracelet to save power. "I've never felt so useful before."

KATE AWOKE WITH THE FEELING OF CLOTH AGAINST HER SKIN. ALEJANDRA must have wrapped her like a burrito in the night with a scavenged blanket. She sat up fast, swatting at the fabric to get it away before her consciousness kicked in. Despite her attempt at speed, it burned in several places. Alejandra slept on the cot, undisturbed by her flailing. Kate picked through the various boxes and items stashed in the tunnel, using a conveniently abandoned crowbar as an intermediary. Little of interest remained; most of the items were trash or too old to be of use. A few shirts and pairs of jeans looked usable, but filled her with jealous anger. Among a cluster of tools, one object, a hacksaw, caught her eye. She hooked it on the end of the crowbar and moved to the cot.

"Alejandra, wake up." Kate poked her until she moved.

The woman sat up, wiping her eyes. "Good morning."

"Look what I found." She dangled the saw in front of the woman's eyes.

Alejandra took it, turning it around in her hands to examine it. "A saw?"

"It's made to cut metal." Kate tapped the welded bolt in the broken restraint. "Cut the bolt, not the band, it's too thick."

"Oh!" Alejandra took it with an eager glint in her eye. She hooked her heel on the edge of the cot and got to work.

Serenaded by feverish scraping, Kate crept to the opposite end of the culvert tunnel, shielding her eyes from the oppressive early-morning sun. She squinted at a few ancient trucks parked by a teal-green building with three white rolling doors. The land was quiet, devoid of life. A heavy metal object hit the ground behind her. Kate smiled as the rapid back-and-forth scrape resumed.

"Slow down, you don't want to break the blade." Kate took a few steps out into the light.

Over the course of several minutes, Alejandra cut the manacle from her left ankle, and hurled it contemptuously against the wall, spitting after it. Kate glanced back at the sound of whimpering, cringing while the woman rubbed at red marks and dried blood.

"If you want me to kill the bastard that sold you, I will." Kate folded her arms.

"He was my husband," whispered Alejandra. "I wish never to see him again, but I have more anger for the raiders who force our people to behave like animals."

"Okay. I'll kill the raiders then."

Alejandra sat for a moment in silence. "I think you have more than enough blood on your hands already. I do not wish to add more."

Kate left Alejandra to rub her wounds and proceeded to search the rest of some long-dead person's possessions. A twist of jealousy at the reminder she could not touch anything without burning it made her look away. Alejandra appeared out of nowhere next to her holding a large red and white axe. Kate jumped, which startled Alejandra.

"Sorry," they both said at the same instant.

Kate started to smile, but kept her expression blank. Such a moment of levity served only to remind her of normal people having normal friendships. She got up and jogged from the tunnel, crossing a barren lot toward the road. An old chain link fence surrounded the teal building and ran for some distance along the highway up ahead. Not wanting a rusty scratch, Kate avoided it and diverted along a dirt access road that curved up to the highway about thirty yards west. At the top, two lanes ran in either direction with a strip of earth between them. She glanced over her shoulder at the building. White letters spelled out 'East Mountain

Pumping' on the road-facing side of the teal garage. Kate pondered whether it might hold anything useful. Smaller white letters below it read 'septic systems.'

Alejandra followed, gasping as her foot hit the baking pavement. "What is it?"

Kate used up a little battery power to check a dictionary app. "Probably a bunch of crap we can't use."

"Oh," said Alejandra, moving back to the dirt.

"I want to follow this road." Kate went west, stepping through a full three-sixty turn to survey the land. "Something is pulling me this way."

Alejandra adjusted the pistol tucked into her skirt and balanced the axe over one shoulder. "Is that good?"

"No damn idea." Kate walked forward with a determined stride. "But, it's all I've got."

21

HIGH NOON

Kate stopped and glared at a large, black raven perched on a peeling metal sign. Whatever '40 Interstate' meant, this ancient paved road seemed to align with the phantom pull. She squinted at the bird, which fluffed its feathers and met her stare with cold, unblinking eyes. It leaned into an upsurge in the wind, head low, wings hunched. Something about its presence felt like more than a simple bird watched her.

Unable to pull her gaze off the animal, she clenched her hands into fists. She hated the feeling of the breeze on her unprotected body, the texture of the paving under her feet, and that she could not be with Esteban. Images flashed across her thoughts: lifted into a hug and spun around, kissing him, being held, maybe even making love.

The bird's ebon beak parted as if it were about to squawk, but it made no sound. For a moment, the world ceased to exist save for the soft howl of the wind, and the black feathers rippling like the anger in her heart. Talons scraped aluminum; the bird's wings stretched to full length, but it didn't break its piercing stare. A strange warbling noise came from behind, chipping at the shell of rage and loathing.

Kate blinked, and the bird vanished from its perch; far off in the sky, a speck of black sailed north. The warble occurred again, morphing into a voice, behind and to the left.

"Kate?" asked Alejandra. "What's wrong? Why have you stopped?"

The urge to silence the nattering sound with fire opened her right fist and heated the air around it near to the point of combustion.

Alejandra crept into view, her face covered in perspiration. "You're frightening me."

Guilt stole the fire from her hand. *That was weird. I was so angry I didn't even know her.* "I…" She looked down. "We're close."

Memory of this woman flooded back to her, a slave she had freed. Despite the sun, the bartered-for flannel shirt remained on, and closed. Kate glanced at the bracelet, the battery meter flashed. The sense of proximity and hope grew strong, and she dialed her outfit up from a bathing suit to a plain white t-shirt, blue shorts, and sneakers.

"You have a glint in your eye." Alejandra gathered long strings of black hair away from her face. "Like you want to kill someone."

"That's because I do." Kate glanced sideways at the fluttering fabric; jealousy rose up unbidden. If she could wear it, she would have already killed the woman to steal it. "I…"

"You are not acting right."

"Not a real child. It made its body look like one to protect itself." Kate walked past the sign, not looking at it. "Not a real child. It made its body look like one to protect itself."

Alejandra seemed spooked by the repeated muttering and faded back a few paces. The air cooled as the road climbed. Kate walked for hours, conversing only with the heartbeat in her mind and the whistling wind. Her companion had become dangerous in her silence; she no longer made soft jingling noises with each step.

Kate shot Alejandra a glare that made her put a hand on the pistol. The woman's brown eyes reminded her of that first deer. Anger at her friend turned inward, and she hated herself even more. Whispered prayers behind her made her feel even worse.

"Sorry. I don't know why I'm feeling so much anger. It's not you."

Alejandra's whisper barely surpassed the faint howl in the air. "There is evil here. The raven is a bad omen. We should turn back."

"I know. It's what I've come to destroy. It knows I'm coming for it." Kate looked to her right, at a smattering of old houses abandoned on the ground between the six-lane road and more distant peaks. Her shadow stretched long over pale brown rocks and clumps of green scrub. "I'm almost free."

"Please, guard yourself." Alejandra let her arm fall away from her handgun.

Kate left the mountains behind, following the highway into the shattered outskirts of a once-massive city. To the south, in the shadow of a cluster of large, commercial-looking buildings, a primitive wall sectioned off a small region. To the southeast, the decaying skeletons of several skyscrapers clustered together. Malice flowed from them, as if the dead city watched her approach. An odd sense of kinship radiated from the ruin. The same anger flowing through her pulsed from the bones of a dead civilization. Kate grinned, though Alejandra slowed.

She climbed down over the side of the highway that had carried her most of the day to a north-south road that followed the eastern wall of the settled area. One old street sign, albeit upside down, marked it as 6th Street NW. Closer to the barricade, the charred remains of dozens of raider buggies and prewar vehicles littered the area. Wind sent whorls of dust into the air in sporadic gusts that caused several bones and a handful of skulls to shift across the pavement.

A glint at the corner of the wall brought her attention to a woman in armor, dark skinned like her friend, raising binoculars to her head, no doubt to check out the two approaching figures. Kate ignored her, but Alejandra waved.

Five blocks later, she hooked right by a sign bearing the words 'Aspen Street' and a warped bullet hole. A block west, a gate in the primitive wall stood below several armed guards. She cocked an eyebrow at their rifles—modern weapons. The last thing she'd expected to see out here. *Damn. That'll hurt.* She rubbed her chest, remembering the last time she felt a rifle bullet. Even melted, the hit had broken a rib. For a moment, she grumbled at her brain, scolding it for being willing to melt bullets but not metal claws.

I guess I'm more afraid of bullets.

Without waiting for anyone to speak, Kate slipped through the narrow gap between two enormous slabs of metal. Inside the wall, a crew to her left paused in their work to cast appraising glances at her. Their efforts looked like an attempt to connect some manner of present day machinery to the gate. Long loops of dangling chains on one end hinted at the barrier's former mode of manual operation. Modern electric motors had been installed to the crude barrier. She squinted at the marriage of high tech and apocalyptic.

What the hell is going on here?

Boots clanked down metal stairs. Kate tossed her hair with a sharp twist of her head, attracting several impolite whistles from the guards and a few phrases in Spanish that went over her head but made Alejandra blush and gasp. Already at the brim of boiling into unchecked rage, she narrowed her eyes. Only the grandfatherly smile radiating from the armored figure ambling toward her prevented a fiery death atop the wall.

Kate lowered her glare from the loudest catcaller. "I am here to see the child with glowing eyes."

The guards fell silent.

"Are ya now?" asked the older man. "You don't seem hurt."

A number of lies swirled around in her brain. Being this close to her goal muddied her thoughts; mixed with building hatred, it kept them out of reach of her tongue. If not for almost twenty armed people above and to either side, fiery murder would have been easier.

"It's not a real child," she muttered.

Alejandra crept up behind Kate, unnoticed by the guards. She remained quiet.

Kate glanced at her for an instant, further enraged by jealousy. Never in her life had she been inconspicuous, always the center of attention. Only when she had been in the wilderness as a child did she know peace, but the loneliness had been too great.

"You must've been out in the desert too long. You've stopped sweating." The old man raised a hand as if to put it around her shoulders. "Come, child. Let's get you some water."

She edged away. "You shouldn't touch me." Esteban appeared in her mind, riding a wave of sorrow that crashed into the urge to kill. "No one can."

"You're safe here, girl. I'm sorry if you was mistreated out there." He hesitated, too far away to feel her radiant heat. "No one here'll make you do anything."

Do I look that pathetic?

"Where is the girl?" Kate advanced away from the gate, trailed by the old man and two of the Watch. "I can feel its presence. It's not really a child; it's a creature from another world controlling everyone."

The old man slid his rifle from his back to his chest, hanging on a strap. Alejandra drew a sharp breath. One man took note of the red abrasions on her ankles, muttering about slavers to the man nearby.

"Where'd you two escape from?" he asked.

Kate bristled at being thought a slave. *How dare you...* She whirled with a glare. "I'm no one's property. I never have been!" *I'm a liar.* In her mind, tiny arms reached out and pounded on a clear tank. Owned by scientists... owned by El Tío...

An arc of fire spread wide in the air behind her; a manifestation of pure anger.

The town's defenders gasped.

"She helped me escape," said Alejandra. "I owe her my life."

One tiny sliver of calm broke the surface of her roiling anger. Kate spun on her heel and headed toward a field of debris. Chunks of concrete and metal fragments littered the road, forcing her to watch where she stomped.

A man closer to the gate wagged his rifle at Kate. "What was that fire?"

Alejandra spoke to the militia in the background; distance warped her pleading words into an indistinct murmur. Something about *El Diablo* having taken her. Contempt welled up within her. She didn't need Alejandra. The woman sounded scared. Useless. *Bah.* Some of the Watch followed at a distance, rifles held short of pointed at her. Street after street of repurposed buildings, former stores turned into residences, passed on both sides. Whenever someone got close enough, Kate called out, asking where the girl with glowing eyes was hiding.

Her tone chased people away, though her model's build and lack of visible weapons seemed to lull the Watch into cautious observation. *Idiots. Maybe those damn scientists got something right after all.* Memories of the lab triggered a surge of loathing that welled out from her core and rippled down her arms into wisps of azure fire.

Something or someone had to die, for no other reason than to provide release.

Kate flung her arm back, fireball hovering between claw-like fingers, ready to throw at the first creature she found capable of screaming in pain. Before she could whirl on the Watch, a startled noise came from a nearby corner. A little boy, barely six, gawked at the scintillating blue sphere.

"Kate! No!" screamed Alejandra, somewhere behind her. "What's taken your mind?"

The boy's awe turned to terror at the look in her eyes. Kate tensed and drew her arm back, ready to kill him. Before she could let go of the flames, the spike of rage collapsed without warning as though someone had yanked a rug out from under her. She recognized some familiarity in the screaming voice, but could not grasp why a woman screamed or who it was.

A huge man leapt in front of the child, who scampered out of sight. Kate stared at the point where the boy's face had been, now containing a thigh as big around as her waist. She looked up, wondering if the hulking figure was responsible for her inexplicable change in mood. Veins swelled from the largest muscles she had ever seen. His skin had the color of saddle leather, and he towered over her, pointing.

"You need to leave," he said.

The fireball dissipated with a *whiff*. No amount of staring at the man triggered anything other than confused calm, neither lust nor fear at what he might do. Alejandra skidded to a halt close behind her, almost grabbing her arm.

He looks like a cyborg turned to flesh. How did a man get that big? Kate still felt nothing when she lifted her gaze to make eye contact. "I need to see—"

"I'm here," said a tiny voice. "What do you want? Why are you scaring everyone?"

Kate let her arms fall slack and took a half step left, shifting toward the voice. A young girl, maybe eleven, stood barefoot in the middle of the street. Her knee-length white dress fluttered in a light breeze, drifting left with her long, blonde hair. Glowing blue eyes fixed Kate with a mixture of annoyance and caution.

Behind her, an older girl with dark skin like Alejandra kept a protective hand on the child's shoulder. Seven more Watch formed a line across the street. The oldest man in the center had a familial resemblance to the teen girl with her arm around the blonde child. The giant took a step closer to Kate.

"Shepherd," said the girl, raising a hand. "Wait. She will not hurt anyone."

"The Prophet," whispered Alejandra, falling to her knees.

"My name is Althea," snapped the girl, a trace of petulance on her voice. "Please, don't bow to me."

Kate squinted at the child. *She looks so innocent. That's on purpose.*

Althea's eyes narrowed; the tiny voice echoed in Kate's thoughts. *What's on purpose?*

What dwelled in the little one's surface thoughts shocked Kate. *You... think you can protect this town? I'm not here to kill anyone but you.*

The girl's stern look faltered for an instant, flashing to horror. *Me?*

Why? What did I do? She squeezed the older girl's hand. The name Karina floated to the forefront of her consciousness. Love.

Kate blinked. The girl was more upset at how her sister would feel if she died than the idea of dying. *I know what you really are.*

Althea's toes gripped the dirt path. Her eyes flickered brighter for an instant. *He lies.*

The priest said you would say that.

Demons lie all the time. Althea's eyes widened, radiating innocence.

Kate squinted at her. *Yes... they do.*

Althea's mouth hung open in shock. *You... think I'm a demon?*

For a moment, everyone stood in silence waiting for someone to make the first move. She felt like a gunslinger at high noon, waiting for the child to twitch first. The image of the plastic doll head bouncing over the road flashed by, followed by the warping face melting into a puddle. Plastic. False. Just like this child.

Blonde.

Blue eyes.

Innocent.

Althea's lip quivered as if she'd burst into tears any second. Unaware of the conversation happening in their minds, the Watch tensed. Shepherd glanced back and forth between them. Kate flashed a haughty smile; as big as he was, she guessed two fireballs would end him. Not to mention he couldn't touch her. *He waits like an attack dog.* The defenders held their rifles a hair shy of aimed at her. The one directly behind Althea had not once yet blinked.

Rather than the expected anger, Althea reacted with a sad frown. "I'm not a demon. How could you think I'm bad?" *All I've ever wanted to do was help people.*

As much as Kate tried to find her anger, an overwhelming sense of hurt and sadness took over her mind. The feeling matched the look on the little girl's face.

"You're trying to manipulate me." Kate figured she had to act fast before the demon's influence went too deep. The anger that had been knocking at her brain beckoned. Kate opened herself to it, trying not to let the idea that the little figure in front of her could be a real child gain purchase.

Althea's eyes glowed bright, and the anger dissipated.

It's too strong...

"I'm not an *it*." The child's voice came calm, soothing. "The old man lied to you. The Many knows you are angry. He feeds from it." She started forward, but Karina held her back. "He is the demon. He wants to use your anger here, to spread pain and suffering. He is afraid of me because he cannot make me evil."

Kate shivered with terror. *What's wrong with me?* She opened her mind, searching for the anger needed to overcome guilt at what she must do. For less than a second, she felt the hatred pass like a cobweb in a dark cave. It evaporated in time with the child's eyes flickering.

You're stealing my anger.

Althea dipped her head in a single nod. "I'm not stealing *your* anger. I'm protecting you from his. I won't let you hurt anyone."

Shepherd snarled. Kate glanced at him, poking into his surface thoughts. He would kill her to defend the girl, without a care for his own safety. She cocked an eyebrow. The man behind her considered himself her father, even though he clearly couldn't have been. He too teetered a hair's breadth from shooting Kate in the heart. Everyone around her seemed willing to die for the sake of this girl. Their devotion didn't feel like thralldom; all their thoughts shone clear and determined.

One final try to get angry failed. Sadness coiled around her soul, a taint of ink creeping through a white cloth. Again she felt like some *thing* outside the world looking in at everyone else. No one wanted her. She wasn't allowed to be part of society. Kate grabbed her head, unable to hold back tears. "Stop making me feel like this."

"I'm not making you feel sad." Althea's voice rang with an eerie calm. She slipped free of Karina's hand and took three steps closer. "When your anger is gone, it no longer hides your real heart. I know you are lonely and sad."

Despite a neutral expression, Althea shed tears as well.

Kate shuddered, sinking into a squat with her hands over her face. Her emotions threatened to drown her. She fought to stop crying. *Weeping is useless.* When Althea's feet crept into her vision, Kate raised her head. The girl had come close enough to touch, pity in her glowing eyes.

"The bad man is making you angry. All he wants is people to suffer. He does not like me because I keep him out of Querq."

"He offered to cure..." Kate fell backward, and landed seated on the road. "Archon said he could fix me too."

Shepherd gave Althea a disapproving look.

"Archon is lying too," said Althea. "He wants you to kill people for him." She glanced to Alejandra and beckoned her closer. "Your friend is hurt."

Kate had no willpower left to do anything but sit and sulk as Alejandra crept up on them. Althea touched the woman's hip near the burn and closed her eyes. The unnatural calm faded. Like a surge of water breaking through a disintegrating dam, a sudden inrush of anger came on. Kate's fury stalled at the sight of the days-old blistering burn shrinking away to undamaged skin. A thin layer of sweat coated the girl, and her face showed signs of exertion. Cuts and scabs around Alejandra's ankles closed and vanished, as did the bruising at her waist from the chain that had kept her in the gunnery pod.

Althea let her hand drop, taking a woozy step back. "Your power is ruled by anger. Those men in white, Archon, and the Many all want to control you."

"Archon was friendly. He said he can help me."

Deep azure eyes bored into Kate's heart. "Your hurt is in your soul. Archon only wants people who do what he says. He wants people to serve him. He is like the king of raiders, only with fancy new things."

"I..." Kate glanced around. *An entire town full of people prepared to die to protect one girl.* Jealousy overwhelmed her. Rage created a wisp of flames around her arm.

"No!" Karina screamed.

Althea made a sad face, and Kate's anger burst into a waterfall of tears.

"All I wanted was someone to care about me." Kate sniffled. "Stop making me cry!"

The child tilted her head. "Why are you so angry?"

Kate's tears wafted off as steam, but she could not stop herself from sobbing.

"You have a long time of crying to let out." Althea reached out to touch Kate's cheek, and recoiled with a yelp.

The Watch's rifles chirped in unison. Shepherd shifted his weight forward, ready to charge.

Althea held up a hand to stall them. "It is okay." The burn on her finger faded.

"That's why I'm like this." Kate stared down at the road. "Everything I touch, I kill. I can't live like this anymore."

Shepherd approached. "Archon would have used her to lure you back to the city."

Althea put her arm around him. "You're right. Kate, you should not trust him. He stole me from my home and tried to make me do bad things."

Shepherd ruffled Althea's hair as Karina ran up and stood behind her, unable to hide her reaction to a painful memory.

Kate shot a jealous glare into the road. Running boots from the side turned heads, including hers. A man and a woman rounded the corner and stopped nearby; both wore form-fitting black uniforms with silver belts—modern clothing.

Division 0? Shit. What are they *doing here?* Kate wanted to get up and run, but couldn't find the urge. Innumerable stories came back to her of what the psionic police would do to her if they ever caught her.

"Why are you afraid?" asked Althea. "They are nice."

"She is confused, child," said the man who thought himself her father. "Another lost soul in from the wilds."

Althea stooped, eye to eye with her. "Archon thought I would want to help you. I will try."

Kate lifted her head, barely able to tolerate the innocence radiating from the eyes staring at her. "I came here to kill you. Why would you want to help me?"

"But, you didn't hurt me." The girl winked, and smiled. "I forgive you."

22

THE ANGER INSIDE

K ate gazed at the cloudless sky. Seated in the shade of a modest two-story home, she listened to the whisper of the breeze, but could not feel it past her aura of heat. A narrow alley ran between two rows of buildings, populated by a handful of curious townies, and a number of Watch. Numerous toys lay abandoned here and there, the children cleared away by wary parents moments before.

Althea knelt nearby, sitting back on her heels while Karina and the man called Shepherd retrieved water from an old-fashioned pump a few houses away. Kate wondered why the 'older sister' had protested Althea going to the pump alone.

"I don't know if I will be able to help." Althea wiped her hands on her dress. "Do you know why you're burning?"

"I've always been like this." It felt like she admitted to the worst crime imaginable.

"It's why you eat so much." Althea grinned. "I eat a lot sometimes too, when there are many hurts to fix."

"How hot is she?" asked Karina, setting down a mostly full bucket of water.

"I'm not sure exactly how hot I am, but wood and cloth ignite right away." She touched a fingertip to the porch step, causing a tendril of smoke to bear the stink of molten paint into the air.

Althea tilted her head. "But, you're—"

"Holograms."

"I'm sorry," whispered Althea.

"What for?" Kate blushed.

"Making you sadder." The girl shivered.

"Why are you shaking?" Kate looked at the man who thought himself the child's father, trying to seem non-threatening. The hardness in his glare told Kate he'd seen the fear in Althea. "I believe you. You're not a demon." *If she stops concentrating on me, will the anger come back?*

Althea made eye contact, speaking in a hushed tone. "I'm scared because I have to touch you, and I know it will hurt." *He will try.*

An impish smile curled the child's lips at Kate's reaction to having her thoughts eavesdropped.

She accepted a metal cup of water from Shepherd, sucking it down before it could boil in her hand. "The anger is trying to sneak in."

"I know." Althea took a breath and reached for her with both hands.

"Wait." Kate leaned away. "I'm not hot when I'm unconscious."

Shepherd flipped the metal ladle over, giving the bowl end—and the back of her head—an appraising look.

"No," said Althea, frowning at Shepherd.

He shrugged.

"I can make you sleep." Althea kept reaching with one hand, aiming for Kate's head instead of her shoulder. "But I still have to touch you."

"Hold on," said a dark-skinned man in a Division 0 uniform.

Kate stroked the heat-resistant bracelet, grateful for its phantom apparel as a Middle Eastern looking officer jogged out of the crowd. Once he got close enough to speak without raising his voice, he pointed to his right and looked at Althea.

"You don't have to hurt yourself. There are sedatives in the medkits."

Kate gave him a distrustful squint. "This is still the Badlands, right? What's Division 0 doing here?"

He smiled at her. She looked away.

"You should keep the magic sticks for when I am too tired." Althea's eyes flared bright and she grabbed the side of Kate's head.

The word "sleep," spoken in Althea's voice, echoed in Kate's mind, drowning out the sound of sizzling skin by her left ear. All the curious faces swirled into a blur of blue, streaked with the colors of the buildings across the street. A little girl's voice shrieked in pain as if a thousand yards away.

Quiet blackness enveloped her. Neither feeling nor sight provided any sense of being. She startled at a distant peal of thunder, rolling over the endless dark. A flash of pink-purple lightning flickered in the shape of a dendrite cluster far ahead, followed a minute later by another heavy crash. More flares lit the dark in an escalating storm. Soon, the world burst with every color imaginable. Distinct snaps of light gave way to a constant shimmering glow. Thick, biological masses surrounded her on all sides, intertwined with an uncountable number of narrow tendrils, each glowing a different hue. With each change in the shimmer came an inescapable, growing roar. Soon, the rumbling felt as though it would crush her.

A chill similar to sudden immersion in icy water seared her nerves, but she couldn't scream. No sense of inhabiting flesh reached her mind; she had become a disembodied consciousness floating amid an alien landscape. Voices bellowed from random directions: yelling scientists, screaming soldiers, and the taunts of the first gangers to find her naked in an alley—followed by their dying wails.

Scraps of El Tío's grandfatherly tone brought warmth. The man did ask her to kill for him, but he had always been protective in a hands-off way. Ignoring the guilt that came with the jobs he gave her to do came easy. Everyone else hated and feared her. She considered it no great task to kill rivals, cheats, and disavowed Syndicate men. Sondra had been the hardest; she'd only stolen money.

The sound of a woman begging for her life filled the air.

She had a son. I could have let her slip away. Kate's instinctual urge to caress the bracelet caused a crackling burst of electricity in the distance, but no motion or feeling. *I can't betray El Tío. He loved me?*

"Does he?" whispered a voice. Esteban floated out of the kaleidoscope of chaos, lip still swollen from a burn. "I'm worried about you, Kate."

Thin strands of lightning leapt across the gaps between the massive dendrites as her brain sent off signals to smile. The chill worsened until she wanted to scream. The giant nerve clusters glowed, brighter and brighter, bleaching her world to a glare of pure white. Pain swam up and down her body, scraps of heat mixed with ice.

"Sleep," whispered an echoey Althea.

Darkness.

Moments of silence preceded warmth, and everything went still.

23

NEW LIFE

Specks of dust floated within a shaft of sunlight before her eyes. The endless whorl of particles mesmerized her for several minutes before it occurred to her she was awake. It took another few to recognize the blurry whitish haze along the right side of her vision as a pillow. Cloth surrounded her everywhere, a bed and blankets.

Kate screamed, sitting up and swatting at the bedclothes until she stumbled, naked, to her feet. The panicked motion left her out of breath and dizzy, swooning on weak legs. She took a step back from the bed as if afraid of being near it. Alejandra's soft moan from behind made her spin. The woman shifted in her sleep, content to rest.

She moved in a slow turn, surveying a small room with two narrow beds, two doors, and a long cabinet of drawers bearing a broken flat panel display. Of the two exits, one looked metal and had a deadbolt, chain, and bar lock. To the left of that door, in a chair, napped a woman in grey-on-grey camouflage and a dull blue armored vest. The other seemed like a bathroom. Pale blue wallpaper peeled away in sheets, patched by haphazard spots of paint, plaster, or nailed boards. Soft warmth surrounded her feet. Frazzled blue strands threaded between her toes from a shaggy throw rug. A rug she stood on—and didn't burn.

The guard leapt out of her chair, fumbling to bring a rifle to bear. Kate backed into the nightstand, raising her hands. At the feeling of a cold surface on her ass, she went wide-eyed and gasped.

"Easy," whispered Kate, as her face reddened.

"*¿Qué es lo que te pasa?*" blurted the woman, fighting the urge to shiver.

"Nothing's wrong with me. I didn't want to start a fire."

"D-don't try anything." The woman kept the rifle not quite aimed at her.

Kate poked into the woman's surface thoughts. She was more embarrassed at seeing her naked than Kate felt at being naked, not to mention terrified of her. A deeper mental poke discovered the woman got stuck here on guard duty because Althea protested them using any form of restraints on her. Rather than a jail cell or chains, The Watch had kept her under guard for…

"Two days?" Kate looked at the rug again. No smoke, no charred footprints. "I know you're scared." *Two days… Did I go out like a candle? Why am I not starving? Can I still stop bullets?* "Look…" She raised one hand. "I'm not going to hurt you. Please don't shoot me."

The woman barely moved; the rifle's muzzle drifted up and down with each breath. Kate risked finger contact with the bed. No fire. Whole hand. Still no fire. Overcome by desire, she dove into the bedding and rolled herself into a cloth burrito. Only a sliver of skin around her eyes peeked out into the world.

Her sudden motion sent the guard stumbling into the wall, weapon shaking.

"I'm…" Kate burst into tears, snuggling into the fabric embrace.

"*Está despierta!*" whispered the woman, repeatedly, into a small black node in her collar.

Kate ignored her, lost in the squirming revelry of being in contact with something other than metal, dirt, or stone. Like a cat claiming its territory, she writhed and rubbed herself into the material for several minutes.

"What are you doing?" said Alejandra, sitting up.

Kate froze, staring out of a gap in the sheets at the strange yellow handmade dress her friend wore. Alejandra broke up laughing. Kate grinned at what she must have looked like, two eyes out from the dark.

"I'm not burning!"

"My God!" blurted Alejandra, scrambling over. "I wasn't sure if you would ever wake."

"What happened?" Kate clung to the blankets, not caring if she grew over-warm.

"The Prop—Althea, touched you and her hand burned. You went to sleep. She mended herself. Then, she knelt over you and put her hands on your head." Alejandra sat on the edge of Kate's bed. "For a long time, nothing happened but the child making strange faces and grunting. All of a sudden, she made the most awful noises. Her hands burned again, but so did you. You got all red and blistered."

Kate shivered. "I don't remember..."

"That huge man almost pulled her away when she screamed, but your skin grew back. The girl was crying from the pain, her hands were..." Alejandra cringed. "She is fine now. They gave her food and she restored herself again after they took you to rest."

"I can't believe it." Kate sat up, letting only her head out of the blanket roll.

"*Baja eso!*" Alejandra waved her hand in a downward gesture at the guard.

The woman backed into the wall, letting the rifle droop a little.

Alejandra gathered Kate in an embrace of surprising strength. A hand at the back of her head pulled her close. She cried at the feeling of fingers in her hair. After a momentary squirm, she gave up trying to fight the blanket, which had become too tight to get her arms out. Her friend held her like a swaddled infant until the sounds of boots outside made them both look at the door. The guard in the room seemed ready to faint at the first loud noise.

"I need real clothes." Kate sniffled, before erupting with sobbing laughs. "I... I can wear clothes!"

"Yes." Alejandra went over to the long cabinet and pulled open a drawer. "They left some for you."

Piece by piece, Alejandra stuffed garments into the blankets: panties, socks, a plain white tank top and blue pants. Kate wriggled into each item in turn, savoring every second of the feeling. She even took the long-sleeved dark shirt and put it on while hiding under blankets.

"You're going to overheat like that." Alejandra pulled on the blanket.

Kate fought to stay under it. "No. I like it here."

"You're acting like a child," said Alejandra, as she won the tug of war with one final yank.

A knock at the door preceded the guardswoman opening it. Kate sat up, clutching fistfuls of linen. Althea, still in a plain white dress, slipped in. She seemed tired, as though recently roused from a deep nap. The man she thought of as Father entered behind her, rifle across his back. Several more Watch waited outside, while the woman that had guarded her for the night took the opportunity to duck out. A brief glimpse out the swinging door gave the impression they were in a motel.

"Thank you." Kate thought back to the Roadway Corporation building and her thin separation from the prisoners. "You were wrong; I'm not a nice person." She pulled her outer shirt closed in a self-hug, staring down.

Althea's bare feet stepped between her white socks. Kate tensed. Gripped by the sudden dread her power may be gone, she feared the wrath of a jumpy enforcer.

The girl leaned forward and hugged her, whispering into her ear. "Doing bad is a choice. You do not need to be angry anymore."

Slow arms lifted to return the embrace; all the while, Kate studied Father's response. He seemed guarded and confused, but more tolerant. His surface thoughts still opened to her prodding; the man did not have much trust in the child's stories of an evil presence in the land.

"You had a lot of little hurts." Althea leaned back and put a hand on Kate's cheek. Her glowing eyes closed, and a tingle flowed through Kate from face to foot. After a moment, the girl smiled at her. "I cannot find any sick."

"What did you do?" Kate rubbed her hand up and down *real* sleeves.

Althea bit her lower lip. "Your thinking shape was like a person running real fast on a puddle of oil. Working hard but not going anywhere." She held her arms up and let them fall against her sides. "I told it to walk."

"Umm." Kate fidgeted. "I don't know what to say. Thank you just doesn't seem enough. You hurt yourself."

Althea shrugged. "You needed help."

Kate squeezed her tight, sniffling. Guilt and joy warred in her heart.

"I know how much pain you had." Althea looked with a somber expression at the floor. "I am glad I could help you."

The child's eyes fluttered, and she started to faint. Kate held on, guiding her to the edge of the bed. Althea recovered a moment later and grasped the mattress.

Father rushed over, taking the girl's other hand. "You should still be resting." Althea remained quiet as he picked her up. "What she did for you made her very tired."

"I'm sorry."

He shook his head. "She must have seen some good in you, or she would not have helped. I'm not sure I trust you not to be a danger."

"Not her," whispered Althea. "The Many."

Kate fell to sit on the bed. "I believe her. There is something evil out there. He showed himself to me. Your daughter"—Althea grinned wide as she said that word—"has done for me what I never imagined possible." She looked him in the eye. "I've never had reason to want to protect anyone other than myself." Again, she cringed away from the girl's innocent face. "I let his lies consume me."

"She has forgiven you," said Father. Althea rested her head against his chest, ready to sleep. "It may take the rest of us more time. What will you do now? Back to your fancy city, or do you wish to petition the Council to stay?"

"Yeah right," mumbled one of the men outside on the stoop.

"I have spoken with some of the strange people," said Alejandra. "I would like to live in this great city where life is comfortable and safe."

"The metal city is bad," muttered Althea. "Everyone is mean and likes to hurt each other." The child shifted, clinging to Father.

A wave of fear spread over the room, leaving Kate feeling like a six-year-old after a scary dream. From the look on Alejandra's face, the effect had hit her the same way. Rifles chirped to life outside the door as the Watch spun around in search of a threat.

Althea drifted off to sleep, and the strange fear faded.

"Perhaps I should stay here," whispered Alejandra. "The spirits suggest it."

Father lowered his powerful voice a notch. "Querq is strong and safe, and we have the support of the Zero police."

Alejandra smiled at him. He held eye contact with her for a moment.

The low-battery chirp from the bracelet reminded her of El Tío. *He treated me okay, but I had to kill for him.* Tiny slits of blue light where Althea's eyes almost closed flashed with a blink. *If I return to the city, he'll ask me to do it again. If they learn I'm fixed, they'll make me an assassin too. This is caveman land, but...* "Umm." *These people seem happy.* "I'm not accustomed to life out here, but I'd like to stay for a while. At least until I've repaid some bit of this favor."

Father nodded. "Then I will speak to the Council." Althea mumbled to him in a half-awake stupor. "She trusts you, but the Watch remain wary."

"I'd watch me too." Kate chuckled. "I need to make a short trip before I settle in. I have to see Esteban."

"The Zero man, Ahmed, has asked us to make sure you speak to him."

Shit. Kate grimaced. "Did he say why?"

Father moved for the door. "Something about not getting your name."

24

TEMPTATION IN BLACK

Kate leaned on the doorframe by the tiny bathroom, frowning at the dry, useless toilet. The bathtub didn't look as if it had seen water in a decade; cobwebs linked two metal pails to the coral-hued fiberglass. She approached a grimy mirror over the sink, unsure why she felt surprised at seeing no dramatic change in her appearance. Doubt gripped her, and she closed the door.

As if afraid to damage any piece, Kate removed her clothes and placed each one on the cleanest spot she could find near the old sink. She set her feet shoulder-width apart on the dingy throw rug, flexing and releasing her toes with nervous anticipation.

"Now or never…"

One arm raised, she concentrated. An azure fireball puffed into existence, many times brighter than the weak light creeping in from the tiny frosted glass window over the tub. It hissed and fluttered, ripples of fire swam around the orb her mind had created. Kate watched the rug around her feet.

No smoke.

She let the fireball dissipate, and made another. Still, the rug showed no sign of damage. Kate 'grasped' the top of the fireball with her left hand and stretched it into a serpent of flame, which coiled around her.

"A-Alejandra?" she asked, surprised at how timid her voice sounded.

"Yes?" A muffled voice through the door.

"Am I awake?"

The woman pushed the door aside and gawked at the streamer of blue flames. She barely registered Kate's lack of clothes.

"What are you doing?"

"Testing," said Kate. "Can you touch me?"

She concentrated on keeping the fire away from the flaking plaster ceiling and the molded shower curtain, turning her back to Alejandra.

After a moment's hesitation, a tentative fingertip poked her shoulder blade, followed by four more, and a full palm.

"You are sweating," said Alejandra. "But so am I. It is stuffy in here." The hand departed, followed soon by the soft *click* of a closing door. "Put something on."

"I was afraid they'd burn." She let the flames dissipate.

Kate burst into laughing sobs and scrambled to dress without falling headfirst into the toilet. She lost another minute reveling in the feeling of fabric touching her skin. After a long stare at herself in the mirror, she held up a tiny fireball. The low-intensity orange lit her face like a scary campfire story. More energy turned it blue and heated it. Her clothing didn't smoke or smolder.

Alejandra had no chance to react when Kate rushed from the bathroom and tackled her into a hug on the bed. Once the initial shock wore off, she reversed it, overpowering Kate with ease and pinning her down.

"What is wrong with you?"

"She did it! She cured the curse." Kate sat up. "I am afraid I'll wake up and find it's all a dream."

"I am awake," said Alejandra. "Which means you are too."

KATE HELD HER UNWORN SOCKS AS SHE WALKED, TRYING TO STEP WITHIN patches of sunlight. Enamored with the sensation of the ground feeling warm, she ran into Shepherd from behind. The impact brought her back to the present; two Division 0 hovercars sat amid the primitivism in the intersection-turned-square.

He dragged a large metal case from the back end of a truck, balancing it over one shoulder. "You okay?"

The sight of him triggered an instinctual prey response; his silhouette brought forth a bad memory of an aug ganger—one time she was grateful to be untouchable.

Shepherd waved a hand past her eyes. "Still nuts?"

"I'm..." An absence of hostility in his expression calmed her. "I'm supposed to talk to one of the zeroes."

He twisted and walked to his left. "Down this way."

Kate ducked the cargo box, not that she had to. His shoulder was over her head.

"They brought in a drop building for an office." He looked down at her. "Please don't look at me like that."

"Sorry. Bad memory of an aug. That, and you wanted to twist my head off a few days ago. The kid thinks I was under the influence of some kind of evil force."

"Maybe. You wouldn't be the first person who started off wanting to hurt her."

"I can't even think of how I was so close before. She's so sweet." Kate blinked. "Wait... what? You?"

Shepherd stopped by a stack of similar boxes, lowering the container in place among them. After clapping his hands clear of dust, he gestured at a side street and resumed walking. "I don't remember all that much to be honest. Mercenary work... Might've been Syndicate. I had a lot of metal. Both arms, headware, strength boosters, at least one eye." He held his hands out like claws. "Reapers too. Nine-inch blades in every finger. Somehow, I wound up with this psycho organ harvester. As best I can remember, I'd gone insane myself... too far from human."

"So how did you run into her?"

"I don't have a lot of those memories left." Shepherd rubbed his forehead. "I think I was his bodyguard, and somehow Althea wound up inside the place we lived. In the state I was then, I saw an intruder and had to destroy it. I didn't know or care she was just a little kid—all I saw was a person that didn't belong there."

Kate gulped, following him through a left turn. "How did..."

"The only memory I have of that night is the face she made." A tear formed in his eye, glistening in the sun as it slid down his cheek. "Such terror in those eyes. In that moment, all my pain and rage twisted into this uncontrolled *need* to protect her, more than my own life."

"She took my anger away too."

Shepherd pointed at a silver box on spring-loaded legs. It resembled an enormous carton that delivery food might come in, only with a door instead of a pull-tab. "The Zeroes think she left a telempathic imprint that programmed me." He chuckled. "Probably true at first, but not now."

Kate put a hand on his arm, a bicep of almost inhuman proportion. "These don't feel metal." She looked down. "Sorry, I don't mean to pry. I'm so confused. I can't believe she actually fixed me."

"She fixed me too." He pointed at the portable structure and winked. "Zeroes are in there."

She remained silent as he jogged away, back to his work detail. Esteban was nowhere near that huge. The memory of the grin in his eyes made her smile. Happiness fell away to dread when she looked at the door. Division 0, the psionic police, the people El Tío were convinced would want to 'put her down like a dog.'

Aurora told her she was Awakened; something they had never heard of and had no preparation for dealing with. Her confidence rushed back. They had hovercars, maybe she could ask them for a ride to get Esteban and bring him here.

Wait, no... He's technically an escaped con. I can't ask the police for a ride.

The door squeaked open, letting her into a modest-sized room with a few desks and holo-terminals. A momentary sense that she wandered amid a dream came on. This place looked as though she had walked into a portal leading from 'primitive world' to real life. Air-conditioning rendered the plastisteel floor frigid. She scrambled to the nearest desk and leapt up to sit on the edge. After brushing dirt from her sole, she started to put a sock on, pausing as a man in black approached.

His uniform clung, hinting at every contour in his chest. No one could accuse him of being a bodybuilder; he didn't even have Esteban's size, but his toned, athletic frame held her attention long enough to create guilt. She tried to look him in the eye, but found herself studying the lines of his jaw. His nose was prominent but not overbearing, a compliment to dense black eyebrows and a neat mass of thick hair. He looked like the kind of man who might appear in holo-adverts for Egyptian tourism.

"I was hoping to see you soon." He smiled. "I'm Officer Ahmed, but you can call me Dave."

She left her sock half on and shook his offered hand. "Kate."

"Something wrong with your socks?" He smiled.

"No one gave me shoes. I didn't want to ruin them walking on dirt and crap. It's so cold in here." She pulled it the rest of the way on and crossed her legs the other way before dusting off her left foot. A weak tremor ran through her brain. "I've never felt cold before. Are you doing something to me?"

"Sorry. Lieutenant Franck hates how hot it gets out here." He gestured to a small doorway. "I'm just reading your emotional state. After the way you blew into town, I"—he chuckled—"was not expecting you to be happy."

After tugging the second sock on, she walked where indicated, into a small interview-style room. A plain silver table had a chair on each side and a loop ring for handcuffs by one of the chairs.

"Don't be concerned." He slid around her. "You're not being detained. Walking into town planning to kill someone is a far cry from actually inflicting harm. We haven't quite become the 'thought police' yet."

She stood stiff as a board in the doorway until he sat. Her fear diminished—too fast. She narrowed her eyes.

"No, that's not exactly ethical, but I don't want to waste more of your time than procedure requires."

Kate lowered herself into the chair, leaning as far away from the eyebolt as it allowed. "So this isn't personal?"

"I wanted to be the one to interview you," he said. "It's not what you are probably thinking. I was intrigued by the emotions going through your mind the other day. I got the feeling you were in need of a sympathetic ear." He fell silent until she looked up at him. "This is an initial assessment interview. Anything you say here stays within Division 0. You are a pyrokinetic, and you have raised some questions."

"What happens if I don't want to answer them?"

Officer Ahmed flashed a 'trust me' smile. "People like us are in an awkward place in society. While the majority of psionics want only to live their lives in peace, a few who use their gifts for criminal purposes make us all look dangerous. Our goal is to protect psionics from the wrath of public opinion as much as we protect the public from the individuals who get out of hand."

Kate shivered, gathering her arms tight around herself. "What are you saying?"

"Want me to turn the A/C down?" Ahmed shifted as if to stand.

"No... I like shivering my ass off."

He stood.

"I'm serious. I've never felt cold before. You can leave it."

"Never?" He eased himself down.

Kate looked into her lap. "Are you making me trust you?"

"No, but I can if you want me to." He winked.

She found his stare boyish at the same time unsettling. "How much did Althea tell you?"

"Almost nothing. The girl's been unconscious as long as you have. Whatever she did to you took a lot out of her." Officer Ahmed fiddled with a screen embedded in a gloss black forearm guard. "Our sensors did register your skin temperature varying from six to seven hundred degrees. Hold up your foot, please." After a momentary confused look, she raised her leg and let her heel *thunk* onto the table. Ahmed held his forearm out, still watching the screen. "Okay, that's good."

Kate lowered her foot. "What was that?"

"Your body temp is a little under normal. That's likely the air set to Antarctic."

Two Officer David Ahmeds stared at her, one real and one a near-perfect reflection in the table's surface. Being an object for men to gawk at was not a new feeling; having him look at her came hand in hand with the painful awareness she could be touched now. She closed her eyes and thought of how Esteban smelled. Ahmed didn't leer, but his gaze felt uncomfortable nonetheless.

"So, tell me about yourself," he said.

"You'll shoot me in the head if I'm honest, and you'll know if I'm lying."

"Are you a serial killer?"

Kate laughed, a little too coldly for his visible comfort. "Not quite. I have killed, but I don't get a thrill out of it. Most of the targets were other criminals."

"Vigilante?" He cocked an eyebrow.

"No... I got involved with the Syndicate. I was like fifteen living on the street and he gave me a place to stay. It started with 'I need you to do me a favor, Kate.'"

"I see." He fiddled with a datapad. "Why don't you start back a bit farther?"

"I don't even know if I had parents. My earliest memories are of being inside a tank of goo in a lab. They let me out now and then for tests and experiments. How hot can I make this box, can I ignite this or that. They couldn't find a way to turn off my constant heat, so they tried to kill me when I was seven." Kate recounted her escape, and subsequent years living like a wood nymph. "I guess I was like fifteen or so when I got tired of being alone. I saw a big metal bird—I didn't know what a shuttle was then—go overhead and followed the direction it had gone until I found the city."

"East City?" he said, recording notes via a holo-panel.

"No, the other huge city on the east coast." She smirked.

"Just clarifying it wasn't one of the settlements in the Scattered Lands."

"I was already in the Scattered Lands. That's where Laughlin-Reed had their lab... but I avoided people whenever I saw them, which wasn't often." Kate shifted, crossing her legs the other way. "I wandered into the city. Some people tried to help me, but they ran off screaming when they burned themselves. I was ashamed and ran until I was alone again in an alley somewhere."

He offered a sympathetic look.

She recounted her experiences with street gangs, and her none-too-gradual change from innocent nature child to nocturnal scavenger. "I got attacked every couple of days at first. I don't remember how many I killed. Most survived though, maimed. Eventually word got around and they left me alone."

"How long did you spend in the disavowed sector? What did you eat?"

"Rats, trash, whatever I could steal from CyberBurger." She explained her encounter with the manager, and El Tío. "He had someone make me this bracelet that projected holographic clothes. I could go out in public without causing a scene. El Tío treated me well, and I'm not going to betray him now. All I'm going to tell you about that is I had to work for him."

"I can imagine," said Ahmed. "No one would see you coming. How many were there?"

"A few dozen." She looked at the face he made. "You're concerned that I don't feel anything?"

"I am."

"It was a job. They were all dirty in one way or the other. Every one of them lied, cheated, stole, or killed. No one was innocent. Except that deer."

Ahmed winced. "You feel more remorse over an animal you hunted, but nothing for contracts on human lives?"

"The deer never tried to hurt me."

"Neither did Althea." At the spike of guilt, he drew a breath. "Sorry, that just came out. I'm curious."

"The only thing I've ever really wanted was to become part of the world. I lived my whole life at arms' length. I was going west to find a man called Archon, who said he could fix me."

"Who is this Archon?"

"Some kind of doctor with a funny accent. I haven't met him yet, only a holo call." She shivered, cupping her hands over her mouth and exhaling warm air into her fingers. "He thinks I'm some kind of special psionic that's more powerful than normal. He's in the west, so I tried to get there. This old man dressed like a priest came out of nowhere in the middle of the night. Something about him scared the shit out of me just from looking at him. At first, I tried to kill him, but he wouldn't burn. He told me there was a demon, an abomination, who had disguised itself as a child. Whatever he was, he wanted me to destroy it to save these people. The closer I got to this place, the angrier I became. I don't really remember the last two hours or so before I wound up kneeling in the middle of the street bawling my eyes out."

"Given the life you've led so far, Kate, I can understand how you would be angry. It's a dangerous thing to hide your loneliness under. Any empath could make it spill over and turn you dangerous. The old man might've been 'The One.'"

"The one?" Kate blinked. "What one?"

"He's a cult leader. Has a 'church' hidden somewhere out here in the Badlands. Psionic suggestive."

"Human?"

Officer Ahmed nodded.

"It wasn't him. If he was human, he'd be dead."

"You're so sure? Perhaps your entire meeting with him was a dream or hallucinatory experience."

"No, I'm sure. I just don't know what to believe. He said the girl was a demon disguised." Kate looked down. "Althea's not a demon. She—"

The door opened. A petite woman in Division 0 blacks walked in, dropped a pair of boots on the table, and left without a word.

"Be my guest." Ahmed gestured.

With the eagerness of a child on her birthday, Kate grabbed them, shoved her feet in, and secured the four plastic fasteners down the side of each one.

"I trust they fit," he said.

"You measured my foot." She shifted her leg side to side, appraising the boots. "Sneaky."

"Call it a deposit on your uniform. They're standard issue... The locals don't have much in the way of footwear aside from moccasins made of prairie dogs, or whatever the heck those things are." He extended the datapad to her, pointing at an open square at the bottom of a blue screen with lighter blue text that looked like a list of clothing items and other random equipment. "Would you mind giving a thumbprint?"

"My uniform?" Her knuckles whitened on the chair. "Whoa... hold on. After what I just said about the Syndicate, you're trying to recruit me? What's the thumbprint for?"

"Just proof you were really here and we really had this interview. A procedural thing." He smiled in a way that made her trust him.

She'd seen a lot of men smile while working for El Tío. None had ever seemed so genuine. She reached over and pressed her thumb to the glass, holding it as a thin green line swept up and down. A digital ghost of her fingerprint remained after she pulled back.

Ahmed leaned back and tapped a few more buttons on the datapad. "In the interest of public safety, and public opinion, Division 0 takes certain liberties. Of course, there will need to be a psychiatric evaluation and possibly a telepath verifying your story, but yes, we would love to have you. Naturally, if you are sworn in, you would no longer be able to 'work' for El Tío."

"I'm not sure that's going to be possible." Kate studied her new boots, unable to look at him. *What am I, in heat or something?* "What about the corporation that ran the lab? *They* are after me."

"What makes you believe you are hunted? Have you seen them since?"

This time, her shiver didn't come from the temperature. "The man outside the lab where they made me... the way he looked at me."

"Kate. Look at me. Your fear felt like a child having a nightmare; I think you may be overreacting to an early trauma. Let me see him." Ahmed reached across the table and held her hand.

Her initial instinct to pull back gave way to an eager grip. Still trembling, she lifted her gaze and thought back to the man on the porch. Sensation spread around her brain, as if the hands of a ghost caressed it.

"Agent Perrin?" Ahmed lifted an eyebrow. He went wide-eyed at her memory of the orange flash. Recalling the lot full of injured soldiers led to a more recent eruption of the same fury—the house full of nibblers. "How..."

"I don't really understand how I did that." She clasped her hands at her mouth and exhaled warm air over her fingers. "Both times I was scared shitless and certain I was about to die."

"I'll post a memo that no one should play startle pranks on you." He couldn't quite bring himself to smile.

"The first time I killed someone, I was seven." Kate frowned at her reflection on the table. "I didn't think about wanting to boil the blood inside his body. It just happened. I hated him. I wanted him to go away." Her gaze flicked up to Ahmed. "He was going to kill me. I was a little kid. A... project that didn't work out."

He squeezed her hand. "I wish I could say I'd never heard stories like that before. Some of the kids in the dorm had their own parents try to kill them. Others were abandoned as young as five once their abilities manifested."

"Are we all freaks?" Kate looked away. Aurora's talk of Awakened made her feel like an outcast even among the unwanted.

"Not all." He kept quiet for a moment. "Some of us have good families and joined Division 0 because we wanted to help others like us. The man you are afraid of looks like C-Branch. If he is, you are right to be concerned."

She tried to pull away, but he didn't let go. "That sounds ominous."

"Military intelligence. I'd say they have a strange relationship with the law, but so do we."

"They told me my genetics were based on a Russian girl named Myshkin, but I'm not an exact clone. The scientists were trying to make me stronger."

Ahmed ran his thumb over the back of her hand. "I feel your confusion turning to sadness. Don't feel alone—you're not. We can protect you, even from C-Branch. If you're on our roster, they can't touch you. I am not sure exactly how that arrangement came to be. That sort of thing is way above my pay grade. You could have a future with Division 0. A real life. A purpose. You can make up for what you did with the Syndicate. That life could be left behind."

"There's a man I have feelings for..." Kate relayed the story of the caravan. "He's got some legal problems, but he didn't try to escape. Bernie was going to murder them all out of panic."

He ran a finger over his lips, thinking. His face seemed too stoic. "It's reassuring that this Esteban fellow accepted your gift. Non-psionics so often condemn us."

"Althea's father seemed to want me to stay in Querq for a while. I think I owe it to them for what she did for me. Can I bring Esteban here?

You won't try to arrest him, will you? If I agree to join, can you do something for his record?"

He let go of her hand. "I'm just a tactical officer. I can't speak for the captain, but I can ask. Do you know what his crime was?"

Kate leaned back. "Something about using stolen parts for repair work on hovercars."

"Oh," said Ahmed. "Nothing violent. We can probably work with that."

"So, what happens now?"

"Well, at some point we'll need to bring you to the city so we can properly assess your abilities. Depending on how that goes, it's possible you could request a post out here. We're fortifying Querq to protect Althea, mostly against corporate aggression."

"Did you try to recruit her too?"

Ahmed laughed. "Yes, we did, but she wasn't interested. She agreed to an assessment and to help us if we asked in exchange for providing material assistance to Querq."

"So she joined but didn't join."

"That's one way to put it." Ahmed got up and offered his hand again. "Are you hungry?"

"Now that you mention it." Kate scratched at her stomach. "It *has* been two days."

25

BLAZING DESTINY

E ndless smears of white paint pulsed on the road, devoured by the front of an electric motorcycle. The faint sound of the in-wheel motors faded under the rush of wind in Kate's hair. Less than fifteen minutes out of Querq, she shot past the culvert where she and Alejandra slept after the nibbler attack. She slowed, looking left at the blast radius. No sign of activity caught her eye. Either she'd burned them all, or any survivors had gone elsewhere. A shiver ran down her spine as the memory of that night came back. She turned away, wanting to leave that particular patch of desert nothingness behind.

Momentary hesitation paralyzed her as she forgot how to speed up. In a few seconds, she remembered a twist of the right hand would do it. She thought of Officer Ahmed and the previous day spent learning to drive. When she had asked for a ride, he had gone to great lengths to explain why he couldn't fly her east without sounding disinterested. He had said something about off-the-leash AI combat-bots running around the northern central region with missiles and a bad temper. The government had sent them into the Badlands to clean up all the mutants decades ago, but they rebelled and built an old city once called Detroit into a deadly war machine.

At first, she thought he didn't want her to leave. Before she could challenge him on it, citing the disappointed look in his eyes, he came up with the small, black bike. Division 0 had sent a handful of them to Querq

· for use by the officers when a car proved impractical or dangerous. When one last urgent stare failed to convince her not to go, he'd offered her a pistol and a backpack with rations and water. She grinned remembering the look on his face when she pointed out how much faster she would return if they took one of the patrol craft.

Esteban would've fainted if a hovercar with police lights landed in St. Louis.

She thumbed the rubberized grip, daydreaming about how it felt to have Ahmed behind her, arms around her waist, talking her through how to ride. Her whimsical mood turned maudlin. One didn't have to be an empath to sense him having more than a basic interest in her; though, had he? Or had twenty-five years of being unable to touch *anyone* made her see things that didn't exist? It had to be that… or just the way men tripped all over themselves to be nice to a woman like her. A woman so beautiful no man would believe she'd even talk to them. Kate grumbled at the scientists who made her 'too perfect.'

Alone, the bike's handling was more responsive, and the first half hour had been nerve-wracking. Any slight movement translated in big ways to the bike. Eventually, trepidation gave way to adrenaline, and she sped up even more.

For a while, she forgot about how excited she felt at the thought of having Esteban touch her and wallowed in the glory of being able to operate a vehicle. She felt like a kid with a new toy, even playing with the emergency lights and siren. Since the bikes were sent into the middle of nowhere, someone had the foresight to pre-load the Navcon with old maps of the interior. While it couldn't anticipate the current conditions of the roads, it did plot a course east along a highway named 40. The route line branched northeast to another road labeled 44. As far as the computer knew, it had chosen the most efficient way there—whether or not the roads it wanted her to take still existed. Not to mention, she had no way to know what waited in any of the old cities.

The system estimated about nine hours if she held her current 120 mph. Kate blinked, surprised that she'd gotten to that speed without noticing. Her body locked up with panic at what a single inopportune hole could do. Ahmed's voice in her head yelled not to hit the front brake first. She made that mistake once. Without his weight behind her, she'd flip if she repeated it. A gentle squeeze at the brake lever caused the number to drop. Cruising at eighty felt like a standstill, but dead girls couldn't have boyfriends.

Shattered countryside blurred by for hours, interrupted by the occasional strange sight. An abandoned trailer, crashed and burned vehicles, a ceremonially stacked pile of skeletons, and a pyramid of blue chemical barrels were the most memorable. An hour past noon, two bears chased her for a short while, but lost interest when she left them in the dust. The shadowy presence of a dead city loomed up ahead, the point where the Navcon indicated she needed to find road 44. Unsettled by the appearance of it, as well as an eerie feeling something was wrong, Kate decided to slow to about fifteen mph and take the bike off the highway. The iron skeletons of ancient buildings ahead held too many places to hide, too many shadows, and radiated an inexplicable sense of hostility. With only an hour or two before nightfall, she wanted to be as far away from the abandoned metropolis as she could manage by the time the sun went down.

Eventually, with the help of the Navcon and a few lucky guesses, she found an on-ramp labeled 44 and got back on course. Travel slowed due to car-sized fragments of paved earth tossed about like broken dice. She walked the bike past the worst of it, getting back up to fifty when the debris thinned. Spent shell casings, bones, and char marks littered the paving on the far side. Based on the amount of damage, she got the sense the debris had been set up as part of an ambush.

As the sun weakened in the western sky, she passed a large vehicle that resembled a self-powered house trailer. She squeezed the brake again and steered off the road, circling back toward it. *Maybe I can sleep in that for the night.*

When she got about sixty meters away, a pack of men and a muscular, shrieking woman ran out the door and piled into a trio of raider buggies. Kate hit the brakes and twisted the handlebars, sending the bike skidding around in a sideways slide that kicked up a wall of dirt. Once she pointed back at the road, she hit the accelerator and straightened out. The spectral whine of electric motors teased at being noticeable over the buzz of approaching ethanol engines. She caught a few inches of air as she hit the edge of the paving, and landed into the start of a wobble. Warning lights flashed on the bike as the auto-compensator forced her to slow down, attempting to correct the stability issue. Kate screamed at it, risking a peek over her shoulder at the buggies, which gained ground.

Varying degrees of damage scarred the highway; stretches of pristine road could give way without warning to barely navigable piles of rubble and sometimes a hole big enough to eat her ride whole.

The raiders flew out of a dust cloud, leaving the dirt access road behind. Tires squeaked and skidded on paving. Kate kept twisting the accelerator, terrified at the sensation of the vehicle ignoring her attempts to steer or control. A wooden projectile clattered on the road to her left. The man in the middle buggy reloaded a crossbow.

"You're shitting me..." She glanced at her speed, a sluggish twenty mph. "Fuck. Go!"

The lead buggy aimed right for her, intending to ram. That fear overrode her aversion to merely dumping the bike, and she brought her left hand around to the rear, a fireball forming between her fingers. Before she could hurl it, the compensation routine ended and the bike lurched forward, as she still had the right grip twisted down. The buggy's front end came within six feet of her back tire before the electric motorbike rocketed up to over a hundred. Fire tamped out under her palm as she clutched the handlebars in an effort not to fly off.

Ahead, a scattering of Corporate War era military vehicles lay on either side of the road, most with large holes blown in their sides. A minefield of craters in the paving caused her to slam on the brakes less than a minute later, screaming. Luck got her past the first few before she slowed enough to slalom the hazards. One crater she skirted by inches contained the ruined fins of an unexploded bomb, something likely dropped by an airplane centuries ago.

One buggy bounced into an end-over-end tumble and eventual fireball when its nose end found a divot. The center one made it through, while the last driver went off-road to avoid the danger, his engine choking on dust. On the far side of the stretch of shredded paving, the highway looked intact for as far as she could see. Against her better judgment, Kate squeezed the grip and pushed the bike up near two hundred miles per hour. The blast of speed almost took her out of the seat. She leaned down and forward, clinging to the frame with every bit of strength in her body.

Both buggies vanished into the setting sun behind her. She sat rigid, staring at the rear-view screen for a minute. Feeling hopeful her pursuers would understand they had no hope of catching up to her, she relaxed and looked up. When she noticed the speed display creeping up on 280, she screamed and eased off the accelerator, letting the bike coast. The electric motors went silent, leaving her with a feeling like flying low to the ground. Her gaze locked on the white numbers over a sky blue display, watching them tick down. Once she'd slowed below 150 mph, she teased at the brake. Any upcoming irregularity in the road could be deadly, and only a little while of daylight remained. According to the Navcon, she was in the eastern section of a region once called Oklahoma.

She rolled to a stop and put one boot on the road, panting. Draped over the handlebars, shaking from the aftereffect of terror, she found herself giggling at the feeling of wearing shoes. When that wore off, she sat up and looked around for cover. The darkness made it difficult to see anything, though the mosquito-whine of an ethanol engine brought her attention to the rear.

"Really?" She sighed. "I guess I'm about to become a cog in the evolutionary process."

One buggy had not given up. The huge woman clung to the back, swinging a chain around over her head with some kind of heavy sphere at the end. Kate smirked and yanked the pistol off her hip. *Bike with lights and sirens, and you give me a gun… You're really trying to convince me, David.* She squinted, grinned, and put her finger on the trigger, making it chirp. The faint *whirr-click* of a caseless round locking into firing position followed.

Kate held the pistol with both hands, one eye looking over the sights. Her aim rose and fell to match the approaching buggy as it went over tiny swells and dips in the road. She suppressed how silly it felt to point a handgun at a vehicle, but remembered the modern firearm would probably put a slug completely through a buggy made out of centuries-old materials.

Ahmed's voice all but whispered in her ear about breath control. The first shot went off before she expected it; the electric trigger had a travel distance less than one millimeter. The next seven or eight came in a rapid series. At least one bullet pierced the front end, the driver, the fuel tank, and hit the engine. The buzz cut out with a sputter, leaving everything quiet except for the squeak of ill-maintained wheels. White smoke billowed forth for seconds before the vehicle burst into invisible alcohol flames. Kate grinned, feeling the pyroclasm in the back of her mind. She called out to it, pouring psionic effort into building it.

Blamf.

The entire fuel tank went up with a blooming roar, ensconcing the buggy in a cloud of light for several seconds. A smoking figure leapt from the back, tumbling in the dirt as the buggy drifted off the road and rolled to its final death in a ditch. Bouncing like a stone, a strange weapon skidded to a halt a few yards away, trailing a length of jingling chain. The sphere had three finger-sized holes packed with crud, and deep gouges in its pearlescent-red shell held dried blood.

Kate started to put the pistol away, but snapped her arm up as the giantess stood. A tumble on the road left her scratched and bleeding, but alive. Aside from a mild limp, she appeared not to have suffered a serious injury.

"Go away." Kate took aim. *Wow, I must be in a great mood.* She wiggled her toes. *I have shoes!*

Armor made of leather and scraps of truck tires would do nothing against a modern pistol. Despite that, the wild woman drew a pair of knives from her belt and continued staggering closer. A shot into the road nearby failed to dissuade her.

"Seriously?" Kate scoffed, gazing at the emerging moon. "For the first time in my life, I'm trying *not* to kill and I run into a psycho."

She holstered the pistol and held aloft a fireball. Glee at her almost-normality lent her a wicked smile. At the sight of the flames, the approaching raider stopped. Kate held the burning orb higher.

"Leave." She waved it about, as if trying to scare off a wild animal.

"Mine," groaned the woman, pointing at the length of chain.

How many people has she killed? Kate frowned. *Like I'm any kind of judge.* "Take it. One step too close and you're dead."

The woman put her knives away and edged closer, eyeing Kate as though she were some manner of demonic creature. She retrieved the improvised flail and dragged it backward several steps before breaking into a full-on limping run. Once the woman was out of sight, Kate shut off the headlamp and crept north away from the road for several minutes, walking the bike.

She chose a decent spot to rest for the night and opened the cargo pod on the back left of the bike. After unpacking a sleeping bag, she sat cross-legged on top of it and took a ration pack from the pod. Her mouth watered merely from looking at the plastic. Some of the locals in Querq had given her odd looks the first time she'd touched food after Althea had cured her. What had to be the most mundane of meals to them, a bean and cheese burrito, had gotten her making noises that sounded more appropriate for the bedroom.

"UCF Enhanced Field Ration – 11V. Spicy chicken vindaloo." She regarded the plain-grey plastic pouch for a second, shrugged, and tore it open.

An assortment of smaller packets fell into her lap, the entrée landing with an audible *plop*. She gingerly peeled the top strip away and held it under her nose. A complex aroma of spices got the inside of her nostrils tingling. She disregarded the pitiful little plastic spoon, and squeezed some of the 'vindaloo' onto her tongue. A new kind of burn filled her mouth, but it came from *flavor* not fire.

Taste.

She didn't have to suck it down before it charred.

Kate closed her eyes and sat still, savoring the texture of chicken mashing apart in an ocean of exotic spices. When she swallowed, she waited a moment to let the essence of it settle before squeezing another mouthful from the packet. The thought of Esteban feeding her got her giggling, and deepened her need to hold him close.

David told her these rations were one rung up the ladder from cat food. He'd offered to take her to a 'real' Indian place back in the city someday. She swallowed, unsure how to feel about him. Having a body designed to be gorgeous had its downsides. Almost every man (and a fair number of women) she came into contact with made passes at her. Yet another reason she'd kept to herself in the black zones, avoiding more reminders of what she couldn't have.

Had Officer David Ahmed been more than friendly or did she imagine that glint in his eye?

Kate took her time with the remainder of the ration pack, including the (according to David) sad, sad excuse for naan bread and plum sauce. After, she removed only her boots and settled in for the night, adoring the feeling of being wrapped chin to toe in cloth.

"THAT WAS RATHER CHARITABLE OF YOU."

Kate's eyes snapped open. The man's voice had come from behind her. She sat up, pushing the sleeping bag down around her waist. A wiry figure wearing a long, dark leather duster coat sauntered around the back of the motorcycle, adjusting a wide-brimmed hat. Despite the change in clothing, she recognized the face of the old priest.

Hard, red eyes shifted toward her, peering out from deepened sockets. His rotting grin broadened, the smell made her regret eating. A palpable air of dissatisfaction surrounded him.

"She was no threat. I had nothing to gain by killing her."

His boot heel ground the dirt as he swiveled to face her. "Since when have you hesitated at taking life?"

"It was a waste of energy."

"Oh, I see." He paced around to the right. "A few minutes with the abomination and your entire outlook changes? I thought you had more resolve. I am disappointed in you."

Kate squirmed out of the cloth cocoon and reached for her boots. "You lied."

"The creature does not belong in this world." He wheezed with a chuckle, gesturing at the bike. "Playing policewoman now? A gun, a motorcycle, and some dime store morals?"

"Althea's not a creature. She is the most innocent person I've ever seen. Even after I stormed in ready to kill her, she helped me without expecting anything in return."

The decrepit gunslinger coughed as if attempting not to vomit. "You really do believe them, don't you?" He spat.

"You can't fake that." Kate used the memory of Althea's smile to ease her fear.

"Those police are no better than the ones who grew you in a bowl of slime. All they want is to use your power. You could be so much more."

"If Althea is lying, why didn't she demand payment? You offered to fix me, but wanted me to murder a little girl first."

His eyes glowed red for an instant. "She's not what she appears."

"I'm not inclined to believe you." Fire swirled into a sphere over her right hand.

The man held his arms out to the sides. "If it will make you feel better, go right ahead. If it will make you angry, by all means do it twice."

To foil his bluff, Kate looked for surface thoughts. Many thousand scenes of death swam in her mind: screaming civilians buried under collapsing buildings, military vehicles rolling over a sea of corpses, followed by soldiers stomping on the dead. Aircraft dropped bombs on panicking citizens. When the smoke cleared, men in grey corporate uniforms shot people lined up against a wall. Disembodied children's voices cried for their mothers and fathers, older voices shouted random names. The pain, fear, loss, and rage of a nation's worth of people rippled over her in a few seconds.

She came to lying on her side, curled fetal and crying.

"Now, that I was not expecting," said the old man. "You see them. You see that of which I am made. I am their vengeance."

"H-how…" Kate pushed herself up to sit. "All those people… how can you justify killing Althea? She had nothing to do with any of that."

"It does not belong here. Part of her soul…" He snarled. "It is pointless; you will not see the truth of it, blinded as you are by your sense of gratitude. Another fool, placated into subservience." Vengeful wrinkles flattened to a conspiratorial smile. "It matters little. You have nowhere else to go and still be free."

"I am free." Kate forced her way out from under the emotional aftermath of the brief visions. "More free than I've ever been."

"In my realm, you could rule. Your power could make you a queen."

"First, I have no interest in ruling a bunch of monosyllabic barbarians that have to flip a coin to decide between eating or fucking what they find. Second, you honestly think I'd believe you'd let anyone have power out here?"

He passed behind her, spurs rattling, and emerged on her left. "You are mortal. For the time you have left, you could know ultimate power. I am but an influence on the world. I do not rule. When your life ends, you will join us… Your rage is only hiding, but it remains who you are."

"It was you." Kate pointed, arm trembling. "You were what made me so angry in Querq. As soon as I saw her, I knew it was wrong, but the hate kept coming. You're doing it again."

Dry air vibrated with a chuckle from deep within his throat. "A fast learner."

"I guess this is where you break my motorcycle or something, right?"

The old man gave the machine a sideways glance, dry lips tightening over rotten teeth. "No… I think I'll pass. You've someone waiting in St. Louis. Why would I get in the way of true love?"

"I'm not going to be your pawn." She flopped down and pulled the sleeping bag up. "If you're just an influence, you can't hurt me."

"Yes, Kate. Go back to your precious oasis of civilization. This land belongs to all of us now, and no one else. That blue-eyed whelp invades our domain like a cancer." Boots crunched distant behind her. "And cancer must be *burned* out."

26

FRIED CHICKEN

K ate paused at the near side of the bridge to watch the great Mississippi river for several minutes. The churning water mesmerized her and took her mind away from the disturbing conversation she'd had with the old man—or whatever. Her mind ran back to that first time her seven-year-old self had found water. She tangled with the nigh-irresistible urge to fling herself into the river. For so long, she had daydreamed of what it would be like to swim. If not for Esteban being less than a mile away, she might have done it. She kicked off the road and accelerated. After a minute or two of guiding the motorcycle past the barricades and wrecked vehicles, she came to a halt at the checkpoint gate.

A startled Private Vickers jumped to her feet, staring at Kate as though she were a ghost.

Kate pulled off a pair of wraparound sunglasses and flicked her hair back. "Afternoon, Vickers. Why so shocked?"

"Well, I'll be damned," said Sergeant Alvarez. He wandered over with coffee in one hand and a pistol in the other. "You're alive."

Anders jogged up to them, followed by another Hispanic man she had not yet met. Once more, Kate felt like an attraction at a sideshow. Vickers stood like a plank while Alvarez put his weapon away and sipped his drink.

"Coffee?" Kate smiled. "It's almost one."

"Never a bad time for coffee." Alvarez waved at Vickers. "Open it."

"Yes, Sarge." The woman let her rifle fall on its strap and hit a button that caused a concrete barrier wall to slide left.

"Fancy bike," said Anders. "Why ain't it melting?"

"I found what I was looking for." Kate winked.

"You do seem... different." Alvarez chuckled.

"I feel a lot better." Kate bit her lip and held her hand out. "Hey... sorry if I was a little short with you before. Had a lot on my mind."

Vickers shook her head. Alvarez gave her a suspicious look. He reached a cautious hand out and tapped one finger on her palm. When he didn't burn, he took her hand. The St. Louis Guard exchanged stares.

After the handshake, she walked the bike in far enough for Vickers to secure the gate. "Is Esteban still here?"

"Who?" asked Anders.

"The mechanic who was with me when I first got here." Kate's heart sank at the lack of recognition.

"Oh, him. Yes." Vickers looked at Alvarez, who found his coffee of sudden interest. "He's umm, in the same apartment."

"Thanks." Kate chuckled at the locals thinking of a motel as housing.

"Remember where you are," said Vickers, gesturing at the bike. "Big city law doesn't mean anything here."

They think I'm a cop? The irony proved too much to hold in and she laughed, earning a frown from the woman. "I promise not to cause trouble."

Alvarez sipped his coffee and waved her through.

A twist of the handgrip sent the bike around the fortification of mobile concrete barriers, zipping into town.

ANTICIPATION MADE TWO TURNS ALMOST-CRASHES; KATE CAUGHT AIR FOR A second on the way into the motel parking lot and skidded to a halt by the door marked 27. Her haste to dismount sent her staggering with the grace of a drunken ostrich until she clamped onto a support post for the awning. A handful of rough-looking prostitutes clustered in the corner left of the entrance ramp. All but one of them gave her nasty looks. Her pleasant mood didn't allow her to waste time worrying about what people like that thought of her.

She ignored them and ran to the door, jiggling the knob, finding it locked. For a moment, she stared helplessly at the barrier. A sad, nervous giggle slipped out of her at the realization her non-holographic clothing had usable pockets. She'd never even thought of taking a key before; where would she have put it? *This is going to take getting used to.*

Kate knocked and pounded on the door, stopping at the sound of a man's groan inside. She clutched her hands to her chest, bouncing like a girl on her birthday waiting for the cake to come out.

With a *click*, the door parted a few inches. Esteban squinted at her from under the haze of unexpected consciousness. Clingy white boxer-briefs left little to her imagination. He sucked a long breath in through his nose and ran a hand up over his head to tame his hair—somewhat.

"Esteban," said Kate, kneading her hands in front of her chest. "It worked!"

"Kate?" His rubbing hand became scratching fingers. "You're, uhh… back."

She grinned from ear to ear. "I'm sorry it took so long; it was crazy. I missed you."

He slipped past the door, pulling it closed behind him and shielded his eyes from the sun. "It's Saturday… and not even noon yet."

"Sorry. I left my 'mini back in Querq." She held up her naked left wrist, and leapt up to kiss him.

He screamed into her mouth, his sleep-addled brain having failed to recognize the significance of the missing holo-projector. Kate squeaked as he instinctively grasped her about the armpits and pushed her away. Esteban squeezed twice, as if testing what his sense of touch seemed to be telling him—physical clothing. She put her hands on his warm chest, her momentary alarm fading back to an alluring smile.

"I'm cured!" As the strength left his arms, she pressed herself against him. "I think I can arrange a pardon for you, but I have to become a cop… Division 0. I need to go back to Querq. I want you to come with me."

"Pardon? Huh? Querq?" Esteban looked her over from face to boot and back. "You're not crisping the shit out of me."

"I know!" She cheered, and kissed him again.

He chuckled. "You kiss like a little girl."

Red swam over her face as she glanced down. "Not like I've had much practice…"

"Ugh, sorry. That was a shitty thing to say. I'm not truly awake yet." He brushed the hair away from her eyes. "I… never thought you'd come back."

"I was thinking about you every day," she said. "That silly glove you had. That was like the most romantic thing ever."

"The oven mitt?" He whistled. "You burned that thing."

Her hands slid around his chest, down his back, and into the waistband of his boxers. "Show me how to kiss?"

What he attempted to say next degenerated into meaningless noises as their lips met; Kate mashed her face into his, attempting the best recreation of what she had watched in vids and seen other people do. As Esteban's stiff posture began to make her feel self-conscious, a squeak from behind him drew her attention to the opening door.

A black-haired woman, maybe a teenager, peered through the narrow gap. Her bare leg snaked around the door, one foot perched atop a blackened footprint facing into the room. Kate's arms tightened around Esteban to keep from falling as she looked up the leg, over the hip, and into the other woman's eyes. All she had on was the motel room door.

"*Esteban, ¿quién es ella?*"

"Kate... I'm sorry..." He slouched. "You were amazing, but... I never thought I'd be able to have anything with a woman I couldn't even touch. It seemed so unreal, what you could do. Never in my life did I expect you would actually find a way to fix it."

Huge tears formed in her eyes and ran down her cheeks.

"When they told me you'd run off into the Badlands without any weapons, I thought you were trying to kill yourself. I got very drunk that night." He put an arm around her, the embrace of a friend rather than a lover. "I can't find the words to say how glad I am you are alive."

"*Esteban, ¿quién es ella?*" whispered the girl in the door.

"*Un amiga,*" he muttered over his shoulder. "*Guardia de la caravana.*"

Kate sniffled. "That's all I am? Only a friend?"

She offered no resistance as he pulled her into a hug. "I'm sorry, Kate. It's my fault. Sometimes I can't turn it off. I wasn't trying to get into your pants, just... we survived some bad shit and you seemed so lonely. I was trying to make your life not suck so much."

"I didn't even have pants then," she mumbled. Despite the sense of betrayal and anger, she held on. "I'm twenty-five and I've never even held hands with a boy." An eerie laugh belted out of her; the other girl leapt back and slammed the door. "The most contact I've had is a pack of ghouls trying to eat me. Last night, I dreamed about when you fed me on the truck. I've never been that happy before." She wanted to giggle at the memory, but it made her cry harder.

"I was at Stephanie's, trying to drink away the guilt. I thought you'd run off because you woke up alone. You should've told me you were going. Mariana saw me and tried to cheer me up."

"I'll bet she did." Kate pulled away, crossing her arms and taking a few steps to the side.

"It's not like that." He held his hands up for a moment. "You were unbelievable, scary, unknown, and a little crazy. I'd never met anyone even close to that."

She smirked, not that he could see it.

"We'd only known each other for what, twelve hours? Almost got killed together… Nothing that happens can break the bond that forms between people who share an experience like that. We'll always have a connection. I'm sorry I assumed you were running off to die."

Kate sniffled.

"Esteban?" asked a mousy voice.

Mariana peered again from the room, having put on one of his shirts, which hung down to her thighs. She reached through the doorway to hand him a pair of dark pants. She was pretty in a girl-next-door sort of way that made Kate feel conspicuous. Even if she hadn't been 700 degrees, she had the kind of looks that would've made her seem unattainable. As Esteban pulled the jeans on, the girl flashed an accusatory, territorial glare at her.

Kate snarled; her clawed hand ensconced with the sudden presence of an azure fireball. "What are you looking at, bitch?"

"*Eeeeeeee! Tu eres una diabla!*" The girl flung the door closed.

Esteban leapt in front of the door, hands up. "Whoa…"

Several thuds preceded the clap of the bathroom door slamming, followed by something metal clattering into the bathtub—*her* bathtub. Kate let the fireball go out; her arm fell limp. The prostitutes on the other side of the motel parking lot muttered amongst themselves, glaring at her. One laughed. She whirled on them.

"If you're the best this town's got, no wonder the goats here run so damn fast."

Her shriek echoed over stunned silence. Esteban cringed.

An emaciated woman gave her the finger. "Fuck off, city bitch! No one here likes plastic. How much did those tits cost?"

"Probably a damn Maya doll," said the woman next to her. "No one's that fuckin' perfect." She tugged at a strained purple mini-dress that would've been snug on Kate, into which she'd stuffed a fortyish 'six kids and counting' body.

Flames covered both of Kate's arms. She started stomping toward them, but Esteban grabbed her shoulders.

"What?" shouted Kate. "Say that again, you dried up old hag. I didn't hear you."

They scattered, running for cover. Two ducked into a room, one ran down the ramp to the street, and one crawled under a parked truck. Three male prostitutes continued leaning on the wall, trying not to look as amused as they seemed to be.

She let the fire fade. *There's my rage, right where I left it.*

Mariana screamed for Esteban from inside the bathroom.

"I wasn't going to hurt her. Just a scare." Her voice trailed to a whisper. "She has no right to give me that face; I was with you first."

Esteban cast a worried look at the door. "I think you succeeded. Look, let me get dressed and we can go talk and sort things out."

"What's to sort out?" Kate stuffed her hands in her pants pockets. Her next words died at the tip of her brain. She looked down, realizing she'd just stuffed her hands in real pockets. Something she'd wanted to do for years.

"When the militia told me you left, I never thought I'd see you again."

"You found a normal girl without all the bullshit I'm carrying around. You're right; I'm dangerous to be with. Maybe I'll get pissed off during an argument and burn you before I can control myself." She kicked one boot at the sidewalk. "I do seem to have anger issues."

"Kate, I'm sorry." He put a hand on her shoulder.

She didn't move as his contact became an arm around the back and another hug. "Stop saying you're sorry. I'm not mad at you. I was surprised you didn't run away from me screaming. I shouldn't have mistaken your being nice for love. I was so... desperate."

"You're so beautiful it hurts." He released the embrace. "I..."

"Don't remind me." She walked to the bike. "The lab coats believed looks could kill. I suppose I'm proof that they can."

Esteban jogged over and held onto the handlebars as she got on. "Don't race off and do something stupid."

"You deserve someone normal." She pulled sunglasses out of her jacket and studied the daylight glint on them. "It was silly of me to think we'd fallen in love in twelve hours. Combat stress." Sunglasses on, Kate chuckled. "I hope you find a happy life here."

He let go of the bike when she powered it up. "Promise me you'll be okay? You probably won't believe me, but I would hate to see you hurt. I'm an idiot; I should have trusted—"

"Stop." Kate let her head sag. "If I was normal and saw someone like I used to be, I'd have run screaming. Thank you for being nice. It's not your fault." She pushed off, letting the bike roll backward in a quarter-circle turn. "I need to figure out who I am. I guess we'll always have that night."

"We will." He leaned against an awning post. "We will."

She drove out of the motel lot before the tears trapped by the sunglasses against her cheek spilled out. A collision of anger, guilt, and sadness left her stranded on an emotional island amid a sea of nothing.

Perhaps because Esteban had mentioned the place, or perhaps randomness led Kate to park in front of the building with 'Stephanie's' written in paint across a wide patch of windowless brick. A string of painted flowers, added by the hand of a child, weaved among the letters.

Walking on autopilot, Kate stumbled into a room full of tables and the scent of fried chicken. She stalled as soon as the aroma reached her, covering her face in both hands, ready to flee from the memories it triggered. A tired-looking, but happy woman with short, reddish hair waved at her from behind a counter on her way to bring food to a booth table where four young girls sat in a giggling cluster.

Kate took a seat on one of the stools and glanced through the kitchen to a hallway full of scattered toys, broken electronics, and the echoing voices of more children, mostly boys, playing in a yard out back. The woman spent a moment fussing over the girls; they all called her Mom despite little if any resemblance. Curiosity led Kate to eavesdrop upon her surface thoughts. She'd taken them in at various points over the years. Her husband's rifle had spared one or two of them horrible situations. She loved them as though they were her own blood, and, as far as she was concerned, they were. Kate closed her eyes, battling jealousy that she had to fend for herself. She thought of El Tío and wondered if Stephanie would ask her children to kill for her when they got older.

The utter ridiculousness of the thought made her laugh.

"Walter, no!" shouted a boy in the rear hall.

The bleat of an inquisitive goat protesting his exile from the building filled the air. The black and white spotted animal ignored the extreme effort on the part of a scrawny eight-year-old trying to pull a leash. Battered sneakers, no doubt on their third or fourth stop along the hand-me-down path, squeaked together as the animal dragged him toward a door. The boy's face formed a mask of determination in spite of overwhelming failure.

"Hi there, hon," said Stephanie. She started to lean on the counter, but turned when Kate pointed at the war in the back.

"Mom!" yelled the boy. "Walter's not listening."

Kate folded her arms over the counter and put her head down, tired from the ride and drained from losing Esteban. *Stupid, Kate. You knew him for less than two days. Impulsive. Since when have I been that desperate?* The fragrance of actual wood in the tiny space between her face and the counter distracted her. Enamored by the novelty of touching things like a normal person, her thoughts spun in random circles as she ran her hand over the texture.

When Stephanie tapped the counter nearby, Kate jumped up.

"Sorry, Miss. What can I get for you?"

"Oh, shit. I left my 'mini at..." Kate raked both hands through her hair and squeezed the back of her neck. "Damn. You have somewhere I could sleep? I could help with like, dishes or something?"

"You have a NetMini?" Stephanie pulled an old machine out from under the counter, as big as a pre holo-terminal computer. The battered thing had several missing panels, exposed wires and circuit boards... but its flat-panel screen still worked. "You can use this to log in if you have your PID memorized." She patted it. "Satellite."

"Okay." Kate tugged it closer, finding the almost seven second load time between screens intolerable. Much to her surprise, the connection back to the GlobeNet worked. "Wow, I don't think I've ever seen a physical screen before. How much for dinner and a bed?"

Stephanie un-leaned from the counter. "What'll you have?"

"Anything but fried chicken."

27

FREE AGENT

Kate squatted at the side of an old-fashioned porcelain bathtub, tracing her fingers across the surface of the frigid water. The sound of playing children outside made her smile at the same time it sparked a twinge of jealousy. She closed her eyes and concentrated on heat. Once the water spawned tiny whorls of steam along the surface, she stood, stepped over the edge, and lowered herself in.

No longer focused on her power, she found the water uncomfortably warm—feeling anything as hot or cold was a foreign experience, but an amazing one. Manual soap seemed strange, but then again so did bathing at all. Lathering up, she daydreamed of finally being able to use an autoshower without causing a steam explosion.

After an inordinately long soak, she toweled off, taking her time to enjoy such a mundane task. A knock on the door turned the towel into an emergency dress.

"The water is almost boiling," said Stephanie, through the door.

"It's okay… I'm done." Kate dropped the towel and scrambled into her clothes. "Be out in a minute."

"Already? What, did you use cold water?" The woman made a shivering noise. "Okay, I'll fix you some breakfast then."

Kate pushed the door open, startling Stephanie with a blast of steamy air. She stared, dumbfounded, until a distant child's voice called out "Mom! Walter's gone over the fence!"

"I can chase the goat if you're busy."

Stephanie's eyebrows went up. "Oh, I couldn't ask you to do that... not after..."

Considering what I did to earn that money... "It's fine. Get something nice for your kids."

KATE SAT ON THE GLEAMING BLACK MOTORCYCLE FOR TEN MINUTES, staring at the console. Inexplicable dread kept her finger away from the on button, worsening each time she thought of Althea.

Cancer must be burned out.

The old man's voice crawled down her back with the tingle of a thousand spiders. Childish giggles from the other side of Stephanie's place brought a smile, then wistful regret at how life had treated her. The emotion turned toxic, collapsing to malignant jealousy. A flash of camouflage caused her to jump, startling a large man with a shaved head, sunglasses, and a long rifle slung over his back. Kate offered a nod of greeting, which he returned.

As much as she wanted to race back to Querq and repay Althea for her kindness, she feared what might happen if she did. *I can't go back. It'll use me to hurt her.* She hit the button. The space between the handlebars lit up as the Navcon displayed a loading progress bar. Aside from an electronic hum too weak to hear over the background noise and a faint vibration in the frame, the vehicle gave little sign of being active.

She took the eastward gate out of St. Louis, finding the roads within the Scattered Lands in far better shape than anything west of the Mississippi. Before she knew it, she had the bike over a hundred and eighty. It rode as though on a cushion of air; if not for the blue number at the top of the display screen, she would never have guessed how fast she drove.

Esteban's 'betrayal' hung heavy in her heart, despite every effort her brain made to blame her for getting too attached too fast. She wanted to be back in Querq, and wondered if the pull to be near the glowing-eyed child was genuine gratitude or that sinister old man, demon, whatever it was, pushing her to do his bidding.

A little more than an hour out, a shimmer to the left drew her attention to a large lake aglow in the sun. Pine trees surrounded it on three sides, and the ruined remains of a cabin sat next to a tiny dock on the westernmost shore. Kate slowed and steered off the road, driving over untamed grass at a little faster than a running pace to the edge of the water. Five or six small islands dotted the surface, two of which were large enough to have trees.

She shut down the bike and got off. After a few minutes of standing in total silence, she felt confident at being alone, and stripped, leaving her clothes in a neat pile on the bike's seat. Kate crept to the edge and stuck a toe in, stifling a squeal at the coldness. For a while, she squatted in ankle-deep water, tracing her fingers back and forth while marveling at how it felt to touch liquid.

Eventually, she waded in and dove under the surface, swimming down to the bottom and gliding over stones coated in fuzzy brown growth. Her auburn hair fanned out in a diaphanous cloud behind her. She swam, twisting and gliding, adoring the caress of water across her body. Here and there, evidence of civilization jutted out of the muck below: beer bottles, a tire, or a bit of furniture. A few fish came by to check her out, though none of them looked threatening. She made her way to the nearest island, where she sat on a rock and basked in the sun, staring up at puffy white clouds.

Her pain at losing Esteban faded to a resigned 'blah.' He probably wouldn't be the last man to do that to her. Not that he really did anything… She couldn't really blame him for doubting she'd ever be cured. Hell, she barely believed it. *I need to be careful. I really am desperate, and I'm going to be gullible. Some guy is going to use me and throw me away.* She wrapped her arms around her legs and enjoyed the fresh air. *Don't be stupid… I can read their mind.*

She laughed, and slipped back into the water.

Two-ish hours later, Kate emerged on the bank by the bike, and reclined in the grass. She debated returning to Querq while drying off, but did not trust that wretched old man. If a sudden spike of anger came out of nowhere with her too close to Althea, the child might not be able to react fast enough to quell it.

Kate shivered at the guilt of what she *might* do.

Once dry, she got dressed and resumed her drive back to the east.

The ease with which any emotion she felt twisted into anger seemed to fade with each mile. Hours later, the blocky shadow of East City darkened the approaching horizon. By the time the console chirped to indicate re-established wireless connectivity to the GlobeNet, Kate couldn't decide how to feel about anything. Text messages and subdued voice chatter came from the controls, reminding her that she drove a police vehicle. Wearing a weak grimace, she switched off the comm system before anyone noticed her listening.

She slowed to follow the curve of the road and dipped the bike into a bouncy left turn. The tires made a *ka-thump* as they went from old paving to modern plastisteel tiles covered with spray-on traction coating. The long, ascending ramp led to the city surface, seventy-five meters off the natural ground. Where the ramp started, a manned access gate with a checkpoint-style bar blocked her way. She hit the brakes, expecting to endure the third degree. Much to her surprise, the gate opened on its own at her approach, before the body-armor clad guard could exit the booth.

Even the gate thinks I'm a cop.

Kate leaned forward and accelerated, not waiting to talk to the man who still came out to see what was going on. To the right of the road, cavernous darkness extended below modern civilization through a maze of metal struts, dangling wires, and tiny white lights. Her time living on the street had provided no shortage of urban legends about the horrors that lived in The Beneath. She had never been desperate enough to go all the way down there past the underside of the plate; black zones were bad, but even the dregs that lived there wanted nothing to do with the 'real Earth' under the city. Being inside the plate was as close as she ever wanted to get.

A little more than a mile later, the bike caught air at the top of the ramp, and landed in a squealing fishtail that came close to soiling Kate's new pants. Several bystanders clapped after she skidded to a halt, panting.

Okay, maybe I should get a helmet. She glanced over her shoulder. *Or not do 110 up a ramp.*

Fading adrenaline, plus a lack of a clear destination, left her driving like an old woman for a few blocks. Her circuitous wandering ended where the Navcon screen warned of a grey zone, and she found a walk-in electronics store. Fifteen minutes later, she was the proud owner of a new *normal* NetMini, not one embedded in the same material as shuttle heat tiles.

She set it on the armored body of the bike between her legs, waiting for it to finish synchronizing with the network. The unit she chose had been sitting in stock for at least three months, and had to download eleven firmware updates and over a thousand app patches. Worry gripped her as she watched the line of bright blue pixels grow to the right. She still had the same PID. El Tío could call her. Kate thought of Esteban and all but felt the oven mitt caressing her hair. She grumbled and stuffed the NetMini in her jacket pocket. Frustration at having waited for him boiled over, and she found herself driving to the nearest bar in search of a man while fantasizing about Officer David Ahmed.

Ugh. Stop it. He was being nice, just like Esteban.

She parked in a small lot outside an orange and pink neon building thrumming with music. The intensity of the sound created the illusion of the walls pulsing to the beat. *What am I doing?* Kate examined her face in the surface of her removed sunglasses. *Looking for dick.* Her attempt to laugh aborted into a shameful frown. *No, that's not me. Oh, what would it hurt? A one night stand just to see what it was like?* She felt cheap at the thought, worse when she remembered the way some Wharf Rat women looked all the time: shell-shocked, like veterans of a never-ending war. The Rats had tried to grab her once, before El Tío arranged for her bracelet.

They learned fast.

No. Not a one-nighter for my first time. Deciding this place far too loud, she drove away, once again aimless. Purple lettering spun through the air over the road some minutes later, spelling out the word 'Destiny.' It emanated from a silver building with strips of violet light around the windows and doors. Something part way between a bar and a nightclub occupied the first three floors of a residential tower. As if some other force took control of her limbs, she parked and went inside.

A too-thin-to-be-human blonde doll in a clingy black dress showed her to a tiny table not much larger than the stools by the bar along the left side of the room. The ambiance was quiet, and the room contained mostly couples. She selected a drink at random from the holographic menu, having no idea what any of it tasted like, and let her weight settle over the table on her arms. Once again, she felt as conspicuous as she did walking naked into CyberBurger. Except for the android hostess, she was the only person in the room with pale skin, not to mention the only one without a date.

Electronic whining drew her gaze toward a floating tray with a tall, narrow glass. Opaque blue liquid settled at the bottom, changing to greenish in the center, and orange at the top. She took the drink, not bothering to smile at the little robotic tray, and fiddled with the straw. The first sip hit her with sweet, which detonated into citrusy alcohol a second later.

Oof. Kate resisted the urge to cough, though her eyes did water. *Take this one slow.*

The level of the drink went down at a gradual pace despite her caution. It tasted wonderful, and before she realized it, she felt lightheaded. Kate admired her stretched reflection in the glass, rambling in her mind about how the scientists made her look like she did on purpose. She was *made* to seduce her way in and kill, or spy, or do whatever the people pulling the strings wanted. Idle daydreams of how things might've played out if she hadn't been 'broken' filled her mind. Would they have trained her how to have sex? Of course, they'd have had to make her so jaded with fucking she could do it without a second thought or any emotional weight. What age would they have started her on that curriculum? Fourteen? Sixteen? Younger? Would the scientists who made her gotten in on that action, or would they have thought of her as their daughter? She scowled. No. They were going to hit the button to kill her. Not a daughter.

What the hell am I doing here? This isn't who I am. Who am I? A desperate, lonely girl. She sighed. Two choices hovered before her: find Division 0 and try to get in touch with David, or go back to El Tío and business as usual. Perhaps business more than usual since she could enjoy all the fancy things he'd always wanted to give her but never could. She swirled her drink about, unable to decide which option appealed more. Division 0 at least had the benefit of not being illegal. With her curse gone, El Tío might make more and more use of her, a career path that almost guaranteed an eventual nasty end, even if the ride would be lavish.

In truth, neither option called to her as much as returning to Querq and protecting Althea. It almost felt as if someone had taken her daughter away and she needed to get back to her before something happened. She flicked her thumbnail at the glass. *If I go back, that* thing *will make me hurt her.*

That's all I am... someone's weapon. Surely, if the scientists had intended her to 'pretty' her way to a target, she could hook some random man for a night. Kate took a long sip from the straw to chase away the shame of the thought.

"I don't wanna cheap fuck; I want someone to care."

A sudden silence told Kate she'd spoken aloud. She tilted the cup in her hand, noting barely a finger of liquid remained at the bottom. Not the slightest urge to blush formed. She couldn't care less if the entire city knew she felt lonely.

"Are you waiting for someone?"

The man's voice to her left made her acutely aware she was at risk of falling off the narrow chair. Whatever she'd just drank, it had hit her hard. With great care, she braced herself on the table and glanced through a wild curtain of red hair at the chest of a dark raincoat with two parallel rows of fasteners running from shoulder to hip. She lifted her gaze upward, past the panel of material covering the chest, and offered a woozy blink at a man's clean-shaven face. He looked about thirty, and Caucasian, with short, chestnut hair.

She smiled at no longer being the only light-skinned person in the room.

"I'm sorry if I'm bothering you. I'm intrigued by fiery redheads. It takes a special kind of woman to wear that look. Did your parents opt for it after birth, or was it your idea?"

"It's natural." *As natural as a tweaked-out clone can get.* Kate inhaled until it hurt, then released. The drink turned her effort at skimming his surface thoughts into a dull headache with a sharp point above both eyes. She made a face and rubbed the bridge of her nose.

"That's a pretty complex drink for a first taste."

"Yeah. I picked it 'cause it was pretty." She chuckled at a whisper, trying to work the pain out of her head with her fingers. "No, I'm not waiting for anyone." Sudden vertigo caused her to flail and grab the table. "Why does every place use these skinny little, tall, fragile chairs?"

He sat. "Good question. Form over function, I'd imagine. I'm Christian."

"I'm not." She laughed.

"Please, call me Chris."

"I was about to ask if that was your name or…" She slurped the last of her drink.

"No." He chuckled. "I'm definitely not one of the fringe crowd."

Kate frowned at the empty glass. "Do you think there's such a thing as fate? Or God? Or…" Her warped reflection in the glass seemed to take on the image of an ancient gunslinger. "…the other guy?" *Normal people ask what kind of music you like. No, that's pretty lame.*

"I don't really think about it. There is little about our world that eludes human understanding these days. We don't need a god to explain what science and intelligence have not already made elementary." He lifted a tumbler glass, a quarter full with a dark brown liquor, from the floating tray. "So, you came to Destiny looking for a philosophy discussion?"

"I'm not sure why I'm here." Kate ordered a glass of water.

"I think everyone has that moment sooner or later." Chris winked. "What are you looking for?"

She flattened her hands on the table, absorbed by the smoothness. "I guess I'm lonely. I guess I came here looking for cheap sex, but I changed my mind." Nearby patrons murmured, glancing at her. "I don't know where I belong or what to do." One arm stretched over the table, taking his hand. "You're warm."

He drew a sharp breath, almost cringing away from contact. Once she touched him, he released an almost unnoticeable sigh of relief. "I think you're putting on a little show. No one gets that tipsy from one drink."

"I've been driving all day. I'm exhausted. And I haven't eaten much."

Chris waved the hostess over. "Do you have any food available?"

Luminous green eyes sparkled as the AI doll smiled. "Buffalo chicken tenders and Kyoto shrimp cocktail with a wasabi-based sauce."

"An order of the shrimp, please," said Chris, without hesitation.

Kate sat up, grateful he didn't choose chicken. "I hope you're not expecting to get into my pants tonight."

"I'd expected nothing of the sort. You don't strike me as that sort of woman."

"What do I strike you as?"

"Hungry, tired, lonely." He sipped his scotch. "I'll match you two out of three."

"You forgot confused." Kate stretched back as the doll came by to set the order on the table.

Eight shrimp, six inches long and at least an inch in diameter hung over the edge of a tall porcelain vessel that resembled a trophy. Pale green sauce half-filled the bowl in the center.

"Have you had wasabi before?"

"No." She took one of the shrimp.

"Be sparing; it's spicy."

Kate nibbled, exploring her tolerance for how much sauce she could get away with before sucking down half a glass of water. She rambled about some of the details of her life, but left out the worst parts. As far as Chris learned, she'd run away from home as a little girl because her father tried to kill her, and had grown up on the streets. His eyebrows came together in a look of amused concern when she mentioned the police wanted to hire her.

"You don't look like the type of woman who's drawn to such a violent profession."

Kate held a shrimp to her lips. "You'd be surprised." She bit slow, aware of the shellfish separating strand by strand as her teeth sheared it. Food was nothing new, but *tasting* it would take getting used to.

He cocked an eyebrow. "You really are a natural redhead?"

"Mmm hmm." She swallowed. "Apparently, I'm psionic too. Zero's got stars in their eyes for me. I'm finding it complicated to refuse. I guess I don't have a lot of choice."

"You're just full of surprises."

She wiped her hand on the small napkin. When she looked back at him, something had changed. Chris's eyes had become fierce, his smile dangerous. "Y-you don't have any issues with that?"

He didn't *look* different, but he felt different. A wave of static charge ran down her chest and settled in her nether regions. Kate squirmed on the stool, overcome by sudden arousal. The perfectly sculpted ridge of his jaw seemed to move in slow motion. His lips shifted to form words she recognized as little more than blurred sound. Her breathing deepened and slowed. She broke out in a light sweat. Warmth spread between her legs.

Chris gathered her hand from the table, stroking his fingers across the back. "I find people with gifts fascinating."

"Fascinating," she whispered. Some part of her mind looked at her traitorous body and screamed. She found herself only able to close her eyes and open her mouth as he leaned in.

His scent flooded her senses as they kissed. Before she thought about what she did, her arms wrapped around him and their tongues crossed like sabers in a duel. She didn't care that the table had fallen over, spilling their leftover wasabi sauce into a green swath, or that the entire room watched her. Chris permeated her soul, and she wanted him right *now*. Kate moaned as he held the back of her head, pulling her tight into another kiss.

Her eyes shot wide open as a squirt of foul-tasting liquid ran down her throat. Chris shifted her so that she coughed and gagged into his chest, muffling the sound. The chemical didn't take long to act, and the room blurred. She tried to speak, but managed only an unintelligible whimper into his coat. She struggled, but couldn't summon the strength or coordination to get away from his powerful arms.

"Shh, be calm." He patted her back, sliding his lips to her ear to whisper. "I'm sorry about the pheromones; we didn't want anyone to get hurt... Especially you."

Kate looked up at the twisting smear of color; some of it ceiling lights, some Chris. "Wa..."

The whorl of color coalesced into a face; a droplet of clear liquid fell from his canine teeth.

"She's had a bit too much to drink," said Chris to a person she couldn't perceive. "I'll get her home."

HOME AGAIN

Dreams of marathon sex ended with the realization of consciousness. Such nocturnal fantasies were hardly new to her, though never had they been so persistent. One or two brief, steamy scenes would interleave with nightmares of running through the woods or random other images. Tonight's X-rated dream had been a relentless parade of partners: Esteban, Officer Ahmed, Wilma, Paul and Leo (at the same time), and even El Tío himself. Kate shuddered. At first, she thought she was sore from all the dreamed intercourse, but the discomfort permeated everywhere.

She frowned. "Sorry about the pheromones…"

Chris, if that was even his real name, had attacked her with synthetic pheromones. Their lingering effect left her horny and aching, and tainted her dreams. The last, and most realistic, scene involved Aurora, a warm beach, and scented oils. Of course, she had still not known a man for real; everything that happened in her dream came from her imagination of what it would feel like.

Kate didn't open her eyes right away, afraid of how much worse she would feel. She lay still for some minutes, taking note of the presence of hard, unforgiving metal beneath her body. A small foam pillow gave her a little comfort. She stretched, rigid and shuddering for a few seconds. Cloth covered her, long sleeves and pant legs. Her toes were cold; someone had stolen her socks.

A strip of ice circled her neck. The oddity of it attracted her hand to a metal collar: one inch tall, a half inch thick, rounded edges, and quite snug. Gripped by the sudden terror of being some gang lord's sex toy, she shot upright and screamed. The expected snag of a leash did not occur, and she half fell, half stumbled to her feet in a blinding white room permeated with the smell of cleaning solution.

Kate yelped at the freezing metal floor, her gaze alternating between walls made of three-foot square white tiles and the bright orange jumpsuit she found herself wearing. The same heat-resistant material her bracelet had been made of covered the cube-shaped space. Aside from the plain metal shelf serving as a bed and one exposed toilet in the corner, the room was featureless. She squinted at the ceiling where the milky tiles glowed from lights on the other side powerful enough to illuminate the room through them.

She grabbed at the collar, frantic to make some sense of it. The metal was smooth all the way around, without a loop for a chain or anything resembling a keyhole, seam, or button. She tried to slip a finger between it and her throat, but it rested too snug to do without choking herself. With a feeble fingertip grip, she pulled and twisted in a lame attempt to break it. Other than being uncomfortably snug and cold, it seemed not do anything at all.

Damn large for a tracker.

The walls offered no indication of anywhere that opened like a door. Someone had to be watching her. She felt like a lab rat all over again. Morning needs made her stare at the toilet. Again, she searched the walls, spotting no obvious cameras. She distrusted the tiny gaps between tiles. Pinpoint cameras had to be everywhere. She flattened the jumpsuit across her stomach with nervous rubbing while trying to get over the fear that someone would watch her pee. Eventually, she glared at the walls and trudged to the bowl. Her suit had one zipper from throat to crotch. With a resigned sigh, she unzipped the suit and let it slide to the floor.

At least they let me keep my underwear. She scowled, trying to cover herself as much as possible while sitting. *Who are these people? Is this what zoo animals feel like?*

Time blurred to an agonizing standstill. She paced, picking and pounding at the wall for a while before sitting on the pillow. Knocking came from everywhere, making her jump.

"Mind if I come in?" asked a man's voice.

"Let me out of here!" Kate leapt to her feet.

Agent Perrin faded into view at the center of the cell. Despite the years, he didn't look much different from the face burned into her memory. The sight of him dredged up childish fear, reducing her to a shivering ball on the bed, pressed into the tiles at her back.

He glanced down at his shiny, black shoes. "I don't mean to frighten you, Kate. All we ever wanted was to help. I'm glad to see you're alive, in one piece, and back home."

"This isn't my home." The weight of an old nightmare faded. She lowered her feet to the floor, uncurling from her fetal cringe. "I don't belong to you."

Perrin offered a condescending smile. "Before you hurt yourself, take note of the device on your neck."

Kate gripped it at her throat, all the color drained from her cheeks. "It's a bomb?"

He looked genuine in his alarm. "Oh, no. I know you don't believe me, but hurting you is the last thing we want. It's a neural-stunner. Have you ever seen the stun rods the police carry?"

"No." *I don't usually associate with cops.* "Why should I believe a damn word you say? You fuckers tried to kill me when I was a kid."

"Incorrect." Hologram-Perrin approached. "A genetics research firm working for us tried to kill you."

"Laughlin-Reed Innovation," she growled. "Get it off me. I can't breathe."

"In time. We have to come to trust you first. For now, know that it is able to detect an attempt to use your gift. Should you try to call upon any psionic abilities, it will scramble most of the activity in your brain for a moment. I assure you it's harmless, but I've heard it's rather painful."

She let her fingers slip off the metal, staring speechless at him.

"Division 0 uses psi-inhibitors. Those devices interfere with psionic power by distracting the wearer on a subconscious level. We find them unnecessarily cruel. All that random sensory input can drive a person insane in a day or two."

Kate pulled her feet up, heels on the edge of the metal shelf, and hugged her legs. "So you're going to keep me locked up longer than that I guess."

Agent Perrin's intangible hand brushed at her hair. "I'd rather you thought of it as protective custody. You're not a prisoner."

"Could'a fuckin' fooled me." She frowned at the orange suit.

"Presently you are 'liberty-challenged,' but we hope to change that."

Kate picked at her eye with her middle finger.

"Cute."

A faint whirr from the left seemed thunderous in the silence. One wall tile opened upward like a hatch, allowing a floating tray to enter from a shaft too narrow for a person to crawl into. The sight of it made her feel even more trapped. It glided over to her bearing a plate of eggs, bacon, and something failing at being potatoes. Despite her situation, the irresistible smell beckoned.

"I'm sure there will be a period of adjustment. We don't want to harm you, Kate. We want to hire you."

She scarfed down the food, unwilling to pause long enough to say a word.

"C-Branch, if you're wondering. Military intelligence. We run the world. You are too valuable to play in the kiddie pool with Division 0. However, we do have some concerns."

"Concerns?" Kate mumbled around a full mouth, swallowed, and glared. "You don't seem too concerned about what I think of all this."

Agent Perrin chuckled. "We are worried about you. Around forty people died when you went rogue. At that age, it had to be traumatic from a psychological standpoint."

"Went rogue?" Her mouth hung open. "I was a fucking child, not a goddamned agent! They were going to kill me. What was I supposed to do, just float there and die like a good little science project?"

"You were never in danger, Kate. The kill button required authorization from my superiors. Ramesh could not have killed you without our okay."

"I'm not seven anymore, Perrin. You'll need better bullshit than that to convince me." She gave up on trying to spear bacon with a plastic fork and grabbed it. "I got numb to it. Ramesh I wanted to kill… everyone else, I dunno. All I wanted to do was get away. My brain translated 'get away from me' into 'burn shit.'"

"You feel no remorse for killing all those people?" Perrin raised an eyebrow.

She chewed for a moment, staring at him. "At the time? No. I didn't know any better. Yeah, I've had a few bad dreams, but I'm over it."

"Your work for the Syndicate indicates you've become rather blasé about killing."

"Every one of those people had their arms up to the elbows in the underworld."

Perrin tilted his head. "That does make it easier, doesn't it? To think of them as deserving of death?"

Kate slouched, staring at the little bits of egg remaining. "Gotta do something, don't I? What choice did I have? I am what you people made me. That's what you want now, isn't it? Wrap me up in a nice sexy dress and send me places to kill people."

"It's not all about killing. It's about protecting our country. All that's a bit of a ways off. We have to know you are... well." Perrin tapped his head before twisting left, as if talking to someone out of reach of the camera creating his holographic presence. "We are quite curious about your recent adjustment. How is it that you are no longer—?"

"A walking pariah?" She finished off the food. The tray hovered back to the hole from whence it came. "I dunno. It just... stopped one day. Maybe I grew out of it."

Agent Perrin smiled. "You'll need some training on subterfuge."

Althea's face came to mind. The girl's wide, innocent stare almost brought Kate to tears. "I can't. Trust me when I say C-Branch couldn't make use of the why, no matter what you threaten."

"Well, perhaps you'll come around someday."

"And what would you do? Try to mass-produce more people like me?"

He sighed. "No, Kate. You were the result of a lucky circumstance. They've been trying to recreate what they did with you since you ran away."

Tears leapt from her eyes without permission. She covered her mouth with one hand. "How many children?"

"You're working it up to be worse than it was." He gestured at someone off camera. "There were sixteen others. Only three came out psionic, and none had your level of ability. What is it your new friends call themselves? Awakened?"

Kate gasped. "You know about them?"

He flashed a shocked face. "Which part of military intelligence didn't you grasp? Do you honestly think you'd have survived on your own without a little help from the shadows?"

"Actually, yes." Kate folded her arms. "If you were really following me, and you're not pumping sunshine up my ass now about 'caring,' why did you leave me out there all alone?"

"Can you handle the honest answer?"

Her smirk went flat. "You couldn't use me for anything."

"More or less. I took some liberties with the project budget. Initially, they wanted to make sure you were not a threat to the population or ran your mouth to the NewsNet. I was trying to keep you safe."

"Gee, thanks, *Dad.*"

"I need to meet with some people. We'll be back in a few hours to conduct a proper interview." He started to walk away, but looked back. "Christopher wanted to apologize for the deception. Based on your background, the doctors think the pheromones may have hit you quite hard. If you're feeling the need to take certain matters into your own hands, I'll make sure the cameras are off."

Kate flushed crimson, flinging herself sideways on the bed with her back to the room. "Go to Hell."

LESSER EVILS

A soft pneumatic squeak broke the silence. Kate couldn't tell how much time had passed. The tray had come and gone again, bearing a turkey, bacon, and tomato sandwich. Despite her current situation, she found herself eating in tiny nibbles to over-taste everything. The texture of the slightly-toasted bread, the contrast of cold tomato, warm turkey, and crunchy bacon. As long as she'd taken to finish it, it had to be vat-grown meat with hydroponic veggies. OmniSoy would've melted back to goop before she was halfway done.

She figured it an hour or so past noon, but the featureless, boring cell offered no clues as to the passage of time or even the hour of the day. Berating herself over being stupid and leaving Querq got her no closer to escaping, so she gave up. Officer Ahmed mentioned something about Division 0 being able to protect her from C-Branch. She wondered if he'd find out they had kidnapped her.

"Kate?" A deep voice flooded the cell.

This guy sounds huge. She shifted onto her back, rolling her head to the right. Sure enough, a large man stood in a space that had become a doorway. He had the build of an augmented special forces soldier; his clingy black shirt accented every ridge and valley of a figure inflated by implanted muscles. Camouflage pants stretched at the thigh, but hung loose the rest of the way to his boots. Behind him, a pair of too-pale-to-be-alive men in sand brown coats and sunglasses waited.

"Can I guess what they sent you here for?"

He frowned. "You have a dirty mind. I'm to escort you to a conference room."

She grumbled and got up. A squeal came out of her as her bare feet hit the icy floor. Once the shock of it faded, she trudged to the door. Another wiseass remark stalled when she found herself eye-level to his pectorals. The metal band tightened around her throat, reminding her she couldn't use her abilities. A tremble manifested in her hands. *Is this what it feels like to be normal? Helpless? Afraid of giant men?*

Eyes downcast, she turned her back and put her hands behind her. "So what do they call you?"

"Agent Jones." He rested a hand on her shoulder and guided her into the hallway. "Kate, you're not a prisoner. We merely need to take some precautions until we know you're on board with the program."

"Jones? Not your real name, huh?" She continued shaking, struggling to process the foreign sense of being vulnerable.

"I can't say." He flashed a mischievous grin. "The two men behind me are synthetics. Unless you can outrun a car, there's no need for restraints. Again, you're not a prisoner."

Kate glanced at her cell. "Yeah... Maybe if you keep saying that, being locked up in a white cube with this fucking thing on my neck will feel just like home." She tried to rub some warmth into her arms. *Guess it's better than being naked in a tank of slime. At least I can pace in circles.*

The huge hand felt like a ten-ton weight on her shoulder as he steered her through a left turn into another hallway to an elevator. She backed into the wall with the three men between her and the door.

"C-can I at least get socks or something? It's f-freezing in here."

"As soon as they trust you won't use them to harm yourself," said the big man.

"With socks? Are you serious?"

The pallid man on the left had no emotion in his face as he spoke. "They could be used to fashion an improvised gravity-assisted strangulation device."

Jones smiled. "He means they're worried you'll hang yourself."

"They clamp a brain-smasher around my neck and they're worried about socks?" Kate growled. "What happened to that whole 'not a prisoner' thing?"

"It will pass. You seem sane enough to me." Agent Jones smiled.

The elevator opened and her escort guided her down a short grey-carpeted corridor to a windowless room. Perrin and a middle-aged woman in a white coat sat at a table. Kate took an immediate dislike to the scientist, glaring as Jones prodded her around to a chair facing them.

"Thank you, Jones," said Perrin.

"I'll be right outside if you need, sir."

Kate sat and scuffed her feet back and forth across the carpet to warm and de-numb them. Agent Perrin gestured at a tray of brownies, cupcakes, and cookies.

"Coffee?"

"Sure," she muttered past a mouthful of double-fudge chocolate chip.

"This is Doctor Mlodzik." Perrin indicated the woman at his right.

The woman offered a slight bow. Short, curled hair touched by the beginnings of grey gave her a look older than her skin seemed. Kate made a sour face at the hand hovering over the table, the same shade of light brown as her cookie.

"I'm aware you have trust issues with scientists. I'm no geneticist, Kate. I'm not even a researcher. I'm a psychiatrist."

"Hi." Kate accepted the handshake with a forced, vapid smile. "I'm a science project. So, at what point is my ass going back in a tank?"

Perrin set a cup of coffee in front of her. "You take it black?"

"I'll take it any way I can get it now." She made a face at him.

"Pheromones still not worn off?" Perrin sat.

"Now who's the one with the dirty mind?" Kate grasped the cup. "I was talking about coffee."

A small amount of color appeared in his cheeks. Kate smirked, the measure of discomfort racked up one minor victory. The coffee was hot, and average. She couldn't help but wince a little as it hit her tongue.

"Sorry, it's government issue." Perrin chuckled. "Cutbacks, you know. Even the coffee took a hit."

"How much did I cost?" She dunked another cookie, trying to give the liquid some flavor.

"I don't have that information. I'd like to build some trust with you, so I'm going to tell you some things that are classified."

"Ooh." Kate perked up. "I get to know about myself? Do I have enough clearance to know that I exist?"

Doctor Mlodzik seemed to be fighting the urge to smile.

Perrin showed no reaction to her attitude. "You did not lose your parents, Kate. You never had them."

She let the cookie fall into the cup, arms limp on the table. It was something she had always assumed, but hearing it—even from him—hurt. Trust and Perrin were far from the same thing, but the quality of his voice rang true. What Archon had shared about the information matched.

"Ekaterina Myshkin?" muttered Kate. "They were trying to clone some old person. Guess they screwed something up."

"I see the file breach found its way to you already." He forced a smile. "Then you know I'm not being deceitful. You were a weapons project, but something went wrong. The constant heat made you unsuitable for any assignments they had in mind."

"Yeah, I got that part." The heaviness of the metal around her neck held back her desperate curiosity to read Perrin's mind. "Right around the time they went to hit me with neurotoxin."

"Unfortunately, the general in charge of the project set an overly demanding deadline. Ramesh decided on his own to stop working on a way to 'turn it off' and start all over."

Kate jumped with a flashback to the man's face as he boiled from the inside out.

"What was that?" asked Dr. Mlodzik.

"I remember Ramesh. I couldn't hear them talking through the tank, so I read their minds. I knew he wanted to kill me. I begged him not to hurt me, but he kept reaching for that button. I wasn't a child to him, just an animal in a tank, a project." She stared at the flecks of cookie floating on the coffee, wavering in a white spot of reflected fluorescent lights. "He was the first person I hated. My abilities picked up on that hate and I boiled the fluids in his body. I didn't know what I was doing. My rage made it happen."

"The site team thought he'd been hit with a microwave weapon," said Perrin. The chuckle underlining his words triggered a disturbed glance from Dr. Mlodzik.

"One of the scientists tried to stop them, but they dragged him out."

"Dr. Aldus Solomon. He was the lead researcher on your project." Perrin noted her eyebrow lift. "Ramesh was the bureaucratic head. He pushed documents, not genes."

Kate slurped at the coffee-cookie concoction, thinking about the old man who wanted to protect her. "Solomon's as close as I've got to a father."

"That's an excellent analogy," said Dr. Mlodzik. "And like a parent, he tried to protect you."

She pouted at her reflection on the dark liquid. "Pity they shot him."

Dr. Mlodzik's smile fell flat.

"Actually," said Perrin. "He vanished. We still haven't located him."

"So much for Military Intelligence." Kate frowned.

"That means one of two things. He's either gone to the Badlands, which I doubt, or he's in the Beneath."

"I'd like to talk about the time between your leaving the facility and now," said Dr. Mlodzik.

Kate remained silent until the feeling of confinement from the guarded door and the metal ring around her neck became too much. In a monotone voice, she spoke of living in the forests of the Scattered Lands, a feral child hunting deer and sleeping on dirt mounds. Mlodzik took particular note of her guilt over the first kill, offering a reassuring expression that encouraged her to continue.

The story rambled through her increasing loneliness and into East City, gangs, and the Syndicate. Figuring she was as screwed as screwed can be already, she held nothing back—except the old priest and Althea. If they thought she'd cracked and started believing in demons, they'd probably just shoot her.

"So, now you want me to work for C-Branch, right? I'm guessing it's not much of a choice. What if I refuse?" Kate held up a hand. "Wait, let me guess. That whole 'you're not a prisoner' thing changes."

Perrin interlaced his fingers, tapping his hands on the table. "You have to understand our interest in protecting the citizens and the nation at large." He swiped his hand over a silver fleck, activating a holo-pane. Images of some of her syndicate kills scrolled by in midair, as well as full motion video of her feeding frenzy at CyberBurger when she burned Alfonso. "The man still wets himself at the sight of you."

"I was starving, still only a kid, wild, and scared shitless." Kate snagged a brownie. "I didn't want to hurt him, but he ran at me with this giant spear thing."

"You may want to slow down. Now that you're no longer burning 24/7, your metabolism's back to normal."

"I think I can spare a few extra calories today." Kate poked herself in the ribs. "So, basically, I get locked up if I don't agree to join you guys." Officer Ahmed's sparkling brown eyes danced in her memory. *Division 0's offer seemed less hostile. Could they really have protected me from these people? Fucking Esteban. Why did I leave Querq?* "I think you're overreacting. I'm not that dangerous."

"Oh?" said Perrin. He poked at the light panel.

The image changed to one from a distant pole-camera, aimed at the front of the remote facility. Little Kate stood on a portable stairway, hands balled into fists, hair in the wind. The diminutive figure looked downcast. Intense light formed around her, seconds before the entire scene erupted in a yellow-orange fireball ringed with smoke. Lines of static tainted the image for several seconds before it cut out to black. When it recovered, a platoon of soldiers lay motionless, military vehicles had melted and warped, and Perrin was gone.

"You did that when you were a child," said Perrin. "You've had a lot more practice since then."

"How is that any different from someone with a plasma grenade? How are my fireballs any worse than someone with a gun? I'm not the kind of psionic that can possess people, mind control people, steal secrets, or do all that other freaky shit. I'm a weapon with tits."

Dr. Mlodzik looked away, blushing.

"Your comparison is not too far off the mark. However, your 'firearms' can pass through security systems undetected. Without a need for weapons of any kind, you could slip into the deepest, most secure places under the guise of a lost tourist or prostitute or girlfriend and then…"

He replayed the explosion.

"If you think I'm going to whore for the government, you've got no idea who I am." Kate leaned forward, pointing at him. "I've killed for the Syndicate, but I've never…"

"Haven't you?" He pulled up an image of that hotel.

They knew about Tyrel.

Kate blushed. "I was unconscious. They had to knock me out to get past the thermal sensors. It was just to get in the door. Even if it were possible at the time, I had no intention of fu—"

Perrin held up a hand. "No one is saying you have to go that far."

"Oh." Kate crossed her arms. "Yeah, that makes sense. Because everything always goes according to plan. I sneak in like someone's paid-for date and not expect things to run off the rails, not even once. No chance of a situation blowing up in my face and winding up with my ankles behind my head to stop something worse from happening. Oh, if you go crazy and blow the shit out of the place, it'll create an international incident. I'm not an idiot, Perrin. I know why they made me look like this." She jumped to her feet. "Be a good agent and take one for the team. Bend over and bear it. It's only a little old man cock. Wait for him to be alone before you kill because dozens of innocent lives are on the line if you make a scene." She unzipped her jumpsuit. "Come on, Perrin. Might as well break me in now. It only took me twenty-five years to be able to wear clothes, and the first thing you people want is for me to take them off again."

Perrin averted his eyes. "Assassinations are not commonplace. Espionage is far more—"

Dr. Mlodzik glared at Perrin. "Enough." The harshness left her voice as she made a zip-up gesture. "Kate, please…"

She closed her jumpsuit and fell into the seat.

"A case where we would need to use you instead of a doll operative are one in a hundred thousand. It may never happen."

"Yeah, sure, like they can't recognize a doll on a scanner." Kate let her elbows land hard on the table and slumped. "What are my options?"

"Well… You could wear that stunner for the rest of your life, eat a bullet, or work for us." He drummed his fingers on the table. "I don't expect you to understand this, Kate, but I do care about you. I've watched you grow up."

She traced a finger across the collar. *He's lying. If they let me leave, they know I'll go to Division 0. They'll get this thing off me. Perrin won't let me go. I'll get a bullet in the back of the head as soon as I think I'm safe.*

"I'll need some private sessions with her before I'm ready to sign anything regarding her suitability for field operations." Doctor Mlodzik faced her. "Kate, I'll be meeting with you soon. I want you to know that you can tell me anything. Even these people don't have the right to breach the confidentiality of a session."

The bullshit never ends. Kate gazed into her lap. They didn't have to know she'd gotten over her demons years ago in the woodlands. Her escape had been a blur of screaming people and belching flames. What regrets could she harbor for people that either wanted to kill her or didn't care to help her?

Agent Jones opened the door and gave her an expectant look.

Maybe she'd waste their time talking about the deer. *That poor animal. It didn't want to hurt anyone.* Her fingers picked at the stunner as she got up and trudged to the men waiting to escort her back to her cell.

She wouldn't give either of them the satisfaction of crying.

30

ANGEL AND THE ALBATROSS

Kate stopped pacing around her 'room' and sat on the edge of the metal slab pretending to be a bed. Teeth chattering, she lifted one foot and tried to rub warmth into it. It was anyone's guess how long ago Agent Jones and the two synthetics sealed her in. She recalled the meal tray coming three more times, or was it four? Five?

"You keep saying I'm not a prisoner," she yelled, staring at the walls until the echo ceased. "How about a goddamned blanket or some socks?"

Her hands clasped the heavy ring around her throat as she leaned forward. Looking down at her feet made her feel even colder. She squeezed the collar, wondering if they'd lied to her. More than the physical weight of the metal, it felt ponderous. Each time she touched it, the burden of helplessness grew heavier.

Do such things exist? She tapped at the device. *Maybe they're lying. Machines sensing psionics? That sounds far-fetched.*

One hand hovered over her feet, focusing on the ambient temperature of the air. *Just a little bit.* It would only take a little energy to warm feeling back into her toes. Kate concentrated on raising the temperature of the air.

In an instant, she went from staring past her fingers at her feet, to lying on the ground with a full view of the ceiling. Cold speared into her head as though an icy lance rammed upward from her heart into her brain. Flashes of blue and white lightning crackled across her eyes, each accompanied by an impact on par with a slap. Convulsions banged her head, elbows, and legs against the hard floor, her body out of control.

The worst headache she had ever experienced rendered the overhead lights intolerable, but her paralyzed eyelids refused to close. Kate screamed in her mind, her attempt to breathe gasped out a glop of foamy spittle that slid over her cheek to her neck and the floor. Still howling in her thoughts, she strained to roll over and curl up. She wanted to cradle her pounding skull in both arms, but she felt as if straps held her to the floor.

Kate lost track of how many minutes passed. She noticed full-body pain only due to its gradual absence. Shivering replaced paralysis. Kate yelled as she forced herself onto her side and went fetal. The skin of her neck felt raw, her head pounded in time with her heartbeat. Every muscle, the ones behind her eyes most of all, throbbed. Her mind seemed only capable of coming up with one reaction to such agony—she bawled like a child.

At the faint hiss of the door opening, she twitched, sobbing became sniveling between staccato gasps for air.

"Well, that took longer than most," said an unfamiliar male voice.

Kate ignored him. Her tenderized brain cringed from the need to do anything.

Dark shoes and a sand brown coat stepped into the edge of her peripheral vision. A second later, a folded blanket landed with a *thump* next to her. Kate strained to raise her head toward it, teeth gritted at a sensation as if her neck muscles tore like dry beef jerky. She startled when a new jumpsuit, folded and smelling of laundry, landed atop the blanket.

"W-what?" She let her head rest on the cold floor. "T-took longer than m-most?"

"Perhaps that is an unfair statement. You are only the third psionic... protectee we have had in custody. The other two both tested the stun ring in less than an hour." He crouched, putting two fingers on the side of her neck.

She wanted to throw him off, evade him, or fight... but her body refused to do anything more than tremble and hurt.

"Try to relax. The device creates the sensation of pain without causing damage to tissues. You were unconscious for several minutes, not that you noticed. The aches you feel now are not true pain, but the muscles' reaction to the absence of stimulation. It will pass."

"If you fuckers wanted to recruit me, did you ever think of oh, maybe treating me like a person?" An attempt to sit up ended with uncontrollable tremors. "Take it off... I'll play along. I swear, just get this fucking thing off me. Please!"

Again, she sobbed like a five-year-old.

"I'm not at liberty to make that call. I'm only an agent." He dropped a packet of underwear, wrapped in plastic, on top of the jumpsuit. "You'll probably want to shower. Looks like you've had an accident."

Her skin had been too numb to notice. Now that he said it, the wetness and smell became obvious. Not wanting to sit in piss, she forced herself onto all fours. A too-pale hand offered to help her up. It hurt to move at all, but she accepted. Despite his thin, almost scientist's build, he lifted her upright with no noticeable effort. Kate wobbled on her feet, unable to suppress a few more tears at the shooting spears of fire in her legs.

"I was trying to warm up." She shivered, unsure if it was from cold. "It's freezing in here."

"Gather your things and follow me."

He waited while she picked up the plastic packet and clean jumpsuit, and walked her a short distance to a room with a number of autoshower tubes. She paused at the one bench and shot him an incredulous stare as he remained with her.

"Do you mind?"

"With apologies, Kate. Until you have clearance, you must be escorted within the facility at all times. Although I am an electronic artificial intelligence and do not have any sense of sexual desire, if you are more comfortable with a live female agent, I can request one."

"What if I prefer women?" asked Kate.

His expression remained flat. "That is the primary reason agents like myself are assigned this detail. I possess no ability to experience sexual attraction of any kind."

"You may be a computer inside, but you still *look* like a man. It's awkward." She unzipped the jumpsuit. "Is this thing gonna explode if it gets wet?"

"No. It is sealed."

The urge to get out of the soiled garments overpowered her humiliation. At the man's utter lack of response to the sight of her stripping, she focused on the thought of him being no different from a PubTran car or menial labor doll. Within twenty minutes, she had showered, changed, and lay once more curled up on the metal plate that served as a bed in her cell. At least now, she had a blanket to wrap around herself.

Hours passed. The solitude crept in as though the walls shrank inward. She alternated between pouting at the floor and picking at the thing around her neck. One by one, the faces of people she killed for El Tío flashed in her memory. *What was it, forty? Fifty? Maybe more if you count that drug lab.* Althea's smiling face appeared next, small hands reaching up to embrace her. *So innocent.* One tear slid down Kate's cheek. *She had no idea what kind of monster I really am. All those people.*

Kate tried to remember herself as a victim, a little girl the government wanted to murder. She had become a feral child living alone in the woods, without a care in the world. A smile almost appeared on her lips until the faces of the dead returned. Screaming, begging, and pleading choked her brain to a halt. Many of them had body counts larger than hers; yet, in her mind, they all became innocent victims.

She stared down the shivering bundle of grey-brown cloth. Kate closed her eyes, thinking back to the Roadway Corp office, and the convicts on the other side of the glass.

I'm where I belong now. They should keep me locked up.

The more she thought, the less she felt like resisting C-Branch. She was a machine made to kill, taking her first life at the age of seven. *What kind of twisted person cries over a deer and feels nothing at killing people?*

The auto-tray arrived with a portion of ziti. It landed nearby, though Kate ignored it. A sense of drifting off to sleep began, but halted with an icy caress down her back. Something tugged at her mind; she sensed an intrusion, though the instinctual urge to resist evaporated under the terror of another shock. The mere thought of getting zapped again almost spilled her bladder.

Nothing happened.

She squirmed around, tightening the blanket.

You look a right hames, girl. Feeling sorry for ourselves, are we?

Kate screamed.

Now, now. Calm down before they think you've gone Cat-6.

She sat up, eyes darting about.

These blokes have got the place locked down hard. This is the only way we have to reach you.

"What? Aurora?"

Don't talk out loud. Just think, dear. I'm inside you. By the way, in case you hadn't noticed, you're quite peckish. Hungry even.

No, I'm not.

The same chill that she felt on her back spread into her arms and legs. As though her brain had detached from her body, she spectated while she sat up and took the tray in her lap. A plastic forkful of ziti hovered at her mouth.

Open up, dear. You don't want me to sing the choo-choo song, do you?

Kate scowled. *I'm not two years old.*

The sound of a woman's voice mimicking a train in the back of her mind became maddening within seconds. She acquiesced and tolerated being fed a few forkfuls before fighting for control of her arm.

That's it, luv. You'll need your strength.

She squeezed the blanket with her toes. *What for? I'm where I belong.*

Rubbish, chirped Aurora. *Archon wants to help you.*

Ziti slid around the plate, urged by an aimless plastic utensil. *C-Branch, Division 0, El Tío, everyone... All they want to do is use me. Archon's no different. I'm just a weapon. A killer.*

Well you're right sick as a parrot, aren't ya? This all over that bloke in St. Louis? I can help you forget all about him if you fancy.

Her left eye winked on its own.

She stuffed another forkful in her mouth. *No. I'm tired of running, and it's not all about sex.*

Twenty-five years untouched, you expect me to believe it's not? Hmm, imagine what the guards watching your cameras would do if I popped out and we messed about. The total clusterfuck that would cause is wicked tempting.

Kate pouted into her lap, reliving the moment with Esteban and the oven mitt. *I want more than that. It's not the physical contact. I'm tired of feeling like it's 'the world plus Kate.' I want to belong with someone.*

Aww, that was so romantic. Her left arm wiped away nonexistent tears.

Stop that. Kate grabbed her wayward hand and held it to her gut. *That's so creepy!*

Her legs crossed, left on top. *I know! Real pisser innit?* Aurora's voice laughed in her thoughts.

Kate shivered and clutched the stun collar. *How is it you're not setting this fucking thing off? Get out.*

Oh, don't throw a wobbly. I'm not using your brain, too. It's watching what you do. It can't see ghosts.

She stared at the wall.

No. Aurora let off a heavy mental sigh. *I'm not dead, but I'm close enough to a ghost to fool that machine. Look, this isn't your place. Buck up, you're leaving.*

She set the fork on the empty plate; the auto-tray floated off and disappeared into its hatch. *Everyone wants to use me. I... I can only think of one person I've met who's been nice to me without wanting something in return.*

Just one? asked Aurora. *What about that spiritualist fellow? The one who got you to thank the dead animals?*

Kate ran her fingers down her hair in a repetitive, nervous gesture. *Okay, two.*

Althea is innocent and naïve. She thinks there is good inside everyone. Can you believe that?

She chuckled. *I'm a killer.*

Are you so sure, Kate? By the way, they can't get you out of here... but once you're out, they can protect you.

"What's that supposed to mean," whispered Kate. "They who?"

Kate, in her blanket-burrito, scooted like an inchworm over the metal cot and leaned against the corner of the cell. She stuck one hand out in the open, gazing at her splayed fingers. For the second time in her life, she felt helpless—at the mercy of others. She couldn't boil her way out of this cage. A brief moment of jealousy toward Althea came and went; the girl had an entire city willing to protect her. Envy gave way to gratitude. Kate had become one of them; she wanted to protect the child. What Althea said hit her out of the blue and hung a leaden weight of guilt around her neck, heavier than the stunner. The old man had manipulated her. *Burn out cancer... He loves misery and suffering. He wanted to scare me away from her.* Kate squinted at the space she thought held the cell door.

I just need to play their game long enough to earn trust.

31

A CHANCE TO VENT

Kate startled awake at the touch of a hand jostling her by the shoulder. A short figure stood beside her iron-hard bed. Kate raised an arm over her eyes to shield them from the relentless ceiling lights. Between the glare and the sudden shift from sleep to conscious, her brain perceived only a blur of color in the approximate shape of a woman. The grip on her shoulder pushed and pulled; her head felt like the yolk inside an egg as someone shook it.

"We don't have much time. Get up and fetch your shoes," said the woman.

"They confiscated them." Kate sat up. "Won't even let me have socks... think I'll hang myself."

"Bother. That's a stack of shit, Kate. They're trying to keep you uncomfortable, make you pliable. Keep you freezing, then give you a blanket. You start to trust them, see them as nice. Didn't it occur to you that you could hang yourself with your jumpsuit more easily than socks?"

A few blinks changed the generic female shape into one she recognized, a diminutive woman with white hair in navy blue coat over black shirt and pants. "Anna? What the hell are you doing here?"

"This is your gallant rescue. Come on." Anna dragged her standing. "Aurora's got the security station man."

Kate fell back to sit on the hard metal bunk. "We'll get shot. Get out of here before you get caught too." She tapped the collar. "I'm useless right now. I'm as safe as I can get here for what I am and I probably deserve—"

"Bollocks." Anna hauled her upright again. "Aurora told me she doesn't think you're in for being used as a killer anymore. Once they figure that out..." She made a finger gun at Kate's temple and a *pshoo* noise. "If not for concern over what you'll do, to keep your existence a secret."

"But..."

"Archon is going to take us away from all of this. You will be safe and happy somewhere far away from the reach of any government or corporation."

Kate sniffed. Burnt flesh. "What's that smell?"

Anna pulled her by the hand to the door. "I think he called himself Agent Jones."

"Dead?"

"No. Just knocked out." Anna peeked out into the hall. "Government types get peevish when you kill one of them. We're trying to get you out of here, not start a war."

"I can't go out there like this... I look like a prison escapee."

Anna smirked. "You *are* a prison escapee. I brought you some things, but they're stashed a bit away from here."

Kate's started to speak, but a noise like the bark of a goose came out of her as Anna lunged forward, dragging her by the arm. Every ten yards along the ceiling, smoke poured out of small holes wherever a camera had been. Anna hurried down the corridor, skipping some hallways and taking two turns without pausing to consider, suggesting she somehow knew the way out.

At the third corner, one of the synthetic agents surprised them, lunging into a stomp-kick that threw Anna into the wall. Kate instinctively drew her hand back in a claw-like shape. Memory of the horrible agony awaiting her stalled her brain before she tried to make the fireball. The synthetic looked at her, taking less than a full second to disregard her as a non-threat.

Kate shivered from the fear of being an ordinary woman threatened by a machine-man stronger and faster than her, and devoid of any sense of conscience. Anna wheezed, looking more angry than worried.

He drew a pistol and aimed at Anna in a motion so fast it created a blurry ghost trail behind his arm. A flash came with a tremendous *bang* that slammed the air from Kate's lungs.

She cringed at the deafening echo. It took her a moment to process what happened. Rather than a muzzle flare, the light had come from a thick bolt of lightning connecting Anna's hand to the synthetic's chest.

Anna growled and clambered to her feet. The synth stood motionless for a moment before falling forward. He hit the ground pistol first, balancing on rigid statue-like limbs. Pale grey foam steamed from the corners of his eyes and mouth—boiling nanobot-laced 'blood.'

When Anna took her by the hand again, Kate clamped on in a hug.

"What the devil's gotten into you?" Anna pushed at her. "We have to get out of here."

Kate tapped the metal band around her neck. "I'm…"

Sapphire eyes widened a touch with a show of sympathy. "Yes, yes… I know. Helpless. You're welcome, now come on."

Three steps into the run, Kate shook off her fear. When she went from drag-along to sprinting under her own will, Anna released her hand. They ducked into a stairwell, heading down.

"Down?" Kate blurted, waving her arms not to fall. "Aren't we underground?"

Anna stopped at the landing halfway between floors and raised both hands. Kate moved up behind, feeling foolish for hiding behind a woman so short. The top of Anna's head barely made it to Kate's chin.

Another pair of synthetics waited at the landing below, compact rifles aimed. Anna closed her eyes. Twin bolts of lightning leapt from ceiling lights, struck the artificial humans, and flowed into her arms. The concussive wave of the blast knocked the door behind them off its mounting rails. Kate tried to grab Anna for support, but wound up on her back, twitching. The smell of ozone and burnt silicon choked the air out of her throat.

"Sorry, Kate. Don't touch me when I'm live." She jogged down to the landing, making an obvious effort to avoid both guns. "Lucky for us, they don't know me."

"What's that mean?" Kate dragged herself upright. Ache ran in throbs down her back and legs; the shock had reawakened a good portion of muscle pain from the neural stunner.

Anna moved into the hallway, muttering. "Synthetics, dolls, cyborgs… whatever. Exactly the worst thing to send after me. They all run on electricity."

"I *hate* borgs and bots." Kate grumbled. "They take so much energy to melt."

Anna smiled. "I find them far easier to deal with than people."

"Killing or... just uhh, 'dealing' with?"

"Take your pick." Anna chuckled as she peered left and right.

Kate snagged a rifle as she stumbled past the twitching synths. *I'd rather be a target than helpless.*

"What'd you take that for?" Anna glanced back while punching in a code by an elevator door.

"I hate feeling like some little girl who needed saving. I don't want to be dead weight." She slid to a halt, back to the wall, and sighted over the rifle at the corridor. "This collar. I'd rather not shit myself twice in one day."

"That was three days ago," said Anna as the doors opened. "If you shoot at them, they won't try to recruit you. They'll just kill you."

"Like they're not going to do that already. Wait... three?" Kate blinked.

"Yes. Mental torture, Kate. Solitary confinement." Anna pointed at the ceiling, and interlaced her fingers to make a step. "Right, up you go."

Kate slung the rifle over her shoulder and put a foot in Anna's hands. After a boost, she climbed up through a hatch in the roof and crawled out onto a ladder. The narrow rungs felt like standing barefoot on icicles, but she weathered the discomfort.

"Climb up a bit and get tight on the ladder," said Anna, before switching to telepathy. *Gonna send the lift to the roof after I disable the cameras.*

Kate pulled herself up four rungs and huddled as tight as she could in the recess that held the ladder, hugging the metal framework. Several sharp cracks echoed from below, followed by the scent of burned electrical components. Seconds later, rattling announced Anna's frantic exit. Once the metal box slid up and past her, Kate looked down. Anna held on to the rungs a few feet below, waving at her to start climbing.

Kate looked up at the receding square of light as the elevator cab ascended. Dangling cables swayed from the underside. The occasional tiny spark flickered between magnets and the tracks it climbed. Anna's impatient tapping grew louder than her breathing.

Dull blue-grey metal stretched overhead in a vertical tunnel. Drawn in the wake of the elevator, wind carrying the scent of metal and grease whipped up from below, filling the legs of her prison jumpsuit and slapping her in the face with her hair. The jolt from the stun collar had left her muscles unable to exert without tremors, every rung she dragged herself up became a battle of willpower. Smears of dark liquid stained the walls here and there around the occasional loose metal flap over a breaker panel or maintenance access. Soon, her hands and feet had gone numb from the frigid plastisteel.

The labor of moving mutated into a repetitious mechanical activity divested of higher brain function. Anna's hands swiped at her feet every few seconds, no doubt a hint to move faster. Kate squealed when one brushing hand turned into a grip about her ankle.

"We're here," whispered Anna. "Slip back down a bit and follow me."

She leaned away from the ladder a little and made the mistake of looking down. Anna peeled the cover from a ventilation shaft, tossed it, and climbed in. Kate's eyes locked onto the slatted grating plummeting into what appeared to be a bottomless pit.

"Kate?" Anna's voice echoed from the duct.

Clatter. The vent hit the wall forty feet below, spinning. *Crack.* It caromed off a pipe and continued spinning into darkness. Her mind filled with a looping vision of falling face-first, the ground rushing toward her with a fatal kiss.

"Kate?" A white pixie-cut poked out from the vent portal. "What is it?"

The telltale mental twinge of incoming telepathy swam over Kate's brain. She didn't dare resist, and had to fight the urge to reply.

"Oh, you've gotta be kidding me. Afraid of heights?" Anna rolled her eyes. "Look, we've got about ten minutes before all bloody hell breaks loose. Guns, dogs, nasty stuff. Look at me, Kate. Don't look down. Look at me."

Kate fixated on the face in the vent. *What's wrong with me? I'm not a coward.* The presence of tight metal around her neck answered her question. She tried to take her mind off her fear of falling by clinging to anger at having the device locked around her neck. Anna grabbed her arms and helped pull her in before she could think about the action. Once inside the claustrophobic confines of the shaft, she forgot all about the deadfall. Anna crawled deeper into the dark. Kate sat for a moment, trying to catch her breath and get her body to stop trembling.

"Will you come on?" Anna whisper-yelled from about ten meters away. "We've got a bit of a schedule to keep."

Kate rolled onto all fours and hurried after. She tucked up behind Anna, trying to peer over her back and make eye contact.

"You do the electricity thing, right?" whispered Kate.

"Yes. Will you please back off a bit? If I stop short, your head's going to go up my arse."

"Sorry. Can you get this damn thing off me?"

"Probably, but not now. It's a complicated device and I'll need to map it out. Once we're in the air, I'll get on it."

Featureless metal vents passed for a minute and change. Kate followed her savior along a series of turns, left, left, right, straight past a four-way turn, then left. Anna moved with such confidence in her route, Kate's fear lessened somewhat. At the end of the next section of shaft, she slid through an opening into a large chamber dominated by a massive air mover. The walls shimmered with chopped-up light as angled metal fan blades big enough to use as beds circled above. Kate crawled out, casting a hesitant glance upward before standing. The chamber's size kept the spinning death machine a good two feet above her head. A few partial rats clung to the walls where the fan had flung them.

"Stay down, if that thing powers up to full speed, it'll suck you in." Anna dragged a large black bag out from a hiding spot among pipes and unzipped it. "Get that kit off, quick."

"What?"

"Lose the jumpsuit." Anna seemed exasperated. "Must you make me say everything twice?"

"Why don't you speak English then?"

"Where do you think the bloody language came from?" Anna rummaged in the bag.

Kate shrugged out of the jumpsuit without hesitation, crossing her arms and shivering in her underwear for a moment until Anna threw clothing at her. She scrambled into a dark, long-sleeved shirt, loose black military-style pants, blessed socks, and boots.

Anna sat, watching her change, but glanced away from the grateful look.

"Why the face?" asked Kate, snapping the last of the boot fasteners closed.

"You've changed." Anna scooted away from the rifle. "I remembered you being colder. You... almost seem like a lost child now."

Kate squatted and recovered the weapon. "Yeah, you were a little freaked."

"I used to be a self-pitying softie." Anna sighed. "I know what the world is really like now. People only want to exploit the kind-hearted."

Kate tilted her head. "You look like you're about to laugh."

"I'm finding it ironic." Anna stood, reaching for a hatch plate in the wall. "The first time I saw you, you made me feel like I was the sweet, innocent thing. Now you're making me feel like the bitch."

Kate followed her into another shaft. "I had some anger issues."

"No, really? You made quite the dog's breakfast of those mercs." Anna paused at a three-way junction to check her NetMini before deciding on continuing straight. "And now you're all peace and love and 'I don't wanna kill anymore'?"

"I destroyed anything I touched. The world didn't want me, and I didn't want it. I mean, I did, but I'd convinced myself I was okay being separated from everything. This girl changed all that."

"You fell in love?" Anna checked the map again and went left at the next junction.

"No... well, I thought I did, with this guy... but as soon as I was gone, he found another woman."

Anna grumbled. "Typical."

"This child somehow fixed me."

The adoring tone in Kate's voice made Anna glance back. A telepathic twinge preceded a gasp. "Althea..."

Kate grinned. "Yes."

"What did she do to you? You're practically ready to kiss her feet."

"She gave me a life." Kate squeezed up alongside her in the shaft, putting a hand on top of Anna's and curling her fingers through. "I don't burn everything I touch anymore. I can wear clothes, use beds, shower, and drive. I'm almost normal." Tears of joy welled in her eyes. "Twenty-five years, I was a science project, some kind of fire demon no one wanted. She... cured me. Even though I'm a killer." Her voice fell to a whisper. "Even though I went there to kill her."

Anna shot a guilty look at the vent wall. "Great. You've gone squidgy."

They crawled in silence for a few minutes.

"How did you manage to get into a C-Branch facility?" Kate whispered. "They made it sound like they owned the world."

"Well, first of all, I'm not an amateur. Second, I have an Aurora. There's no defense against her. Thirdly, they made the mistake of hiding their facility under a residence tower. The levels they held you on were inside the city plate, twenty meters below the surface. That building goes all the way down to actual ground."

"So?"

"So, they can't have a military garrison around it without attracting attention. They were relying on stealth. And they still don't know what they're dealing with."

"They know about Archon."

Anna whirled. "What did you tell them?"

"Not much, they already knew more about him than I do. All I said was that he'd contacted me and he's got brown hair and a funny accent."

Another minute of crawling took them to a large slat grating. Anna slipped out first, and Kate wasted no time leaving the tight space. The corridor felt like they were in an ordinary middle-class apartment.

"Leave the gun in the vent. We're trying to look like citizens."

Kate clenched it. "Normal citizens carry guns."

"What if it's got a tracking chip?" Anna gestured at the vent.

Reluctantly, Kate slid the weapon out of sight. When she turned back, Anna had gotten half a hallway down at a stairwell entrance. Vulnerability fell on her like a wet blanket as she ran for the door and scrambled down the stairs. Anna grabbed the bar of an emergency exit, a dozen crackling sparks flew from her fingers into the alarm mechanism, killing it and letting the door open in silence. Sunlight flooded the hallway. Anna jogged a few paces ahead and knocked a punk off an iridescent blue motorcycle with a blast of lightning. The young man hit the ground twitching, trying to scream, but his jaw wouldn't open.

"No stealing." Anna stepped square on his chest on her way to the bike. "Come on! We've got seconds left."

The man wheezed and rolled to the side.

Kate hopped on, wrapping her arms around Anna's waist, clinging tighter as the machine took off. City blurred; to avoid getting Anna's skull to the jaw a second time, she nestled her chin into the small woman's shoulder. Metal squeezed her throat. Gunshots rang out behind them.

Without her pyrokinesis, she felt more naked than she had ever been.

NO TIME TO THINK

S peed reduced Kate's surroundings to a smear of colored lights and blaring horns. When Anna took a section of sidewalk to avoid traffic, screams added to the mix. A hail of NetMinis and various other objects crashed over them, flung from a crowd of pedestrians diving for cover. Warm liquid splashed on her face from a disposable cup bouncing off the windscreen. Anna sputtered and wiped her eyes.

Kate basked in the scent of it. "Can we stop somewhere? I really want coffee now."

"Ask them," yelled Anna, nodding to the rear.

A pair of black hovercars skimmed over traffic, closing in fast.

"Oh, shit." Kate clung tighter.

"That's one way to put it." Anna threw her weight to the right, skidding into a turn. "Bloody handling is in the bog with two people."

"Bog?" asked Kate.

"Loo."

"What?"

"Shitter!" shouted Anna. "Bloody hell!"

Anna pulled into the space between lanes of slow-moving traffic and accelerated. They barreled past a red signal, narrowly avoiding cross traffic. The headlights of a forty-ton articulated cargo transport bore down on them, passing within three feet of Kate's face, and inches of their rear tire. She clamped her eyes shut, unable to look, cringing and holding back the urge to leak from both ends. When she felt confident she would neither vomit nor wet herself, she risked a peek.

A spherical advert-bot hovered at speed, projecting a holo-panel with offers for protective motorcycle gear on one side and driver's insurance on the other. Kate locked on to a shiny, red helmet—a steal at seven hundred credits. One arm unclamped to reach for the intangible screen, when the hovering robot disappeared with a *clank*. She blinked and looked back; a sparking, smashed metal orb wrapped around a bent Citycam pole. Kate blinked, staring at it. When her brain managed to ascribe meaning to her surroundings two seconds later—that Anna jumped the bike onto the sidewalk—she screamed.

"You're going to kill us!"

"Oh relax," said Anna. "Not like I'm heading for the tube."

"What?" Kate spun to face forward again. "Tube?"

"Forget it," grumbled Anna.

Shouting erupted on either side as the bike parted a crowd. An unexpected right turn sent them toward long outdoor stairway. Kate let out an uneasy wail of protest.

"Calm down, I've done this before," yelled Anna, fighting for control. "Stairs look a lot worse than they feel. Lean up and forward... now!"

Both women shifted their weight; Anna pulled a wheelie and they cruised up the stairway, shuddering from a milder-than-expected vibration. The bike leapt the top step, landing a few feet later, and smashed a pair of sliding glass doors. Dozens of people turned at the explosion of glass bits resembling snowflakes as the bike skidded through the entryway of a shopping mall built into the fourth floor of a century tower. Shrieking children ran in random directions. Tires squealed over the polished tile floor. Several people leapt out of their way, flying into a fountain pool as the wobbling vehicle shot past them on the verge of wiping out. Faced with a choice of running down a little girl or taking a merchant stand head-on, Anna aimed for the pretzel cart and hit the brakes.

The bike came to an abrupt halt on impact, though the vendor's pushcart rocketed away in a shower of pastries, powdered cinnamon, and salt. A short distance from where it had been parked, it punched a hole in a small railing around an open atrium and fell out of sight, likely onto an unsuspecting crowd one story down. They'd missed the child by less than two feet; the girl, who couldn't have been older than seven, froze like a deer staring down a truck, seeming too afraid to move or make a sound.

"Off the bike, now!" shouted a man in a grey jumpsuit with a dark blue DuraFib armor vest; he ran up behind them and took a stance with a pistol in a two-handed grip, knees bent.

"Great... mall cops," muttered Anna. She put on a placid smile. "Is there a problem, officer?"

He blinked, straightened his stance, and glanced at the trail of devastation through the mall.

"I'm sorry, was I going too fast?"

Kate kept her head turned away, so the officer couldn't see her on the verge of giggling. People stared at her as they got back to their feet. Most looked shocked, some cursed at her, others laughed. The kid Anna almost ran over continued staring at them in wide-eyed fear.

"Get off the goddamned bike now!" shouted the security officer. "Dispatch, I got a situation on four, central concourse. Get the pol—"

Crack!

Kate jumped at the sound of a single, sharp stroke of lightning between Anna's hand and the man's chest. Steam peeled away from his face, which had frozen mid-word with a look of surprise. After a second of stillness, he fell over backward like a board.

The crowd's increasing anger turned to terror. People ran in all directions. The little girl seemed to recover from shock enough to start crying.

"Go to your parents," yelled Kate, waving.

Anna stooped, grabbing two cinnamon-covered hot pretzels. She handed one to Kate. "Care for a munch?"

"Isn't this stealing?" Kate's straight face only lasted a second before she laughed.

"It's fair game on the floor."

Anna twisted the handlebars, holding the treat in her teeth, and drove left, heading for the walkway past the railing. Panicking shoppers leapt to the side yelling, despite their tame speed. More security officers chased on foot, shouting at them to stop. One skidded to a halt with a pistol out. Kate lunged forward, forcing Anna down over the bike. A window up ahead exploded in a flash of shattering flakes; people scattered in all directions, screaming. She cringed as the bike picked up speed, but a quick glance to the rear brought relief at the sight of other officers tackling the trigger-happy guard.

Anna caught a downward escalator, forcing people to leap the dividing rail to the ascending half. The undulating shudder of driving down stairs tightened Kate's arms again, and pounded her tailbone.

"Bloody hell, you're squeezing too much," yelled Anna. "You're gonna make me shit."

Kate closed her eyes so as not to see the blur of stores and screaming people going by. Tires squealed on tile, and cries of surprise rang out on both sides. Severe acceleration dug Kate's arms into Anna's gut. Shouted curses faded into the distance before the people could finish two words. A sudden shift in the sound of the e-bike's motors made her look; they zoomed down a clear-walled tunnel. People flattened into the sides of a skyway connecting the mall to an adjacent parking deck.

Some genius decided to make the whole thing (including the floor) transparent.

A comedian had painted graffiti of crashed advert-bots on the sides, like bugs stuck to a windshield.

"For the love of..." Anna tugged on Kate's arm. "In some countries, the way you're pawing me would count as marriage."

Kate loosened her grip after the free-fall simulator ended with an opaque concrete deck between her and the ground. "Sorry."

Forty yards of parked vehicles passed in an instant. Anna slowed and steered onto the exit ramp, stopping to catch her breath once solid wall blocked off any potential attack from the skyway.

"Are you trembling?" Anna glanced over her shoulder. "You are, aren't you? What happened to that cold-hearted 'it's just a paycheck' thing?"

The metal around her neck seemed to tighten. "Heights. Can't burn gravity... and this fucking thing on my neck. I *am* as helpless as a child right now. You wouldn't believe how much it hurt."

Kate's trembles worsened with anticipation as a mental vibration spread across her brain.

"Oh, bugger all." Anna's accusing glare softened before she frowned at the stun ring. "Damn government wankers. I think I'd rather be shot dead. That's just cruel."

"Can you fry it?"

A black hovercar slipped into the windowless gap, squeezing between the ceiling and gliding over parked cars. Windows cracked and body panels crumpled in its downblast. The other one circled outside, a streak of ebon against the building across the street.

"Yes, but not right this second. Hold on." Anna hit the accelerator, crouching low to the frame as the bike zoomed in a corkscrew down the ramp.

Kate clamped her arms around Anna, screaming through gritted teeth until the bike bottomed out when it leveled off at the end. The shock kicked her in the crotch and set off a string of curses, which made Anna laugh. They avoided the waiting car, making liberal use of the sidewalk, and took off in defiance of traffic signals for several blocks in a straight line.

The Navcon chirped with a danger notice, a grey zone approached fast. Two streets later, they rounded a corner and Anna hit the brakes hard enough to smoke both tires at the sight of a road filled with old, wrecked cars. While Anna slalomed the bike among the wreckage, Kate stole a few rearward glances.

"They're right on us."

"Can you drive one of these?" yelled Anna.

"Sort of." Kate looked up. "Not very well."

"Trade places. I'll go up and over, you scoot forward."

"Are you fucking insane?" shrieked Kate.

"Fine then, you fireball them out of the sky." Anna came close to losing control after hitting an already-dead small animal. After recovering, they went sliding into a hard left. "Shit!"

Kate squealed as the bike dipped enough to let ground scuff at the fabric by her knee. "I can't. Not with this thing on my neck."

"I was being sarcastic," yelled Anna.

Flecks of debris floated past in the air. The bike picked up speed down a more open patch of the abandoned city. Judging from the decay, they had already passed into the blacked out area. Half-broken buildings formed a canyon of glass and steel; shattered windows glittered amber in the fading day. Tires kicked up a haze of water vapor from hours-old rain, and a patch of traction-coated plastisteel gave them three blocks of open space in a straight line. Numerous vagrants prairie-dogged out of trash piles to check out the oncoming noise.

"Well, then, grab the handles behind you. Let go of me. I'll jump over you."

Anna aimed the bike down the centerline.

"You are crazy!" screamed Kate, squeezing the air out of Anna's chest. "Just go!"

Trash, shredded plasfilm posters, cups, and fragments of packing cartons whorled into a horizontal tornado behind them. Anna wheezed, glaring at the rear-view monitor. She steered with one hand while trying to pull Kate's arms loose from her middle, giving up as the straightaway ended. Kate closed her eyes at the sensation of rapid deceleration; her resolve not to scream again failed when the bike twisted sideways and kept sliding against its tires. When she looked, they faced sidelong to the way they'd come, stationary at the end of a twenty-foot pair of skid marks. Two black hovercars hung in the air, nine feet off the ground.

"What the hell are you doing?"

Anna flicked her thumb at the right handgrip. "They're herding us."

"What?"

Smoke billowed into the air as the rear tire spun up and fishtailed the bike around, pointing it straight at the hovercars. Kate crushed a gasp out of the smaller woman when the bike lurched forward. The hovercars glided backward, nosing together as the women got closer. Anna raised one hand. A great concussion wave slammed into Kate's back in time with a deafening *crack* and flash of blue that left a coppery taste in her mouth. A shadow shot overhead. Vagrants shouted and ran for cover; a second later, a heavy metallic *whump* rocked the air. Anna forced the bike into a skidding left turn, barely controlling the too-fast maneuver. Behind them, both hovercars sat dead on the ground, clusters of sparks pouring from their ion thrusters.

Kate yelped at a sharp static jolt to her hands, instinctively releasing her grip around Anna's gut. While she flailed in an effort not to fall off, the little woman coughed and drew a great breath.

"Sorry, luv. Was about to pass out."

Fear of falling overcame fear of another shock; Kate clamped back on, but not as tight.

"The only time you *see* military intelligence following you, they're either herding you where they want you to go, or everything's gone pear-shaped."

"Pear whaa—"

Kate ducked her face against Anna's neck as they swerved at a half-collapsed dumpster, using the inclined metal as a ramp to jump through a blown-out second story window. They landed in the hallway of an abandoned apartment building. Cans, spent autoinjectors, and shredded bits of carpeting flew everywhere. Anna threw her weight right; the bike swerved into a sideways slide for a few feet before coming to a halt.

"Pear shaped. Means all cocked up. Gone to hell. So that's what Lauren meant by use the dumpster..." She twisted around to look behind her. "You all right?"

Kate gawked at the swinging pieces of drop ceiling, wires, and dangling LED light tubes between her and the smashed window they'd flown in from. "No... I don't think so."

"What'd you see out in the weeds, hon? That little sprog have your bollocks in a jar now?"

"Can you speak English?" Kate released her death grip and breathed into her hands.

Anna gave the bike a little throttle, navigating past a number of apartment doors to the end of the hall. She hit the brakes, but they kept sliding due to the peeling carpet and skidded to a stop with a *thump* as the front tire hit a closed elevator door. She leaned forward and poked the button.

"Ever since you went out to that wretched wasteland, you've been different. Did that little girl reprogram your mind like she did to that lumbering dogsbody?"

The elevator opened with a ping.

"Bugger me... I wasn't expecting this thing to work." She walked the bike inside. "Be a dear and hit the button for six please."

Numb, Kate twisted to her left and did as asked. Anger at being cut off from human contact had protected her from guilt over taking life. Even the label of self-preservation didn't seem enough to justify what she had done anymore. She killed to please El Tío, and for money. Kate had been so desperate for his approval, a parental connection—for any connection, but he had seen only a useful tool.

Kate considered the possibility Althea had tinkered with her mind. Of course, the girl *had* to do something to her brain to fix what had been wrong with her. *Did she change my personality?* Kate thought back to the glowing, innocent eyes and trusting smile. She recalled the feeling of the anger fading, like water out of a tub once the stopper came free. Without her anger, she knew the old priest for what it had been—malice.

"No... I don't think so. She's so sweet."

A soft *ping* emanated from nowhere in particular, and the doors slid open.

Anna walked the motorcycle out until the rear wheel hit the wall. She jockeyed it back and forth to turn, and drove to a stop at a four-way intersection. Each hallway had an identical number of apartment doors, with an elevator bank at the end of the east-west hall and floor-to-ceiling windows at the ends of the other one. The entire area reeked of mold and booze. Anna turned left, driving at about a walking pace to the window and brought them around to face the opposite end.

"Lift your weight up a sec." Anna waited for Kate to stand, and propped the rear wheel off the ground on the kickstand. "Okay, sit. That girl's *too* sweet. There's more to that child than she seems. People aren't that nice. She's up to something."

"She could've thrown me out of Querq," whispered Kate. "She hurt herself to help me even after what I almost did. That thing made me want to kill her."

"What thing?" Anna glanced back to press Kate on the issue, but a not-too-distant explosion snapped her attention forward. She hit the accelerator, spinning up the rear wheel. "Shit. Hold on."

"But you said—"

"Window."

Kate squeezed. Anna flicked the switch to retract the kickstand into the frame. As soon as the tire touched down, it shredded what little carpet remained. Scraps of smoking rug and flecks of molten rubber hit the transparent panel behind them. Smoke billowed up around them, gagging Kate with the stink of burned wood and tire. When the wheel caught a grip, the bike took off like a bullet, hurtling for the distant window.

"It's not glass!" Kate screamed, but the small woman either didn't hear or didn't care.

Seconds before contact, Anna threw all her weight back to lift the front end. The bike barreled into a panel of bullet-resistant polycarbonate; the unexpected *whump* of it tearing loose left Kate trying to scream with empty lungs. A short period of weightlessness came as they shot out into space, flying over a two-lane street. After seconds that felt like minutes, the motorbike slammed onto the fifth-floor roof of an abandoned parking structure. Kate's body crashed into the seat, sending a spike of pain into her skull by way of her spine.

"Shit! Shit! Shit!" screamed Anna.

The front tire went into a terminal wobble, but before the bike could dump, it struck a steel railing. Both women catapulted over the handlebars, sailing clear of the wreck. Kate's brain had not processed the reality of an imminent face-first meeting with the concrete surface a half-story down before she came to a midair halt. Anna floated a few feet in front of her, also stationary.

Cinnamon sugar bubbled up into the back of her throat.

Full body pressure wrapped her like a too-tight bodysuit. Kate pedaled her legs and waved her arms, trying to swim, but it did no good. The crash of the motorcycle hitting the deck some distance ahead of them snapped her out of the daze.

"Well, you two certainly know how to make an entrance."

A man's voice, tinted with superiority and a British accent echoed up from below. Kate stopped struggling and let her body go limp, trying to make sense of the figure in the long, tweed coat ten feet away. Copious brown hair fluttered in a breeze that appeared to annoy him. He lowered his arm; their hovering bodies moved as if in response to the gesture, and settled to a gentle landing on their feet.

"Christ, James..." Anna sounded flustered. "You could've met us on the street."

"And risk being seen?" He walked away, heading for a gold Halcyon-Ormyr luxury hovercar parked on the fourth deck.

Anna stormed after him. "What about me? They've bloody well seen me now."

His gloved hand waved dismissively back at her without a glance. "As long as I remain an unknown quantity, I can repair any sloppiness."

Kate gathered her arms tight around her chest. Every muscle from fingertip to shoulder throbbed from such a prolonged death-grip on Anna's middle. She walked in a zombie's half-sideways shuffle, trying not to anger her already sore tailbone.

"Sloppiness? We just managed to get Kate out of a C-Branch holding facility, James. You do realize these people are not the CSB? There's a modicum of competence here. And they won't hesitate to kill us."

"The Bureau is more competent than you give them credit for." Archon winked. "Friends were cack-handing things on purpose. For *your* benefit."

Archon stopped by the driver-side rear door, opening it. His grin exuded smug confidence. Something about the glint in his eyes took the enthusiasm from Kate's steps. The government was right behind them, no doubt. The whirr of circling hovercars echoed off bare concrete from every direction.

Kate almost tripped, twisting to follow the Doppler effect. This man had kidnapped Althea. Of all the things the girl could have said about Kate's wanting to kill her or her being an evil bitch who took lives for money, she had warned her not to trust this man. The child had spent more time warning her about Archon than she had the old priest.

Kate stopped.

Anna looked back, one leg in on the passenger side rear. "Come on. You can ride up front with Aurora. Don't dawdle, they're right behind us."

No malice lurked in Anna's face, just impatience—and fear. Kate took a step, not trusting that man alone with her. Aurora glanced back with a bored smile, and took her time fiddling with the car's Navcon.

"Is something amiss, Katherine?" Archon tilted his head.

"She's a bit funny in the head since she ran into the sprog," Anna muttered, closing her door behind her.

"Sprog?" Archon lifted an eyebrow. "Oh, you have got to be kidding me. You've met our precious little Althea?"

"I couldn't take a shuttle to the west." Kate halted ten feet from the car. "They don't much like it when people light their seats on fire. Tripped over her in the Badlands. She..." Kate's eyes welled with involuntary tears of gratitude. "She fixed it..."

"Wonderful. Brilliant." His expression hardened with contained annoyance as he leaned toward her. "Get in."

"She said you want me as a weapon, like everyone else. Is that true?"

Sirens grew close. A car door slammed nearby.

He sighed, pinching the bridge of his nose. "I do not have the time for this."

Kate edged backward. "I... need to think."

"Katherine. You are Awakened, and a rather potent example thereof. Don't trust them. We are your future. Either you are with us or you are against us. Our cause offers no room for hesitation."

"Why did Althea tell me not to believe you? What did you do to her?" Kate narrowed her eyes.

Archon stared at her, eyes widening. *"Get in the car."*

His voice pierced her brain, crushing past hesitance and worry. A scrap of Kate's psyche recoiled; a reflex to knowing he forced his will into her mind. Althea's warning rang true. He would take what he wanted, regardless of her feelings. She tried to scream, but her body lurched forward on autopilot. The overwhelming desire to obey, to make this man pleased with her, took over.

Step by quivering step, she rounded the rear fender, reaching for the handle to the passenger door. Archon's voice ran in an endless loop within her head.

Get in the car. Get in the car.

Kate swallowed hard; the gesture tightened the ring about her throat. Her eyes shot open.

The ring.

Her fingers closed around the door handle; her mind rebelled. She channeled her panic into the desire to make something burn. The tiniest puff of smoke appeared before a cascade of agony swam into her brain. Her legs gave out. Cold concrete cracked her in the back of the head; the sound of her boot tapping the car door rang louder than the sparks that sizzled in her ears. Hot spittle dribbled down the side of her cheek, and her mouth flooded with the taste of copper.

A circle of blur closed in from all sides, shrinking until everything turned white.

FALLING DOWN

A massive crash sent a shockwave reverberating through the concrete with enough force to bounce Kate's chin an inch off the ground. Against the wishes of her tenderized brain, her eyes peeled open at the sound of echoing squeals. Tiny sparks lapped at her cheek, connecting to the puddle of rainwater in which she lay. The weak charge scratched at her skin like a hungry cat trying to wake its owner. Rubber chirping on concrete grew louder, but she couldn't gain control of her twitching body to move. Every so often, one of the sparks seemed to exist inside her eye, making the world flash blue. She gritted her teeth and screamed a mixture of agony and rage at a sensation like a lattice of burning wires closed around her skull.

Hot plastisteel around her neck reminded her of how she wound up face down on the floor of a parking garage. A twenty-minute e-bike chase replayed in seconds. Growling, she pushed herself up enough to get her mouth out of the puddle.

A van slid past, spun sideways, and leapt into the air. Voices amplified by loudspeaker cried out in panic before another crash—much like the one that jarred her awake—came from beyond the range of her sight. All at once, her situation flooded back, lifting her out of a dazed fog. Archon had tried to do something to her mind, to make her obey.

Althea is right. I have to run.

Gunfire erupted. At first, it seemed as though a violent holo-vid played from speakers covered by a blanket. The sounds of fighting had been present for some minutes, only now able to puncture the bubble of her separation from the real world. Kate screamed and forced one arm to move to cradle her cheek. Her muscles burned as if they had fused in place, and stretched to the point of fraying. She gasped for air, taking in small droplets of dirt-flavored water from the puddle, gagging. Each convulsion caused a ripple of pain and involuntary tears.

You did this to yourself on purpose. She chanted several times in her head, trying to fight the crippling pain that protested every motion—including blinking eyes. Kate gurgled, clearing her mouth of a mixture of spit and vomit. She dragged herself away from the car while Anna and Archon focused their attention on armed men in black bodysuits. Several feet later, a railing ran the length of ramp. Beyond it, a drop to the next level beckoned. Her right leg continued a sporadic dance beyond her control, and her left dragged limp. Terror chilled her nerves at the sense of paralysis from the waist down. Still, she crawled elbow over elbow to the edge.

The damnable ring at her throat didn't let enough air in; lightheadedness threatened to send her back to sleep. She reached out and grabbed the eight-inch concrete curb at the edge, hauling herself up and over. She slid between it and the metal banister, somehow managing to find the strength to cling while her body unfurled beneath her and dangled for a few seconds. Her arms gave out and she fell onto jellied legs that dumped her to the floor one story down, flat on her back.

Bright stars danced along the ceiling.

Kate stared up at lights that seemed to drive needles into her eyes, overwhelmed with too much pain to feel it. Heavy crashes, dazzling flickers of azure sparks, and gunfire continued. One digitized voice said something about police before it broke into a terrified man's scream and cut out.

"Gone? What do you mean she is gone? She was unconscious!" Archon's yell echoed from above.

Laying there in the pose of a snow angel, Kate's urge to move rolled over and went back to sleep. The sound of Archon speaking made her want to sit up and triggered a full body convulsion. She whipped upright into a ball, both hands clutching the metal around her throat. Spit and bile slipped off her lower lip.

"Find her," said Archon.

Kate shuddered, clenching her jaw to keep from screaming as she stood despite her body wrapped in scorching. Reluctant muscles burned as though she tore them free from her bones; her body shambled in a zombie's stagger past rows of parked cars to the nearest barrier in front of another drop. Shouting, gunfire, and the intermittent *crack* of lightning bolts continued somewhere behind her. Desperation to get away from Archon added speed to her loping gait. Snot dangled from her nose, blasted loose by cries of pain her jaw refused to let out.

Her legs had almost become obedient by the time she reached the edge. Kate flattened out on the floor and lowered herself through the space between the metal barrier and the concrete. She dangled by her fingertips until she stopped swaying side to side, and dropped to her feet. Her legs refused to absorb the weight of landing again, and she rolled backward to the ground, though the fall only inflicted enough pain to make her scream, and didn't cause a blackout. Both legs seized as if in the throes of a nocturnal cramp. She rolled over on her front and forced herself to crawl. She tried to stand a few yards later, stumbled, and got herself upright into a stick-person walk without bending her knees.

Snarling, she tried to get her fingers under the collar and pull. *Whoever put this fucking thing on me is going to die.*

Another car went flying somewhere overhead, announced by the squeal of tires sliding sideways, a short period of silence, and a tremendous metallic *whump*. Kate tuned it out, stumbling down the ramp in search of a passage to daylight that did not involve a three- or four-story fall. Ten steps later, her knees decided to work again, and she picked up speed.

Gravity pulled her in a stagger, which ended against the side of a column at the bottom. A large numeral 2 painted on it gave her hope she neared freedom. For a moment, she felt a twinge of betrayal toward Anna, guilt for leaving her with that man, but she was in no shape to do anything about anything. She grabbed the ring with her other hand, growled, and tried to tear it apart.

Several large, armored figures rounded the corner. Kate jumped at the cluster of rifles pointed at her. Althea's cure of her curse had left her in doubt as to whether or not she could still melt bullets, but it wasn't exactly high on her list of things to test. Staring at the police firing squad in front of her, she resigned herself to being a tool of C-Branch, at least for the time being.

Althea had given her no specific warning about them.

Weary muscles gave up, and she collapsed to her knees in a shaking fit.

Her attempt to speak came out in random, unintelligible noises. Kate attempted to point upstairs but her arm swung about in an uncoordinated flailing gesture.

"No weapons," said one voice, ending with a static crunch as his loudspeaker cut out.

"Probably one of the vagrants," said a female.

An armored glove clutched the back of Kate's jacket, lifting her upright. "Your turn, Rina."

The man guided her into the grip of another blue-armored figure, a woman. *They think I'm a vagrant?* Kate's disbelief added to the aftereffect of the neural stunner must have made her look strung out on chems. Of course, the way she'd been walking, they would assume she'd gotten wrecked. The rest of the Division 1 police jogged up the ramp, leaving her alone with one.

"Come on, ma'am," said the officer. "We need to get you out of here. It's not safe."

As if on cue, a heavy *thud* came from overhead.

The parking deck melted into a swaying blur. Patches of white glare on the smooth concrete made her dizzy. She closed her eyes before the urge to vomit became too strong, and let the cop escort her to the ground floor and out to a cluster of waiting police vehicles.

"What did you take?"

Bright light right in her eye felt like a bullet to the brain. "Ngh... I dunno."

"Your clothes seem new... Looks like you've had some expensive gene work." A gloved thumb brushed dirt from Kate's cheek.

Ten seconds after the fact, Kate cringed from the light that no longer shone in her face. In her mind, she said, 'Just ran away from the Syndicate,' but what came out of her mouth sounded like a foreign language. Making up a story about being forced into prostitution could explain her amped-up looks and the stun collar, if the cop even noticed the device as something more than a decorative choker.

"Damn, girl." The officer eased her into the back seat of a patrol craft, leaving the door open. "You sit here; I'm going to call for a medical unit."

Kate looked up at a flash, managing to point at the fourth floor. "Bwaa!"

The cop spun about as five armored figures sailed off the deck, propelled by a car flying sideways, roof first. Bodies rained around them, some moaning, some still.

"Son of a bitch!" The officer sprinted for the deck, rushing back inside.

The gold hovercar zoomed out from a gap between the fourth-floor deck and ceiling, orange sparks raining from the undercarriage as it scraped. A row of Division 1 police armor ran up on the edge, all firing at it. Something passed overhead, a barely visible shape with thin wings and a long, pointed nose shimmering in the air. Kate squinted at the patch of distortion. Momentary awe chilled to dread.

Military intelligence. Downdraft washed over the area, coppery air laden with the charge of ion thrusters. *Bastards have an invisible aircraft.*

Kate leapt out of the car, waving her arms as the noodles someone replaced her legs with gave out. She fell on all fours near a dead or unconscious officer. Without thinking, she grabbed the pistol lying a few inches from his hand and scrambled up to a drunkard's run. Tears of pain streamed backward into her ears as she forced herself to move despite the agony in her muscles. Instinct guided her deeper into the decaying city, the parts civilized people referred to as 'disavowed sectors,' the sections blacked out of the Navcon database because no one belonged there.

No one but her.

Kate's legs gave up a few blocks later, dumping her to the ground in a foul-smelling alley. She dragged herself to the side, instinctual habit seeking out a patch of bare metal behind an ancient dumpster. Her last conscious thought was to tuck the pistol out of sight.

THE STINK OF PISS GAGGED HER AWAKE. KATE MOANED AND PUSHED HERSELF upright. A few pieces of windblown trash fell off her as she surveyed the alley with bleary eyes. It had gotten dark, though she felt as sluggish as if she'd slept two days. Pain had given way to soreness all throughout her body. A band of hypersensitive skin around her throat burned even at the touch of smooth metal wherever it made contact with the collar.

I gotta get this damn thing off. She frowned at the stained, rusting dumpster. *No shit.*

She choked back the sickening stench of urine, feeling a little better when a quick pat down revealed it as an ambient aroma rather than a need to find new clothes. An odd feeling of reassurance battled her sense of vulnerability. The last time the stunner went off, she'd made quite a mess. *Maybe I'm getting used to it?* After a stretch, she pulled herself upright, and stretched again. *No, it hurt a lot more this time.* Her head sagged forward. *I hope this thing doesn't cause permanent nerve damage.*

Kate worked the stumble out of her step in a few minutes, feeling sore but not to the point of limping. She considered her options: go back to El Tío, try to get to Querq, seek out Division 0 in the city, sit still and wait for C-Branch, or wait for Aurora/Archon to find her again.

El Tío could probably find someone to get rid of the damn collar. She rubbed it. Of course, that would make her feel indebted to him all over again. Now that she could wear clothing and be normal, he'd be all the more inclined to use her. That might not be so bad.

I could finally enjoy the giant apartment and all the fancy things he's been wanting to give me for years. I could live well.

She cringed from the remembered image of Althea's smile. *Why the fuck do I care what that kid thinks of what I do?* Her arms folded over her stomach, trying to press away the want to eat. For minutes, she tried to justify working for El Tío as a necessary means for survival, but always, Althea's disappointed tears filled her thoughts.

Is Anna right? Did that girl do something to me? She closed her eyes, pausing for a breath. The deer advanced out of the darkness, pleading black eyes fixated on her. Kate sank into a squat, rubbing the side of her head. *That's a helpless animal. It's not the same as killing people. I only killed them to survive.* A clattering can bounced in the wind. She glanced down the abandoned alley, eyes drawn to every flutter of trash or waving scrap of curtain. *C-Branch made me to be a killer, but it's not what I wanted.*

No, she couldn't return to El Tío.

C-Branch would be no better. They were little different from the Syndicate, though rather than trade in drugs, weapons, and sex, they traded in power. She'd rather work for El Tío; at least his people admitted being criminals.

No, C-Branch was out.

She wanted most to repay Althea for the priceless gift she had given her. The urge was easy to label unnatural, as much at odds as it felt with her personality. She trudged without direction, walking just to walk, peeling back layers of logic. The girl told her she used anger to hide from sadness. Kate cried. The horrible images of the lab seared into the memory of her child's psyche came back. Men screaming and burning, little Kate killed them without wanting to. Her desire had focused on survival and escape, but her awful power had translated her urge into death. Each grotesque sight had terrified her more, which only intensified her emotion and made the next one even worse.

She never *wanted* to kill them.

A sunken stairway to her left offered a welcome place to hide from the world. The recessed stoop had a dull green door that looked as though it had not opened in decades. Kate trudged into thigh-high trash at the bottom, one story below the road, and curled up on the ground against the wall. All the guilt and loneliness hit her out of nowhere. One by one, the faces of her victims faded in and out. She sobbed apologies to empty air. The deer had been food.

"It is the way of all things, child," said the wild man's voice. "Be grateful to the deer for its sacrifice, for it gives up its life to sustain yours. Its spirit will return, as do we all."

The deer had become her guilt. Everything she could not feel for the scientists, she had put on the animal. She *was* every bit the monster the old priest had said. She *would* have killed Althea without a second thought to get what she wanted, killed a child to satisfy her desire for Esteban.

Kate cringed, feeling dirty and ashamed. She didn't deserve to be in Althea's presence; she didn't deserve the gift she'd been given.

I'll just sit here until they find me.

She didn't look up when the door to her right scraped open. Tattered green pants, one boot and one bare foot, stepped into view.

"Someone order pussy?" asked a man.

Replies emanated from deeper inside the building: "Huh?" "No." "Thursday!"

"Cool, then we got a freebie."

Kate jumped as the man seized the shoulder of her jacket, hauled her upright, and shoved her through the door into a stumble that ended in the middle of what had once been someone's living room. Four glass orbs, a former light fixture, hung above her head. To the right, three men sat at a folding table. One cleaned a pistol, while the other two busied themselves repacking liquid drugs into used autoinjectors. Breath caught in her throat as the smell (and flavor) of damp, sweaty socks mixed with mold pervaded her senses.

One of the repackers blinked, hunching over his work as though she would steal it with a look. "Thursday!" He pointed at her, one eye wider than the other. "Don't trust the blue turkey!"

A woman reclined on a sofa so far gone it was impossible to tell which parts had rotted to mildew and which were supposed to be that color.

Too-large eerie lime-green eyes shone from a caramel-hued face. Almost cartoony, they stood out as an obvious cosmetic mod trying to make her look like an anime girl. What she likely got hoping to create a look of innocence had left her creepy. Her torn microskirt, striped leggings, sneakers, and pink sweatshirt lent an air of psychotic preteen to a body that looked a few years older than Kate.

Flickering light painted the wall between the sofa and the boarded-up front window where a frighteningly thin naked man had draped himself over a coffee table. A wire connected him to a battered net deck, its damaged holo-projectors responsible for the blur of color. Thumbnail-sized derm patches, black and red octagons, drew a line down both arms from wrist to elbow. He hadn't even bothered removing the spent ones.

Past the couch, a doorframe led to a darker space where plaster dust hung in the air. Walls had crumbled or been battered down. Large portions of several separate apartments had become one large area filled with half-walls and mounds of scrap. Several old mattresses littered the ground a few paces in, some stained with blood.

"Badge hasn't come out of C-Space since his pet bitch got herself shot," said Creepy Girl. "You can have her bed if you want."

Kate gulped.

"Wow," said the one cleaning a pistol as he dropped it, jaw hanging open. "That bitch is fucking hot!"

Old anger returned. She held her hand up in a claw shape and grinned. "You have no idea."

"This one still smells city fresh," said Grabby. "Bet she's gonna run. Twitch, you still got those cuffs?"

"Yeah," said the man at the table, ignoring his gun. "Do we have to?"

"They ain't for you this time, dumbass." Grabby winked at Kate.

The stun collar grew heavier in her mind. Kate froze. Hundreds of encounters with horny gangers replayed in her mind, each one ending with flames and screaming. Her left hand teased at the choker, fingers slid between the metal and her neck. Stuck in the damnable psionic restraint, she had no options aside from those of a normal woman—a normal woman of slight build, average strength, and little skill at fighting.

A normal woman that, at that instant, felt vulnerable.

"Ooh, I bet this one's a freak." Grabby put a hand on her arm. "Likes the leash?"

Kate rolled away, twisting to face him as she backed for the inner doorway. Something hard poked her in the ribs as he tugged at her jacket.

The gun! A forced smile showed teeth. She ran a hand down her stomach and slid it into her pants.

"That's it, baby," said Grabby, advancing on her. "Take it off slow."

"Nah, nah… Hell with slow." Twitch ran up behind him, tossing a pair of handcuffs to the other man before he yanked his tight blue shirt off over his head in one smooth motion. "Let's do this."

Grabby pushed her to his left, pressing her into the wall before she could get through the doorway. She turned her face aside, redirecting his attempted kiss onto her cheek. He growled with lust and ground his stiffening crotch into her. She pulled her hand out, caressing his stomach for an instant before covering her left breast. He took a fistful of her hair, pulling her head around and holding her tight. Grabby didn't notice her hand slide from her breast into the jacket as he forced his tongue into her mouth.

More than anything, Kate wanted to burn him. Reason barely kept instinct at bay; if the stunner went off now, she wouldn't want to wake up to the aftermath. She shifted her weight to her left leg, squirming. Grabby took her writhing as interest instead of the revulsion it was and relaxed his hold on her hair.

Twitch pulled at him. "Dude, let her get naked first."

Her fingers found the gun and slipped around the handle. Grabby leaned back enough to reach for her belt. She swung her arm out, bashing the handgrip into his teeth. He tripped over some cans, landing on his back while clutching his bloody mouth.

Twitch dropped the cuffs.

The urge to reach for pyrokinesis held back by threads, Kate clutched the weapon in both hands and fired. Her first two shots went high, holing the floor on either side of Grabby's head. He tried to take advantage of her poor aim and lunged. She fired again, and the back end of his skull exploded. She stared through the small finger-sized hole below his right eye, at the room behind him.

The *thump* of the body hitting the ground spooked her, and she fired several more shots into the corpse's chest. Shouting snapped her out of the fog; the two men at the table scrambled for their guns while Twitch jumped in a flying leap for his half-assembled pistol.

Kate rolled left and darted into the doorway as they opened fire. Plaster bits and fragments of Epoxil simulated wood flew overhead. She stumbled, not noticing she had tripped over a mattress until she somersaulted back to her feet. Clanks and pings danced in the dark. The voice of El Tío made fun of holo-vids in her mind as she scrambled behind a half-crumbled wall.

When her world consisted of a four-foot square heat tile in El Tío's office, she had little to do but watch him watch movies. He found the ricochet thing silly, as guns didn't do that anymore unless someone happened to fire one at an armored military vehicle. Modern firearms had enough energy to penetrate most materials—especially helpless psionic women. She gathered herself in a shivering ball, digging her fingers under the collar and tugging at it with all she had. It had no seam, no controls, only smooth silver metal the whole way around.

That's impossible. It's gotta open somehow! How did they put it on me?

"You fucked up now, bitch!" shouted an unrecognized voice. "You're gonna die."

She gave up on the idea of tearing the stunner apart, and squeezed the pistol. Boots crunched on debris, getting louder. For an instant, she debated popping up and firing over the small barricade, but chickened out. Confidence borne of expecting bullets to melt on contact had abandoned her. Even if Althea's 'fix' would still let that ability work, it would certainly trigger the stunner. Terror at what bullets would do to her raised a rattle from her shaking pistol. She cowered as another hail of shots rang out. At a break in the gunfire, she dove into a rapid crawl, headed for what looked like a doorway into a corridor that once ran between apartments. Fragments of plastic and glass embedded in her hands and bit her knees through her pants.

"There you are!"

A face and a handgun peered over the irregular curve of a crumbling cinderblock wall thirty feet behind her. He fired without sighting over his gun, and missed by several meters. Kate shoved herself sideways, landing on her back. She wasted a second trying to aim at his head before she thought of the ricochets. She flinched as his second teasing bullet whistled past, close enough to spray her with bits of wall.

A hail of wild shots barked out of her police-issue sidearm, disintegrating fist-sized holes in the wall where she guessed his body to be. His gun slipped from his grasp, blood seeped out of his mouth. He regarded her with utter confusion—the last expression he would ever make.

"You... cheated," he wheezed, sliding to the floor.

In the wake of her rapid barrage, the tromping of two pairs of boots got closer.

"Fuckin hell," yelled Twitch. "She shot Pillbox right 'froo the damn the wall."

"Yeah," replied a voice slowed to a disinterested haze, likely by drugs. "You can *so* freakin' do that, man. This ain't Cyberspace where missiles stop on office cubes." Two bits of wall exploded as the druggie fired back. "See... right goddamn through it. That's such bullshit, man. I fuckin' had Ceebo dead to rights, but the god damned cube wall stopped my rocket."

"This ain't a fuckin' game." Twitch's voice had raised to near-feminine pitch.

Between her barrage and a few pot shots from the other side, the wall had taken enough damage to afford her an unobstructed view of Twitch and one other man. They stuck their guns in the holes, aiming at her. Kate fired in their general direction, trying to break their concentration while scampering backward to her feet. The gangers dove for cover, giving her a chance to get up and run deeper into the building.

An explosion of shattering glass erupted behind her; she spun to look back. Twitch ran headfirst into dangling, broken light tubes, swinging his gun to bash them out of his way. A little bit of old Kate showed itself as she aimed and fired without hesitation. The first bullet cored his left thigh; the next five riddled his chest. She shot him once more after he hit the ground, causing the body to twitch.

She laughed at the irony of it. "Well, Twitch. For what it's worth, I did help your body emit fluid."

"Fuck this," whispered a man's voice from somewhere out of sight. "Hey, bitch..."

"Don't fucking call me that." Kate shot at the approximate source of the voice.

A man shrieked. "Hey... whatever... Make you a deal?"

"I don't want to make a deal with someone who was ready to kill and or rape me." *Holy shit, I just killed three people and I'm not even tired.* She stared at the gun. *This is so much easier than making fire.*

"Relax woman!" he yelled. "I was loadin' up some spent stims wit some fresh chem. Look, you don't want my stash and I don't wanna get shot. I take the stash; you don' get shot."

"Is that supposed to be an offer or a threat?" She backed up, gun raised. "What guarantee do I have you're not gonna fuck me over?"

"Bunsen's too high to even walk," whispered a woman, behind her.

Before Kate could react, a thrown knife plunged into her left bicep, scraping bone and poking out the other side. She screamed, firing several shots where she'd been aiming as she slumped to her knees. A wet splat preceded a moan and a gurgling wheeze.

The large-eyed woman pounced, tackling her face-first into the floor. Two fistfuls of hair pounded Kate's head into the debris-covered concrete.

"Think you're fuckin' pretty huh!" shrieked the woman. "You need some more work."

Roaring, Kate flung her right hand backward, trying to hit her attacker with the pistol. The woman caught her forearm in her teeth, biting down. Kate screamed; the woman let go of her hair and grabbed her wrist, smashing her hand into the side of a broken cinderblock protrusion until she dropped the pistol.

An attempt at a left cross hit the woman in the cheek, but the pain from the embedded knife sapped all the strength from her arm. Large, unnatural eyes widened even more, the lime green irises phosphorescing in the near dark. She tried to bite, but Kate kept teeth from finding her cheek with a raised knee. The woman's canines elongated to fangs with a faint mechanical whirr. The sight of the dagger-teeth gave her enough of a scare to kick the woman off and sit up, grunting. She grasped the handle sticking out of her arm, but couldn't summon the will to pull it out.

Kate lunged for the pistol, but the woman dove on her legs and pulled her back. Fingers smeared clean trails in the dirt inches from the weapon. She kicked backward, a feeble effort that her attacker avoided with ease. A hand around her belt hoisted her off the floor high enough to receive a kick to the gut, which flipped her on her back. The screaming woman fell on her again, six-inch metal claws sprouting from each finger.

"Fuck!" screamed Kate.

Kate caught both wrists, ignoring the hot smear of pain in her left arm. They rolled over each other several times, the woman's advantage in strength and experience offset by Kate's panic. One slip up let the fangs get too close. Fortunately, the stun collar got in the way, resulting in a mild cat scratch on the side of the neck.

Kate shimmied along the floor, locked in a deadly game of mercy with razor-sharp claws. The woman bent her hands forward, trying to slash the arms holding her.

"I'm gonna flay that pretty face off!"

The woman tried her best impression of a vampire's hiss, which cut off as Kate lurched upright and smashed her forehead into the woman's nose. A second head-butt left the freak dazed and bleeding from the nose.

Finger blades retracted as she cradled her bleeding face. As soon as the woman went from trying to claw her to pulling back, Kate flung her to the side and scrambled for the handgun.

She fumbled with the pistol while rolling over. The panic that had given her the strength to keep frenzied claws at bay left her confused at how to hold a firearm. Kate scooted backward until her shoulders hit a wall; she raised the gun in a weaver grip at the same moment the screaming ganger pounced. The woman grabbed both of her wrists, sending her shot high. Kate screamed from the knife still embedded in her bicep as the woman pinned her arms to the wall over her head, keeping the gun out of the fight. She hopped forward and sat in her lap. Kate struggled as the big-eyed off-gridder leaned in to sink her cybernetic fangs into Kate's cheek. Growls of frustration came from her attacker as Kate fought her to a stalemate. Creepy Girl traded to a one-handed grip on her crossed wrists and punched her in the head.

Dizziness threatened to pull Kate under, but the pain of the knife wrenching loose from her arm brought her back. The woman held the blade like an icepick, aiming for the thigh. Kate thrust her legs up, twisting her hips and throwing the crazy bitch off her lap to the left. The knife went flying. After leaping to her feet, she aimed the pistol, but her shot went wild as a kick to the ankle swept her legs out from under her.

The claws sprouted again, and Creepy Girl tackled Kate over backward. One blade-fingered grip pushed Kate's shoulder into the ground with all of the woman's weight. Four droplets of blood formed where the tips of her right-hand claws teased the tender front of her neck above the stun ring.

Green eyes flickered brighter. "Got anything to say before I bleed you out?"

"Look down."

After a seconds-long suspicious squint, the woman risked a quick glance. Kate had the pistol through a hole in the ganger's shirt, right between the breasts.

"You think you're faster?"

"If you cut my throat, I won't die right away. I'll have plenty of time to fire."

"If you shoot me, I won't die right away. I got time to cut you."

Kate grunted, trying to stretch her neck away from the four sharp points. "Call it a draw?"

"You got a gun, bitch. Soon as you're up, I'm dead."

"Touché." Kate squirmed. "Why are we fighting?"

"You killed my friends!" hissed the woman, spraying Kate in the face.

"How did you meet them?" whispered Kate.

"Just like you." Lime-eye grinned. "They found me onna street and dragged me in."

Kate stared at her. "They forced you to fuck?"

The woman bit her lip. "Not exactly."

"Huh?"

"They said I could do them or they'd kill me."

Kate smirked. "That's not a choice."

"Uhh…" Creepy Girl's face twisted with confusion, sadness, and anger.

"Are you on something?"

"Yeah, I'm high as hell. Took some smileys, a hit of SynSD, and a couple puffs of Basket. Want some?" She spent four seconds giggling, and cried for another two before finally looking serious.

"No, thanks." Kate prodded her in the sternum with the pistol. "Look, those weren't your friends. You were kidnapped."

"They weren't?" She blinked. "But they brought me food and clothes and chems and toys."

"You were a pet to them. A warm body to get their rocks off with."

The woman blinked. "I never thought of it that way."

"There's no reason we have to kill each other."

The woman's eyes glowed brighter. "'Cept it would be kinda funny."

"No, it wouldn't."

"The face you made when you saw my teeth was funny." She showed them off again.

"Killing each other wouldn't be funny."

"Okay, maybe truth. But you're still gonna shoot me if I get up."

I'm going to shoot you if you don't. "I promise I won't."

"Nobelieve." The woman retracted the claws digging into Kate's shoulder, but left the others at her throat. She wound her fingers around the knife handle. "'Cause, I stabbed you in the arm."

Kate clenched her jaw at the sensation of the metal blade sliding out of her. "If you trust me, you might live. If you don't, you definitely won't. We're both victims here. Let's just walk away." She made the same face that failed to convince Ramesh not to hit the neurotoxin button.

"Okay. But if you kill me, I will kill you."

"Umm." *Not worth it. Let it go.* "Deal."

When the claw tips retreated from her throat, she let herself take normal, deep breaths again. The woman sat up, staring at the pistol until Kate lowered it. She backed away from the woman's offer of assistance standing. *That is so creepy. Why would anyone get that done to their eyes?*

"What's the story with the deck pilot?" Kate waved the gun to the left.

"He's always plugged in. They called him Badge 'cause he wears all his old derms. Some kinda military-grade performance stuff for the net. Cops want him bad, but not bad enough to come in here." She backed out of sight around a broken wall. "Remember, you promised. No kills."

Kate cradled the pistol in her lap, her sigh of relief stalled in her teeth when she noticed the '02' glowing on the side.

Shit, I thought it was empty.

DARK SPIRAL

The pistol hung heavy on the left side of Kate's jacket, tapping her side in time with her stumbling walk. Her right shoulder burned from five shallow puncture wounds, her left bicep throbbed where the knife had been. She had not noticed inside; however, the moonlight revealed the odd stickiness in her hand to be a coating of blood. It oozed from the knife wound and dripped off her fingers as she walked.

Logic said she should find help. Her best chance would be to try to contact Division 0, but at least half the population thought they didn't exist. Going to the normal police might help, but she feared they would have made a connection between her and Archon by now. Even if they didn't, her face had been in clear view of the one officer's helmet camera for quite a while. C-Branch was sure to have their hands armpit deep in the police systems.

She stopped at an intersection a couple blocks from the punk's crash pad. For a minute, she stared down at the pat of red spots appearing next to her boot. Kate smiled and wiggled her toes inside the *real* boot. A sense of calm took over at the thought her first time having sex wouldn't happen against her will. Elation lasted only seconds before her mind replayed dozens of attacks. Back then, she had been too hot to touch. Regardless, it had taken months for word to spread through the underground society in that sector. At least four times a week, someone tried to assault her.

Here she stood in the heart of a *different* black zone.

New territory, somewhere she had never been in before. It looked worse than the place she called home. This area held char-blackened buildings that resembled the aftermath of serious warfare. A handful of cyborg parts emerged from the shapeless debris, too many to be runaways. This had to be a failed attempt to retake a 'disavowed sector' with a military assault. That meant she'd wound up west of old DC. Far out of Wharf Rat range, though the legend of what lived here had reached up north.

Afraid something would catch sight of her out in the open, she ran to the nearest building with a breach in the wall. Scorched wreckage in the road still exuded the scent of burned plastic as she weaved among the long-dead vehicles. The blast hole looked like it would let her inside, but it contained a cave in of building guts. Grumbling, she followed the wall to the corner, but froze in place at the panorama waiting for her.

An entire city block had been reduced to a burned field of junk mounds; buildings, cars, and anything else that had been there vaporized by some long-ago event. Rats scurried along old pipes, one rose on its hind legs to sniff the air at her approach. Speechless at the devastation, she skimmed against the wall and climbed past an archway into a large room that had once been a cube farm.

She collapsed on an old wheeled chair, which tolerated her weight for less than a minute before it collapsed and dumped her to the ground. Kate lay on her side, giving the finger to the broken furniture. With one hand clamped over the knife wound, she forced herself to sit up and leaned on the wall, hissing through her teeth.

"Althea, if you really are some being from another place... I could really use some help now."

A faint breeze carried the scent of burned things off the clearing, mixed with a subtle trace of rat piss. She ignored the wild hair dancing over her face, content to let it flop wherever it wanted. Blood oozed between her fingers as she put pressure on the wound.

"Yeah, I'm gonna catch something nasty."

She debated attempting to cauterize it, but bristled at the weight of the metal around her neck. Once more, she hooked fingers under the collar and pulled, twisted, and tried to crush it. The device ignored her.

Shivering from pain, she got her left hand involved as well, though it added little strength. She spun it around her throat, still unable to find any seams or gaps.

"Fucking thing... Does it have to be so tight? I can't breathe." She tugged at it until she ran out of energy and let her arms fall limp in her lap. "I'm a victim waiting to happen..." The urge to cry, to feel sorry for herself grew harder to resist. "So stupid... I should've played along with them till they took this piece of shit off me."

More futile pulling failed to affect the ring, though it let her entertain the idea that she at least tried to do something other than mope. She didn't feel confident about her ability to get back to Querq like this. Even Alejandra had recognized the advantage of her power. Kate gathered her jacket tight, adoring the sensation of being dressed. Now normal, able to touch and be touched, she found herself as helpless as anyone else.

"I got my wish," she muttered, and let out a halfhearted laugh. "I asked for it."

For no reason she could ascribe logic to, she considered the old man who wanted her to kill Althea was responsible for this. *He'd probably adore this... He, it, whatever the fuck. Burn out cancer...* She turned the stunner in a circle to the right. *Maybe he was going to catch me in a weak moment, make me angry enough to...* The rising lump in her throat made the collar constrict. *No, I can't go back there. I can't thank her for wasting her time.*

Guilt brought tears.

If I didn't go there, I'd still be cursed. C-Branch wouldn't want me. She sobbed. *They're going to find me wherever I go. Anywhere I could hide... I'm helpless, just a piece of meat to these savages.* Rumors that the gangs out here tended to torture for pleasure and partake of cannibalism more than they caved in to lust made her shiver. With nothing else to imagine, her mind went back to the nibbler camp and that poor man devolved by pain into a primal beast.

My creators didn't want me.

She covered her face with the jacket, sniffling.

El Tío only wanted a weapon no one would see coming. She frowned at the wall. *Giving me an education doesn't mean he cared. I had to be useful. A primitive naked wild-girl isn't useful. If he cared, he wouldn't have asked me to kill.*

Kate tried to summon anger at the way he used her, but wound up feeling like an ungrateful shit.

The man I thought loved me didn't want me. She stopped crying at the memory of Esteban.

Division 0 made an offer, and I was an idiot. A few scenes of her ride east replayed in her mind. She wondered what Officer Ahmed thought of her now, promising to come back and disappearing. Would he blame her for that, or would he suspect something happened. *He's an empath; he had to know how grateful I felt.* She spent a few minutes daydreaming about the day he'd spent teaching her how to ride an e-bike, picturing his arms around her from behind.

I can't trust Archon. He's just like El Tío.

She stared out a once-window, squinting into the wind. From here, she found it easy to imagine the entire city as nothing but a destroyed wasteland full of rats. *Can they really protect me from C-Branch? I doubt it... everyone lies.*

She pulled the gun from her jacket, rubbing her thumb over the ammo counter, which still read two shots. Kate tilted it back and forth, letting a glint of waning sunlight play on the grey plastisteel. It was almost silly how something so light could be so deadly. The weapon had the mass of a plastic toy; all the heft had been in the ammo, of which she'd used most.

For hours, she sat, staring between the pistol and the broken city. Every few minutes, she'd think of how her life had been either killing something or feeling isolated. Scraping got her attention from outside.

A lone figure rummaged the debris across the square. Metal arms gleamed in the harsh glare of the pre-dusk sky. He grunted and made noises far from anything a human should produce. Still in the relative dark of her shelter over a mile away, Kate remained unseen. Her eyes tracked him as he trailed off to the right until he vanished out of sight past the wall. The sun crawled west, sliding past a notch in the side of a distant century tower, where a long-ago explosion twisted girders into tangled black strands.

I'm helpless. Her fingertips traced the front of the collar. *The next time punks find me will be the last time punks find me. Two bullets won't be enough.*

All I ever wanted was to belong somewhere, to be able to touch without destroying, to have anyone care about me. She tilted her head forward. One tear spattered on the back of her right hand. *Anna was wrong. Althea didn't change me; she let me out of my cage. I don't belong to this world. I shouldn't even exist.*

I wasted her time. Kate took a deep breath and let it out her nose. *I'm sorry, kiddo.*

She raised the gun, barrel in front of her right eye. At the far end, the square, blue face of a caseless round peeked back at her.

Kate closed her eyes. "No one gets to use me again."

35

EMPATHY FOR THE DEVIL

"**P**lease don't do that," said a man.

Kate froze with her thumb by the trigger, whispering, "I'm sorry, Althea."

"I'm not Althea," said the man. "We need to talk."

Kate remained still. "There's nothing to talk about."

"I don't want you to hurt yourself."

Blurry slits of light expanded into the world as she let her eyes slide open. One man, thirty-something, sand-brown coat, neat hair, sunglasses—C-Branch. He stood a step inside the shattered wall, hands in his pockets.

"You fuckers are good."

"I wanted to apologize for the stunner. Please understand we had no idea what we were dealing with. The brass hates not knowing."

"It doesn't matter. I don't want to be your assassin any more than I want to kill for the Syndicate."

"We can negotiate that, Kate." He seemed to want to move closer, but didn't. "Our interest is one of national security. To employ you as a field agent against your will would be idiotic."

Kate touched the trigger, not enough pressure to set it off. "One millimeter of travel takes a life."

"That's rather morbid."

She couldn't hold back tears any longer. "Paul used to say that. One of El Tío's leg breakers."

"You're bleeding all over yourself. Please, put down the weapon and let me get you some help. There are operatives all around us. You are perfectly safe."

Bright light swiveled outside, lengthening the skeletons of buildings into apocalyptic shadows. Several hovercars came in to land; Kate shut her eyes again to ward off the glare.

"You are giving up too fast. You're young. The whole world is ahead of you."

Kate shivered at the sound of a shoe scuffing closer. She couldn't ping his brain with the damn thing on her neck. If he was a synthetic, he'd be on her before her finger could move a killing distance. Then, she'd be back in the cage.

"Kate, please," called out a familiar voice, laced with concern.

The man whirled. "Who are you?"

Depression, like a bubble of tar, burst. Suicidal feelings vanished to blah neutrality. Kate felt nothing at all. Cold logic pointed out she had a gun an inch from her eyeball. She lowered her arm, as it seemed reckless and dangerous to point a weapon at herself. A serenade of crunching footsteps approached outside after several car doors slammed.

"Officer David Ahmed, Division 0 Tactical."

"Back off," said the C-Branch man. "This is an intelligence operation. Who is your commanding officer?"

"At the moment, that would be me," answered an icily calm male voice. "Lieutenant Commander Niles Ashford, Division 0."

Kate opened her eyes again, blinking away the blur of tears. The agent had shifted to his right, staring with fear at a stark white man in a black long coat. *Who is he that C-Branch is wetting their pants?*

"Operative." The pale man seemed devoid of emotion as he offered a single, curt nod of greeting. "This individual is an as-yet undetermined type of psionic. I am here on direct order of Director Burckhardt to secure her safety. She is an active-duty member of Division 0. Your agency compatriots have already turned around to go home. I suggest you do the same."

"Active duty?" asked the C-Branch man, also without emotion.

Commander Ashford extended his arm, bearing a datapad. "She has been officially on the roster for eight days. The boots and vehicle your abduction team collected are Division 0 property."

The C-Branch man showed a trace of a frown at the datapad. "You're stretching a technicality."

Ashford tucked the datapad in his coat pocket, tapping it down. "Stretching technicalities is half of all government work. You should be quite used to it by now."

Officer Ahmed rushed to Kate's side, taking her attention off the staring contest ten meters away. "Kate..." He put his hand on the gun, pinning it to her lap. "I'm sorry I muted your mood. I had to. I couldn't bear to watch you take your own life."

She withdrew her hand, letting him collect the gun. "I..."

"It's okay. A lot of psionics bottom out like that. You've nothing to be ashamed of." He slid an arm behind her back.

"Ow, shit!" she screamed.

He tugged at her shirt, exposing her clawed-up shoulder. "Looks like you've had a bad day."

Kate laughed and wept at the same time.

Ahmed opened a belt case, taking out two stimpaks, which he pressed into her shoulder and arm one after the other. Cold seeped under her flesh, setting off pins and needles wherever blades had touched. Bloody foam exuded from the puncture wounds. When the oozing ceased, he wiped a towel past the mess, revealing clean, new skin.

"How do you feel?"

"Dizzy," she whispered.

"The wounds look pretty superficial. Worst part was the blood loss." He pulled her arm around his neck and stood with her. "You need something to eat and a long nap."

She had the strength to walk on her own, but found it nicer to let him support her. Her awkward smile faded as the C-Branch man stepped in front of them.

"Do we have a situation?" asked Ashford.

"There is one small matter regarding asset retention." The man in the brown coat stared at Kate with a look equally capable of protecting or killing her.

Ashford pulled down his dark glasses. "She is not a military asset."

Tension rendered Officer Ahmed into a man-shaped board. He stared at the confrontation.

"I'm not referring to the woman." The agent returned his intense stare to Kate. A second later, the stun collar chirped, hissed, and popped open, setting off a wave in her skull as though her brain had crushed into a tiny speck and snapped back to full size. "This device is proprietary technology. Classified. Even to you people." He snatched it out of midair before it hit the ground. "You fools want to juggle a live grenade, by all means do so. Don't blame us if you get burned."

Mr. C-Branch edged around Lieutenant Commander Ashford and strolled out in a flutter of brown coat. Ashford gave a simple nod to Ahmed before he walked outside to a waiting unmarked hovercar.

"Thanks," she whispered, her free left hand clutching her tenderized throat.

He helped her walk out the breach in the wall and guided her toward a different hovercar—plain black and bearing transparent police bar lights flickering with rapid snaps of blinding azure light.

"It wasn't me that found you." He stopped at the side of the car, letting her lean against the door. "We just followed the chaos."

"No... I mean for stopping me from..." She looked down. "I've never been much for crying before. I think I've cried more this week than in my entire life."

"I can't even begin to guess at what you've been through, but I'd like to help you deal with it."

Kate looked up, her legs weakened as they made eye contact. "I was afraid of being used again."

He lifted the gull-wing door. "We can keep C-Branch away from you."

"But I have to join Division 0?" She glanced at the car seat. "Am I being arrested or escorted?"

"You kill anyone recently?" He chuckled. "And, technically, you've already joined."

"Yes, three men."

His face went flat. "You're serious?"

"Yeah." She explained what happened.

"Oh." He mimed wiping sweat off his forehead. "That was self-defense. No, Kate, you're not being arrested. The brass is interested in learning about you. The only thing that would be required is to consent to a little testing. We're not going to force you out on tactical duty. As far as your duties go, you can fly a desk in the admin section if you want. Maybe sort history books or babysit dorm brats if you pass the psych board."

She crawled into the seat and let him close the door. The scent of technology enveloped her; for a moment, she felt like a child with a new—expensive—toy as she tried to make sense of all the displays and controls on the dashboard.

Ahmed climbed into the driver's seat and winked at her. "Somehow, I don't think you're the type to be happy sitting behind a desk."

"I don't know. Maybe I've had enough violence already." Gazing into his eyes sent strange tingles down her body. Perhaps he had been looking at her that way back in Querq. Was his concern for her personal? "Are you doing that to me or am I just pathetic?"

He pulled on the control stick, sending them straight up. Kate forgot about the dancing butterflies in her stomach and grabbed the 'oh-shit' handle above her window.

"I'm not manipulating your emotions now. I'm only authorized to do that in emergencies." The smile he tried to give her became a concerned stare. "Need a jolt of calm?"

"Heights." She almost lifted herself out of the seat. "I'm not good with heights. Wait, I take that back. I'm fucking terrified of heights."

"Really? You've never once been in a hovercar before?" He blinked.

"It's a long story."

Her terror melted away.

"We've got about an hour's ride."

"That was you." She watched buildings go by below, knowing deep in her gut she should be shaking. "You're keeping me calm."

"You'll get used to flying. Fear is the mind's natural reaction to the unknown and to things which appear dangerous."

Absent her usual reaction to being this high off the ground, she reached over and put a hand on his arm. "What about other things I find unknown and dangerous?"

"Your long story first." He winked.

36

NOTHING TO HIDE

Kate sat on the edge of a heated Comforgel pad. A woman in a white coat caused little chirping noises to emanate from a nearby holo-terminal each time she poked the screen. A snug white sports bra and clingy spandex shorts left her feeling exposed and cold everywhere except where her rear end met the heated pad.

"I'm almost done with your medical scan; we shouldn't be too much longer." The woman in the coat glanced at her with a pleasant smile that verged on patronizing. "Oh, how did they forget that? Kate, what's your last name?"

"Umm." Kate swung her feet back and forth. "I don't have one. The government made me in a lab, remember?"

The Medtech pinched her nose and let off a sigh. "Well, make one up then."

Kate thought. At first, she considered 'Althea' but that sounded odd, strange, and a touch sycophantic. After a moment of pondering, amid increasingly loud tapping from the medic, she remembered the old doctor who had tried to save her.

"What about Solomon?"

"Sounds peachy to me. Okay, make sure you remember it." Kate cringed at the way the woman emphasized the t. "From here on out, you're Kate Solomon, unless you'd rather Katherine."

"No, Kate's fine." She squinted. "Doc?"

"What is it, dear?"

Kate lowered her voice to a whisper. "Since when are you British?"

The medic smiled and leaned close to check her eyes. "As of a few moments ago, luv."

"Aurora?"

"You're sharp as a bag of wet rats, aren't you?"

"You knew?" Kate blinked.

"Why aye!" She stuck something metal and cold in Kate's ear. "I'll let Anna know you're grateful for the bailout. She's okay by the way."

Kate cringed at the device invading her head. "Ouch, fuck. Do you know what you're doing? She's not like him."

"No bloody clue," whispered Aurora. "I'm no medtech. I'm just sticking metal bits in random holes that seem to be the right size." She rummaged about a tray on a nearby cart for a few seconds. "Ooh, this is a nice thick one! Bend over, please. And yes, I know. She'll be all right when the dust settles."

Kate glared until the woman giggled. "You knew I was—"

"Going to naff off? Yes, of course. And I know you're going to ask why I didn't stop you or warn them." The medtech put her hands on her hips and shifted her weight. "Future's not always a guarantee, and sometimes what I see doesn't happen. He's a bit full of 'imself, and sometimes takes my advice and tosses it. For one thing, I didn't want the argument, and for two things—I find it amusing to watch him throw tantrums."

"You're strange."

"Thank you, luv." The medic glanced at the door. "Right, about time I sod off then."

"But, what about…"

The medic blinked, shivered, and leaned on the equipment table. "What about what?" No trace of British accent remained. She gave a bewildered look at the light pen sticking out of Kate's ear.

Kate smirked at the lack of accent. "Nothing. Is the scan done yet? Can I get dressed?"

"Not yet," said an older man in a white coat, as he walked into the room. "We'd like you to come with us."

Behind him waited two people in Division 0 uniforms: an Asian woman who looked to be in her mid-twenties, and an even older man, balding, with a fringe of white hair around the back of his head. He had a permanent grumpy look to him, as if irritated at the world for existing.

The medtech pulled the wand out of her ear, still making a face suggesting she had no idea how that got there.

"Like this?" Kate waved a hand over her underwear-clad body.

"Might as well. No sense ruining anything nice," said the scientist. "I'm Doctor Talbot. Behind me is Division 0 Deputy Director Johannes Burckhardt, and Officer Yuki Kurosawa."

Kate met Burckhardt's appraising squint without fear. He looked at her the same way Ramesh had, wondering how useful she would be. "Why do I have a feeling this is going to hurt?" She slid from the table, wincing at the cold floor.

"It shouldn't," said Dr. Talbot. "Though, if something unforeseen does occur, you are already in the medical facility."

Talbot took the lead, walking past Kate deeper into the room and past a pair of automatic glass doors, the lower half frosted. She padded along after him, uncomfortable at the way people seemed to drop whatever they were doing to stare at her; some even followed.

He stopped at a door marked 'Testing C' and swiped an empty hand past the panel. A chirp emanated from the wall and the door opened. Inside, a featureless white room held a few machines, one of which looked like something out of a targeting range. Most of the area was empty.

"Okay, Kate. What we're doing here is an evaluation of your psionic talent."

"I did this same exact routine two days ago with Doctor Rama...something."

"Ramachandran?" asked Talbot.

"Yeah, that's it. She was very thorough. Apparently"—Kate faked a shocked expression—"I'm a pyrokinetic. I'm also a little telepathic, and she said I've got some potential at self-healing, though I've never consciously used it." *That explains why my hair survived, I guess.* "I always thought I never got sick because I was too hot for germs."

"Oh, yes." Talbot crossed his arms over a datapad, bowing at her. "That's not what we're evaluating. We need to see the extent of your pyrokinesis. As you may or may not know, pyrokinetics create fire that looks like... well, fire."

Kate blinked. "Wow, that's impressive. You have a doctorate?"

Burckhardt made no effort to hide his smile.

"What I mean is..." Talbot's face reddened. "Other pyrokinetics we have studied have created red or orange flames."

"Oh, and because mine are blue… Yeah, okay. I guess C-Branch didn't want to share what they did? Tell me again why I had to stay in my underwear for this?"

"The report indicates your skin temperature—"

"It doesn't do that anymore. Look, just tell me what you want me to do and let's get this over with."

He pointed at the long wall, which appeared to be made of blunt-cornered cubes stacked on top of each other. "A series of target drones will come out and fly around. Use your weakest ability on them."

Great. I'm seven again in the 'game room.' "I can't kill machines. It's hot, but not hot enough to melt bots."

"No, we're testing accuracy. You don't need to destroy them."

Yuki frowned.

Kate indicated the woman with her thumb. "What's her problem?"

"He is asking you to start fires on a moving target. That is extremely difficult." Yuki gestured at Talbot. "Pyrokinetics cause materials to combust by concentrating on them; we are not firearms."

"You can't make fireballs?" Kate blinked.

Yuki stared at her with an unreadable expression.

"That is why you are here," said Burckhardt. "Please, humor us."

Talbot raised his hand and a terminal screen appeared in hologram to his left. When he poked a button, a head-sized orb bot exited a port on the wall and zoomed around in a semi-random pattern. Kate watched it for a moment, held her hand up, and whipped a small fireball at it. She felt like it missed, but the drone chirped to indicate a hit, likely due to the heat of the blue flame.

Yuki gasped. "How did you do that?"

"Like this." Kate nailed the second, slower orb with another one.

For a few minutes, Yuki made faces at her empty hand while Kate shot fist-sized fireballs at a series of orbs of various speeds. Some moved in circles while others zipped about in random patterns. Behind her, Talbot and Burckhardt commented on her accuracy.

"Okay, that's the end of that test." Talbot smiled and hit another button. A single orb bot floated into the center of the target area with a silver square dangling on a cable below it. "Try to inflict as much heat on that plate as you can. While you do that, Officer Kurosawa is going to attempt to interfere."

"Interfere?"

"Two psionics with the same gift can attempt to counteract each other.

I am not gifted myself, though I have heard it described as a battle of wills."

Yuki looked up from her still-empty hand. The woman's 'I want fireballs too' pout made Kate chuckle as she walked closer to the swaying target. She gathered the essence of heat around her body and thrust one arm out, creating a swaying serpent of fire that shifted from red to orange to blue within a second.

Again, Yuki looked despondent.

Tingling crept over her brain, a nagging resistance to her psionic energy. Kate powered past it, concentrating on the point at which the stream of fire met the sensor. She pictured the head of the C-Branch man who'd put the stunner on her hanging in place of the sensor panel. The fire splash turned from blue to yellow and teased at becoming white for seconds at a time. Exertion manifested as sweat. Yuki's grunting swam somewhere in the indistinct morass of sensory input containing everything that wasn't the torrent of flames gushing from Kate's hand.

She felt the fire burn through the sensor and stretch to eighteen feet. The distraction of the sudden change in length lapsed her focus back to 'just making fire' as opposed to 'as hot as you can get it.'

"Kate!" Talbot's scream pierced the fog of concentration. "You can stop."

A bit out of breath, she stumbled backward and wiped perspiration from her face. "How'd I do?"

"You destroyed the sensor," said Talbot, sounding annoyed. "It's rated to three thousand degrees."

"Sorry… guess I got a bit angry."

Yuki shifted, taking a step back. "I… I couldn't. It's like she didn't even notice me try to stop her. I held up an umbrella to stop a crashing starship."

"I felt a tingle," said Kate.

The woman glared at the floor.

"It's not as fun as it looks." She fanned herself. "That British guy said something about 'order of magnitude.' I guess that means I'm unusually strong or something."

Officer Ahmed entered with another man, who went to Burckhardt's side.

David walked up to her. "Looks like they're making you work already."

She shrugged, accepting a bottle of cold water from a lab assistant.

"They want to see how hot I can burn. I guess I'm doing better than they expected."

He handed her a towel, which she hung around her neck unused until she had sucked down three-quarters of the bottle. She wiped herself off, dabbing at her face and forehead. Noting her hesitance at touching her neck, David offered to help.

"There's no deep tissue damage."

"I know. It's mental." She turned her back on the room, finding she didn't mind when he stood closer. "They told me they used that thing because the inhibitor is cruel. I don't want to know what the hell one of those is like if it's worse than the stunner."

"It's not as painful, not even close. The inhibitor disrupts psionic activity by injecting an endless stream of random stimuli into the brain. It feels like whispers and strange hallucinations, smells, and feelings."

"Sounds like being high." Kate leaned until her back touched his chest. "That doesn't seem cruel."

"If left on someone too long, it's been known to cause insanity. If you decide to accept an assignment with a tactical squad, you'll be required to suffer through wearing one for about twenty minutes to get certified to use them. If you decide to stay in admin on a desk or working at the dorm, it's not an issue."

"That's stupid," she muttered. *Why isn't he putting his arm around me? Am I that bad? No, I'm just doing the same thing I did with Esteban all over again, mistaking 'nice' for interest.* After pouring the rest of the water down her throat, she chucked the bottle over her shoulder and glared at Talbot. "We done yet?"

Ahmed gave her a 'calm down' look, but did nothing telempathic. She softened the expression she aimed at the scientist from 'die in a fire' to 'you suck.'

"One more test." Talbot mumbled at the console, shying away from eye contact. "If you'd be so kind as to stand on the green dot."

A holographic circle appeared out in the middle of the target area. She chucked the towel to Ahmed and trudged over to it. Fourteen orb bots emerged from portals in the ceiling, surrounding her in a spiral pattern of increasing distance from two feet away to about fifteen meters. Sensor modules dangled on cables from each.

"You mentioned a radiant thermal event to Dr. Ramachandran. Would you be so kind as to recreate that?"

Kate laughed as though he'd told a joke of genuine humor. "Sorry. I can't."

"Please, explain," said Talbot.

Burckhardt's right eyebrow went up.

"Two problems." Kate crossed her arms. "One, despite your best efforts, I'm nowhere near angry or terrified enough to do it. I've only gone off like that twice in my entire life, and both times I was scared shitless as well as in immediate danger of being killed by a large group I couldn't run away from."

"Let me guess." Talbot held up a hand with a light pen stuck between his fingers. "The second problem is that it drains you unconscious for a few days?"

"No." Kate let her arms fall slack. "None of you are far enough away to survive."

Burckhardt's other eyebrow went up. "Perhaps we can skip an active recreation of that test." He moved to the edge of the target area. "Miss Solomon, would you be so kind as to think about when you last used it?"

The telltale squirm-inducing feeling of a telepath knocking on her brain sent a ripple from head to toe. Despite her effort to recall only the abandoned house swarming with nibblers, the emotional scar of her escape from C-Branch as a child brought both events to mind. The last thing she expected was to see Burckhardt smile.

I'll find it quite a welcome change not to be the only one around here everyone is frightened witless of. He faced Talbot. "I figure the range at about fifty to sixty meters in all directions from where she's standing. As best I can tell, she is correct about it being a subconscious reaction to extreme duress. I doubt very much she has the ability to create an explosion of that magnitude as a conscious act."

"So, are we done yet?"

"Yes, yes..." Talbot waved her over. "That's quite enough for now."

"One more test," said Burckhardt. "How do you melt bullets?"

At this point, the man who entered with Ahmed removed a small Class 1 handgun from a carrying case. The tiny size made it resemble a child's toy.

"What?" Officer Ahmed shot a questioning glance at Burckhardt. "That's completely without sense... Sir. You can't be serious. That is so far outside protocol I don't even know what to call it."

The Deputy Director appeared to take a few seconds to suppress the reflexive need to lash out at the enlisted man. "Need I remind you, *Officer*

Ahmed, that her very existence is far outside of protocol. It is necessary for the greater understanding of what we may come to deal with in the not too distant future."

"I don't even know if it still works." Kate stared at the man holding the pistol. "The last time I was shot, my skin was constantly hot enough to burn anything I touched. I might not even have the ability to do it anymore."

Burckhardt clasped his hands behind him and leaned back and to his left. "Lieutenant, aim for her leg."

The Lieutenant offered an apologetic look.

"Sir, please reconsider," said Ahmed.

Kate felt a rush of warmth in her face. *Is he standing in front of me? Or, am I ducking behind him?*

"Miss Solomon," said Burckhardt. "If the ability no longer works and you suffer a wound to the leg, you can begin your active duty period with one month paid vacation. The intelligence value of this test is too high to—"

"Worry about ethics?"

Thinly veiled anger cloaked Burckhardt's voice. "Officer Ahmed, you are dangerously close to an official reprimand for insubordination."

"It's okay." Kate put a hand on Ahmed's shoulder. "It's only a little pea shooter, right? In the leg. Maybe it'll work." She leaned up to him, whispering, "Don't get in trouble for me."

She walked out to the center of the target range, fists clenched, and rotated to face the Lieutenant.

"Is there anything we need to know to increase the chances of it working?" asked Burckhardt. He gestured at Talbot. "Send for a medic, just in case."

Officer Ahmed looked at the wall, unable to watch.

"Even if it works, it's like getting hit with a pipe." Kate shivered. "It hurts. It used to melt before it pierced, but it still slaps me like a hammer. I doubt it works on the asteroid-metal bullets... uhh indirium. And, I have to see it coming. It's a subconscious thing."

Kate, don't do this. Ahmed's voice rang in her thoughts.

She jumped, startling the Lieutenant who had raised the pistol.

She concentrated on him. *Don't distract me. I'd rather not enjoy a free month.*

"Proceed, Lieutenant. One shot only."

The man mouthed a silent apology and aimed. Ahmed closed his eyes.

Kate stared at the weapon, trying not to tremble hard enough for anyone to notice. At the sight of a muzzle flash, a wave of hot and cold came over her. Compared to the hand cannons she so often had pointed at her, the tiny pop this one emitted almost made her laugh. If not for the sensation of a hard punch to the left thigh, she would have. Smoke wafted past her face, carrying the scent of molten plastic.

A brush of cold air caressed her naked breasts.

Burckhardt pursed his lips and turned a shade of red. The Lieutenant averted his eyes. Talbot gawked. Yuki covered her mouth. Officer Ahmed whirled about and attacked several pushcarts in a hasty search.

Kate attempted to maintain an air of dignity. Her sports bra and shorts had vaporized. A soft whimper slipped past her clenched teeth as the re-solidified bullet burned her leg.

"It burns. Ouch. That's certainly new."

A spatter of re-hardened lead clung to her thigh. She peeled it away from a darkening bruise and smirked at two black footprints melted into the floor. Tossing the misshapen lump of metal from hand to hand, she limped up to Burckhardt.

"Still works." She reached out, grabbed his hand, turned it palm up, and dropped the warped metal into it. Wearing a defiant smile, she closed his fingers over it. "Burns now."

The old man's jaw clenched, but he tolerated the hot metal without flinching. If anything, he seemed... impressed.

"I didn't get a temperature reading," whispered Talbot. "It surpassed the upper limit of this equipment. Likely several thousand degrees for only the span of a microsecond. I'll need some time to set up for the next test."

Kate tilted her head at Burckhardt, hands on her hips. Twenty-five years of being naked 24/7 left her beyond shame. "When do we test how many fireballs it takes to make a scientist beg for his mother?"

Ahmed tore the lab coat from Doctor Talbot and wrapped her in it. Kate threaded her arms into the sleeves and rubbed the blistering bruise. The Lieutenant unloaded the weapon and put it back into the box. Yuki opened her belt case and offered a stimpak.

Kate held up two fingers, and injected the first one.

"Loss of uniform could prove quite inconvenient in the field," said Talbot. "Did it hurt?"

She glanced at the fading six-inch bruise. "You're the doctor. You tell me."

A GIFT IN BLACK

Kate reclined on a plain white sectional, wrapped in a soft robe and the scent of lilac. The apartment was a simple one-room modular where the Comforgel sleeping pad mounted to the bottom of a rotating sofa that folded into the floor. Overall, her new home had about as much space as a half-length trailer of a cargo transport truck. One window in the center of the outside wall offered a modest view of the building across the street. A counter with a food reassembler occupied the area to the right of the window; to the left, an autoshower stood wedged between a toilet and the wall. Rather than a partition or separate room, the shower used a near-opaque plastic tube, which still emitted the warm fragrance of recent use.

She swished one hand over the holographic control panel every four or five seconds, trying to find a channel on the vid with something worth watching. After settling on an animated fantasy intended for kids, she went over to a white box mounted at about head-level on the wall. It ignored her when she pushed the single button at the bottom. A pounding fist caused a plastic-wrapped packet of pale grey cloth to plop to the carpet at her feet.

"A soft couch and all the pre-packaged panties I could ask for." Kate ripped the pouch open and slipped them up under the robe. "Guess this is the sweet life."

Once dressed in a full-sleeved shirt and loose pants, she tossed the bathrobe over the autoshower door's handle and dialed up a turkey sandwich on the 'sem. It whirred and chugged; the level of beige goop in the OmniSoy tank dropped by an inch and a half and the machine went into a banging, beeping fit.

"That doesn't look—"

Bang.

The reassembler hatch flew open, spattering her with ooze the approximate consistency of hot cottage cheese that smelled of Spanish olives and sardines. She pursed her lips, wiping her eyes clear.

"Yeah… So this is paradise."

"Are you okay?"

Kate whirled, startled by the voice of Officer Ahmed standing in her doorway. Distant squeals of playing children echoed in from the cramped hallway behind him. "I was just conducting an experiment involving molecular reassignment of protein strands. You could have hit the buzzer."

"Heard the explosion, used the override."

Her glance shifted to the box under his arm. "What's that?"

"I wanted to bring you something; mind if I come in?"

"You're already in." She pulled her fingers through her hair, squeegeeing out handfuls of OmniSoy slime, which she threw into the autoshower. "Give me a moment to clean up."

He sat on the couch with his hand on the box next to him. Kate ran a towel over herself, considering another shower, but decided against it with a guest in the room. After changing her shirt, she flopped on the other side of the package and swiped her arm at the air to turn off the holo-vid.

"This is for you." He patted the box and removed his hand.

She slid the gift onto her lap and examined it. It took a moment to find the clip holding it shut, and the upper half opened like a hatch. A layer of shimmery black fabric with a metallic sheen sat inside. Grasping it, she found it cool to the touch, and the fabric took on the shape of a Division 0 uniform as she held it up. The material went from black to indigo when light struck it at certain angles.

"Indirium nanofibers. It won't burn if you take a bullet."

Kate lowered her arms, still clutching the fabric. "Sorry."

"Why are you apologizing?"

She wanted to look at him, but couldn't. "I must've made you uncomfortable in the testing facility. It…" Her hands kneaded the uniform. "I read too much into the way I thought you were looking at me."

"Ahh." He leaned forward, elbows on his knees. "I'm surprised no one commented when you leaned into me like that."

He noticed? Kate's face warmed with blush. "Sorry, that was... I didn't mean to make you uncomfortable."

"You do realize he is the deputy director of Division 0? There's five layers of command below him... Directly under Burckhardt is a regional commander, then two area chiefs, director of field operations, a couple lieutenant commanders, and finally, Captain Hollister, my immediate superior. They call that fraternizing."

She stared at her lap. "It's okay; you don't have to make me feel better. I know I'm seeing what isn't there. Just like with Esteban."

"That man you went off in search of?" Ahmed laced his fingers. "I was disappointed when you left."

Kate looked up at him. "You *were* flirting with me then? I thought—"

He chuckled. "No, you weren't imagining it. Maybe I should've been more obvious, but I didn't want to scare you off. You seemed like someone who understood how it felt to be isolated. Then, you mentioned that man..."

"Isolated? You?" She wrinkled her nose.

"As soon as women learn I'm an empath, they assume their emotions are unnatural. Even if they're genuine, once they hear the word 'telempath,' there's no convincing them I'm not manipulating them to make them have feelings for me." He glanced at her. "I saw that same loneliness in you, and felt a connection. Still, I wanted to help you... even if you had your heart set on someone else."

Every muscle in her body tensed upon eye contact. She became vaguely aware of her pulse picking up as she reached over and slid her fingers between his. He didn't scream, burn, or pull away. *Twenty-five years and I've never been able to even hold hands before. What are you waiting for? He's here. I'm here... No, don't ruin it.* Kate closed her eyes, brought close to tears by the touch of his thumb across the back of her hand.

"Would you like to go somewhere for a drink?" He glanced at the splattered beige mess. "Perhaps food?"

She leaned into him. "I don't know. I don't handle liquor well. The last time I had a drink, I wound up in a clandestine prison."

David put an arm around her. "You don't have to worry about that anymore."

Kate grinned. "That fingerprint... in Querq when you asked me to e-sign that pad."

He smiled. "Sometimes a minor technicality is a major help."

"All right." She lifted her head from his shoulder; the energy in his eyes filled her heart with the stirrings of a connection she craved for her entire life. "I don't know my way around the civilized parts of the city. Did you have anywhere specific in mind?"

"I was thinking of this rustic little place named Tumbleweed's." He winked. "It's a bit of a ride, but the locals are quite friendly."

Fin

THE OLD CITY

Author's Note: The Old City is a short story I wrote soon after the original completion of Daughter of Ash. I am including it here as it has become canon to the Awakened series, and so readers can have the entire story in one place.

Home offered a sense of security that Althea struggled to accept. Being alone in the house reawakened old worries. Though she hummed to herself while stuffing empanadas for later, she glanced at every shadow and found herself freezing still whenever the building creaked. Over and over in her mind, she planned out how she might react if someone did try to kidnap her again. She wouldn't let that happen. Her spike of determination made her mash the spoon down too hard, spreading filling over the side of the dough. She bit her lip and grimaced, as if Karina would've seen her mistake and been disappointed in her.

The city police wanted her to visit them for a little while today. She shifted her weight onto her right leg and tapped her left big toe absentmindedly at the floor while scraping the stuffing paste into a nice lump in the middle. Each excuse she tried to come up with for not going to see them made her feel like more and more of a liar. Anything from the big city took her back to being separated from her family, and made her

322 | DAUGHTER OF ASH

think sad thoughts. Still, the psionic police did help Querq as they promised to. She had to keep her promise.

A few more empanadas, and she'd go see what they wanted.

Karina had made a mush mostly consisting of black beans and shredded chicken, with some chopped up herbs. Her sister wanted to try some of the new 'spices' the city police had brought in. Even Father seemed pleased by sniffing the jar. Despite that the powdered seasonings came from *that* place, she couldn't argue they smelled good. The fragrance made resisting her urge to taste it uncooked difficult, but Karina had specifically made her say 'I promise not to eat any before they're done.'

Althea jabbed the large spoon into the bowl of filling and scooped out a dollop, which she plopped into the middle of a new dough square before leaving the spoon upright in the chicken-bean mush. She folded the dough to make a pillow and sealed it by pressing around the edges with a fork as Karina had taught her. After adding it to the tray, she glanced out the window at the position of the Sun. *Late afternoon.* At the time, she huffed a sigh that made her hair jump away from her face.

"I said I'd go…"

She draped a cloth over the tray of unbaked empanadas, another over the bowl, and eyed the sink. The Water Man had gotten the faucet working, a feat that most people in Querq still considered an act of magic. Althea didn't want to 'waste' the faucet water just washing her hands, so she ducked out the back door heading for the water pump. Despite the street empty of people, the sight of the place where Dean kidnapped her with a tranquilizer gun tightened her throat. Karina still didn't want her going off alone, but she no longer feared the stinging green needles. Now that she knew what they did, she could protect herself… not that she expected anyone to try that again.

Althea stepped into a warm puddle on the boards around the pump; an involuntary squirm climbed her legs and continued into her back at the sensation of mossy slime squishing underfoot. She pumped twice to get water flowing, and rinsed food and flour from her hands before rubbing them down the front of her simple white dress to dry them. It didn't hang as long as her beloved skirt had, stopping about halfway down her thighs. The white dress Archon made her wear had been longer; at least she could run in this one.

Wanting to get home as soon as possible, she ran past the pump to the end of the alley, and hooked a left on the street. Cool dirt gave way to warm paving. Despite the small group of city police, and the fancy things

THE OLD CITY | 323

they brought with them, few cars drove through Querq. Only the Watch had working vehicles, three 'pickup trucks,' as Father called them… which didn't make a lot of sense. They couldn't pick anything up. She pondered that while walking down the centerline of an ancient strip of blacktop. Here and there, scraps of reflective paint glinted at her. She skipped from one coin sized spot to the next, grinning, daydreaming about what it must've looked in the before-time when the whole street glimmered yellow in the Sun.

Mrs. Alvarez wandered by, offering a wave and a pleasant greeting; her three grandchildren also smiled and yelled hellos. Althea grinned back at them, savoring the joy the woman had shown once clear of pain. Most of her bones had looked strange around the joints, and it hurt her to move at all. She remembered fixing the youngest boy's broken ankle once, and tending to the nine-year-old granddaughter, Belinda, when she ran through Jorge's scrapyard and got a hunk of metal stuck in her foot.

The grandkids broke formation long enough to hug her one after the next, and followed Mrs. Alvarez off to the street leading to their home. The odd machine smell in the place came back to her. She'd visited to mend the woman's bone sicks. Their home smelled like metal and the underside of a car. It had to be from whatever happened there before it became someone's house. Father said most of the places in Querq from the before time had been shops and such. Corinne and her husband lived in something called a 'pizza place.'

"Pee sa. Peetz uh." She tilted her head; the effort of thinking about a word slowed her walk. "Piza. Piz-uh. Bah."

Two blocks later, she emerged in the center of Querq, where the city police made their home. They'd even brought their own building, a rectangular metal box elevated off the ground on fat metal legs. Various small components on the roof glittered with tiny flashing blue or green lights. One emitted a continuous whirring. Some of the smaller kids could run underneath the city police's house without ducking. Althea bit her lip, feeling a twinge of shame at her reaction to the noise of the flying machine that had brought it here. It had taken Karina a good hour to talk her out from under the bed. Even though it had felt like their home would shake itself apart, she didn't want to come out.

Unlike the rest of the children of Querq, who all came running to watch the flying machine set the enormous box down in the middle of the city, she wanted nothing to do with anything that could make her home tremble. Two black sky cars sat near the long wall of the rectangular box, identical to the one she'd been riding in when Archon first appeared to her. From the outside, where they should've had windows, they had slabs of black metal.

Althea blinked, certain the one she'd been in had windows. People can't see through armored plates. She shook her head, dismissing it as 'stupid city stuff,' and gave them both a wide berth on her way to a metal staircase attached to the side of the boxy structure. She gasped as soon as she stepped on it, as hot as a cooking plate. With a yelp of surprised pain, she raced up the four steps and hopped from leg to leg while knocking, though her small hand didn't make much noise.

"Hello?"

She bounced on tiptoe to keep her feet from cooking for a moment, but no one answered. A small metal box perched on the wall to the right of the door. Looked like another tiny door, perhaps for mice. Figuring it more 'stupid city stuff,' she leaned her face close to it.

"Hello?"

When nothing happened, she stood straight and frowned. Annoyance got the better of her and she pounded her fists on the door, but made only a slight bit more noise than knocking. She screamed, "Hello!" at the little box. Seconds later, she opened the tiny door to reveal a glowing green square about as big as her palm. *Eep! Glowy!* She leaned away and slammed the small door. A few seconds later, the door split down the middle with a loud *pfshh.* The two halves retracted into opposing walls, releasing a blast of freezing air.

"Eep!" She jumped back.

A man in a clingy black uniform with a silvery belt smiled at her from the doorway. Darkish skin and black hair almost made him seem local, but he didn't look like everyone else here. "Althea?"

"Yes, sir." She stood with her feet together, arms at her sides.

He backed up, gesturing for her to follow. "Come in. I'm Officer David Ahmed, but you can call me David if you like."

Having acclimated to the scorching metal porch, the inner hallway felt like walking on ice. Gleaming white walls caught the glow of overhead lights, forcing her to squint. Despite it being a clear day, the light inside seemed brighter than the sky. Teeth chattering, she gathered her dress as tight as she could around herself and followed the man through a short hallway to a square room with two desks at opposite corners. He glanced at one for a few seconds, chuckled, and went past it to a smaller room with two cushioned black seats catty-corner against the wall. Each looked a little like Father's sofa, but only big enough for two adults. He sat in one and gestured at the other.

Althea perched on the edge, hands on her knees, back straight and rigid. Her body wouldn't stop trembling from the cold. An odd sense tugged at her mind; she looked up at him, somehow knowing he attempted to 'read' her emotional state. Probably to figure out if her shivering came from cold or fear. She didn't fight him.

"Would you like a blanket or something?" He smiled and crossed to a small storage cabinet by the wall. "I'm sorry it's so cold in here. Lieutenant Franck, my superior, can't stand heat. That dress is so thin, and you've got no shoes."

"Is this going to take long?" asked Althea. "I have empanadas I need to finish making."

Officer Ahmed took a plain grey blanket from the cabinet and returned to the adjacent mini-couch. "I understand you've had a difficult time of it before you arrived in Querq." He handed her the blanket. "This won't take too long, but I would like to meet with you somewhat regularly to offer any help you might want coming to terms with what's happened to you."

Althea cocooned herself in the blanket, pulling her feet up under her on the soft cushion. She clutched two handfuls of plush fabric at her chest and waited a few seconds for the shivering to lessen. "What does it mean to come terms?"

He rested his arms over his knees and laced his fingers. "People react to traumatic things in different ways. I'm aware you don't fully trust Division 0, but my interest here is only to help you heal any mental or emotional wounds you've suffered from your ordeal. Coming to terms means reaching a point where bad things that happened to you in the past no longer affect you as strongly."

Her telempathy read genuine concern from him, without a trace of deceit or greed. Not like the old man back in the city... Burkhardt. He'd initially felt like a raider finding treasure, until he learned 'all she could do was heal.' He couldn't use her as a weapon, so he couldn't care less about her. She looked down at her lap; blonde hair draped down her front touched her legs. "Like how I wanna hide when the sky gets loud?"

"You're frightened by storms?" Officer Ahmed raised his right eyebrow a little.

"No." Althea brushed the blanket at her chin to chase away a minor itch. "I'm scared of fly machines. I like rain. I always go outside when it rains."

He nodded. "Are you worried that whoever is in the aircraft is coming to take you?"

"A little." She looked up, smiling. "But I can stop them. I'm scared it will break an' hurt someone when it falls. Metal boxes aren't s'posed ta fly."

"You can stop them?" He slid a flat bit of plastic, one of those 'datapad' things, into his lap and tapped at it. The surface facing him lit up blue and green, painting his features in colorful shadows.

"Yes." She flexed and relaxed her toes while staring off into nowhere. "I used to be scared to, but I'm not anymore."

"Afraid to protect yourself? Didn't it bother you the way people kept treating you?"

Althea's mind filled with memories of cages, rope, handcuffs, leashes, and locked doors. She pressed her arms to her chest, wishing Karina or Father sat at her side so she could cling to them. "The Wagon Man took me all over. Alla people inna Badlands know I can fix hurts and sicks. They wouldn't do bad to me. If I did mystic things, they'd be scared and wanna kill me." She slipped a hand out from under the blanket to wipe a stray tear. "I feeled good helping people, even if I hadda be in a cage."

He typed for a few seconds. "Sorry... that's no way to treat a child. I'm... You don't seem as traumatized as I'd have expected for a girl your age having spent so much time in captivity."

"I'm scared of being tied." Althea looked down again. "I don't like it." Silence hung thick between them for a little while before her mood lightened and she raised her head to make eye contact. "I have a home now. A family. I'm not scared to say no when someone wants ta take me." A spread of embarrassment warmed her cheeks. "I used ta always let people take me. I promise not to run away, an' I don' run away. That way, raiders don't tie me." She gave him a pitiful look. "Much."

"You've got to be the most potent telempath I've met... that Division Zero has ever recorded. *And* you've got a passable grasp of suggestion." He stared at the datapad. *If this kid wasn't so damn innocent, command would be losing their minds.*

Althea tilted her head. "I won't take away your commands' brain shapes."

Officer Ahmed chuckled. "Listening to my thoughts?" He let off a resigned sigh. "Normally, we consider that a breach of manners... but given the life you've had, I'm sure it's developed as a survival instinct. Also, considering your situation... it's probably best that you keep checking people out. For security reasons, of course. I don't mind if you peek."

Althea considered the mixture of pity and concern swirling around him for a second or two before peering into his thoughts. He seemed to have expected her to be more upset, constantly crying or wanting to hide from people. That she acted relatively normal both relieved and intrigued him. "I can make people not do bads. I used ta be scared people would hurt me if they knew I could." She recalled the image of a mystic, a scrawny man in a handmade skirt and wild-colored headdress who led a band of raiders against another tribe that had captured her, one that had kept those handcuff things on her legs so she couldn't run away.

Of course, being a mystic hadn't stopped an enormous raider from knocking him senseless with a pipe.

She leaked some of the memory of watching him scream and burn, chained to an iron beam, into Officer Ahmed's mind. The kind of fear that glowed from her captors at the mere sight of a mystic had terrified her. They believed they had to kill him by burning, or he'd just keep coming back from the dead. Rather than try to explain it with words, she sent a shade of her fear that if she'd done anything other than heal, it would've been her lashed to a metal post and lit on fire. Everyone knew her as the Prophet, the healer. They'd take her away—some groups would keep her tied, some would be nice and treat her more like a person—but she would never stay in one place for long. She'd been with the Wagon Man the longest, but only because she hadn't been famous yet. Once the entire Badlands knew her, she changed owners every few weeks.

As long as her captors allowed her to heal people who suffered, she tolerated her lack of freedom. After all, back then she didn't have a home, somewhere she'd rather be. Wherever she went, she'd only get taken again. And so on.

Officer Ahmed shivered.

Her love for Karina and Father bloomed, an unintentional radiance made the city police man flash a dopey grin. Sensing her power running away, she backed off.

"I still did somes." She shifted in her seat and stretched her legs under the blanket. "I stopped real bads, like wifeing. But"—she puffed up her chest—"I have a home now. I'm not scared."

He tapped again at the datapad thing. When he finished, he smiled at her. "Aside from holding you against your will, did any of the people who abducted you do anything to you that you didn't like or that made you feel uncomfortable?"

Althea looked him right in the eye. "You mean did they wife me?"

He coughed. "I'm sorry? Wife you?"

"Put boy parts in my girl parts."

Officer Ahmed blinked. "Umm..." Discomfort fell away from him in sheets.

She shook her head. "Not right 'cause I'm too young. Some raiders have harems. They make me help the women when they get hurt from wifeing. If they were too mean, I sometimes made them stop." Althea fidgeted, thinking about Rachel's fear of being wifed... almost as strong as Althea's dread of it. "No one wifed me. I would not let them."

"You've witnessed, umm, women being..."

"Wifed?" She nodded. "Yes. If they were real scared, I'd take 'way the raider's..." Her face scrunched up as she searched for how to explain.

"Urge?" asked Officer Ahmed, a second after a tingle in her mind. "You... interesting. Dampened their desire."

"One woman wasn't even as old as Karina." Althea looked down. "He was gonna wife her, but she was so scared. I made him guilt. Strong. He helped her 'scape."

Officer Ahmed fidgeted and leaned on the armrest. "Well, I'm very happy to hear that nothing like that happened to you."

"I wouldn't let it," said Althea in a matter-of-fact tone. "I rather burn onna post."

He nodded. "I think I would too."

"Why are you surprised?"

"From what I've read here, you were taken by this guy with the wagon when you were five or six years old, and put in a cage for about a year... you've been kept prisoner on and off since, and been surrounded by violence more or less the entire time." He exhaled into his hands for warmth. "And that mess with Archon in the city... I guess I expected you to be more, umm... damaged. It's remarkable how unscathed you seem from a mental standpoint."

She tilted her head to the side. "Is that good?"

"Quite... but somewhat unsettling too. A child your age going through that... it's astounding me that you're not showing much mental trauma." He tapped and poked at the datapad again. "Perhaps knowing you had the ability to leave whenever you wanted to, and staying of your own choice helped?"

She opened her mouth to protest, saying they'd kept her bound or caged... but if she'd been less afraid of being thought a mystic, she'd had the power to force them to release her. In a way, she had chosen to stay a captive.

Althea looked down at the little tents her feet made in the blanket. "Before, I only wanted to help everyone I could. 'Cep for wifed, I did what they told me." She rolled a marble of an idea around her head, smiling to herself at taking more and more risks as she got older. She hated being tied up, and used her 'magic' to manipulate her captors to avoid it. Small pokes at their emotion wouldn't make them think of her as a mystic.

"Well..." He leaned back, smiling. "I'm honestly surprised and relieved that you're so resilient."

She stared at him, eager to get back home.

"I understand you've already given the Admin people back west a good idea about that Archon situation."

Althea frowned. "He's not a nice person. I don't wanna see him again." She looked down and to the side as Aurora's words floated in her memory. *The time will come when you will not save his life. You will watch him die.*

Officer Ahmed rubbed his chin. "It's distressing we weren't able to find him at the abandoned power station. Though, I'm more curious about the entity you mentioned, the one from the garden."

She shivered despite the blanket. "The Many... Bad." Althea shook her head rapidly side to side. "Not good. Hates everything."

"Some people think the reason we haven't reclaimed the Badlands to modern civilization is due to supernatural influence, though they're somewhat of a laughed-at minority."

"I don't know what you said." Althea narrowed her eyes.

"You've seen the city in the west."

She made a sour face as the urge to run home welled up within. "I don't like it there. You said I didn't have to go back."

He raised a placating hand. "You don't. Please calm down. I'm only saying that people think it's odd that modern technology hasn't spread back across the country. Before the war, people didn't live in two massive cities crammed against the coastlines." His datapad projected a map of North America, and he pointed out cities here and there throughout.

"People are trying to understand why, since the war has been over for four hundred years, we haven't spread out again."

Althea looked down, speaking in a near-whisper. "Because he won't let them."

"That's what a few people say, but no one believes them. Most think it's due to money… it would be too expensive. There are still issues to be dealt with: weaponized mutants the corporations released during the war, runaway androids, environmental damage, and so on."

"He told me that he's made up of all the people who died. They're angry and want other people to suffer too." She looked up at him, eyes wide, searching. "I don't understand. Why does he want to make other people hurt just because they got hurt? Making pain doesn't fix pain."

Officer Ahmed gave a mild shrug. "I wish I could answer that. I don't think there is a good answer for that. Alas, being cruel is not an exclusively paranormal trait. Some people are like that."

"That's bad." She shifted to sit straight, moving her blanket-encased feet to the floor. "People shouldn't be bad… even if they're already dead."

He chuckled.

Althea smirked at him thinking her 'adorable,' but held her tongue. 'Aww how cute' didn't bother her anywhere near as much as 'ooh, the Prophet, grab her.'

"I find it interesting that none of the reported manifestations of equipment malfunction have occurred here since we've arrived."

She stared at him for a moment, blinked, and kept staring.

He bowed his head. "Sorry. It's oddly easy to forget you're ten years old."

"Twelve."

A sly grin pulled his lips to the side. "Maybe I'll meet you halfway and say eleven. Though we really don't know what effect such an overclocked accelerated healing would have on your body. Maybe you are twelve and you've been spending so much energy using your abilities on others, your body hasn't been growing. Maybe you've got a subconscious fear of being 'wifed,' and your power had been keeping your body childlike as some kind of defense mechanism."

Althea huffed. "I'm sorry. I didn't have the school. You are talking words I don't know."

"Forgive me; I was more muttering to myself there." He read from the datapad. "I wonder if your presence here somehow interferes with that apparition's ability to break machines. You are such an unusual case."

"I'm not a case. I'm Althea," she muttered.

He closed his eyes, smiling away the frustration.

"Sorry for making you upset." She scooted her feet back and forth to warm them.

"It's okay. What I meant is that you have quite a few psionic talents. Healing of course. Your telempathy is the strongest we've ever seen. Your eyes... you see in the dark, correct?"

"Yes. Bio... loom nis ant." She beamed with pride at remembering the word.

"They always glow blue." He tapped a finger on his chin. "We have seen astral sensates who can see in the dark by shifting their vision half into the spirit world, but their eyes radiate white light, and only while they are using the ability to see in the dark... or to see spirits."

"Spirits?" asked Althea.

"Ghosts? Apparitions of people who have died. Have you ever seen one?"

She shook her head. "Just The Many."

"Interesting. Well, psionic potential doesn't always translate to ability... like any other muscle, it needs to be developed. You've got a bit of suggestion, clairvoyance, and telepathy as well."

"If you say so." She shrugged.

"You can order people to do things sometimes and they do it?"

Althea nodded. "The woman in the bad city already told me 'bout it. I don' like doing that 'cause it's mean. Only when someone's gonna get hurt if I don't."

He radiated relief and pride, much the way Karina and Father felt when she'd finally gotten the fork to work. He thought about people being frightened of 'suggestives' the way people out here thought of mystics. Her hesitance at using it made him happy.

"Most psionics exhibit anywhere from one to three separate abilities. You've got potential in six, though your healing and empathy are by far the strongest."

Althea slipped an arm out from under the blanket and flexed her bicep.

"Indeed. A well-used muscle."

She grinned.

"Well... I can't say I was expecting you to be so well adjusted. I'm glad." He leaned forward and patted her on the knee. "I'm glad that you've found a light at the end of that long tunnel."

Her brow knit together. "I wasn't in a tunnel." As Officer Ahmed chuckled, she thought back to running away from those two raiders in the Lost Place. "Wait. I was... for a little."

"I see why everyone here loves you." He took her hand and squeezed it. "You make everyone near you happy."

She shifted her weight forward. "Can I go home now?"

He nodded. "Yes. Thank you for visiting with me. If you ever want to talk about anything that happened to you, or if you have any questions about your abilities, please find me."

Althea stood, letting the blanket fall to the cushions behind her. Cold air swam up under her dress, bringing a chatter to her teeth in less than a second. "Thank you for being nice. Sometimes I get bad dreams in my head, 'bout people who wanna take me, but Father said it will need time."

Officer Ahmed stood and patted her shoulder. "After the life you've had, a couple of bad dreams are to be expected. He's right. It will take you time to accept that you're safe here. Your dreams tell me you love your family very much and fear losing them."

"Yes." She smiled. "Father said the dreams will stop once I find a *confee onza.*"

He chuckled. "Confidence?"

"That's not what he said." She blinked.

"*Confianza.*" He chuckled. "It's Spanish. Means confidence."

She flattened her eyebrows. "I'm not stupid." That she'd been searching around Querq to find a 'confee onza,' made her blush.

Officer Ahmed pulled her into a brief hug and patted her on the back. "You are too much." He chuckled.

She shot him a confused look for a second until she read his mood. He didn't mean to sell her; he'd meant 'too much' as some way to say he thought her adorable. Eager to get home and finish the empanadas before Karina returned from her farm job, she waved at him and found her way back down the little white corridor to the door. A few voices murmured from a nearby room, discussing something about 'Gee-ball scores.' One woman thought of being stationed in Querq a bit of a vacation, while a man in the conversation felt it a punishment. The scent of coffee hung in the air, along with a fruity-sweet smell.

Althea couldn't imagine how anyone could *miss* being in that big, awful city. Every time she thought of the place, it made her want to curl up and cry. So many people so close together, how could they be anything but miserable? All in a hurry; always angry. None could even be bothered to offer a kind word to a lonely child. She wrapped her arms around herself at the memory of being pushed aside, called a pickpocket, and stuffed headfirst into a trashcan. Before the tears started, she thought of Karina and how happy she'd be that Althea had finished her chore on time.

She stood at the exit waiting for a minute or two before Officer Ahmed walked up behind her.

"Something wrong, sweetie?"

"The door isn't letting me out." She pointed at it.

He smiled and pointed at a small green square on the wall to the left. "You have to push the button."

"I don't touch things that glow." She shook her head. "It's not safe."

"This isn't radioactive or harmful. It's an electric light." He gestured at the ceiling. "Like those, only smaller."

Althea raised a tentative hand and poked the green square with her finger. She cringed, expecting it to burn, but it felt neither warm nor cold. The door opened, letting the warm outside air fall on her like a comfortable blanket. She flashed Officer Ahmed a grateful smile, and hurried down the steps before they could burn her feet too much, and spent a few seconds basking in the sunlight, letting it chase away the chill.

"There she is," said a woman.

A group of ten or so people hurried over, forming a horseshoe around her. She didn't recognize most of them, though except for one blond man, they all resembled locals with sienna skin and black hair. All of them seemed about Father's age, and wore backpacks and gear that suggested they'd been traveling. Sensing no malice in their emotions, she decided to stand still and quiet.

They gathered closer, about half knelt before her.

"We have journeyed for weeks to see you," said a man.

A woman a little older than Father bowed so deep her hair tickled Althea's toes. Her clothes smelled like wood smoke. "Guide us. What shall we do?"

Althea's stomach knotted with unease. "Please don't bow to me."

The woman sat up. "As you wish."

"She is real." A man leaned closer and put his hand on her arm. "I can feel her power. She is the one."

"Blessed child." A man in the back raised his arms to the sky.

"Stop." She edged back a step. "I'm just Althea. I don't know what you think I am, but I'm only a girl who can help people."

"So humble," whispered a younger woman. "We should be like her."

Murmurs of agreement swept over the group.

"Please don't pray to me. I'm only a girl." She caught fleeting glimpses from their surface thoughts; they all thought she'd come from some place called 'Heaven.' A few thought her to be sent by someone named God, one thought she *was* him... or her. "Please, don't. I'm just a person like you."

"Beloved, believe not every spirit, but try the spirits whether they are of God: because many false prophets are gone out into the world," yelled a woman to the right.

Althea glanced toward the voice. A thick-bodied woman with a square-jawed face and a weathered tan ambled closer. She didn't look at all familiar. Her dress and boots appeared to be made of the same type of leather, fringed with goat fur. Numerous pouches and packs hung from her belt, and she carried a pre-war rifle over her back on a strap. A strand of pewter-colored hair hung over her face, the rest held back in a bun.

"Please don't call me that. I don't like Prophet."

The stocky woman raised a hand at the group. "Beware of false prophets, which come to you in sheep's clothing, but inwardly they are ravening wolves."

Not trusting the outsider, Althea scanned her thoughts. Fortunately, she did not intend to abduct her. This woman believed she wanted to hurt people, wanted to be worshiped, that Althea committed a great crime against the same 'God' person that the others thought sent her here.

Althea scowled. "You don't understand. I don't want to hurt anyone."

"Fools," said the woman. "This girl is lying. She is not of God, or of heaven. Do not be deceived by her false innocence."

"Why do you hate me?" Althea leaned away from the palpable emotion. "Do you need me to mend your ear-shapes, or are you just stupid? I *told* them not to bow to me. I don't want them to."

"Leave her alone," shouted a man.

The angry woman fixed her with a glare. Her thoughts swirled in confusion; she hadn't expected Althea to deny wanting followers. A scowl formed as the woman regarded her claim as a lie. *Of course, the Devil will claim it does not want what it wants.*

"She's not what you think she is," said a woman behind Althea.

Althea twisted around to peer at a Division 0 officer descending the metal porch, boots clanking on the steps. She stared at the nameplate, but the funny marks, the frozen word, didn't mean anything to her. The officer looked like a local, with caramel skin, a rounded face, and black hair, but her English had no trace of a Spanish accent.

"This one spreads false testimony, seeking to lure the sheep away from the flock," said the angry woman.

"Operative word there being *sheep*." The officer folded her arms. "If your magic sky daddy has a problem with Althea, why doesn't he pop down from the cloud castle and say something?"

Everyone, except Althea, gasped.

The angry woman closed her eyes and wagged her head side to side. "The Lord works in mysterious ways. It is not our place to question."

"Right. Easy to keep the mindless sheep obeying your bedtime story when they're trained not to expect to see anything happen." The officer put a hand on Althea's back, smiled, and filled her voice with concern. "Are you okay, hon?"

"Yes. These people are confused, and that woman hates me, but I don't know why."

"Maybe *He* sent her?" shouted a man, pointing at Althea.

Althea stomped. "No one sent me. I live here. I don't want... followers, or people bowing. All I want is to help people."

The crowd stood in silence for a little while before the angry woman scoffed at the man who'd suggested this 'god' person sent Althea. The would-be worshipers surrounded her and got to arguing about what this entity wanted. Amid their trying to shout over each other, all of them seemed to lose notice of her.

Althea crept off to the side and started to make her way home, but stopped as a telepathic voice entered her head.

You let me know if these people bother you again, hon. The officer winked at her. *These Cat-3 people can be dangerous sometimes.*

Althea blinked. *None of them have cats.*

The officer laughed, and hugged her. *Oh my, you are so adorable.*

Althea hugged back, basking in the affection. She loved Querq, and how everyone (well almost everyone) here treated her so well.

It's short for category three. It's a rating system for mental problems. Cat-3 is religious delusions, those who commit crimes and attempt to justify it with religion, or those who've detached from reality and allow their mythology to cause real harm. The law considers them to be suffering a psychological condition.

While the words mostly sailed over her head, she picked from the woman's surface thoughts to help understand. *How can made-up stories hurt people?*

The officer rolled her eyes. Contempt fell off her in sheets. *Oh, you'd be surprised. People used to kill each other for believing in the wrong fairy tale. Or sometimes people would believe their Easter Bunny would magically cure sickness and wouldn't take their kids to a doctor. They'd sit there and watch their own babies die expecting some made up 'god' to zap them fixed.*

Althea's eyes widened at the images in the woman's mind. Of course, it had been a long time since that happened. As far as the officer knew, few people in the area still paid attention to this 'religion' thing. Most of that occurred in other parts of the world. The officer regarded 'religious' people with almost as much contempt as the angry woman had for Althea. She didn't *hate* them the way the woman regarded Althea as some kind of evil thing; the officer thought them stupid and primitive.

In a brief moment of dark logic, Althea wondered what The Many would think about the idea of a 'god.'

I should go home. Althea offered a pleasant smile.

The officer nodded. *Okay, hon. I need to stay here and watch these idiots so no one gets shot.*

Althea's eyes widened. She did *not* want anyone to get hurt because of her, or because of an argument about 'religion.' She stared at the arguing group and projected a wave of calmness. A shouting man cut off in mid word, staring dumbfounded at the angry woman as if he couldn't remember why he'd gotten so worked up.

Satisfied, she left them to exchange confused glances, and walked back the way she'd come. It struck her as silly to argue about a 'sky-man' who may or may not exist. The officer did make sense in a way. If this 'god' person really did have an opinion, why didn't he show up and say so? The Many had no trouble appearing to torment her. If such an entity did exist far above the clouds, it either didn't care or approved of things.

She shrugged, and let daydreams of fresh empanadas replace pointless thoughts. She walked about three blocks before pausing at the sound of someone running up behind her.

"Althea!" yelled a boy. "Please, help!"

She stopped and whirled around.

A pair of boys, both shirtless and in jean shorts, sprinted out of an alley. Santiago, on the left, had waist-length straight black hair and a thin build that often got him mistaken for a girl from behind. His best friend Diego kept his hair short by decree of his mother. They rushed to her side, both standing more than a head taller than her. A thick layer of grey dust covered them, as well as dozens of small cuts and scratches on their forearms and legs below the knee. Diego also appeared to have broken a toe, though it didn't affect his walking. Something had scared him good.

Her heart sped up as she realized Pedro wasn't with them. The three friends had always been together whenever she saw them, and the look of fear on the boys' faces got her worrying.

"What happened?" she asked. Her gaze dropped to a trail of blood running down Santiago's left leg. She took a knee and pulled up on his shorts, exposing a deep cut a hand's width above his knee. "Stay still."

"Pedro's hurt. He needs help," said Diego.

She touched his leg near the wound, despite the pair of them tugging on her. Her mind linked to his body. Amid the darkness of her closed eyes, his life shapes appeared one by one. Bones as lines of white, followed by muscles and the inside bits. She directed her attention at his leg, where a blank spot in the muscle form revealed a puncture wound deep enough to swallow her whole index finger. Small black lines and smudges appeared in place of dozens of small cuts and abrasions.

A quick mental nudge disabled his sense of pain, and she willed his body to mend itself. The minor hurt sealed in seconds, a trivial exertion.

Diego pulled her to her feet. "Althea, please... He's dying."

Her eyes snapped open. "Where? What happened?"

"He fell through the floor in Old Town," said Santiago.

Althea gasped. "We're not supposed to go there."

"Please don't tell anyone," said Diego. "But can you help him? I think his leg broke."

She put her hands on her hips and sighed. "They told you not to go to the Old City, didn't they?"

Santiago bowed his head. "Yes."

"Yeah," said Diego.

"Well, then, you *should* get in trouble. If you listened, Pedro wouldn't be hurt." She gestured at the alley they came from. "Let's go... Take me to him."

"I thought you weren't gonna go, sayin' we were told not to." Santiago jogged off.

"Someone's hurt because you broke the rules," said Althea. "Going to help them isn't breaking the rules."

"Oh." Diego hobbled along to keep up.

She waited for him and took his hand as soon as he got close enough to reach. Eyes closed, she linked to his life essence, concentrating on the broken bone shapes in his foot. The second and third toes had both snapped, and one of the muscles along the arch looked fatter than it should be, with a small rip. It took her about ten seconds to force his body to mend itself, and a small growl came from his gut.

Hers answered.

"This way," shouted Santiago.

She released Diego's hand and sprinted after the long-haired teen. He raced down the alley, hooked left at the end, and darted across a street into another alley. Althea had little trouble keeping up on the run, barely feeling the exertion by the time the boys stopped, winded, beside a building that made up part of the eastern wall.

Althea looked up at the walkway upon which the Watch patrolled. Blue-painted steel covered by mismatched awnings and stretches of fabric supported on poles passed over the roof of a two-story brick-shaped structure with three garage style doors on the right, and a normal door on the left. The roll-top doors appeared welded closed, and what had once been an office had large metal plates secured over a giant window. A row of small bricks surrounded a dirt strip by the wall that likely used to have grass.

"You climbed the wall?" asked Althea.

"No." Santiago gave her a cheesy smile. "The metal cracked." He grasped the knob and yanked open the door.

Althea followed him in to a room empty save for a cluster of ancient papers on the wall, bearing images of women. At first glance, they seemed naked, though a triangle of bright yellow covered one's 'girl parts.' She stared for a second, confused why anyone would bother wearing clothing so small. It wouldn't do anything for warmth.

Scratches on the floor suggested where a desk or some heavy piece of furniture had been dragged to the entrance. Santiago crossed the room and headed past an interior doorway to a large room full of old mechanical junk well advanced into the process of becoming a single heap of rust along the far wall. Hulking metal frames took up most of the middle of the room, separated by pushcarts littered with junk. Scraps of yellow and red plastic flaked on the ground by a few fragments of snipped copper wiring. Matching insulation decorated nubs on one of the carts, suggesting someone had scavenged wire. Aside from empty steel shelves, and a small window peering back into the first room, blank grey cinder blocks surrounded them on four sides, darkened in mold-covered trails where water had leaked in.

"Watch out," said Diego from behind. "There's traps in the ground."

Althea started to turn to look back at him, but his arm slid past her face, brushing her nose, as he pointed ahead. Three rectangular pits in the floor lined up in front of the garage-style doors. Santiago headed across the room to the most distant one, and sat on the edge.

"Don't fall," yelled Althea, while running over.

"Come on." Santiago eased himself off the edge and wound up standing on something inside.

She bit back the shout of alarm and rushed to a halt at the edge of the pit. He stood on a wheeled ladder/cart that left him at about eye-level with her. It wobbled and creaked as he made his way to the floor inside the pit. She didn't trust it, but if it held his weight, it didn't seem likely to break under hers.

Diego offered his hand. She held it and stepped from the floor to the top panel of the ladder, which held a wide, shallow pan. She squeezed his fingers as the cart shimmied underfoot. After a second to find her balance, she let go and climbed down the steps to the concrete. A scattering of small white cylinders littered the floor between her and Santiago, who waited up ahead. The front end of the pit, opposite the garage doors, connected to a walkway that linked all three chambers, and continued off to the right.

Santiago bounced on his toes by the tunnel. "Come on... hurry."

Her foot clipped one of the cylinders as she rushed ahead, which had a lot more weight than she expected. Althea gasped and limped for a few steps, trying to rub her ankle and run at the same time.

"Ow."

The boys ran down a narrow passageway lined with more empty steel shelves. A short distance later, it opened into a square room with yet more empty shelves and a number of pallets stacked against the wall. Santiago went straight to a concrete stairway that led up to the ceiling, and a metal cellar-style door. He gave it a heave, and the doors opened with a grating screech.

She followed him up the steps and out into the Old City, in the shadow of Querq's wall. Althea regarded the metal hatch with worry. "Does anyone else know about this door?"

"No," said Diego.

"Hurry... please." Santiago jogged backward down the street, away from Querq.

Althea pointed at the entrance. "The Watch needs to know about this way out."

"You can't tell them," whined Diego. "If they know, they'll close it up and we can't go exploring."

Althea leaned at him, imitating the way she'd seen mothers act. "If we can go out here, bad people can come in here." She gestured again at the cellar door. "Do you want raiders sneaking in at night? People could get hurt. You should have told the Watch right away." After a quick look around, and up at the wall, she sighed. "Where is Pedro?"

"Two blocks over. In the big place." Santiago took off at a sprint.

Althea ran after him, boosting her stride and endurance with a small psionic tweak. Diego let off a startled noise as she left him in the dust and overtook Santiago in seconds. She slowed to keep pace with him. He didn't look back, but sped up a little as the clap of her feet on pavement came up behind him. They passed two cross streets and cut diagonally through an intersection of a third before he clambered up a severe hill onto the grounds of an enormous three-story building. It sat adjacent to a sprawling field containing the decaying remnant of some manner of coliseum. A fork-shaped pole stood at either end of a field of fake grass, some of which had peeled up in sheets.

A shiver took her at the sight of it, picturing raiders and bandits jousting with motorbikes or unwanted slaves forced to fight each other. She forced the image of a severed hand flying overhead out of her mind and chased after Santiago, who had disappeared into a double front door.

The room contained numerous wood-framed cases, lined with jagged bits of long-broken glass. She stepped with care, mindful of debris in case any of the shards remained in her path. Whatever had happened to the shelves must have been long ago, as the floor appeared free of sharp dangers.

Santiago raced through another set of double doors and jogged past doorway after doorway on both sides of the corridor. He hooked a right perhaps sixty yards in and went down another hallway lined with narrow vertical doors. Most hung open, or simply didn't exist, revealing chambers she probably could've squeezed into. Padlocks secured the few doors that remained. She cringed, wondering what sort of horrible person made such cramped cages for children... and so many of them. Though they had air holes, she didn't want to look for fear she'd find skeletons. Maybe the war that ended the before-time had been a good thing after all.

"In here." Santiago paused with his hand on a doorjamb. The distant wails of another teenage boy echoed from beyond. "Be careful… the floor just fell out below us."

She nodded.

He crept in.

Althea followed into a large room with a ruined wooden floor. Loose narrow boards peeled up in places, and several holes in the ceiling revealed the upper level, with more holes in its roof. Dirt and debris gathered in dried whorls left behind by past rain. Thick yellow ropes hung like a forest of slender trees a short distance away, over cushioned pads. She grasped one of the ropes to brush it out of her way, and her hand clenched tight. The muscles in her back and legs locked as her mind leapt back to another time.

The rope extended past her face, close to her chin. Her arms and shoulders ached, the insides of her legs burned from where they gripped the rope. The overwhelming need to climb flooded her thoughts; fear of ridicule for failure built stronger and stronger. An indistinct man below shouted phrases like 'move your ass, Adams,' 'come on, boy. The rope won't climb itself,' and 'you're halfway up, come on, couple more feet. Pull!'

Fear built to a peak. She gazed out of the eyes of a memory, an emotional imprint in the rope, at a crowd of adolescent boys all pointing up and laughing. The climber looked down and got dizzy at the floor so far away. Hot ran down his legs; the laughter got louder. Terror paralyzed him; he couldn't climb up *or* down, and burst into tears. The shouting man turned soothing, beckoning the boy down. His grip failed, the rope fell away, and Althea snapped back to reality.

She shot a stare at the floor, and breathed a sigh of relief at not standing in a puddle. It had felt so real; she squirmed.

A distant wail of pain pulled her attention to the right. The boys hadn't gotten too far away; the vision must've only taken a second or two. She took two steps after them before Pablo's screaming changed tone from pain to terror.

Althea sprinted in the direction of the screaming, heedless of the small bits of wood jabbing into her soles. She zoomed past the boys and stopped short at the edge of a hole large enough to swallow one of the Watch's trucks. The floor below looked deeper than single story, though not quite two. Pablo lay amid a mess of debris, likely what remained of the floor that gave out. His right leg twisted at an unhealthy angle, and he struggled to drag himself back while screaming out for his mother.

A man-like being with dried, mottled dark green skin shambled toward him, growling and emitting a shrill whining sound as if trying to scream despite a jaw he couldn't open. It had no clothes, but also no man-bits to cover. The creature radiated hatred, directed toward Pablo.

"There's stairs over there," said Santiago.

She concentrated for a second on toughening her legs… and jumped.

Both boys behind her yelled in alarm.

Her toes hit the floor first, and she let herself fall into a somersault that dumped her on all fours; a dull ache spread through her left foot, though nothing felt broken. Pablo ceased screaming, staring in awe at Althea. She rose to stand, grasping hold of the creature's emotion and pushing its hatred aside. It lumbered to a halt a few paces away. From here, the armor-like texture of its scabrous skin confirmed her suspicion. Scrags called them 'ghouls,' though unlike what some of the legends claimed, they hadn't died and returned.

"You don't have to hurt anyone," said Althea.

It emitted a confused moan.

"*Mi pierna está quebrada*," wheezed Pablo.

Althea turned toward him, but kept half an eye on the ghoul. "Sorry. Too fast. Broken? Oh, your leg. Yes."

The ghoul advanced a few inches, reaching toward Althea. Its right eye widened, though the left remained a veritable slit.

"Run," screamed Santiago from overhead.

Althea swallowed; her toes gripped the old concrete. She'd never been so close to one of these beings before. Always, raiders or settlers, whoever had kept her, had shot them from afar, fled, or sometimes risked a close-in fight. From the aftermath, mending shattered arms and crushed bones, she knew the ghouls had strength greater than the biggest raider juggernaut. Letting it get so close unsettled her, this person-thing who could crush her with ease.

"Hi," whispered Althea. "You don't have to hurt anyone. Maybe I can help you."

"Get away from her," shouted Diego. He threw small hunks of wood or concrete from above at the ghoul.

It ignored the pelting.

"Help," whined Pablo.

Althea took two steps sideways to the right, toward Pablo, her gaze locked on the ghoul. "I don't want him to hit us when I fix your hurts."

The ghoul's anger began to return. She quashed it and probed deeper into its mind. Its armored skin hurt whenever it moved, a burn as though inflexible plates ripped away from muscle. Althea raised her hands.

"Don't hurt me. I want to help you." She bit her lip, wondering if she could do for this creature what she'd done for the canid.

It remained motionless as she crept up to it and put a hand on its dry, scratchy chest. The skin didn't feel at all like that of a living creature, closer to the vests some of the Watch wore while standing post on the wall. Despite its hardness, her attempt to link to its life essence worked, proving she touched living skin. Life shapes unfurled in her vision, close to that of a man, but some of the inside bits didn't look right. The ghoul had two heart shapes, low in the belly where the bean-shaped blobs usually belonged. Lighter smears surrounded the inner bits, not quite as pale as bone. A few seconds' probing revealed a dense coating around some of the organs, similar to a thick fingernail.

She couldn't guess where to begin to make it human again; the change—if it had even been changed and not born this way—seemed too drastic. Would de-growing the armor around the inner shapes hurt it? Should she force the heart shape back where it belonged? And what about the second one?

Her fingers went cold. The life shapes glided away from her as if pulled back by an unseen force. At once, she felt the presence of The Many. The Sentience, as Aurora called it.

He is mine, child. You cannot save him.

Althea scowled despite her closed eyes. *Did you do this to him?*

Dry chuckling circled around her mind. *No. But I sustain him.*

She tried to force her power into him again; a faint hint of his life shapes appeared far away, drifting closer.

You cannot help him, child. He has been a weapon of war for centuries. There is no mind left to save.

She emitted a faint snarl. *I don't believe you.*

Again, The Many chuckled. *You may think me evil, but not everything I speak is false. Look into his mind for yourself.*

Althea opened her eyes and gazed up into a pair of pale yellow spheres. Where perhaps once a human's eyes had been, the ghoul had orbs of a single, solid color, which emitted a weak glow. Reflected blue from her luminous stare glinted off smooth patches of its facial armor. She opened a telepathic connection to the ghoul's thoughts. At the surface, it tried to comprehend why it wasn't bashing her to death. It hadn't hesitated out of hope, pity, or curiosity. It simply couldn't understand why it had stopped.

Little of any memory existed beneath its surface thoughts, only the need to kill anything that moved, and attempt to feast upon whatever remained after.

I speak truth, child. You can only help this wretched creature by ending its sad excuse for a life. Go ahead, child. Kill it.

Althea stared at her hand against the creature's abdomen. The dense, hard plate of skin rose and fell with wheezy breaths, flooding her senses with the stink of rotting-meat. She wanted to pull away, but couldn't bring herself to. The Many had attempted to trick her before. It wanted her to kill someone. She had killed a bonedog, but the alpha had melted away into shadows. Was it a real dog, or had it been The Many in disguise? Perhaps she hadn't taken a real life? She thought back to the millipedes, too simple for her to manipulate, too stubborn for fear to work on them. Bugs didn't count. Especially mean bugs that wanted to eat people.

"I can't kill him."

So, you would choose to leave him to suffer an eternal agony? He will never die from old age. He will spend years and years in constant torment. Many years after you are no longer here, this creature will remain, still suffering. You could spare him that.

Althea looked down. "I… It's wrong to kill."

Is it? The Many laughed; though the sound existed only in her mind, her bones shook from the deep timbre. *If a raider was about to kill Karina, and the only way to save her life was to kill him, would you?*

Tears streamed down Althea's face as an image overwhelmed her thoughts: walking into her bedroom, a man on top of Karina, knife at her throat, about to kill her after wifeing her. A gun in Althea's hand. Seconds to react. Anger welled up inside her. Anger like she'd felt toward Hector.

Ahh, there it is. You would do it after all.

Althea wept. *You are awful! Why did you make me see that? Why did you show me him wifeing her?!*

I did not show you that. I showed you her after.

She let off a rageful scream in her mind.

A spidery caress passed across her shoulders as though The Many walked around behind her, tracing his fingers across her back. *It is nothing you have not witnessed before.*

But not Karina!

The Many appeared in her thoughts, smiling. The ancient man in a leather duster coat, cowboy hat, and boots offered a resigned shrug with upturned palms. *Of course, I wanted to hear you say you'd kill him, to feel your anger. Even one as innocent as you is not free of wrath. I had to give you the proper motivation. If Karina was in endless pain, would you take her life to stop her suffering?*

Althea snarled. *No. I'd make the pain stop.*

An exasperated sigh scratched across the back of her mind.

"Althea?" asked Santiago, sounding close. "Pablo is hurt."

Kill this wretched creature, or you own the rest of its suffering.

She looked up at the ghoul. Still, its surface thoughts held a battle of confusion. It wanted to smash her, but couldn't summon the urge to do so. That it couldn't left it bewildered. Pablo's moans of pain crept into her consciousness as the essence of The Many receded. As much as she hated to admit it, the dark spirit had not lied. This creature, she couldn't help. She pondered commanding its heart-shapes to stop beating, but couldn't see it as anything but killing.

The ghoul snapped out of its stupor and raised its fist, its jaw opening and shifting left with a sharp *snap*. Thick saliva trailed off its teeth, fluttering in a bellow that wafted the stink of fetid carrion across her face.

Santiago let off a high-pitched shriek.

Althea gathered her fear at imminent death and threw it forward, filling the ghoul with dread and amplifying it. For an instant, she felt like the boy on the rope, a hair's breadth from wetting herself. The tone of the ghoul's roar shifted to terror; it fell over backward, flipped onto its hands and knees, and dragged itself across the room as fast as it could crawl. Some thirty or so feet away, it dragged itself upright and sprinted through a doorway, howling.

She took a deep breath and held it. *It's gone. Calm. Calm.* Her heartbeat slowed back to normal. With the ghoul distracted, she rushed to Pablo's side and knelt. He looked up at her with adoration in his eyes. The way his leg had twisted, she expected it to have broken in at least two places.

"I'm sorry."

He shook his head. "I understand. It would've killed us if you looked away."

Althea put a hand on his bare stomach, and commanded his body to stop feeling pain. "I need to move your leg. It won't hurt, but you shouldn't watch." She took hold of the rubbery limb and pulled it out straight, unsettled by the lack of rigidity.

Santiago doubled over and vomited while Diego stared with fascination.

She linked her mind to his life essence. The bone-shapes in his leg had become a scattering of small fragments in three places. His hip had broken, as well the bones below the knee, and his ankle. Althea poured energy into him, commanding the splinters to move back in place and stick to each other. Shard by shard, his leg came together. A minute or so later, she directed the blood shape back where it belonged, and mended some rips in the muscles where the sharpened bits of bone had cut.

By the time she opened her eyes, a thin layer of sweat covered her.

Pablo sat up and wrapped his arms around her. Despite being bigger, he clung like a boy to his mother and cried. She smiled, sensing his tears came from happiness and relief.

A loud *smash* echoed from the hallway where the ghoul had run off. Hissing and moaning followed.

"Time to go," said Santiago.

Diego grabbed Pablo's arm and helped him stand. "I got you, man."

"Is okay." Pablo bounced on his feet. "She is amazing. It's like I never broke it." Overcome, he hugged her again.

Althea allowed herself a second or two to enjoy feeling loved before she squirmed away. "He's right. We need to go back to Querq before the ghoul finds us."

As if on cue, the ghoul let off an anguished wail.

Diego glanced in that direction, shaking his head. "That didn't sound good. I don't think 'dat ghoul be findin' anything."

She stared at the doorway where the ghoul had run, more than a few feet in, the corridor turned black and white. A cloud of dust obscured the view, likely from whatever had caved in. She didn't trust this building not to fall on their heads. Scratching, skittering, and hissing echoed off the walls. The ghoul roared and wailed. A wet, squishy *crunch* followed. Diego edged up beside her, transfixed on the hallway as well.

Pablo studied the hole he'd fallen in from. "How are we going to get out of here?"

"There's a stairway." Santiago pointed off to the side.

Scratching grew louder in the hallway.

"Come on." Diego pulled on Althea.

She glanced to the side; the stairway Santiago wanted to use sat ten feet to the left from the corridor full of scary noises. They'd have to walk *closer* to go up. Diego and Pablo didn't seem to care much about the crunching and scratching, and started walking toward it.

A long tubular shape emerged from the dust, weaving toward them.

They froze.

"Somethin's movin' in there," whispered Santiago.

"What's that?" asked Diego.

A giant millipede spattered with greenish ooze slithered out of the darkness into the large chamber. Althea had seen ghouls shot before—green blood. This millipede looked larger than the ones that had attacked her when she'd been in the desert with Rachel and the escaped harem. Its body looked thicker around than Shepherd's thigh. She lashed out with fear as a reflex, but her telempathic assault didn't faze it.

Three fourteen-year-old boys hid behind her.

"Scare it off," whispered Diego.

"Can you kill it?" whispered Santiago.

"It's poisonous," said Pablo. "The pincers are red tipped."

Gleaming black shell plates undulated as it propelled itself closer.

Althea closed and opened her empty hands. Even if she had a spear, she doubted herself strong enough to break its shell. The giant millipede fit right in the middle of the category of 'bug.' Worse, *stubborn* bug. She wouldn't have hesitated to smash it, but lacked the means. Her left foot tingled with the memory of venom paralyzing it.

"I can't scare it. It's too mean." She locked stares with it. "I'll make it come after me. I can run faster than it. Go. Get help."

Diego put a hand on her arm. "But—"

Althea poked it with anger. Venom exuded from its mandibles and it hissed at her. She channeled her power inside, strengthening her legs and fortifying her endurance. The instant it surged forward, she darted to the right. Her feet clapped the old wooden floor like tiny gunshots, echoing off the bare walls. Scratching and hissing followed her. She barely noticed the boys' shouts and the creak of a metal door in the distance.

The millipede slid wide to the right, its pointy legs scraping on the bare concrete, as she cornered to head for an opening on the side of the giant room. A pile of blue padded mats twice her height blocked her path. She leapt onto it and climbed, grabbed the top of frayed canvas, and hauled herself up to stand on top. When she tried to jump to the floor, her feet squished down into the spongy obstacle, reducing her great leap into a near-fall. She scrambled for balance after landing, waving her arms about to keep from wiping out.

Knowing the millipede would be on her if she tripped, Althea squealed in fright and forced herself to run as fast as she could. Smears of grey walls, dark blue paint, and debris shot past her. Seconds later, everything went black and white, a sign she'd run into darkness. Maybe the millipede couldn't see without light? She glanced back over her shoulder and screamed at finding the enormous insect barely ten feet behind her, and showing little sign of slowing.

Her gait took on a bounding deer-like quality as she further strengthened her leg muscles. Althea leaned forward, pumping her arms, trying not to think about the clicking, scratching horror behind her, and focused entirely on the end of the hall thirty yards ahead. Twenty yards. Ten.

"Aaaaaah!" she screamed as she dove between a set of ancient steel double doors.

She whirled about and tried to slam them closed, but the creature got its head in the gap. Althea rammed the slab of metal against the bug, trying to crush it, but succeeded only in pinning it. The fifteen-foot long monster thrashed and whipped about in the hallway outside. Venom dribbled from snapping mandibles inches from her face.

Her bare feet couldn't gain purchase on the dusty polished wood; the harder she pushed on the door, the more she slid away. Althea grunted and struggled to keep from letting the millipede shove its way in. It gained a few inches, carapace scraping on steel.

"No!" she yelled. "Go away!"

It hissed, wrenching itself in a rotating back and forth motion. Althea pressed harder into the door, her feet pushing clean smears through the dust. She didn't like whoever had decided to cover the floor with such slippery shiny stuff.

"Go away!" She strained, grunting

When its tail pincer punctured the door an arm's length above her head, she screamed, high, loud, and clear.

The millipede didn't react to her terror. This creature felt no hatred, nor particular animosity. It wanted dinner. It didn't know anything other than eating and defending its territory from things it couldn't eat. She stared at the twitching mandibles. Her throat dried out. She worked her legs, walking in place, barely able to keep up enough resistance on the floor to prevent the creature from barging into the room.

Althea twisted, bracing her shoulder against the door. Wide-eyed, she stared at the millipede's 'face,' dreading touching it. Out of desperation, she sent a surge of blood and adrenaline into her left arm.

And pounded it on the nose.

It emitted a sharp shriek and recoiled; the door slammed closed. She bowed her head to exhale with relief, and spotted a small metal stake that looked as if it would slide down into a hole in the floor. She kicked at it until it locked. A matching one near the top of the door hung out of reach. While she stared at it, the door rocked with a loud *slam*. Althea kept pushing it closed.

Mandibles pierced the door at thigh level.

She screamed and jumped back. It tore the holes wider as it ripped itself free of the door. Seconds later, it bit through again, a little above the push bar, striking with a *slam* that shocked the air in her lungs. Again and again, it attacked the barrier; Each time it crashed against the steel, it seemed as though the entire building shook.

Althea padded backward, unable to stop staring at the thrashing horror. She drew her hands together at her chin, and cried out with her mind for Father. When that awful man had left her tied to a post blindfolded for the night, she'd called out the same way, and the canid found her. Knowing that Father would sense her beaconing for him lessened her fear. Back in Querq, he'd get a feeling that she needed him, and he'd come running. Hopefully, the feeling would guide him to her instead of leaving him wanting to find her and not knowing where to look.

The millipede rammed itself into the door four more times, its mandibles making holes big enough for Althea to stick her arm through, and causing the metal to bow inward. By the time the creature gave up, it had riddled the door with so many gouges she had a clear view into the hall. She shivered at the sight of the massive black-shelled horror slinking off into the distance.

She deflated to sit on the floor and slouched, gasping for breath while staring at the boards between her legs. Like the room with the climbing ropes, the floor had so much polish it appeared to have a layer of glass above the wood grain. She traced her fingers over it, wondering what kind of stupid person would want to make a floor slippery.

A moment of terror came and went as she pondered what might've happened to her if it had caught her. Involuntary tears and sniffles broke the heavy silence. Althea trembled for a few seconds until she felt gratified that the boys had managed to escape unhurt. Once her heart stopped racing, she looked up.

Painted lines adorned the wooden floor from wherever padded blue mats didn't cover it. A little ways behind her stood a strange little bridge made from a pair of metal frames holding a thick beige bar off the ground. The span had a smooth top and rounded sides. More pads surrounded it on the floor. She stared past it at a large row of bleacher style seats, covered in dust and debris from the collapsing ceiling. Curious, she stood and walked over to the purposeless bridge. The surface hovered about at her shoulder level. Maybe someone built it to cross the holes in the floor? But why would they make a bridge so narrow a person had to put one foot straight in front of the other?

The second her fingers made contact with it, her mind filled with a vision.

People filled the bleachers, dressed in strange clothes she'd never seen before. A line of girls about her age stood off to the side, in bizarre garments that covered only their arms and bodies, leaving most of their legs bare. She looked down at herself, finding a similar garment wrapped around a body that didn't belong to her. The girl who had left the emotional imprint had skin of a rich chocolate hue, and a much curvier shape despite being close in age.

Althea hovered like a spectator in a body moving on its own. The girl climbed up and stood on top of the spar. Flashes of light came from the crowd, snapping from random places. The cheering audience reminded her of the arena where Vakkar made men try to kill each other. A clench of worry filled her heart; did these people make young girls fight to the death?

The girl on the beam tried to keep herself calm, though the emotion left in the bridge said otherwise. She thought of the spar as a 'balance beam,' and had to do 'moves' on it to make her parents, and someone called Coach happy. Such intense nervousness at being in front of so many people left a permanent mark on the beam. She hated being watched by the crowd. She wanted to go home and be alone. The girl splayed her arms to the sides, brought her hands together, and bent forward, tumbling into a cartwheel. As the familiarity of a well-rehearsed routine set in, confidence overtook nerves, and the imprinted emotion faded.

Althea blinked away the vision, a hand on her belly to swallow the anxiety she'd picked up. As worried as the girl had been about falling off,

Althea wondered what would've happened to her if she failed? None of the people in the vision appeared to have weapons, and no one looked angry or hostile, yet the girl seemed as nervous as those men who the raiders made fight.

Althea grinned and pulled herself up to stand on the beam. She walked back and forth twice, face scrunched up at how people could think the task difficult. In a moment of adventurousness, she mimicked the girl's motion and rolled into a handstand.

Her dress fell down around her head.

She brought her legs down slow and found her footing after a little feeling around blind. She eased her weight from her arms to her toes and stood, smoothing her dress back in place.

"I guess that's why they didn't wear dresses." She fidgeted with discomfort at the idea of those odd garments being so snug between her legs. Except for being pretty and shiny blue, they didn't cover enough to have been meant for warmth or protection. She scrunched up her nose thinking of the little yellow scrap the woman on the wall of the other building wore. It made no sense at all why they would wear something so tiny. Why bother with it at all?

She shrugged. Perhaps the girls who played on this beam wore those things for decoration? They seemed to be putting on some kind of show for everyone watching. *They're too young for a harem... what did I see?* She scowled. *The before-time is strange.*

Althea folded her arms, trying to make sense of what she'd seen. She walked back and forth on the beam, cartwheeled once more, and shrugged. "Is this supposed to be hard?"

She bit her lip and used the edge of the beam to scratch the underside of her foot. Those girls didn't have her gifts. Maybe they didn't grow up having to run and hide to stay alive. Elders had told her that life in before-time was quite different. People lived in relative safety. Perhaps anyone nimble enough to do something like this had been rare enough to be worthy of being a spectacle. Sometimes settlers would dress funny and dance for amusement. Maybe that's what these girls had been doing? Some kind of festival.

The millipede had evidently given up for good, as it hadn't returned... though she'd only spent two or three minutes playing on the beam. *I'm not helping anyone now. I should go home. I'm not supposed to be in the Old City.*

After hopping down, she turned in a circle, searching for a way out. She didn't want to go back through the ruined door toward the millipede.

Fortunately, another double door offered an alternate exit on the opposite side of the enormous room.

Althea walked past two more beams, and a set of smaller ones much higher up at two different heights. Those looked like they might be difficult to walk on, but she didn't bother playing. A glint caught her eye from the floor about halfway across the room. She stooped and brushed at the accumulated dirt and silt, exposing a silver disc on a rotten red white and blue ribbon.

As soon as she picked it up, another vision came to her.

Her perspective changed to that of a girl standing on a small platform to the right of another girl, on a somewhat higher platform. She looked down at a skin-tight white and red garment like the others had worn, only this one covered the backs of her hands, connected to a fabric loop around her middle fingers. The girl peered down at the silver disc hanging around her neck. Shame crippled her, mixed with dread. Pale fingers caressed the silver amulet. She'd come in second. She didn't win something. Her parents were going to be angry. So much so that she stared at the medallion she'd won, and contemplated not even going home after the tournament. She would run away. The idea of never seeing any of her friends again felt better than going home to face her parents' wrath for *merely placing second.*

Althea gasped and dropped the medallion, backing away from it as if it were an evil thing unto itself. She melted to her knees and wept into her hands, overwhelmed by the shame and sense of worthlessness the ancient twelve-year-old had imprinted on the lump of metal. It took her a moment to gather herself enough to stop bawling. She wiped her face, hoping that the girl hadn't run off. She couldn't imagine *wanting* to be separated from her family. She scooted a little farther away from the medallion, lest it make her feel that way again.

How had the medallion remained here? Did the girl who won it leave it behind, disgusted with herself for merely doing great as opposed to perfect? Did the war start while they were in here? She clambered to her feet and jogged around it, heading for the door. It didn't matter why it wound up here; that girl would've been dead hundreds of years ago, even if she'd lived to old age.

Reading that girl's desire to flee her family made Althea want Father and Karina more. That millipede could come back and attack the door again at any moment, and from the amount of damage it had done, if it tried hard enough, it would break through.

She couldn't be here when it returned.

Althea ran to the other door, raising her hands to the push bar. She intended to ram it aside in a hurry, but changed her mind at the last second, and pressed it gently. Old instincts returned. Noise meant death. She eased it open and peered through into another plain hallway lined with white-painted cinderblocks.

Benches along the side appeared grey to her, as did peeling paint on the walls that formed words she couldn't read. Father wanted her to learn how, but so had Archon. The idea of 'school' learning made her think of him, so she'd done all she could to avoid it.

She took the first left, some thirty feet in from the door and found herself standing between two rows of those narrow vertical cages. Unlike the ones in the other hall, these seemed smaller and all had their doors. Only two hung open, though they contained some folded clothing rather than the skeletal remains of a young prisoner.

Althea looked down, feeling a touch stupid. The before-time people hadn't used them for cages; they put stuff in them like closets. She approached one and tugged the door open. A scrap of cloth hanging from a hook fell apart as soon as she touched it.

"Everything here is dead."

She sighed and moved to the end of the row where another doorway led to the right. She hurried to it and let off a disappointed moan when she walked into a dead-end room covered in white tile. The outer wall consisted of numerous individual segments, each with a faucet mounted high on the wall. She made confused faces at them for a little while before remembering seeing similar things on walls elsewhere, but still couldn't figure out why people would put faucets so high up or fail to include a sink.

Althea turned on her heel and headed back out, passing between two different rows of the small metal cabinets. In one open door, she spotted a twelve-inch plastic doll. The too-skinny false woman wore the same kind of clingy garment the girls she'd envisioned had on. She stroked its hair and puffed dust off it. Maybe she'd 'rescue' it and take it home.

"Are you lonely?"

She peered into its plastic eyes and felt the tug of an imprint. The city police had called it clair voy ants, but that didn't make any sense. *That's silly. Bugs aren't sigh-onic.* She hesitated, fearing another awful memory like the medallion, but curiosity got the better of her in a few seconds.

She closed her eyes and opened herself up to the psychic energy embedded within.

A girl about Karina's age with a larger bosom cradled the doll to her heart like a girl much younger. She cried and rocked it side to side. Althea got the sense this girl had brought the doll with her to competitions for years, believing its presence somehow gave her luck. The emotional imprint held worry and love for her father. A war seemed likely to start soon, and he would probably have to go fight. The teen sat on a bench, crying harder while clinging to the doll. She dreaded having to leave her home, this school, her friends, everything she's ever known because of the danger. Her mother wanted to move west, trusting the government's promises of a safe zone, while Dad thought they should stay since he'd gotten a great new job.

She tried to put her anxiety aside so she could compete tonight; her thoughts turned toward getting into something called college in two years. To do it, she needed to win tonight. After a moment, she kissed the doll on the head, asked it to give her luck, and tucked it in the locker where Althea had found it.

The room seemed to age four centuries in seconds as the vision faded. White paint became grey, cracks appeared, and lights went from glaring bright to smashed and missing. Althea looked around. *This was a school? It's bigger than Querq!*

She frowned.

"No it isn't. I'm just lost and frightened. It only feels big."

A faint man's weeping emanated from the hallway outside the locker room. She tiptoed to the end of the row and peered out. A couple paces left of the opening, a man in a baggy grey uniform slumped on one of the benches, clutching his hands to his armored vest. Blood seeped through the fabric of his jumpsuit. For a foot or two on either side of him, the benches appeared blue, before fading to grey.

Althea rushed over to him. "It's okay. I can help you."

He didn't react until she grasped for his bare hand, and gripped only air.

At her attempt to touch him, he looked up. Dirt and blood caked around his mouth; his expression twisted with great anguish, though not from any physical wound. This close, Althea noticed the wall appeared through him; his body shimmered like one of those holler-grams the city police made.

After a brief mournful stare, he disappeared. The bench faded to grey. He must have been emitting light.

Althea took a step back. The corridor hung heavy with an eerie presence that hadn't been there before. At first, she blamed her fear of millipedes, but the longer she stood in place, the more she felt that man watching her.

"Are you still here?" she whispered.

Sorrow thickened the atmosphere. It seemed as though he wanted to make her sad, but she didn't allow it to affect her. Officer Ahmed said she had 'astrals,' but she'd never seen a ghost before. What else could he have been?

Althea clenched her fists in determination. That man needed help. An odd compulsion deep inside her made her want to do something for him, but she couldn't tell where he'd gone. She thought about wanting to see him. After a moment of squinting, concentrating, and probing around in her head, he reappeared—only he no longer looked transparent. While the bench, and the corridor around her remained in black and white, the man looked normal—and in color.

She figured him for a little younger than Father, perhaps in his early or middle thirties. He had short brown hair, had gone a couple weeks without shaving, and wore the most sorrowful look she'd ever seen on the face of a grown man. His black armored vest had a small patch with a word on it, a red mark to the left of white letters. He carried a handgun in a hip holster, and she recognized magazine pouches for a rifle around the side of his belt.

"Who are you?" wheezed the man. "Have you seen Madison?"

"I don't know anyone named Madison." Althea shook her head. "You've been shot." Again, she tried to touch the man since he looked so solid and real, but her hand passed through him, as if she'd stuck it into a cloud of that 'air conditioning' again.

He exhaled. "You're talking to me. No one else talks to me. No one else has seen my daughter. Bob won't tell me where she is."

"Who's Bob?"

"My boss. He's not answering the radio." The man sniffed. "You have to help me find Madison… my daughter. She'd be seventeen by now."

Althea stared at him for a moment. "You were in the war?"

"Yeah. What are you doing here, kid? It's not safe."

"I know. But the war is over." Something welled up inside her, and she knew this man did not belong here. "You don't need to be here anymore. I'm sorry… but you died."

He looked down at his chest. "Madison…"

"I don't know what happened to your daughter, but she can't be alive anymore."

"What?" He reached for her, but his hands passed through her shoulders. Grief shifted to anger. "What happened to Madison!? Tell me!"

"The war ended a long, long time ago. Couple hundred years." Althea shook her head. "She probably got old."

"Hundred years?" He stared into space for a little while. "Madison went to this school. Is the war really over?"

"Yes." Althea put on her most sympathetic look. "For a long time." She took a breath. "Why did people fight?"

"Companies disagreed with the government about taxes. They didn't think we needed politicians anymore. They were right." He waved disgustedly to the side. "Bastards in Washington just sit there like fat leeches sucking money out of everyone. The rich keep getting richer and the politicians keep bullshitting us. Yeah, the corporates are just as bad, but why have both of them sucking us dry? Government took our money because they could, and didn't do anything. Sure the corporates are rich fatcats, but at least they ran business and made jobs and stuff."

"You fought the gov-mint?" She blinked.

"Yeah." He chuckled, shaking his head. "Though, I guess 'fought' isn't the right word. Verizon hired me as a security guard. I got the job like three months before things got bad. I should've quit when they gave us armor and military-grade weapons, but they paid so god damned much. A hundred and fifty thousand bucks a year to sit on my ass watching security screens. I couldn't turn that down. Madison needed to go to college."

She scrunched up her face. "They gave you deer?"

The man laughed. "Yeah kid, sure. So, things got worse and worse. The telcos were the first ones to tell the government to go f—orget themselves." He glanced to the side, muttering, "damn kid."

"I'm sorry you died."

"Never saw it coming. I don't know what Bob was thinking. They never even trained us or anything. Couple hours a week on the range… fu—ming special forces guys hit us. We didn't have any warning. I didn't even get a hand on my gun before I died. Heh." He laughed. "Now that you reminded me I bit it, it's all comin' back to me. After they took me out, I watched the whole thing. They killed thirty of us in two minutes. Not one of 'em said a damn word. Like a machine. We didn't have a god damned chance." He leaned his head back, tears streaming out of his eyes. "My daughter... I never even got to say goodbye. She went to this school."

Althea held up the doll. "Was this hers? You appeared right after I touched it."

"That doll..." He reached for it. His body became transparent again, and he grabbed the plastic woman as though he'd become solid. "Yeah. We got her this when she turned seven. She was so into gymnastics... took this doll with her to every practice, every competition."

"For luck," said Althea.

"Yeah." He stared at her. "How did you know that?"

She clasped her hands in front of herself, fidgeting with her dress. "She left her 'motions in it. I saw them. I'm sigh-onic. She was scared you would have to fight, and she didn't want to leave home."

"What's sigh onic mean?"

She smiled. "I guess it means I can do stuff."

"Like what?"

Althea shrugged. "Like talk to ghosts."

The man bowed his head with a sad chuckle. "We decided it would be better for them to go. Debbie couldn't be reasoned with. She trusted the damn government. I decided to stay with my job, send them money when I could. The pay was too high to walk away from... stupid. Stupid. Stupid."

A twinge nagged at Althea's soul. An urge blossomed into action. She raised her arm. "You don't have to stay here anymore. They are waiting for you." She reached at nothing, and pulled aside the air like a curtain, revealing a shimmering silver doorway. Part of her mentally leapt back in shock, though the energy emanating from the opening bathed her in security, as welcome and reassuring as the scent of Father's house.

"Dad?" A woman's voice floated out of the silver rectangle. Seconds later, a thirty-ish woman with short auburn hair appeared. "Oh, God, Dad..."

"Maddie?" The man stood. "You're so... young."

The woman laughed. Another woman, a little older, appeared behind her. "I made it to ninety-four, Dad. I passed on in my bed, surrounded by grandchildren. Appearance is all in your head on this side. I think I looked my best at thirty-two. Everyone's here waiting for you. It's been many years..." She smiled at Althea. "You found Gina, my doll." Madison looked downcast. "I never did compete again after we evacuated. I always told Mom it was because I'd forgotten Gina, but that wasn't the real reason. Gymnastics always made me think about Dad." She beckoned her father to follow her.

"Thank you," whispered the man. He walked past Althea into the doorway of light, which closed like a theater curtain behind him.

For a few seconds, the sounds of an emotional family reunion echoed in the hallway.

Althea breathed a sigh of relief. She held on to the doll and hurried down the corridor, wondering what the heck just happened. Maybe she would talk to Officer Ahmed about it, but she'd have to ask Father first. She expected ghosts to scare or unsettle her, but something about meeting that man made her feel *right*. A part of her seemed at ease with what she'd done.

She rounded a ninety-degree corner and took the first door on the left, finding a large bathroom. Sensing a dead end, she pivoted on her heel to leave, but froze at the sight of herself in a huge mirror over a row of sinks. Her eyes glowed bright white, not their usual blue.

"What?"

Althea crept up to the sinks and stood on tiptoe, hips against the edge. She leaned close to the mirror, studying her phosphorescent eyes. They no longer appeared to have pupils or irises, resembling eye-shaped holes filled with pure white energy.

"What's happening to me?"

She reached out to touch the mirror beside her reflection.

The room shifted; decay, mold, broken tiles, and dirt vanished. Four hundred years ago, a girl sat on the sink shelf, bawling hard into her hands. She looked about sixteen or seventeen, and had a small, but telltale swell of a baby. The boy she loved had told her to go away and never come back. She didn't want to tell her parents she had a baby coming, afraid they'd make her leave the house. She worried about something called 'finals,' and dreaded being a mother would ruin her school.

Althea squinted, trying to understand how getting wifed would make someone do bad at learning. She forced her way out of the vision, and pictured the girl's emotions in a box, which she kept at arm's length. Whatever happened to that poor woman happened too long ago to get upset over. Her baby could've had a baby who had babies who'd grown old already.

I need to go home. Father is going to be worried.

She stared at herself in the mirror, afraid she'd broken herself by making her eyes change color. The instant she wanted her eyes normal again, they changed back to their usual azure glow. She blinked in surprise, but grinned at the elation of not doing something bad. Perhaps that—why they changed color—would be a question for Officer Ahmed.

Althea headed out into the hall and turned left. It hadn't been *too* long. She could still finish the empanadas before Karina got home from the farm. She rubbed her belly, looking forward to eating. Mending Pablo's leg had left her ravenous. The hallway went for some distance, and turned another corner. Alas, nothing looked like a stairway.

A rattle high and left made her look up. Less than a second after she glanced at a ventilation duct near the roof, the millipede burst out of it, hissing, swinging its head side to side in a searching manner.

Althea screamed her lungs empty.

As soon as the giant insect lowered its front end to the floor, hundreds of legs gripping at the wall, she took off at a hard sprint. She cleared to the corner at the end in a few seconds, and screamed again at the sight of a cave in. Before her brain could kick in to process that she ran *toward* the creature, she doubled back for the nearest doorway, fortunately one made of steel. She ducked past and slammed it a second and a half before the millipede crashed into it.

Two mandible points pierced. Venom dripped from the tips as they wiggled, testing the door. With a grinding screech of stressing metal, the millipede closed its jaws, scissoring the door. It couldn't fit through the inch-high slit it made, but it wouldn't take long to eat the door.

Althea backed up and whirled around.

Her heart fluttered in her chest. She'd found a room with no other way out save for a tiny window near the ceiling in the back. From the amount of shelves in here, she assumed the space had been used for storage. Her body twitched each time the millipede crashed against the door, piercing and tearing.

Again, she beaconed for Father. She couldn't stop shaking. During her years drifting around the Badlands, she'd been comforted by the knowledge everyone regarded her as too valuable to hurt. As long as she obeyed, even the meanest raiders would protect her. She had never known true terror but once, when bad-Shepherd wanted to smash her. This creature, this millipede, was one of those monsters that didn't care about her being the Prophet. It would kill and her with as little remorse as settlers killing Squealers for food. No one thought much about killing the enormous prairie dogs. She rather enjoyed the taste of their meat as well.

Being the meal, however, horrified her.

Althea ran to the wall under the window and sucked in a breath to scream for help, and choked on dust. Her heart seemed to synchronize with the millipede's assault on the door, thudding in her chest each time the monster slammed its face into the failing barrier.

She glanced back; the door had warped in, shredded in long gouges wherever the creature pincered slashes into the metal. The Many had to be laughing at her. It wanted her gone for reasons she couldn't guess. But that's what evil creatures do: they want innocent people to die. She held back the want to burst into tears and scream, and forced herself to look around. It would take too long to get up to the window and escape; the creature would eat her before she could get away. She had no choice but to stand her ground… somehow.

Sticks protruded from a huge box on one of the shelves. She considered arming herself, but they looked too long and thin, with a weird L-shaped bend at the end. The box next to it held hundreds of rubber discs about an inch thick. She grabbed at the next box, which held decaying head-sized balls with white and black panels.

A loud groan of protesting metal stalled her frozen. She glanced back over her shoulder. The millipede forced a flap of the door inward, wriggling through the hole it had made. Inch by inch, the creature squeezed into the room with her.

Althea yelled in surprise and pounced on the next box. Small hard, white balls with red stitching. She pulled it out of the way, sending them scattering on the floor toward the creature. Maybe they would slow it down. The next box filled her with hope. Wooden clubs.

She grabbed one and pulled it out, grasping it with both hands. Another one caught her eye, metal. She dropped the wooden one and drew the metal club from the box. Black tape flaked off under her grip, but the weapon itself felt solid.

Holding the club high, she took a wide stance in the middle of the room, and concentrated on the muscles in her arms and back. As the millipede worked its way in, she channeled psionic energy into her body. Her biceps swelled; her already sinewy arms grew more defined. She moved her right foot back, watching the creature, waiting, pouring more and more energy into herself.

The millipede got enough legs in contact with the ground to gain traction. It dragged itself forward, its strength and mass bending the flap it made in the door with a wail of stressed metal. It spilled into the room and rushed straight at her, its head rising, mandibles poised to take her head off at the neck.

Althea let off a war cry and brought the metal club down with every bit of strength she could milk out of her tiny frame. The impact of metal on chitin jolted her fingers with a painful shock, but rewarded her with a wet *crunch.* Yellowy ooze sprayed on her face and chest.

The millipede waved itself side to side in a spasmodic, repetitive motion. It slithered backward over itself in a continuous spiral motion, unwinding, and coiling again. She backed up, holding the club in a ready position, but the creature kept thrashing about as if it had forgotten entirely how to control its body.

She stooped to pick the doll back up and darted past the writhing millipede to the door, but the warped metal slab refused to open. She eyed the jagged hole and considered trying to crawl through, but didn't trust making herself that vulnerable near the millipede in case it snapped out of the daze.

Althea raced across the room to the shelf by the window and climbed. Much to her surprise, the metal-and-glass pane opened inward with little difficulty. She stretched her leg across the open space between two shelves, straddling the gap below the window with a foot on either side. The opening led out to an alley, only a few inches above the paving. Her momentary amplified strength made pulling herself up and out a triviality. She crawled into the alley, rolled onto her back, and gulped down lungful after lungful of fresh, dry air.

She lay there for a few seconds trying to catch her breath. Her arms and back muscles spasmed as they shrank to their normal size and strength. A dull ache came on after, but she smiled, thrilled to be alive.

Home.

With a grunt, she sat up and got to her feet.

A moan behind her made her whirl, raising the club.

The same ghoul, torn up and bleeding in several places, stumbled out from behind a large metal dumpster and glared at her. Millipede mandibles had ripped great sections of its armored skin away, but new tissue bubbled up already, growing over the wounds.

Althea sighed.

She thought about making it afraid. *It'll only go hurt someone else.*

She eyed the club and considered… killing it. *I… can't.*

She considered attempting to 'heal' it. Perhaps instead of making it human again, she could permanently disable its ability to feel pain? But it's mind had seemed so simple… that might not even help. The brain between those hardened green ears made the canid mutant seem like the town doctor.

Unable to decide what to do, she bolted and ran when it charged her.

Her sprint came to an abrupt halt as soon as she reached the street at the end of the alley. A strange metal truck with six huge wheels, as tall as a man, sat in the road. Four people in dark blue jumpsuits with rifles similar to the ones the city police had given the Watch spun around to look at her. Three men, one woman.

They smiled and waved.

The ghoul, moaning, came shambling out of the alley.

Althea dropped into a ball and plugged her fingers into her ears, knowing what would happen next.

All four of them opened fire on the ghoul. She winced at the icy feeling of a departing life, and frowned. When the gunfire ceased, she opened her eyes and looked up. The people lowered their weapons and again smiled at her. A reaction one might expect from normal people finding a lost child.

She stood and returned a friendly wave.

"Hey sweetie," said a pale man with black hair. "Would you like to see inside our fancy rover?" He pointed at the strange vehicle.

She opened her mouth to politely decline, but stopped at the notice of a symbol on his chest. A round octagonal letter with another letter inside it. She remembered Archon's learning datapad enough to recognize a G with an I inside it. The image haunted her for some reason; time seemed to freeze.

Her memory leapt back. Framed by a haze of grey fabric, her vision contained the chin of a blonde woman, viewed from below, as if the woman carried her. Pale skin caught the reflection of blue light, and the same GI logo sat upon the woman's chest, near Althea's face. The world jostled in a rapid back and forth; the woman ran.

That's me… I'm a little baby. My mother… She blinked as reality came back. *How can I remember that? No one remembers being a baby.* Althea reached out a psionic feeler; all four of them radiated eagerness, the same sort of eagerness raiders always had when they found The Prophet.

She took a step back. "No. I'm going home."

"Real smooth, Ed. You might as well have tried, 'hey little girl, want some candy?' Idiot," said a dark-skinned man with short, curly hair.

"Bite me, Joe." Ed took a silver pistol from the back of his belt and pointed it at her. "We've been looking for you for a long time. Come on, sweetie. You don't belong out here in this shithole. Please don't make me dart you. This is for your own good."

Althea poured herself into his thoughts. They worked for a corporation... Gravion Interstellar Incorporated. These must be the 'corporations' the city police warned her about. The reason they let her live out here in Querq. She frowned at the little silver gun. They didn't use money to hurt people; they had guns too. He thought of it as a tranquilizer. Something that would knock her asleep.

"You're bad. Go away."

The woman quick-drew a similar gun and shot her in the chest. Althea peered down at a two-inch metal dart with green fuzz at the end. The delirium of drugs encircled her mind, but she'd readied herself for it. A seconds' worth of concentration sent a stream of chemical running down her leg to the road. She grasped the dart and pulled it out with a twist.

"That wasn't nice." She glared at them, tossed the dart aside, and leaned forward in an aggressive pose.

Before the confusion of how the drug hadn't done anything could wear off, she released a blast of sorrow.

"You hurt my mother!" she screamed.

The four adults crumpled in place. Ed and an Asian man who hadn't spoken burst into tears. Joe stared into space, as did the woman. Althea's lip twitched with a light snarl. This corporation already took her away from her mother. She would *not* let them take her away from her home.

"I'm sorry," whispered the woman. She dropped the dart gun and reached for a larger pistol. The slowness of her motion made Althea hesitate until the woman lifted the weapon to her own head.

She backed off the sorrow and clubbed the woman with calm.

Her gun arm went limp, the handgun clattered to the road.

Althea stood tall. She forced her way into their minds. None of them had any memory of her mother beyond reading files explaining that 'an employee' had run off with 'an unusual child' that the company had expressed interest in studying. Her mother had refused to let the company doctors touch the baby, and fled. A 'recovery team' proved unsuccessful in locating the infant. Althea growled with desperation at their lack of knowledge as to her mother's fate.

In Ed's mind, she found a memory of him sitting in a meeting where a stern-faced woman with caramel skin told the four of them that Gravion Interstellar had maintained a facility in the Badlands which had suffered an unexplained catastrophic failure eleven years ago, in which forty-six of fifty-nine personnel died.

Althea looked down at her feet. *I guess I'm not really twelve.*

After a few seconds to process that—being eleven made her feel like a 'child' more than calling herself twelve had—she shook off the somberness of wondering about her mother, and glared at them. She radiated dread, a slow, building sense of ominous doom rather than 'scream-and-run' fear. These people would remember Querq; they would believe that something *horrible* would happen to them if they ever came near the place again. They would fear it so much that they would tell their whole company never to go here.

"Go away. Don't come back and try to kidnap me. I'm not the Prophet anymore. I won't let anyone take me away ever again." She stomped toward them, making all four adults cringe. "Querq is my home, and you aren't allowed here."

A final blast of dread sent them scurrying back into their six-wheeled machine.

"Here!" a man shouted in Spanish from the end of the street.

The large vehicle lurched into motion and lumbered past her heading north.

Two blocks down, a man wearing the telltale blue denim of the Querq Watch waved. In seconds, six more men as well as Father rounded the corner and came running toward her. Overwhelmed with joy at having a father to run to for protection, she dropped the metal club and sprinted into his arms. He mumbled in Spanish too fast for her to understand, something about Santiago and the boys... and how worried he became out of nowhere.

"Thea...?" He patted her back. "Did you call for me?"

"Yes." She nodded into his chest, and explained about the millipede and getting lost in the building.

The Watch decided to leave it be, figuring she'd likely killed it already, and headed back toward the gate.

Althea snuggled into Father's embrace. She cradled the doll to her chest, and basked in the feeling of being held by a loving father.

"The boys told us about their secret door," said Father.

"I told them to."

He made a noise part way between grumble and laugh. "I thought so. They also said you came out here to help Pablo."

"Yes. He'd fallen and his leg broke. I'm sorry for running off without telling anyone."

"You worried he might have been dying, but you could've sent one of the boys to get the Watch."

"Yes, father."

He brushed her hair back and looked at her. He exuded relief that came after a brief period of intense worry. "They also said you lured the 'pede away from them."

She gave him a guilty look. It had seemed like the right thing to do, since she could outrun it, but she'd been *so* scared.

Father hugged her to his chest and carried her in silence for a minute more.

Althea got the sniffles from thinking about the ghoul.

"It's all right, Thea. You're safe." He rubbed her back. "Those 'pedes scare me too."

"I'm not crying about that." She wiped her face. "I couldn't fix the green man."

"Those mercs must've shot the ghoul," said Alonzo, at their left.

Luis, at the front of the group, called up to the Watch above the gate. Soon, the belabored whine of an electric motor started, dragging the great doors open.

"You cannot fix everyone," said Father, his tone somber. "But you wouldn't be you if you didn't try." He kissed her atop the head.

Althea smiled as he carried her past the gates of Querq—her home.

Karina raced out of a side street about three blocks from the house. She rushed over and pawed at her. "Thea, what happened?"

"I'm sorry!" Althea looked back and forth between Father and her sister, awash with as much guilt as if she'd accidentally burned down the house.

"What? What for?" asked Karina.

"It's all right." Father patted the older girl on the shoulder. "She's had a scare."

"Not that," said Althea in a small voice. "I didn't finish the empanadas."

Karina and Father exchanged a glance, and burst into peals of laughter.

After a second or two of feeling foolish, Althea grinned and laughed as well.

ACKNOWLEDGMENTS

Thank you for reading Daughter of Ash, book four of the Awakened series!

Mark Woodring – You have my thanks again for another wonderful job editing. It's always a pleasure to work with you.

Thanks to Jackson Tjota for the cover illustration and Alexandria Thompson for the title layout.

ABOUT THE AUTHOR

Originally from South Amboy NJ, Matthew has been creating science fiction and fantasy worlds for most of his reasoning life. Since 1996, he has developed the "Divergent Fates" world, in which *Division Zero, Virtual Immortality, The Awakened Series, The Harmony Paradox, and the Daughter of Mars series* take place. Along with being an editor at Curiosity Quills press, he has worked in IT and technical support.

Matthew is an avid gamer, a recovered WoW addict, Gamemaster for two custom RPG systems, and a fan of anime, British humour, and intellectual science fiction that questions the nature of reality, life, and what happens after it.

He is also fond of cats.

Visit me online at:
    Facebook: https://www.facebook.com/MatthewSCoxAuthor
    Amazon: https://www.amazon.com/author/mscox
    Pinterest: https://www.pinterest.com/matthewcox10420/
    Goodreads: https://www.goodreads.com/author/show/7712730.Matthew_S_Cox
    Email: mcox2112@gmail.com

OTHER BOOKS BY MATTHEW S. COX

Divergent Fates Universe Novels

Division Zero series

- Division Zero
- Lex De Mortuis
- Thrall
- Guardian
- Harbinger

The Awakened series

- Prophet of the Badlands
- Archon's Queen
- Grey Ronin
- Daughter of Ash
- Zero Rogue
- Angel Descended

Daughter of Mars series

- The Hand of Raziel
- Araphel
- Ghost Black

Virtual Immortality series

- Virtual Immortality
- The Harmony Paradox

Prophet of the Badlands Series

- Prophet's Journey

Divergent Fates Anthology

(Fiction Novels - Adult)

The Roadhouse Chronicles Series

- One More Run
- The Redeemed
- Dead Man's Number

Faded Skies series

- Heir Ascendant
- Ascendant Unrest
- Ascendant Revolution

Temporal Armistice Series

- Nascent Shadow
- The Shadow Collector
- The Gate to Oblivion
- The Queen of Discord

Vampire Innocent series

- A Nighttime of Forever
- A Beginner's Guide to Fangs
- The Artist of Ruin
- The Last Family Road Trip
- The Phantom Oracle
- How Not to Summon Demons
- Ordinary Problems of a College Vampire
- A Vampire's Guide to Surviving Holidays
- An Introduction to Paranormal Diplomacy

Standalones

- Wayfarer: AV494
- Axillon99
- Chiaroscuro: The Mouse and the Candle

- The Spirits of Six Minstrel Run
- Sophie's Light
- The Far Side of Promise anthology
- Operation: Chimera (with Tony Healey)
- The Dysfunctional Conspiracy (with Christopher Veltmann)
- Of Myth and Shadow
- The Girl Who Found the Sun

Winter Solstice series (with J.R. Rain)

- Convergence
- Containment
- Catalyst

Alexis Silver series (with J.R. Rain)

- Silver Light
- Deep Silver
- Silver Quarrel

Samantha Moon Origins series (with J.R. Rain)

- New Moon Rising
- Moon Mourning

Vampire For Hire series (with J.R. Rain)

- Moon Master
- Dead Moon
- Lost Moon

Maddy Wimsey series (with J.R. Rain)

- The Devil's Eye
- The Drifting Gloom
- Dark Mercy

Samantha Moon Case Files series (with J.R. Rain)

- Blood Moon

Immortal Operative series (with J.R. Rain)

- Broken Ice

Four Elements series (with J.R. Rain)

- The Elementalist
- The Black Rose
- The Wakefield Curse

Young Adult Novels

The Eldritch Heart Series

- The Eldritch Heart
- The Cursed Crown

Evergreen Series

- Evergreen
- The World That Remains
- The Lucky Ones
- Nuclear Summer

Standalones

- Caller 107
- The Summer the World Ended
- Nine Candles of Deepest Black
- The Forest Beyond the Earth
- Out of Sight

Middle Grade Novels

The Adventures of Ubergirl series

- My Dad is a Mad Scientist
- Aliens Ate My Homework
- The End of all Halloweens

Tales of Widowswood series

- Emma and the Banderwigh
- Emma and the Silk Thieves
- Emma and the Silverbell Faeries
- Emma and the Elixir of Madness
- Emma and the Weeping Spirit

Standalones

- Citadel: The Concordant Sequence
- The Cursed Codex
- The Menagerie of Jenkins Bailey

www.ingramcontent.com/pod-product-compliance
Lightning Source LLC
Chambersburg PA
CBHW020512260626
47156CB00006B/1983